NO WAY
BACK

NO WAY
BACK

KELLY FLORENTIA

URBANE
Publications

urbanepublications.com

First published in Great Britain in 2017
by Urbane Publications Ltd
Suite 3, Brown Europe House, 33/34 Gleaming Wood Drive,
Chatham, Kent ME5 8RZ
Copyright © Kelly Florentia, 2017

A CIP catalogue record for this book is available
from the British Library.

ISBN 978-1-911583-40-0
MOBI 978-1-911583-36-3
EPUB 978-1-911583-35-6

Design and Typeset by Michelle Morgan

Cover by Julie Martin

Printed and bound by CPI Group (UK) Ltd, Croydon, CR0 4YY

urbanepublications.com

To Joe, with all my love.

NO WAY BACK

CHAPTER 1

"AUDREY? AUDREY, WAKE UP!" Nick's voice is loud in my ears.

I stretch my legs across the bed, feeling for him as I drift in and out of sleep. It's a bedtime routine he's become accustomed to over the years; whenever we share a bed, that is, which is at least five nights a week, either at his place or mine.

He usually welcomes the slither of my feet caressing his long limbs in the mornings, especially if he's feeling a bit frisky; but, strangely, is none too pleased on wintry nights when I unexpectedly fasten my freezing cold feet against his warm calves. On those occasions, he leaps to the edge of the bed in fury, screaming expletives at me, complaining that he's not a frigging radiator. I can't think why he freaks out over it. I mean, come on, it's a girl thing, isn't it? It comes with the territory, and is surely much better than wearing off-putting bed-socks.

I wriggle my toes in contentment. His side of the bed is empty but his scent is still lingering, wafting through the Egyptian cotton sheets. A subtle odour of perspiration infused with fresh, citrus cologne and a hint of tobacco. His smell. So familiar. So masculine, that even after eight years I still find him incredibly sexy. I can't wait to marry him. I've been counting the days, crossing them off my office calendar with a thick red marker in large diagonal lines.

"Audrey." His voice again, only, this time, more persistent. I force my heavy eyelids open and try to focus on his hazy image crouched by the bed. Oh God, what does he want? What day is it?

It's morning, I know that much because the sunshine is pouring through a gap in the blinds, filling the room with a dim light. My head feels as if it's about to explode. I'm never drinking again.

I catch a glimpse of the outline of Nick's face, his perfectly shaped nose, strong jawline and wavy, unkempt brown hair, before a sharp pain zooms in on my right temple and my eyes close. Jeez, how many drinks did I neck last night? I want to cry.

"Audrey…honey," he whispers urgently in his slight Irish twang, "can you hear me?" I groan and turn my face into the comfort of my pillow. What time is it, for goodness sake? It's far too early to be up. Nick knows I'm not an early bird, what is he thinking?

Church bells are ringing, louder and louder, gently lulling me back to sleep, then suddenly it hits me. Today is my wedding day. That's why Nick is desperate to wake me! Oh, my God. I've got to get up. I've got to shower. I've got to get dressed. Where's my dressing gown? What time did Chloe book me in for hair and make-up? I can't remember. My brain is frazzled.

I start to rouse as last night's events slowly slip into my mind like a film trailer. A Greek taverna by the sea. Mum and Dad's smiling faces, talking, drinking, enjoying the ambience. Loud, lively music, and mouth-watering fish-meze, which I barely touched, spread across a crisp, white tablecloth in front of us. Bottles of Thisbe upturned in ice buckets. A handsome, roguish, young waiter taking my hand for a group dance – everyone egging me on, "Opa, opa, opa!" - laughing, singing, clapping.

I try to swallow but my mouth feels like it's been pumped with a litre of compressed air by a sadistic dentist. Oh Christ, did I make a complete fool of myself? I know I did as I shamefully recall attempting a high kick and then stumbling back on my heel before collapsing onto a fellow diner's lap. My arms instantly wrapped around his neck like an octopus as I struggled to regain

NO WAY BACK

my equilibrium. And then I gaped at him, bleary-eyed until he slowly came into focus – dark blonde, forties, and quite fit.

"I bet you're married," I slurred, "the good-looking ones always are." And he smiled, embarrassed. Shit! Nick must've been watching in the distance, no wonder he's all narky and shouty this morning. "I know what," I yelled, "let's take a selfie together, yeah? I'll post it on Facebook so that all my friends in drizzly, cold London can see what a fit bloke I met in Cyprus. Where's my iPhone? Muuuuum!" I waved my arm aimlessly in the air demanding that someone fetch me my handbag. "Oh, look," I giggled as I swivelled back towards him, "you've got two heads."

The good-looking man held me in his strong arms as I limped awkwardly back to my table. One shoe on my foot and the other…. where was my other shoe? And then the tears, so many tears. Mum's arms around me, comforting me, telling me that I'd had too much wine and it was time to go home.

Why on earth did I do it? I know that I've become a frigging lightweight since turning forty who gets wasted after a measly three glasses of wine. And as I probably knocked back the government's recommended fourteen units a week in one binge session last night, I now have the hangover from hell. On my wedding day!!

My breathing calms. I wish Nick would just stop gawping at me, go into the kitchen and fetch me two strong painkillers and a jug of water, but no chance. He's still here, being persistent, as usual. I suppose that's the most annoying thing about Nick, his stubborn nature.

"Audrey?" He moves closer. I grunt as I strain to open one eye, the other feels like it's been sealed down with superglue. "My God," he breathes, running a hand through his longish hair, which I must say does look like it's in dire need of a wash, and he hasn't even shaved yet. He seems troubled. His eyes are red.

I think he's been crying. I wonder if everything's okay. I don't want any hitches, not today of all days. Nothing, and I mean NOTHING, can go wrong. I frown, which only accentuates my headache - bad move. "You're so beautiful," he murmurs. I don't think so, not after the boozy night I had, and I'm still wearing last night's makeup. "I've been a complete dick. Can you ever forgive me?" He lowers his head for a moment then suddenly looks up, eyes brimming with tears. "Listen, I don't want you to worry about me, Foxy, do you hear?" Foxy is his pet-name for me. He usually reserves it for when he wants to get onside. So, obviously something's wrong. "I just wanted to let you know that I'm really, really sorry and I'll do my best to get back to you as soon as I can. Okay? I love you."

"Huh?" I try to speak but my mouth feels as if it's about to crack. What is he on about? Where's he going? We're supposed to be getting married, for goodness sake! I force my eyes wide open, and for a few fleeting moments, our eyes lock. I blink and then he's gone.

I turn on my back quickly; my camisole clings against my damp skin. I'm wide awake. Nick's isn't here. He never was. I've been dreaming about him. AGAIN. I roll onto my side hugging my knees like a foetus, eyes stinging with tears. My stomach feels like it's spun an 8kg load of washing. I think I'm going to be sick.

A hum of voices and the shuffle of movement feeds through the bedroom door, then everything starts to slot into place, piece by piece, moment by moment. I cover my head under the duvet as reality hammers its way wickedly into my mind. Today was SUPPOSED to be my wedding day. I howl with grief.

"Darling?" There's a tap at the door, "Are you okay? Can I come in?" And before I can reply the door flies open and my mother swiftly wafts into my bedroom on a gust of warm air and Chanel

NO WAY BACK

N°5. She's holding a wooden breakfast tray and looking like something out of *The Stepford Wives*.

By the time I gather the energy to protest she whips up the blinds effortlessly with one hand, balancing the tray in the other. I shut my eyes as the garish light streams into the room, and wince as the terrace door clanks into the security latch. Has this woman ever heard of a hangover? And then the room is flooded with warm, soothing air, washing over me like a healing light.

The church bells are still chiming in the background, and I remember that there's a beautiful church right behind our apartment.

"Never a dull day in Cyprus, Audrey," Mum trills, "Blue skies and sunshine all day, every day." I want to throw up. I heave myself up on my elbows, squinting as my eyes adjust to the daylight.

"How're you feeling?" Mum plumps up the pillows behind me then perches on the edge of my bed, and I almost vomit into her lap. "Rough, I expect, after last night." Leaning forward, she smooths back my long brown, tousled hair, then holds my face in her soft, warm hands that smell of baking, and suddenly I feel as if I'm five years old. "You really shouldn't drink so much, darling." She narrows her hazel eyes and presses her petite nose against mine, a feature, I'm pleased to say, I've inherited from her. "It's terribly bad for you."

"I didn't have that much," I protest, "that wine must've been off." Mum raises an eyebrow giving me a "nice try" look, and I grouchily deflate into my pillows.

"I know what day it is," Mum says darkly, picking an invisible thread off my red, silk camisole, a gift from Nick last Valentine's day, only I've no recollection of changing into it last night. "He's not worth your tears, Audrey. You're well rid of him. I always said he wasn't in it for the long haul, didn't I? Right from the start."

She's referring to the way Nick eats his meals. Mum has this theory, you see; she reckons she can analyse people by the way they eat their food. "Always saving the best till last means you're a procrastinator." She fills a glass from the water-jug. "You never get anything done, and I was right, wasn't I?" She shakes her head knowingly, not expecting a reply. I take the glass from her hand. "I don't want to say 'I told you so', Audrey, but I did warn you about the age difference too." At thirty-six, Nick's five years younger than me, big flipping deal. "But would you listen? No."

I want to tell her to leave me alone; that I miss him so much that I physically ache. That I dream about him constantly. Think about him every waking moment of the day. But I know it'd only kick off an argument. I stay silent, taking large gulps of water. The cool liquid coats my dry mouth, sliding down my throat, and I start to feel semi-human again. I stretch my arm out for a refill.

"Time's a great healer, darling, you'll see." Yes, so people keep telling me but they're not the ones that were left red-faced ten days before their wedding day, were they? It's a good job I had Louise on hand to cancel everything and let all the guests know. She's always had my back, ever since our first day at primary school.

We lost all our deposits, of course - the venue, the honeymoon, the lot. The Bridal Wear shop refused point blank to take back my beautiful silk, handmade strapless dress. I didn't bother taking out any wedding insurance, didn't think that after eight years together there'd be any doubts, to be honest.

"George rang this morning to see how you were getting on." Mum pours coffee from the cafetiere into a tall, white *Villeroy* mug, which she brought with her from London because she won't serve coffee in anything else.

"Oh," I say, feeling touched by my brother's noble gesture. With just over a year between us, George and I have always been close.

"That was nice of him," I manage a small smile. "How're Vicky and the kids?"

"Vicky's lost her job again," she says, exasperated. "Let's hope she doesn't take an aeon to find another one this time."

"She's a smart girl, Mum. I'm sure she'll find something else." I take a sip of much-needed coffee, wondering if Vicky's baby blues is lingering on a bit longer this time. She suffered from mild postnatal depression when she had Florian but it was over within a couple of months; it's taking much longer with the twins. I frown, concerned, and a thump over my right eye reminds me that I'm still in the dog-house.

"George said it's because she's been taking too much time off sick." Mum waves a hand. "Only God knows how they'll cope with three children on your brother's school teacher salary. I had enough trouble with two."

She can say that again. Mum's not really the maternal type. Although George and I weren't deprived of anything as children, she always put her marriage and social life before us. I resented her for it at the time, especially during my teens. But I now know that I've probably inherited her non-maternal gene. Nick made it very clear early on in our relationship that he didn't want any children, and I, having never really felt the burning desire to have any, agreed.

Mum takes the half-empty mug from my hand and places the tray on my lap. "Anyway," she continues briskly, "I've made you a light breakfast." The smell of the omelette makes me heave. "And I'll see you downstairs when you're ready."

As she walks towards the door I reach into my open handbag by the side of my bed. "Your mobile phone is on the kitchen table where you left it last night," she snaps as if she has eyes in the back of her head. "And no, it hasn't rung or bleeped with any text messages." My heart sinks, the very least I expected was a text message from Nick, especially today of all days. "Oh, and by the way." She spins on her heel, resting a hand on the doorframe, "The restaurant called this morning; they found your other shoe. It was under a table, one of the customers handed it in - ha. Dad's gone to fetch it for you."

Thank God for small mercies, they're *Louboutins* and cost me a week's salary.

CHAPTER 2

I KNOW THAT MUM AND DAD MEAN WELL, but after a day visiting monasteries, local bazaars, and shopping in Nicosia, the bright lights of Ayia Napa aren't doing it for me. And I've had a niggling headache all afternoon, which I can't seem to shift. I rub my temple as I follow my parents like a grouchy teenager.

Dad has chosen a busy, elegant restaurant in the heart of town that he and Mum frequent whenever they're over. We're quickly seated at a table by the window by an eager short, plump, balding waiter who addresses them by name. My parents are really fitting into the Cypriot lifestyle. This is their fourth visit in eighteen months. It's nice to see them so happy and relaxed.

I sink into the soft leather high-backed chair as the eager waiter lights the candle on our table before handing us the menus tucked under his arm. Greek music drones softly in the background, black uniformed staff whizz around the packed restaurant, weaving between the tables like a choreographed dance group. But all I can think about is an early night and a good book, preferably a weepy.

Dad orders us a bottle of house white and a large Keo Beer for himself as I gaze out of the window, elbow on table, chin in hand. The resort is buzzing with people clad in shorts, t-shirts and strappy dresses, enjoying the balmy evening without a care in the world. A young couple saunter past, arms wrapped around each other. I smile sadly. I was there not long ago. I check my mobile phone for the umpteenth time. I really can't believe that Nick hasn't bothered to get in touch with me. Did I really mean that little to him?

"Kalispera." A tall, dark, and quite handsome, waiter has appeared at our table. He's wearing a thick gold chain around his neck and a matching bracelet. Where's the eager, bald one gone? I liked him, he was jolly; this one has an air of arrogance about him. "Eiste etimi na parankiledeh?" he says, looking at me, pen hovering over his notepad. I've been mistaken for a local several times during my stay. It's probably down to my dark features, and my newly acquired tan.

"We'll have a few dips to start, please - tarama, houmous, tzatziki," Dad says, taking control, "with extra pitta bread." The waiter scribbles away on his notepad, nodding all the while. "And for mains. I'll have the Stifado, please."

The waiter inclines his head and nods. "Good choice, Sir." Then mouths, "I'm sorry" at me. Perhaps I was hasty. He does have a nice smile.

"And my wife will have the same. What about you, Audrey? It's a lovely beef stew type dish. Do you want to give it a go?" Dad drums his fingers joyfully on the table.

"I'm not that hungry, Dad." I scan the menu quickly, the words a blur. "I'll just have a Greek salad." I close the leather-bound menu with a thud and hand it back to the smiling waiter who's now blatantly staring at my cleavage. I tug at my V-line white cotton top feeling my cheeks burn. Perhaps I should be flattered, but it's a bit difficult to feel enchanted when the man who's flirting with you is wearing a thick gold band on the third finger of his left hand. Goodness, is this what I'm now destined for? A married man's bit on the side?

"You really should have something more, darling." Mum leans forward on her elbows, fingers entwined, and looks at me worriedly. "Look at you, you're wasting away." A chance would be a fine thing. I could only wish for a body as sculptured as hers. Although I've inherited my mother's looks, George and I have taken after Dad where physique is concerned. We only have to look at a cream cake to gain weight. Okay, maybe I've lost a few pounds these last few weeks due to the stress of my break-up, but at 5'7" tall, and only an inch taller than mum, I'm still a size fourteen, hardly a waif.

'So, how's the long holiday going?" I ask brightly, changing the subject.

"Good. Nice and relaxing." Dad takes a swig of beer and glances at Mum. I must say, the tan suits him and he does look a lot more relaxed these days. Albeit he's put on a few pounds. "Just what we need at our age."

The apartment they've rented is on a newly-built complex. The contract was originally for four weeks, giving them plenty of time to enjoy a nice break before my wedding. But when that went pear-shaped they decided to extend it so that I could join them for a while, to give me *a little time to get over it* as Dad put it. But I'm going to need a lot longer than two weeks to get over this heartache. It's torn me apart.

"You're looking well," I tell my parents truthfully, glancing at my mobile phone on the table as it lights with a Twitter notification. "Cyprus suits you." Mum swirls a strand of sleek grey hair around her index finger, giving Dad a mischievous grin.

"Oh, Audrey," Mum drones, placing a French-manicured hand over mine, "We didn't want to tell you, not just yet…not with all the problems you've had recently. But…oh, you tell her, Lionel." Mum always does this to Dad, starts something off and makes him finish it. Dad's cheeks are on fire. He hates being told what to do.

"Not now, Ruby," he replies sternly, pushing his dark-rimmed spectacles up the bridge of his nose before folding his arms.

"But, Lionel, she's got to –"

Dad gives her a warning look. "Ruby."

"Oh, what is it, you two? Come on, tell me?" I insist, my curiosity rising, "I'm a big girl. I can take it." I tear a piece of warm pitta and dip it into the houmous. "You're not renewing your vows are you?" I laugh, biting into the bread.

"We've decided to buy a little house in Larnaca and stay," Mum trills, clapping her hands like an excited child. "Isn't that fantastic? Just think, you and your brother will be able to pop over whenever you like." I almost choke on my mouthful. I stop chewing and stare at them in horror. They can't be serious. What about me? Have they forgotten that I've just been abandoned by the love of my life? They can't walk out on me too. I don't think I could bear it.

"But you can't just leave," I cry. A heavily tanned woman with a blonde bob at an adjacent table glances at me quickly as she reaches for her cocktail. I lower my voice. "What about the house, your friends……your grandchildren, for heaven's sake."

"It won't be for a while yet, love," Dad adds quickly, fiddling with the napkin tucked into his tight collar. "We've got to find a place here first, sort out the house in London. It'll be ages yet." Not with Mum on the case, it won't, her middle name is *efficiency*. I want to cry.

Picking up my wine glass, I down half of it in one go. "But… but…" I take another large gulp. The heavily tanned woman says something to her partner as she curls her blonde hair behind her ear, and he gives me an indiscreet look, face red from the sun against his silver hair. "You can't even speak Greek, how will you communicate?" I grumble, because right now I'll do and say

NO WAY BACK

anything to put them off this ridiculous idea. George will be livid when I tell him. Livid!

We're wordless for a few moments, and I'm suddenly aware of my heart thumping hard against my ribcage, then Dad says, "Come on, love, most of the locals do speak English." He's right, Cyprus is very accommodating to the British, but I'm desperate to dissuade them.

"Well, it's not as if you live with us, darling," Mum points out, "we hardly ever see you."

"What?" I reach out for the wine bottle. "I ring you most days, don't I? And besides," I add loudly over the babble of voices from fellow diners, "at least I know you're there, that I can pop round whenever I like, and what will happen if…"

"You're a grown woman now, Audrey," Mum cuts across me, "You've got lots of friends. And George has his own family now." She looks at Dad for support but he's staring at her through narrow, angry eyes. "Well," she huffs, fanning herself with the dessert menu. Mum always gets defensive when she's outnumbered. "There's still a lot of organising to do. Your dad's almost seventy-five now, you do know that, Audrey, don't you? The milder climate will do wonders for his arthritis. Our GP's been telling us that for years. It'll be a new lease of life for us." Then she looks at me, hurt. "We thought you'd be pleased," she says in a quiet, remorseful voice, "having a holiday home on tap." She looks around her in awe, "On this beautiful island."

But the news has dampened the mood. My entire world is crumbling yet everyone else seems to be getting on with theirs - making plans, changing jobs, EMIGRATING. I down the rest of the wine in one. Mum and Dad exchange glances.

I feel lost, bereft, abandoned. This holiday was a mistake. What the hell am I doing here? I should've sweated it out at home on

Dukes Avenue instead of coming on this ludicrous escape. I press my lips together hard to suppress the tears from springing to my eyes, and as look out of the window a gush of heat spreads through my body like wildfire. And that's when it happens.

"Oh my God." I scrape my chair back and shoot to my feet. A few diners at adjacent tables look round, heavily-tanned-woman and her red-faced partner gawp at me, enjoying the floorshow. "I can't believe it ...I ..." A waiter knocks into me, almost tipping the plate from his hand, and says something in Greek. I think he's swearing.

"Darling? What is it?" Mum asks abruptly, "Are you okay?"

"I...I..." The words catch in my throat. My tongue feels like lead. I look down at my trembling hands. Sweat is beginning to slide down my cheekbones.

"Ruby," Dad says urgently, "she's gone pale! Didn't I tell you to wait until we got back to London before telling her we're moving? Didn't I?"

"Lionel, she's a grown woman. It's not my fault if..."

"Oh, you really know how to kick a person when they're down, don't you?" He yanks the napkin from his collar and tosses it onto the table furiously. Mum and Dad continue to argue, their voices a wispy, snappy buzz in my ears. I stumble against my chair, my legs feel like jelly. Dad jumps to his feet, grabs my arm, then yells, "Someone get her some water for heavens' sake!"

Muffled murmurs and gasps fill my ears. And then everything seems hazy – as if I'm in some sort of dream.

"Oh, my goodness." Mum leaps to her feet and yells at a waiter, "Please...Bambos, hurry." I feel her hands curve around my waist. "It's my daughter...I think she's..."

I look back at the window. The room is spinning. I can't seem to focus. His figure is a blur but he's still there, wistfully pressing

NO WAY BACK

his hand against the window frame. He's come to find me. He's changed his mind. He's come to take me home.

"Nick," I whisper before slumping over the table into darkness.

CHAPTER 3

GEORGE ISN'T SURPRISED TO HEAR about Mum and Dad's plans to move to Cyprus, when I call him with the news the next day.

"They've been behaving like a couple of newlyweds all summer," he sniggers, not sounding the least bit distraught.

What is it with me? Why am I feeling so crushed? But then, I've always been closer to our parents than George has. He left home as soon as he could, living in student digs while he studied for his maths degree, taking on bar and restaurant work to make ends meet. I, on the other hand, held onto my mother's apron strings until I was well into my twenties. They had to practically shove me out the door.

"Be great, though, hey, Sis?" George says enthusiastically, "Rent-free accommodation whenever we feel like it on a beach resort." Mum's words exactly. He really is his mother's son. "Florian will love it." I smile at the mention of my nine-year-old nephew. I can just imagine the pair of them in long shorts, baggy t-shirts and flip-flops. George has always been a bit of a beach-bum. He had a stint as a holiday rep in Rhodes one summer while he was in-between teaching jobs, which is where he met Vicky and where Florian was conceived. But, that was back in the day when George had a full head of hair, a six-pack and a string of girls chasing after him.

"So, how's my favourite boy?" I ask as the doorbell rings. Mum said that Maria was due round this morning. Maria's a lovely

NO WAY BACK

Cypriot woman with grown-up children. She's part of the cleaning team on the block, and, despite her English being very poor, we've struck up a bit of a friendship, even though she can't pronounce my name properly.

"Maria," Mum said, on my second day here, "this is my lovely daughter, Audrey."

"Oddly?" Maria looked puzzled, "Funny name, Mrs Fox."

"No, Maria, not oddly. Audrey, A-U-D," Mum spelt out.

"Ah...A-U-D, like the car, yes?"

"Yes!" Mum and I said in unison, pleased that we were making progress. Maria puffed her chest out, blew a strand of loose hair off her round, olive-skinned face and beamed at us proudly.

"Audi," she said, shaking my hand heartily, "I *very* please to meet you." So we settled for Audi, well it's better than Oddly, isn't it?

I open the door and wave Maria in, miming, "Hello and sorry." She presses a finger to her lips and whispers, "Okay, Audi," as she scurries past me into the kitchen.

"Vicky's taken him to a birthday party," George goes on, to the pelting soundtrack of Maria filling her metal bucket at the sink, "and Josh and Nathan are with her parents, which means..." I know what it means - the sofa, the remote control and lager, "I've got the whole afternoon to myself to watch the match in peace."

George doesn't ask me how I'm coping with my break-up and I get the feeling he's treading on eggshells in an attempt to avoid the subject altogether. He was livid when he found out that Nick had left me, threatening to go round there and sort him out, as brothers do. You see, apart from Nick being his future brother-in-law, they'd become good mates over the years, often spending the weekend in front of the TV cheering on ManU, sometimes even travelling up to Manchester to watch their heroes live in action. I'm sure he misses him too, although he'd never admit it, of course.

So we don't talk about my shambles of a wedding. I don't mention that I dread going to sleep each night for fear of dreaming about Nick, nor do I embarrass myself by telling him about my "episode" last night. Dr Charalambos said my faint was due to stress and dehydration. I also overheard Dad whispering to him outside my bedroom door, telling him that I said I saw my ex-fiancé just before passing out, yet that was impossible as he's in England. The doctor told Dad not to worry, assured him that I'd be fine, it wasn't unusual for patients to hallucinate under extreme pressure or stress.

Maria wanders into the lounge humming under her breath and starts polishing furniture as I read out my return flight details to George.

"Everything okay?" I ask dubiously, pushing a hand through my hair, he sounds a bit put out. "If picking me up is a problem…"

"No, no, of course, it's not a problem," he croaks, then clears his throat, "Everything's fine. I'll pick you up as planned."

"I'll see you in a few days, then." I put down the phone and chew the inside of my lip. I know when George is lying to me.

I spend my last day in Cyprus on the beach with Dad. Mum's gone to a yoga class with Maria. I can't believe how quickly she's settled in, making friends, taking part in local activities. I often feel quite homesick on a fortnight's holiday.

I find a secluded spot away from toned, bronzed, bikini-clad bodies. I don't want to feel more depressed than I already am. I used to be quite slim when I was younger but that was way before I began my love affair…with food. Nick always said that he loved my voluptuous curves, told me I didn't need to lose any weight. He insisted that I got rid of all my size-ten-for-when-I-get-thinner outfits stored at the back of my wardrobe. Naturally, I ignored him. Nick always told me what I wanted to hear, which is how we got ourselves into this mess in the first place.

I throw my orange beach towel onto the sun lounger while Dad secures our belongings onto the metal steeples of the straw umbrella, the sun beating down onto his bare tanned shoulders. I hope he doesn't burn. Dad is quite fair-skinned. "September's the perfect time to visit Cyprus," he says, grinning. "The kids are all back at school, not so many tourists, and 30°C is just about right for us." He reclines onto his lounger and opens his newspaper, sighing contently.

I strip down to my black bikini and recline on the sunbed. It isn't long before I feel the scorching sun stinging my shoulders, despite the fact that I've smothered myself in Factor 30. Why do I always burn? Nick goes a lovely golden brown almost immediately. Oh God, I've got to stop thinking about him.

I close my eyes and try to relax as Maria's words sweep into my mind.

"Audi, no thinking about that bastad Nik," she warned, waving a finger as she climbed into the car next to Mum this morning. "Glear your mind and breathe."

"Clear my mind?"

"That's o'right."

"Well, that's easier said than done, Maria. I can't…."

"Ah." She reached out and covered my mouth with her warm fingers. "Breathe in one, two, three, breathe out one, two three… juuuuuss relax."

The smell of the salty sea whisks its way to my nostrils as it gently laps against the shore, slowly lulling me to sleep. One, two, three, inhale – four, five, six, exhale.

"Shamishi, Locmades, Bommbes, Nero," yells a voice. I hoist myself up on my elbows, squinting at the sun. There's an elderly man holding tightly onto the handlebars of a pushbike kiosk. His white, colossal moustache beaming against his tanned, leathered skin, shielded from the sun under a fisherman's hat. So much for a meditative snooze. I glance at Dad. He's cradling his knees and staring out into the ocean; thin, white hair blowing in the warm breeze. I haven't seen him looking this content in a long while.

A middle-aged couple with a young boy have just arrived with portable chairs and an umbrella. "Townies," Dad says from the side of his mouth as if the family are aliens, "no beach in Nicosia."

The man whips off his top immediately to reveal a large hairy belly, then plunges the umbrella into the sand like a warrior before running and diving into the sea. Dad and I exchange knowing glances and smile.

"Dad," I say, after a while.

"Yes, love?"

"I am happy for you, you know." The wind has picked up and it's humming in my ears. I lean my head back and gaze up at an aeroplane soaring through the sky, descending towards Larnaca Airport. "It was just a bit of a shock, that's all. Of course, I want you and Mum to be happy."

"I know, honey." He smiles as a light gust blows through his maroon t-shirt, ballooning the chest and the sleeves. "And you can visit us anytime. You know that, don't you?" I nod vigorously and press my lips together hard, beating back the tears. When did I turn into this quivering, vulnerable wreck of a woman? This isn't like me at all. I used to be strong, independent, fun to be around. What's happening to me for Christ's sake? I can't let a man destroy me. I'm worth more than that.

The middle-aged man is back, a welcome distraction. He's wet from the sea, his bits semi-erect in his tight black Speedos.

"I'm going for a dip," I announce.

NO WAY BACK

"Right you are, my darling." Dad has made a start on the newspaper crossword, one of his favourite pastimes, which requires no interruptions.

"Won't be long, Dad." I stand up. Speedos-man catches sight of me as I saunter towards the ocean and gives me a long, leery stare. I feel his eyes burning into my back as the sea tickles my feet.

I'm usually frightened of the sea. I'd only dare venture in if Nick was close by to rescue me from drowning. I can't count the times he tried to teach me how to swim, to no avail, of course. But today, I don't seem to care. Its warmth envelopes me as it laps smoothly against my chest. I bounce blissfully on the soft sand beneath my feet, the waves gently carrying me further and further into the ocean. I close my eyes and tilt my head back. Water gushes into my ears, encasing me in a bubble of dark solitude. My toes brush against the soft grains. If I let go I could just float away from all this angst, all this pain. It could all be over in a matter of minutes.

But I'm too much of a wimp, and besides, that's the coward's way out. The foamy sea swishes around my legs as I awkwardly make my way back to shore, hobbling from foot to foot in a vain attempt to avoid the sharp pebbles from digging into my feet. My eyes sting, my feet are glued with sand, then as I pluck my wet bikini bottom out of my left bum cheek with a twang, a male voice says, "Hello, Cinderella."

I turn around and look up at a handsome face, using my hand as a sun visor. I don't recognise him and I'm in no mood for getting picked up on the beach by a stranger.

"Hello," I say, suspiciously. He's holding two bottles of mineral water that he's just bought from the old man on the pushbike kiosk. He gives me a wide, friendly grin, flashing a perfect set of white teeth. His skin is tanned and smooth, even the hairs on his well-toned chest and arms are golden. Clearly, this man spends hours in the gym.

"Did you get your other shoe back?" he asks in an accent similar to mine, another Londoner on holiday. I furrow my brows; what's he on about? "You know, the one you lost trying to do the Zorba the other night. We found it under our table after you'd gone, so I handed it in to the manager. He said your folks were regulars and that he'd make sure you were notified." He glances around the beach as if my parents will materialise from thin air. "They did contact you, didn't they?" Then it dawns on me. He's the man I fell onto when I was drunk at the restaurant.

"I'm really, really sorry about that. I don't usually get drunk and fall over." My face is getting progressively hot. "And yes, I did get it back, thanks for handing it in, they're my best pair."

"S'okay," he says cheerfully, crinkling his slightly curved nose. He sweeps back his short, golden brown hair with his free hand, showing off his toned biceps, and then wipes the sweat off his forehead with the back of his forearm as if he was shooting an advert for *Emporio Armani* or something.

I like the fact that he hasn't dyed the tufts of grey in his hair or cut it into a style to disguise his receding hairline. I don't usually find men of my own age attractive. "Don't worry, we've all been there. It was fun," he laughs, kindly. Then he looks over his shoulder. I follow his gaze. In the distance, a little girl plays in the sand with a bucket and spade. A slim, young woman with blonde hair piled on top of her head is kneeling beside her. She clocks us, jumps to her feet and calls out to him.

"Dan! Hurry up, we're parched." I knew he was married.

"You'd better get back to your family," I say as the beating wind whips up strands of loose hair and lashes them onto my face.

"Er…yeah." He nods, and then lowers his aviator Ray Bans. His deep blue eyes, the shade of the evening sea, hold my gaze, his full lips part, he's about to speak and then…

"Dan!" his wife screeches, waving her arms in the air manically, almost tumbling out of her white skimpy bikini.

"Anyway." I look away and nod towards my sunbed. Dad lifts his arm lazily in acknowledgement and the handsome stranger responds with a shy wave. "My dad's waiting," I say, pulling hair strands out of my mouth. "I'd better get back." I'm really in no fit state to be flirting with anyone so soon, and the last thing I want to do is get involved with a married man. "Thanks for saying hello…" I back away, "and for finding my shoe."

"No worries," he says, and then he's gone.

I watch as he struts along the beach, taking long, smooth strides. I wonder if he's a professional model, he certainly has the right height and physique for it. Or, perhaps, he's some kind of ex-athlete. I can just see him on the racetrack in navy shorts and a red, white and blue vest, pounding across the finishing line, his strong arms raised in triumph to the roar of the crowd. Hmmm… I wonder; and just then he looks back and waves. I drop my head quickly, hurrying back to my sun lounger with a small smile on my face. Men. They're all the bloody same, aren't they?

CHAPTER 4

ON OUR WAY BACK TO THE FLAT, Dad and I stop off at a café on St Lazarus Square in *Scala* for a Greek coffee, a taste I've come to acquire and will miss terribly when I'm back in London tomorrow.

We sit in companionable silence, sipping from our espresso cups as we gaze at the 9th century Byzantine church of *St Lazarus*, just feet away from our table. The faint sound of bouzouki drones into the street from the café radio. Cyclists swish up and down the road, drivers beep, beep, beep their horns, yelling at each other in Greek.

"I know how much you miss him," Dad says suddenly, his eyes fixed on the limestone block building. "And I'm not going to lie to you, love, Nicholas was a good man. We all liked him." He shakes his head and stares at his open-toed sandals, stretching his toes. "The stupid bloody sod." I swallow hard. I can't bear talking about Nick in the past tense as if he's dead. Dad glances at me briefly, then puts his cup down and faces me. "Look, Audrey, love, he may be able to weave his magic through a camera lens." Nick's a professional photographer, passionate about his art. "But with a job like that," he complains, "well, he's not the marrying kind, is he? We did all tell you that from the start." I don't know what Dad is talking about, Nick's work gigs were never a problem, no matter how far he travelled. I trusted him completely. Dad isn't helping.

I stare silently into my cup. A trickle of sweat rolls down my spine, a man's voice yells, "Sophia!" I jerk my head up and watch as he chases a little girl who is running amok, weaving through the legs of tourists outside the church. The town is heaving. It's always busy on a Saturday. I feel hot, sticky, uncomfortable. Why did I agree to come here? We should've gone straight back to the flat for a shower and a change instead of stopping off for coffee in the lunchtime heat.

"What I'm trying to say, love, is…" Dad's voice again. He licks his dry lips as if trying to summon up the words that will miraculously make my pain dissipate. "Well, you've just got to move on now, don't you?" he says finally. I look at him blankly. Isn't that what I'm trying to do? "You've still got your friends, your lovely home." A two-bed Victorian garden flat in Muswell Hill stacked with memories of Nick. I bought it a few years ago on the cheap because it needed complete renovation – everyone told me it was a great investment, and they were right. Nick helped me to restore it, and although it took the most part of two years it was worth it in the end. It's more than doubled in price. "And you've still got us." He covers his warm hand over mine and gives it a good shake. "And your career."

"I'm an I.T. assistant, Dad," I whine. I work for a friendly team of web-designers on Cavendish Square in central London, "Hardly a career." Dad seems irritated by my negativity; beads of sweat have formed at his receding hairline and are beginning to slide down his temples.

Dabbing his face with a napkin, Dad glances up and acknowledges a waiter who's just placed two glasses of iced cold water onto our small wooden table. "You'll meet someone else in time, you'll see," he says, once the waiter is out of sight, his voice as unconvincing as his portrayal of Father Christmas. Florian and the twins know that it's Grandpa dressed in a red suit and a beard. "Audrey, I want you to promise me one thing." Oh, here we go, another lecture. I suppose this coffee stop-off was just an excuse for a father-daughter talk, no wonder Mum didn't want to come. "If Nicholas calls you begging for another chance, promise me you'll say *no* this time, no matter what."

He's referring to the short, yet painful, separation we had eight months ago. We'd been bickering all week over his refusal to give up his pokey one-bedroom flat in Crouch End and move in with me, and I was itching for a row. I couldn't see the point in paying for two properties, especially as he was practically living at mine. But mostly, I was sick and tired of his fear of commitment, of him dragging his feet and delaying our wedding. He knew how much it meant to me and he didn't seem to care. I think that's what hurt the most. I finally reached boiling point one Saturday night and we had the fallout from hell over something completely trivial. I'm pretty sure it was over whose turn it was to order the takeaway. Anyway, after launching into a string of accusations and letting rip some home truths, I threw him out in a mad frenzy. It took two long weeks of apologetic texts, phone calls and pleading voicemails before I caved in and took him back. I wish I hadn't now.

I huff in a high-pitched tone. "If he wanted to be with me, Dad, he'd have married me when he had the chance instead of calling it off at the last minute." I shake my head incredulously, tears sting my eyes. I don't want to cry again – not here, not now. I wish Dad would just stop nagging me.

He stretches back in his chair, cupping his bare, bony knees. "You can mock all you like, Audrey, but I've been around the block a few times. Good women like you are hard to find. You mark my words. He'll be back with his tail between his legs once he gets fed up with the boozing and the clubbing. That's what us blokes are like, we love the initial freedom but it hits us later. And harder." I frown at him. I wonder if he's speaking from experience. "Just listen to your old dad, will you, and beware."

It's Sunday. I'm standing in front of the living room mirror smoothing down my freshly blow-dried hair in preparation for my flight home. Maria has many talents other than domestic goddess and mindfulness coach. The sleekness in my otherwise frizzy mane is remarkable. I told her this morning that if she ever fancied a job in London I could quite easily get Leeroy in Mayfair to employ her as a stylist.

"Ah, you very nice lady, Audi," she said as I forced twenty euros into her palm, "but I can never leave Kypros. Is my home."

My suitcase is packed and Dad has called a taxi to take me to the airport. I study my reflection in the mirror. I've got a tan, a healthy glow. Two weeks in Cyprus with my parents has been a real tonic, which does rather surprise me because I always thought that the only real tonic was one with a large vodka in it. And I think I've finally come to my senses too. Painful as it was, that pep-talk with Dad seems to have worked a treat. Nick is no good for me. I've got to stop wallowing and move on, start again.

Squaring my shoulders, I stand back. I don't look bad at all for forty-one. It's funny how things turn out, isn't it? Life's full of curves and twists and it doesn't always follow your idyllic path. Maria told me that it's the knock backs that make us stronger, perhaps she's right, but only time will tell. The toilet flushes, there's a shuffle, then Dad emerges from the loo with a newspaper folded under his arm. Old habits die hard.

"You look great, love," he says, smiling at me in the mirror.

"I'm getting there, Dad, thanks."

"You'll be all right." He pinches my nose, "You're a Fox remember." I lean forward and kiss his cheek, his skin bristly and rough against my lips. I'm going to miss him terribly. Then he gives me his signature wink and wanders off into the kitchen whistling the theme tune of *Reservoir Dogs*.

On the balcony, Mum is gazing into the distance thoughtfully, cigarette in hand.

"I thought you'd given up." I nudge her lightly with my elbow, pressing my torso against the black curved railings.

"I only have one when I'm feeling tense." She throws me a nervous smile, arms folded. Below, a middle-aged balding man looks up at us briefly, all the while talking loudly into his mobile phone in a foreign language (not Greek), his fat, tanned body astride a sun-lounger by the deserted pool. We stand side by side, staring down at him, yet through him, in silence.

"Is it okay if I give Louise a quick call, Mum?" I turn around and fold my arms, "I just want to let her know that I'm on my way home." Mum nods furiously then stubs her cigarette out into a nearby ashtray, blows the smoke over my head and pulls me into a tight hug.

"I'm going to miss you, Audrey Fox," she whispers into my hair, "it's been so lovely having you here with us…almost like old times." I squeeze her tightly, she smells of cigarettes and Chanel N°5, a nostalgic, comforting concoction.

"Thanks, Mum." I pull away and we gaze at each other longingly for a few seconds. "For everything. I really mean it." Our moment is broken by the sound of Dad's voice bellowing from the kitchen, he's made us all a fresh brew, it's on the table. We disentangle and walk inside, arm in arm.

"Don't be long, Audrey," Mum warns, handing me the phone, "the cab'll be here any moment, and Stephanos doesn't do waiting." Christ do they know all the tradesmen by name? "You don't want to miss your flight."

Louise squeals with delight at the sound of my voice. I tell her how therapeutic my trip has been, how lovely it was to spend time with my folks but that I've missed my friends and Dukes Avenue more than I can say.

"I can't wait to see you all," I say, "and stuff Nick, frigging prick," I laugh. There's a short pause. I can just imagine Louise's face, full of concern, because we both know I don't really mean it. "Anyway," I say, exhaling loudly. "How're things with you? Any goss? Anything I should know about?" Silence. "Lou?"

"Oh, Audrey…I've got some good news and some bad."

"Tell me," I demand, intrigued, "Good news first."

"I'm pregnant!"

"WHAT?" I yell as Mum appears before me, pointing at her watch, eyes wide.

"I said, I'm pregnant!"

"You're JOKING!" I shush Mum away with a hand gesture and she stomps off, complaining that this isn't the time for a girlie catch-up and it won't be her fault if I miss my flight. "Seriously, Lou?"

"Yes, absolutely. 100%. I've done six tests! Look, I'll tell you all about it when you get back. I can hear your mum in the background," she laughs.

"My God! I can't wait." I rake a hand through my hair, forgetting that I've just had it blow-dried. "This is just awesome. I'm so… so…" I'm gobsmacked, absolutely thrilled for her. Louise is already mum to nineteen-year-old gorgeous, bolshy Jess from a previous relationship, but she and Gerry, her lovely, dependable husband, have been trying for a baby for years. The last time we spoke they said they were looking into the adoption process. "Nothing you can say can dampen my mood now. So, come on, hit me with the bad news."

"Well," she says carefully, the joy fading from her voice, "actually, it's about Nick…"

"Audrey," Dad shouts, "taxi's here, come on, love."

"What about him? Oh no, please don't tell me he's seeing someone else already." My heart picks up speed.

"Audrey," Mum cries, "come on, you two can catch up tomorrow. You'll miss your flight."

"Quick, Louise, I've got to go. I've got a cab waiting."

"Ohhh," she exhales loudly, "I wasn't going to tell you this until you got back, George and I agreed not to put a dampener on your holiday, but I wasn't expecting you to call me today and…" I don't let her finish.

"Please, Louise, I'll miss my flight if I don't leave now."

"Okay, but promise me you won't freak out." The taxi driver honks the car horn repeatedly, Dad yells at Mum to hurry me along, Mum repeats his instructions word for word even though I can hear him quite clearly - Stephanos is leaving, he's got other passengers to collect, the aircraft won't wait for Audrey flipping Fox.

"I promise," I cry, my voice shaking.

She takes a deep breath. "Nick's been in a horrific motorcycle accident. It's not looking good."

CHAPTER 5

"OH MY GOD," I CRY, "what on earth happened? Is Nick all right?"

Louise is quiet for a few seconds and then, "We don't really know, Audrey. Ronan called Tina looking for you. Apparently, he still had her mobile number from when they were dating years ago." Ronan is Nick's cousin, it's how I met Nick. "He said he couldn't get a hold of you, tried your landline, but obviously, you're away, and didn't have a mobile number." That's true. Ronan would call Nick at my flat occasionally, but he and I never bothered exchanging mobile numbers, didn't see the point, really. We hardly saw Ronan since he moved to Dublin, anyway. I think the last time we got together was about five years ago when we flew over for his daughter's christening. Nick invited them all to our wedding, of course, and although we were expecting the whole family to attend. Ronan turned up on Nick's doorstep two weeks beforehand. Alone.

"Doctors have confirmed that he was over the limit, though," Louise goes on. "He's lucky to be alive." Her sigh crackles down the line. "I can't believe it happened on the eve of your wedding day. How ironic is that? Talk about Karma." I clamp a hand over my mouth. My stomach twists. How could she be so cold at a time like this? A tear rolls down my face, curves over my lip and slides into my mouth. "Audrey, are you still there?" I feel as if I've been winded. I swallow back a big ball of guilt. This is all my fault. Nick's a sensible drinker. He'd never ride his motorbike if he'd had too much. I drove him to it; he was feeling guilty because of me, because I refused to postpone our wedding. What have I done?

On our way to Larnaca airport, I sit quietly in Mum's arms in the back of the taxi, gazing ahead in a tearful stupor, catching worried glances from Stephanos the driver in his rear-view mirror. Mum strokes my hair lovingly, reassuring me with platitudes – it isn't my fault, he's a grown man. It was his decision to jump on that stupid motorbike of his and put his and other people's lives at risk. "I always said that bike was dangerous, didn't I?" she complains. "It's a good job you weren't on the back of it. Can you put your foot down please, Stephanos, we're running late."

"Sure, Mrs. Fox."

We race along the dual carriageway, wind blowing in my face from a gap in the window. "I caused it," I say flatly, laden with guilt. "How can it not be my fault?" And then I suddenly pull away, panic-stricken, "What if he dies? Oh, Mum, I don't know what I'd do," I gasp.

Mum bites hard on her lips for a few moments, grimacing, and I realise that I'm digging my nails into her flesh. I let go. "Audrey, I don't mean to be harsh, sweetheart." She closes her eyes, exhaling loudly through her nose. "But he's not your responsibility anymore, is he? You're no longer together. He's just your ex, love." I stare at her in disbelief. How can she be so callous? What if he doesn't make it? "He called off your wedding, remember? What kind of a man does that to a woman he loves, hmmm?"

"Well, at least he didn't leave me at the altar," I say defensively, annoyed that she and Dad aren't as devastated as I am. They've known Nick for years. He was part of our family. "At least he had the decency to talk to me about it face to face." And I don't miss the worried look that Mum shoots Dad as he studies us in the

NO WAY BACK

sun visor mirror. The rest of the journey to Larnaca Airport is in pained silence.

There is nothing more annoying than sitting next to a stranger on a five-hour night flight to London listening to him snoring loudly and profusely to the backdrop of a roaring aircraft's engine. People at adjacent seats are getting ratty, shifting uncomfortably in their seats and throwing him annoyed glances, which is futile really as he's fast asleep, but very British nonetheless. I resist the urge to get up, shake him awake and tell him to stop being so damned selfish and give us all a frigging break because we're all bloody exhausted. But only just, mind. And why do flight attendants assume that just because you are sitting next to someone of the opposite sex on an aeroplane that you're an item?

"Does he want anything?" whispers the air-steward politely. He places a miniature bottle of vodka and tonic onto the table in front of me and nods at the snorer.

"I don't know," I say lightly. "I don't know him." The plane swerves and my stomach flips as the *ding* of the seatbelt alert plays in the background, flashing on the overhead panel.

"Oh, I am sorry." The steward has gone slightly red, "I thought you were together." Why? I want to scream. I know I'm a forty-something woman who's just been jilted by her ex-fiancé who now just happens to be lying helplessly in the Critical Care Unit of a north London hospital, but don't you think I'd chose a partner who wasn't old enough to be my grandfather? I look at my fellow traveller sleeping soundly next to me, his head tilted to one side, giving a bit of movement to his two-toned wiry toupee.

"He has only just nodded off," I offer.

"We'd best leave him be then," the steward says, "he does look knackered."

Reclining my head on the padded headrest, I remember how tired I was the very first time I met Nick. I'd had a crap day at the office and all I wanted to do that evening was crash out at home with a takeaway and a lovely glass of ice-cold *Moscato*, but Tina, my second bestie, had other ideas.

We bumped into Nick the moment we walked through the doors of *The Crown's Head* pub in Camden. Tina had just started dating Ronan and was all loved up. I wish she'd stuck with Ronan, instead of marrying that smack-head Mickey. Their marriage only lasted four months. I told her to leave him on their wedding day when he tried to sell me cocaine outside the church.

The pub was heaving. Tina, Nick and I spent the entire evening huddled around a wooden, glass-stained table, drinking Cabernet Sauvignon and telling tales. Nick made me laugh so much that I almost wet myself. He was so easy to talk to and very easy on the eye too, and, unlike many other men I'd met, he didn't spend the entire evening talking about himself or trying to impress us. He listened and was actually interested in what we had to say. I liked him. A lot.

It was almost seven months before our paths crossed again, at a smart little Italian restaurant in Crouch End where Louise worked as Sous chef. Tina and I were sampling her latest gastro creation when Nick breezed in.

"Hey, Audrey," he said after exchanging preambles with Tina. He remembered my name, I was impressed. I didn't bother getting up, so he leaned over and kissed me on both cheeks. The smell of tobacco and his citrus aftershave lingered in the air, "How's it going?" An attractive, slim brunette with striking red lips and big hoop silver earrings stood close beside him, her haphazard long plait flung forward over her left shoulder like a Spanish temptress. Clearly not too pleased to see us, she spent the entire time huffing

NO WAY BACK

and rolling her eyes whilst giving me and Tina intermittent evils, all the while holding onto Nick's arm so tightly that I'm surprised she didn't cut off his blood supply. We exchanged the usual pleasantries - Tina asked after Ronan, and when Nick said that Ronan was engaged to a local girl called Catherine, I didn't miss the flicker of disappointment in Tina's eyes, and, I later found out, neither did Nick.

"Listen, girls," Nick said, swiftly moving on. "I'm having a little flat-warming party next week. If you've no other plans why don't you drop by? I'd love to see you both."

As it happened, we didn't have any other plans, and Tina, being a fun-loving party animal, almost tore Nick's arm off when he handed her his business card with his address scribbled on the back. Louise got her usual childminder for Jess and the three of us turned up on his doorstep with a bottle of *Veuve Clicquot*. The memory of that night still makes me smile. Minus the Spanish temptress girlfriend, Nick and I danced the twist all evening because it's the only dance he can do - two left feet, I'm afraid. It was the best party I'd been to in ages, and by the end of the night, or should I say early hours of the morning, I was smitten. I knew from that moment on that he was *the one*. The rest, as they say, is history.

CHAPTER 6

I LOOK UP AT THE SMALL SCREEN IN FRONT OF ME. We're flying over Munich now – almost home. The 'snorer' is still asleep, mouth ajar, but the snoring is now a bearable muffled grunt. Most of the other passengers have woken up, anyway. A pretty little girl with long strawberry-blonde, corkscrew curls has been visiting the toilet at almost ten-minute intervals, spending only a few seconds in there and then rushing back down the aisle shaking her wet hands. I wonder if she has OCD. George had a spell of OCD when he was about eight. He used to wash his hands three times in succession and perform other rituals. I used to watch him silently with great intrigue until one day my curiosity got the better of me and I quizzed him over it.

"If I don't do it," he warned heatedly, "something bad will happen to all of us." Terrified, I ran and told Mum immediately. It soon emerged that he was being bullied at school for being a little overweight and the stress of it all had brought on the condition. It took a while, but he recovered with the help of our lovely GP and lots of TLC.

The child rubs her little hands together and gives me a small, timid smile, then dips her head and scuttles off down the long aisle.

I adjust in my seat. I need a wee for the umpteenth time. A queue of women a mile long has assembled outside the toilet cubicle, so I can forget it. I do sometimes wonder if my bladder is the size of

NO WAY BACK

a pea. I cross my legs. A teenage boy wearing a headset catches my eye. He's staring at a glowing screen in front of him, flicking back his long black fringe and chuckling intermittently. I smile sadly. Nick loved all the in-flight entertainment. He'd watch whatever film was on offer while I'd read a novel from cover to cover.

I feel exhausted. I've got to stop thinking about the past. I rest my head back to the hiss of a can being opened and the muffled hum of conversation. My eyes sting from sleep deprivation. If I could rest them for just a few moments.

"We'd have been on our honeymoon now if I hadn't been such an idiot." Nick's voice bellows in my ears. I open my eyes wide. I can't fall asleep now. I won't let myself dream about him again. I don't think I can take the strain. But it's true. We'd have been in Goa now, living it up in a five-star luxury hotel as Mr and Mrs Byrne if he hadn't called our wedding off at the last moment. My mind rewinds to the night of our break up.

"We've got to talk," he said as I loaded the dishwasher hurriedly.

"What now?" I huffed, glancing at my watch. "I haven't got time. I've got to finish this, then go round to Louise's. She wants to go over the final details of the wedding menu. But I'll be home by…"

"No, Audrey," he cut across me. "It's important."

I followed him into the living room complaining all the while, I'm going to be late, Louise has got an early start, can't this wait until I get back? We sat on my oversized chocolate coloured sofa. He refilled our glasses with red wine, and, with a slightly trembling hand, passed one to me.

"There's something I need to tell you," he began with a shaky voice. I knew in an instant what was wrong but I didn't want to believe it. I tried to stay focused, positive, telling myself that it's probably Ronan, he's let him down, he needs to fly back to Dublin urgently and wants me to ask George to be his best man, or at least something equally fixable. When he dipped his head, my heart fell into my stomach. He'd been acting strange all week. I braced myself, I knew what was coming. "I just...I...it's..."

"You don't want to marry me, do you?" I said coldly, eyes fixed on our untouched wine glasses on the coffee table.

"No. I mean, yes." He ran a hand over his unshaven face. "But... just not now. I'm not ready." He stood up and began pacing the room, running his fingers irritably through his greasy hair as if he had some kind of infestation. I'd never seen him like this before, he looked drained, dishevelled and loaded with frustration. "I need more time," he blasted, making me jump, "what's the rush?"

"Rush?" I cried incredulously. "Rush? It's been eight long years." Tears sprang to my eyes. "How much time do you need, for heaven's sake?"

"I dunno. I feel trapped, you're *all* suffocating me." He reached for his cigarettes in his shirt pocket, then, remembering I don't like him smoking indoors, shoved them back in again angrily. "Why can't we just postpone it for a while, hmm?" He clasped his hands at the back of his head, exhaling loudly. "Say about six months or so."

"You're unbelievable." I took a large gulp of wine then slammed the glass onto the coffee table, spilling some of the ruby liquid onto an invite that was meant for Louise's mother-in-law. We'd had a last-minute cancellation from my uncle Jack in Scotland and there was a spare place. I picked up the invite, brushing the stain away with my thumb but it was too late. The wine had caused the paper to swell. A big, fat tear fell onto the card. Tears and wine. It was ruined now.

"You know I'm no good at all this, Audrey," he complained, resting his hands across the wooden surround of the fireplace, his back to me. He'd spent hours restoring that fireplace when

NO WAY BACK

I first moved in, sanding it down, buffing it up before applying a thin varnish in meticulous soft strokes. Who'd have thought that a few years on he'd be using it as a prop to leave me? "It's all happening too fast," he snapped. "If you'd just…" And then the penny dropped.

"There's someone else, isn't there?

"What?" He spun round, face ashen.

"You've met someone else." I cupped my hands over my mouth, my stomach clenched. "Oh my God, how could I have been so stupid? The signs were all there. Who is she? Do I know her? Is it someone you met through work, or –" I was blabbering but I couldn't seem to stop myself, and I didn't really care.

"For God's sake, Audrey, stop it," he cut in loudly, "there's no one else. I can barely keep up with you let alone have an affair. Besides, I'd never do that to you, you know that."

"Promise me," I demanded, wiping my snotty nose with the cuff of my sleeve, inhaling the teary phlegm. "Swear there's no one else."

"Okay, okay," he said finally, "I swear on my mother's grave." I knew then that he was telling me the truth. He adored Coleen. But if there wasn't anyone else, what was it then? Why the sudden change of heart?

"Why, then, Nick?" Silence. "Come on, you owe me that at least."

"I just don't feel ready for marriage," he replied, but he couldn't even look at me. Then, for the briefest of moments he seemed to come to his senses and I felt a sliver of hope. "Oh God, what the hell am I doing? Look, Audrey." He took a lungful of breath and exhaled loudly. "I love you so, so much. You're my world." I looked up at him then. This was a blip, a meltdown, last minute nerves; everything was going to be fine. A trickle of confidence danced in my chest. "But…well, if I'm honest, I'm not sure I'll ever be ready for marriage." I squeezed my eyes shut. I couldn't believe what I was hearing. I felt like I was on a carousel, that my life was spinning, spinning, spinning out of control.

"And you couldn't tell me this months ago, hmm?" I rose to my feet. He looked at me wordless, face dark with remorse. "Before I ordered my dress." I tapped the invite lightly on the palm of my hand as I slowly walked towards him, "Before I booked the venue, perhaps?" I pointed the card at him as if it were a loaded gun. "Before I sent out all the bloody invitations!" I screamed. I flicked the card across the room, missing him by inches as he ducked out of the way.

"You seemed so excited," he said in a quiet voice, startled by my outburst. "I didn't want to hurt you."

"And what the hell do you think you're doing now, Nick? You're breaking my heart."

He took a few hurried steps towards me. "I don't want to lose you, Audrey. If we could just…"

"No fucking way," I cut in, raising my hand to silence him, "no rescheduling, no postponing." I'd waited years for Nick to agree to this marriage, spent endless hours organising our wedding day, making sure that everything was perfect - from the buttonholes to the honeymoon, the bridesmaids dresses to the cars. And although like any other excited bride-to-be, I was walking on cloud nine, I also felt completely shattered. There wasn't a chance in hell that he was going to persuade me to come round to his way of thinking, not this time.

"It's now or never," I said gravely, wiping my cold tears with my fingers, willing him to change his mind. The deafening silence that hung between us for those few decisive moments was unbearable. I can still hear the wail of a police siren in the distance as I

NO WAY BACK

collapsed onto the sofa, wrapping my arms around my quivering body, gulping back the tears. Swallowing hard, I looked up at him. "So, what's it to be, then?" Blue and yellow lights flashed through the window, demanding our attention. The blaring sound of the siren screamed in my ears, louder and louder before drowning into the night.

"I can't do this," he confessed. I closed my eyes and covered my ears, blocking out his words as he rambled on and on with pathetic excuses. I couldn't believe what was happening. That this was the end. Questions flapped around in my mind - what was I going to tell everyone? How would I cope without him? Was this it for me now? Would I end up a spinster surrounded by a thousand cats in a six-bedroomed house? I'd put my heart and soul into this relationship, eight years of my life, and in a flicker it was over.

"You're going to regret this, Nick, think carefully about what you're doing," I pleaded, feeling pathetic.

With his hands loosely on his hips, he stared at the wooden floor, a solitary tear trickled down his face. "You deserve better," he murmured, "I'm sorry."

Pushing my trolley through the sliding doors of Heathrow Airport's arrivals always gives me a bit of an adrenaline rush; makes me feel as if I'm some kind of celebrity. Perhaps it's the barriers that section off the area that do it, and the crowds of people hanging over them with eager, excited expressions. I scan their faces quickly, looking for George.

"Audrey!" George's voice bellows through the arrivals lounge, my eyes flit from face to face as I search for him in the crowd. "Over here!" There's a loud whistle and then I spot him bouncing in the background, arms outstretched above a line of taxi drivers with blank faces, notice boards in hands. I rush through the barriers. We hug tightly like long lost relatives reunited by Holly Willoughby in an episode of *Surprise Surprise*; I've missed him.

"You're tanned," he says accusingly, wrenching his sleeve and pressing his pale, hairy arm against mine. "It's almost October. We've got the bloody heating on at home." He takes control of my trolley; a man thing, I know.

I link my arm through his. "It was twenty-nine degrees yesterday," I say, as we walk across Terminal Five, "I was lying on a sunbed almost every day." I scratch the back of his shaved head playfully. George scrunches his face, I know he's forty but he's still my kid brother. "How's the family?"

"Oh, you know, kids screaming, Florian being a nuisance and Vicky…well, you know how low she's been feeling lately. So what's new?" My brother looks tired and haggard in his baggy jeans and khaki parka coat. I feel a pang of guilt for dragging him out of his warm bed at this ungodly hour. I should've just jumped in a cab. What was I thinking? He steers the trolley into the lift and gives me a warm grin.

"I hope you've taken the day off tomorrow," I say, pulling my cardigan around me as we step into the car park to the sound of whistling aircraft.

"Bloody right I have. I could do with a few days off from that madhouse, anyway."

I listen to my brother's anecdotes with a smile as we soar along the M4 heading for north London. It's good to be home.

My flat is just as I left it – only tidier. I notice immediately that all pictures of me and Nick have vanished. And gone too is the pop-art canvas of the two of us that adorned the eggshell coloured wall above the fireplace. Vicky must've been around with a duster and gotten rid of all traces of Nick. Vicky's great like that, always

NO WAY BACK

thoughtful, always compassionate. She stayed over the night Nick left me, consoling me, making me hot drinks, wiping away my tears, making sure I didn't do anything stupid – not that I would've. I'm not that daft.

"We had a bit of a tidy-up, watered the plants, sprayed the garden," George calls out from the kitchen. "Hope you don't mind." He reappears with two mugs and a teapot. We sit side by side on the sofa. I'm glad to be home but it feels odd knowing that Nick will never walk through my front door again, that I'll never fall asleep in his arms on this sofa. A cold, eerie feeling crawls over my skin and I quiver. "Oh, before I forget," George says. His hand disappears into his coat pocket. "Better give these back." He hands me my door keys, smiling. "And if you don't mind, babe, could you help with house-sitting Mum and Dad's pad? It's been a bit difficult for me trekking up to Whetstone from Archway three times a week, what with Vicky feeling so tired all the time."

"Of course, I can." A tinge of guilt pinches my skin. "I'm sorry I left you in the lurch." I lean onto him, closing my eyes, and he wraps his arm around my shoulders. It's almost daylight. We're both exhausted. He presses his chin over my head affectionately and Nick's face propels into my mind. I pull away quickly.

"Are you okay?" George looks startled.

"Yes, it's just that smell…I…"

"God, I don't smell that bad, do I?" He sniffs under his coat. "I have washed, you know, and I splashed on that aftershave Vicky got me last Christmas. One you recommended she said." Dior Eau Sauvage. Nick's favourite.

"Of course, you don't smell, you numpty." I lay a hand on his forearm, the other over my stomach. "It's just that scent. It made me feel bit nauseous, that's all."

George looks horrified. "You're not…" It takes me a few moments to register what he's implying.

"Don't be so stupid, of course, I'm not pregnant."

"I was going to say, what with the news about…" he falters. My poor brother's eyes are red, he needs to sleep. I should tell him to go.

"It's okay," I smile. "Louise told me about Nick's accident."

"Yeah, I know," he groans. "I did tell her…"

"Don't be angry with Loulou." There's no way I'm going to let him land this on her. Louise has been my rock. I don't know how I'd have coped without her these last few weeks. "I made her tell me," I insist. George grunts and takes a slurp from his mug. He knows Louise and I always stick up for each other, no matter what. We always have, even as kids. "Any news on Nick's condition?" I ask casually, refilling our cups from the teapot.

"I dunno," George fidgets with his key fob. "Look, I feel sorry for the guy and that, and I hope he'll be back on his feet soon, but he's got nothing to do with us anymore, has he?" I watch silently as he flicks the key in and out of its fob. Thud, thud, thud. "And quite frankly, I don't know why that cousin of his tried to contact *you*. Had he forgotten that he jilted you and humiliated the lot of us?" He hisses loudly through his nose, then suddenly puts his mug down on the coffee table and faces me. "I hope you're not planning on visiting him in hospital," he warns, knotting his thick, dark eyebrows.

"As if." I pull a face, then blow onto my hot tea. Clearly, I'm not going to get anything out of George. "I just wanted to know if he's okay, that's all. Jesus, am I not even allowed to ask how he is?" I say rhetorically. "And I think you're forgetting that I'm the injured party here, George, and if I can have some compassion for him…" I tail off, taking a large sip from my cup, forgetting that it's hot. My lips burn.

George picks up his mug and draws it to his lips, all the time regarding me dubiously. He doesn't provoke me further, and we finish our drinks in silence.

CHAPTER 7

SLEEPING IN UNTIL 2 P.M. IS UNHEARD OF FOR ME, but I really needed those seven hours. I bet George is still snoring. "Don't call the flat until after school," he warned, squeezing me in his arms on my doorstep this morning. "Vicky's got a coffee morning on with some of the mums from nursery and I don't want the phone going off every flipping five minutes. You know I can't get back to sleep once I'm awake."

I pour myself a coffee and shuffle into the lounge with it, sipping from my mug. A neat tower of mail is waiting for me on the dining table. Vicky must've assembled it, George doesn't do tidy. I sift through it quickly - a few cards, probably wedding ones, which I really can't face right now. The rest is bills and junk mail. I toss them to one side and sink into the high-backed chair at the table, wrapping my hands around my warm mug. I'll deal with them later. There's no rush. I've got all day. I'm on compassionate leave, anyway.

Closing my eyes, I'm suddenly aware of the ticking clock on the mantelpiece – tick, tick, tick in time to my beating heart. Apart from the muffled sound of traffic outside and the odd tweet and ruffle coming from the birds in my garden, it's deadly quiet in here, and I'm not sure I like it. Perhaps I should get a cat or a dog. I've heard that pets reduce stress levels, and it'll be nice to have something pottering around the empty flat.

The bare wooden floors creak under my weight as I walk towards the French doors. Nick was supposed to change a couple of dodgy floorboards, but, what with the wedding and everything, never got round to it. He was good at DIY and gardening, fixed most things when they went wrong, decorated my flat singlehandedly. I wonder how he is today. If he's okay. If they're looking after him well. I wonder if he's thinking of me too. I shake my head, gazing into the garden. We almost had it all. When is this aching going to end?

A bird lands on my garden fence. "Hello, Mr Magpie," I say, saluting it, although I'm not quite sure why; could my luck possibly get any worse? The bird hops along then spreads its wings and takes off. I watch enviously as it soars into a blanket of grey sky. We had big plans for this good-sized garden - bedding plants along the foot of the raised decked patio with a splash of colour on either side of the green; tulips, daffodils and gerberas.

"And a couple of rose bushes, Foxy," Nick had said last summer, standing on the lawn in his army green wellies, shovel in hand, sweat trickling down his heaving bare chest, "And I think a camellia too. In the far corner, just there." He nodded towards the gazebo he'd built the year before, wiping the sweat off his hair speckled torso with his rolled-up vest. "My mum loved camellias."

Nick loved working in the garden. It may as well rot now.

I knock back the last dregs of tepid coffee, then fire up my laptop. I need to catch up with all the latest news on social media and sort out my work emails. The last thing I want to do is lose my job.

"Take a few weeks off, Audrey," Raymond, my boss, had said when I called him the day after Nick broke off our engagement. "We're all thinking of you."

I love working at Blue Media. I get to meet lots of new people and my colleagues, bar Callum, are a good, friendly bunch. Nick got me the job there two years ago. He was doing a photo shoot for them for a well-known fashion label when an admin job came up. I'd just been made redundant from Blackshore Finance and was desperate for work. Nick put my name forward and Raymond offered me the position on the spot, and, after a short spell in admin, I was promoted to text editor. I now help Fearne, one of the webmasters, with her new clients. Raymond suggested sending me on a web design course recently, and although I was fleetingly tempted I was too busy organising my wedding to give it any serious thought, but now…

My stomach furls at the sight of my profile picture on Facebook. It's of me and Nick on the night of our engagement, cheesy, I know, but I just couldn't help myself. We're smiling into the camera lens, cheeks pressed together, glass of champagne in hand. "Oh, Nick," I hear myself say, touching his image on the screen with my fingertips, "what on earth happened to us?"

I regain my composure and start typing quickly, there's no time for tears. There's work to be done. The sooner I get back to some kind of normality, the better. I change my relationship status to single, upload a new photo of myself, which Maria took of me on the beach in Cyprus, then type a quick message saying I'm back. I scroll through my timeline. Raymond's status was updated a few minutes ago. A short post about how busy they are, followed by an update on *www.weloveflowers.com*, a new online florist we'd recently published. Raymond's posts are mostly work related and he always encourages us to do the same.

"Social networking sites are useful marketing tools," he'd said, a few weeks ago during one of our meetings, "let's use them to our advantage."

Raymond's a self-made thirty-eight-year-old entrepreneur. He set up Blue Media from his spare bedroom five years ago and now employs four full-time staff members, which includes me, Fearne, Callum, and Stacey, our personal assistant who steps in when I'm away and does my job too. We also use freelance photographers and illustrators, one being Nick. We're like one big happy family working from his prestigious office in the heart of London. The boy's done good.

I bite my nail thoughtfully, a bad habit, I know, but Mum's not here to slap my hand away. I'm supposed to be off work until next Monday, but what's the point in moping around here all day in my dressing gown feeling sorry for myself? I need routine, distraction. Getting to my feet, I glance at my watch. Stacey should be back from lunch by now. I'm sure they'll be glad of an extra pair of hands, especially as they're rushed off their feet. As I reach for the phone it rings alarmingly in my hand. It's Louise.

"Wow, you're eager," she says brightly, and I get the feeling that she thought I was sitting by the phone waiting for it to ring. "Welcome home. How was your flight?"

She howls with laughter when I complain about the snorer, and tuts sympathetically when I tell her about the little girl who kept washing her hands, how she tugged at my heartstrings, reminded me of George when he had OCD. It isn't long before the subject of Nick slides into our conversation.

"I kept having all these dreams," I explain, "I was even convinced I saw him outside a restaurant in Ayia Napa last Saturday. Can you believe that? And then I bloody well fainted. They had to carry me out and bundle me into the car in a semiconscious haze. It was so embarrassing. My parents even called a doctor in."

"Oh God," Louise groans. "Dreaming about him is one thing, but if you've started hallucinating, well, that's just not right." I hear her breathe heavily down the phone. I can just picture her, hand on hip, thin, blonde eyebrows gathered worryingly. "Are you sure it wasn't just someone who looked like him? I mean, he has got that kind of face, hasn't he?"

"What, a one-face-fits-all?" I ask, a hint of sarcasm in my tone. Louise never misses an opportunity to put Nick down.

"Oh, you know what I mean," she whines. "I'm only trying to help."

I feel a pang of remorse. She's right. I shouldn't be taking out my frustrations on her. I apologise immediately. "I don't know what's happening to me, Lou." I hold my aching head in my hand, "Sometimes, when I close my eyes I can even smell him, as if he's still here, lying next to me in bed." A shiver tingles through me as the image of him kneeling by my bed in Cyprus flashes in my mind. "Am I going mad?" I ask, half-joking, half-meaning it. "Perhaps I should go and see my GP."

"You've been mad for years, love."

"Oh shut up, you," I say, and we both giggle. I've missed my lovely friends. I ask her about her pregnancy and she explains how she weed on six sticks while Gerry sat outside the toilet door, how they can't believe their luck, can't wait to be parents.

"Honestly, Aud, after all the disappointments we've had, and then all that stress over the adoption." Gerry wasn't keen on adopting and I know that they were having some heated debates over it. "We just can't believe it," she squeals. I can almost feel her excitement travelling down the phone. "Sometimes I just have to pinch myself to make sure I'm not dreaming."

Despite my sadness, a warm smile spreads across my face. If anyone deserves a break, it's Louise. Life hasn't always been easy for her. Her first partner walked out on her the moment he found out she was carrying Jess. She lost all hope in men after that. A devoted mother and chef in the making, Louise rarely had time for relationships. Until Nick introduced her to his accountant

Gerry, that is. Then everything seemed to change overnight. From Michelin craving career woman she turned into a domestic goddess, her sole objective to have a family with Gerry.

"Gerry must be a happy bunny," I smile down the phone to the clank of car doors followed swiftly by the rumble of an engine.

"Errr…yeeeesss…he is, err," she murmurs, sounding a little distracted, "but he's…erm…Will you be back before six?"

"Six?" I ask, glancing out of the window as Alan from upstairs zooms off in his old silver Mercedes SL, leaving a trail of fumes behind him.

"Oh, just a moment, Audrey." There's a kerfuffle of hissing, mumbling, keys jangling and then the slam of the front door. "Sorry about that, you were saying?"

"Was that Jess?"

"No, no, Francesca's staying with us for a while." She sniffles quickly, "Another business trip."

"Oh no, not Francesca." I grumble. Francesca is Gerry's twin sister. She lives in France with her rich, successful husband Jean-Pierre.

"I know," Louise drones. "But what can you do? She's family."

"I hope you're not putting up her entire brood again." Francesca has three children by three different men. I had the pleasure of meeting her youngest son Marcel, a charming little boy of five going on twenty, when Gerry and Louise had him over last summer while Francesca and Jean-Pierre went on a Mediterranean cruise. She packed the other two off to their respective fathers.

"No," Louise affirms, "she's on her own this time. The kids are with Jean-Pierre and the nanny. She's flying back tomorrow night, anyway."

"So we won't get to meet her again?" Our paths never seem to cross, but from what I've heard, it's a blessing.

"Afraid not," she sniggers, "Lucky you. We've barely seen her ourselves, to be honest. She's either out partying with friends or shopping at Westfield. My hallway is crammed with designer shopping bags." Francesca treats their house like a hotel. I don't know why Louise puts up with it. This'll be her fourth visit since Louise married Gerry, and it's not as if they can't afford to stay in a hotel. Louise always says that "this time is the last time" and then caves in when Gerry gives her the puppy-eyes look. I don't blame her. It is very hard to say no to Gerry and he does do very good "puppy-eyes".

"So, how did Jess take the baby news?" I say, changing the subject. I get a vision of Jess in her skinny white jeans and lace black top, her neck adorned with numerous chains, clanking every time she moves; blonde, wavy hair tumbling over her shoulders. Jess and I are close. I'm like her surrogate aunt. I watched her growing up, and was chief childminder when Louise had the odd night out. Jess was the only person I texted back when Nick dumped me. Even through my grief, I couldn't bear to ignore her consoling message - **The shit head freak. R u ok? Luv u x <3**

"Brilliant," Louise replies, sounding surprised, "she can't wait to have a little brother or sister. She can't do enough for me around the house." Well, that'll be a first – doesn't sound like the Jess I know. "Mind you, she is busy with a new boyfriend." Ah, that explains things, then. Jess can have her pick of boyfriends, with her good looks and curvaceous physique, they're lining up to take her out. Her phone never stops pinging with messages.

"So," I say, tentatively, "any news on Nick's condition?" My iPhone throbs on the coffee table. I glance at it quickly as a message lights up the screen.

"No, I haven't heard anything else," she says, voice suddenly cold. "Why should you care, anyway? You're not together anymore."

There's a short pause as I retrieve my text message. It's from Vicky, welcoming me home and asking when we can get together. I slip my mobile into my pocket. "Look," Louise huffs, "I know how you must be feeling but…" Annoyance flares through me. How could she know? She's not me. She's not in the arena. I wouldn't wish this kind of agony on my worst enemy. "This has come as a terrible shock, I'm sure," she says as if she's reciting a paragraph out of a self-help pamphlet. "But he made his choice, didn't he? Before the accident, I mean. You've got to stop pining for him, Audrey."

"Pining?" I ask, surprised. Is that what they all think I'm doing? Looking for a way to get back with him? "What are you talking about?" Distracted by a noise outside, I yank the net curtain back. A young builder in a blue hooded sweatshirt is throwing bricks into a wheelbarrow outside the house that's having a loft conversion a few doors down.

"I'm saying that you're well rid of him, that's all. You'll meet someone else."

"So everyone keeps telling me," I say dryly, moving away from the window.

"Well, what do you expect, Audrey? Have you forgotten what he did to you? He treated you like shit. If that were me, I'd…"

"Of course, I haven't forgotten," I cut across her. Louise always says it how she sees it but I wasn't prepared for this backlash from her. I thought she'd be more compassionate, given the circumstances. "But aren't you all forgetting," I add defensively. I've had enough of being patronised. "That if I'd agreed to postpone our wedding, none of this would have happened. We'd still be together and he wouldn't be on a hospital bed."

"Oh, so it's your fault now, is it?"

"Some of it, yes," I admit, cheeks burning.

"Audrey! Will you just listen to yourself? Why are you trying to make him out to be like some kind of saint just because he's injured?"

"Stop twisting things, Louise. I'm concerned about his welfare, that's all. We were together for eight years, in case you've forgotten. Anyway, you wouldn't even be with Gerry if it wasn't for Nick." I pause but she doesn't answer. She knows I'm right. "And he did love me. He got cold feet, that's all. I pushed him too far." I thrust a hand through my hair restlessly, another crash of bricks land in the skip.

"Oh, Audrey, you don't know what you're saying."

"So, I'm mad now, am I? That's what you're all thinking, isn't it?"

"If you go and visit him in hospital, which is what I think you're planning on doing then, yes, you are!"

"Don't be so stupid."

"And if you're considering taking him back, well…" she sighs irritably.

"I could do a lot worse." I can't believe I just said that out loud.

"Audrey, he's not the man you think he is."

There's a brief silence as I process what she's just said, and then, "What's that supposed to mean?" I demand. I can hear my heart pumping in my ears, her breath heavy down the phone.

"Nothing, forget it," she snaps.

"No, no, come on. You've started now, what do you mean?" I can't believe that Louise and I are arguing over Nick. Oh my God. Are we about to fall out again?

"Look, you're taking all this the wrong way. What I mean is, he's not worth it, that's all," she says firmly. "When push came to shove, he couldn't hack it. He showed his true colours. Anyway, you've always been too good for him."

My mind starts racing. What the hell is she talking about? Nick was devoted to me, she knows that. Then it suddenly dawns on me and I feel the colour drain from my face in an instant. "You're jealous!" I say furiously. "You've always been jealous of me and Nick."

"Audrey!"

"Just because I had a man who loved me. Just me!" I poke my chest with my index finger. "Without any Ts and Cs." Anger rips through me like a tsunami. I know I shouldn't be saying these hurtful things to Louise but I can't seem to stop myself. I'm like a woman possessed.

"I can't believe I'm hearing this."

"Yes, well the truth hurts, doesn't it?"

"Jealous of what exactly? A commitment phobic loser?" she laughs incredulously. "You are way off track, Audrey, way, WAY off track."

"He loved me, everyone said so, apart from YOU, that is."

"Love? Ha! Don't make me laugh. If he was so in love with you then why did he do a runner, hey? Why did he abandon you ten …"

I slam the phone down hard before she can finish. Looking down at my trembling hands, heat sweeps through me, the room spins. I think I'm going to faint again. The phone rings almost immediately. I let it go to answerphone.

"Audrey," Louise's voice is thick with emotion. "Audrey, I'm sorry, okay? I was out of order. I know you don't want to talk to me right now but I didn't mean to upset you. I should've been more sensitive. It's my raging hormones, Gerry will tell you," she laughs softly and my heart thaws. "Look, I know you didn't mean any of the stuff you said either." No, I didn't, she knows me so well. "We're a right pair, aren't we?" More soft laughter. Poor Lou. My hand reaches for the phone and then… "Oh, God," she exclaims and I move my hand away quickly. "I hate talking into these machines. Just call me… Please." She blows her nose loudly. "Please don't let him come between us again," she says with a nasally voice. Oh God, I've made her cry. I hate myself. "I'll be home until about four-thirty, then I've got to pick Jess up from the station. Bye for now. Love you."

My hands are still trembling as I dial Tina's number.

"Audrey! Arrghhhhhh... hi!" It's so good to hear her jovial voice. She must be in a bar or restaurant. I can hear a lot of commotion - voices, clatter and the drone of background music.

"Tina. I've missed you, how are you?" I try to control my wobbly voice. Tina has always had the capacity to lift my spirits.

"Fine, fine. Listen, how are you?" She sounds a bit pissed, which is good because she's more likely to cooperate. "You sound dreadful, is everything okay?"

"Yes, I'm fine, it's just hay fever." I know that Tina won't bother questioning why I've got hay fever at this time of year, she doesn't do cross-examinations.

"In the last week of September?" Damn.

"Yeah, spores, you know," I sniff for impact. "Where are you?"

"Having a bite to eat at a pizza bar," she says cheerfully, "with a few friends from the office. How was Cyprus?" I tell her it was the perfect place to convalesce and did me the world of good.

"Listen," I say tentatively, "I heard Ronan contacted you about Nick, has he been in touch with any more news?"

"Oh God, I know... poor Nick. No, I haven't heard back from Ronan. I'll have another glass of Pinot Noir," I hear her say. "Sorry, Audrey, I've been trying to get the waiter's attention for the last twenty minutes. A girl can die of thirst around here. You were saying?"

"You wouldn't know which hospital Nick's at, would you?" Tina doesn't possess the high morals of Louise and George. She's more

NO WAY BACK

of a follow your heart, life's too short, kind of person. If anyone is going to give me any information about Nick, it'll be her.

"No, Ronan didn't say... Another pause as she speaks to the waiter again, "Oh, a large one please, thanks."

"Tina, I'll call you when you're less busy... tomorrow, perhaps?"

"Okay, Audrey, we'll talk properly then."

"Oh, and one last thing, Tean."

"Go for it."

"Can I have Ronan's number please?" Silence. "You do still have it, don't you?"

There's a pause and then, "Babe, I don't." She sounds nervous, unsure. She's lying. "I never kept it in my contacts and erased all my log details a few days ago. Sorry. Look, we'll talk tomorrow, yeah?"

Damn. I fling my phone onto the sofa and start chewing my nail. Clearly, George and Louise got to her first. What's the matter with everyone? Have they no compassion at all? What do they think I'm going to do? Jump on an injured man?

I stand up then sit down again, rubbing my chin thoughtfully. I've got to see Nick. Just one last time. I need to know that he's okay, that he's being looked after. If I could just talk to him, say goodbye properly, then and only then will I have a fighting chance of moving on.

My phone throbs then flashes with a message. I glance at it quickly. It's from Louise. I can't read it, not now, I'm too wound up. I lean my head back on the headrest, staring up at the coving. I need a plan, a strategy. I could ring round the hospitals. Or I could contact the police, surely they'd have a record of the accident. But that'll take hours, and will they even disclose any information to me? Isn't it confidential? I'm not even his fiancé anymore. Then as I go to stand up I catch sight of the flashing red light on the answering machine. *"Ronan couldn't get a hold of you, didn't have your mobile number."* Louise had said, which means he might've left a voicemail. Bingo.

CHAPTER 8

NICK HASN'T REALLY GOT ANY FAMILY, apart from Ronan, that is, and a few scattered relatives here and there, which is one of the reasons why we were so close. He used to love family get-togethers with my lot, possibly a lot more than I ever did. I think it probably had something to do with him being an only child. He'd often comment on how lucky I was to have a brother and nephews.

Nick was brought up single-handedly by his beloved mother Coleen (with the help of his grandmother and Aunt Meghan, Ronan's mum). A close-knit family, they all lived on the same street in Malahide, a small village north of Dublin, which, I expect, was convenient as far as childminders go. I can't count the different babysitters George and I had when we were little, none of whom we particularly bonded with, they didn't stick around long enough. But at least we grew up with both parents. Nick's father, a plumber from Cork, died when Nick was only five-years-old from a genetic blood disorder, so he never really knew his dad. It was the main reason why Nick didn't want any children of his own.

"What if I've inherited the faulty gene, Audrey?" he told me, shortly after we started dating. "Or worse still, what if it skips a generation? I couldn't bear to pass it on to one of our kids." And I knew in that moment that he was in it for the long-haul.

Coleen never remarried, even though she was only thirty when her husband died. When I quizzed Nick over it once he just shrugged his shoulders and said that she wasn't really interested in anyone else after she lost his dad, that no one could match up to him. But Ronan told me, once I got to know him a little better, that the real reason Coleen never remarried was because she didn't want another man bringing up her son, couldn't bear the thought of anyone coming between them, which I thought was rather sweet yet sad in equal measure.

I really wish I'd met Coleen, she sounded like quite a woman, but, sadly, Nick lost his mother a few weeks into our relationship, she'd been ill for a while. And now he's lost me too and is lying in a hospital bed – alone.

"What happened, Ronan?" I ask, after spending an hour trawling through a mass of voicemails to retrieve his message. His was number seventy-nine.

"I dunno exactly." He exhales loudly down the phone. I imagine him smoothing down the back of his red hair with his palm. "It was a pretty normal Saturday night, few cans in the fridge, game on the Xbox, when he got this phone call and went all weirdy on me."

"Weirdy how?"

"Erm…he just went a bit pale, looked as though he was about to throw up, to be honest. To begin with I thought it was you on the phone." I'm sure that Ronan isn't deliberately trying to be offensive, but does he really think that a phone call from me would cause Nick to gag? "But then he snatched his keys off the coffee table, said he was off to see a man about a dog, and shot out the door." He pauses, I think he's lighting a cigarette. "The next thing I knew the police called round, said he'd been involved in a collision and that the impact threw him off his bike."

"Jesus," I say finally, "And then what happened?

Ronan sounds dreadful. I can tell he's uncomfortable, wants to stop even, but I keep pressing him for details. I want to know everything. How many beers had he sunk before leaving? Were

NO WAY BACK

there any other casualties? Did he mention me at all before he left, did they discuss our break-up?

"We spoke a bit about you, yes," Ronan explains, and my stomach stings. "He only had half a lager before the call came through, we were just getting started, and no, no one else was injured." Thank you, Lord. At least I don't have to feel responsible for any other poor soul. "A witness said he skidded off the road and smashed into a parked car." I can't believe what I'm hearing, Nick rode that bike like a professional. "There must've been something wrong with the brakes, I reckon." I hear him blowing out smoke. "Anyway, when I got to the hospital I was told he'd had a blow to the head and a few other injuries."

"A blow to the head? Oh, my God," I gather the lapels of my dressing gown tightly, "Is he all right?" Silence. "Ronan!"

"Audrey, he's been in a coma for five days, love, didn't anyone tell you?"

The piercing pain in my right temple seems to come out of nowhere. "Whaaaat?"

"But he's stable now and off the respirator. The doctors are quite optimistic." Fear burns in my chest. I think I'm going to be sick. I can't believe what I'm hearing, there must be some mistake. I stagger into the bathroom, legs like jelly, and heave over the sink. Angry thoughts flit around in my head as I swallow back the bile with a handful of cold water from the tap – Louise, George and Tina must've known how serious Nick's condition was. Why didn't they warn me? How could they be so cruel?

"A coma? A respirator?" I blub. "That's bloody serious."

"Calm down, Audrey, the worst of it is over," Ronan says soothingly. "Just take a few deep breaths. Come on now, love." But I'm in no fit state for mindful breathing. I knew his injuries were serious, but I was thinking more along the lines of broken limbs, fractured ribs, that kind of thing. Normal accidenty things. But a coma? I've heard that some people never regain consciousness. My goodness, is he going to die? Will the words, "Get out of my fucking flat, you pathetic little piece of shit," be the last he'll ever hear me say? "Look," Ronan's voice again, "he's had all the tests done and…"

"What kind of tests?" I cut in urgently, running my sleeve over my snotty nose in front of the bathroom cabinet mirror. I look like shit. I turn away.

"Well, you know, the usual kind." No, I don't know, I want to scream, I'm not a flipping doctor. "Blood tests, an ECG, CT and MRI scans, they've run the lot and he's doing well. There's a little swelling on the brain but they're treating that with drugs, nothing to worry about."

"Will he wake up?" I quiver.

"Yes, of course, he will. Once the drugs kick in, he'll be fine. I promise." I know Ronan's trying his best to put my mind at ease but it's not working.

"I want to see him," I blurt. The lip of the washbasin digs into my lower back as I lean against it. "Will you take me to him?

"Yes, we can go first thing…"

"Now, Ronan."

Ronan exhales loudly down the phone. "Audrey, I'm shattered. I literally just got off the plane, but I can go with you first thing in the morning. Visiting times start at…"

But I don't let him finish. "You mean he's there all alone?" I can't hide the alarm in my voice. "When did you fly back to Dublin? I thought you were here looking after him."

"A few days ago." He clicks his tongue, annoyed. "Look, Audrey." I can hear the guilt in his voice and I feel a little sorry for him, but how could he leave Nick alone at a time like this? What if he'd died? "I had to go back home," he claims, "Catherine couldn't cope

NO WAY BACK

with work and the kids, and I –"

"What?" I ask incredulously, my anger returning. "Couldn't she ask her family for help for Chrissake?" Catherine's one of six children, they're a close-knit clan. I march back into the lounge, pluck a tissue out of the box and blow my nose loudly.

"Audrey, they're my family. I –"

"Nick's your family too, Ronan." I knot the belt of my dressing gown angrily, phone jammed between my shoulder and jaw. "He needed someone with him."

"I know, I know," he tuts, "I really didn't want to leave him but I had no choice. That's why I called *you*. I shouldn't have really but I was desperate. I didn't know who else to turn to. I didn't know you were away, of course, and I'm sorry if I spoilt your holiday." I tell him that he didn't, that I only found out on the last day, anyway, although I wish I'd known sooner because I'd've taken the first flight home and Nick wouldn't have been alone.

"So, what happens now?" I ask, raking a hand through my hair. "What about Nick's flat, his work?"

"I've taken care of all that. I've cancelled all his shoots, everyone's been very supportive. I've squared it with his landlord and sorted out his wrecked bike. He's being well looked after, Audrey. He's got round the clock monitoring. NHS has been brilliant. The nurses are lovely. There really isn't much you or I can do at the moment, but if you're desperate to see him today," he pauses, and my spirits lift for a moment. Maybe he's changing his mind, maybe he'll take me today. "He's on the second floor in the critical care unit of the Whittington hospital." I slump onto the sofa, defeated. "He's in bed four. Just buzz and tell them I sent you. I'll give Rosie, one of the nurses, a call to let her…"

"No," I interrupt, logic kicking in. I can't face walking in there alone. I need Ronan with me. "Tomorrow morning will be fine."

CHAPTER 9

I'M NOT USUALLY ONE TO BE SQUEAMISH but I cover my mouth and gasp. Nick's face is unrecognisable. Swallowing hard, I take a step closer. I want to scream. I want to pull out all the IV tubes, yank off the monitor cables and climb into bed with him. I want to hold him in my arms, kiss away the swellings, the cuts, the bruises. Tell him that I'm sorry, that I didn't mean any of those things I said. I want to turn back the clock and say, 'Yes, of course, we can postpone our wedding, honey'. But I can't. There's no going back. Ronan takes my hand, his fingers are cold.

"You should see the other guy," he jokes, squeezing my hand gently. I look at him and manage a small smile. I'm so glad he's here. "Right," he says, then spins round, hands on hips, staring wildly around the ward. I glance quickly at the Nurses Station then give him a reproving look as he drags two comfortable looking armchairs towards me, legs screeching against the floor. "It's ok," he whispers with a dismissive wave, swerving them into position, "They're all out of it in here, anyway." Trust Ronan to make light of such serious circumstances. "Sit," he demands, "go on." We sink into the chairs simultaneously with a loud squish, he in the green one and I'm in the smoky pink. "Because pink is for girls," he winks.

I inhale warm, hospital air, unbuttoning my beige raincoat. "It's so quiet in here, Ro," I whisper after a few moments, glancing around me.

"Yeah, but at least there isn't that horrible smell of hospital food." He pulls a face and adjusts his jacket as if it's crawling with fleas. "These guys are better off with IV nutrition, I can tell you. Jeez man, I feel so dehydrated I could do with a bag of that saline myself." Ronan loves a swig of Jack Daniels. In fact, I'm sure I smelt a whiff of whiskey on his breath this morning as he climbed into my car.

He pulls a crumpled tissue from the inside pocket of his jacket and wipes his eyes and nose. My eyes widen. Surely, he hasn't come in here with a virus. "Don't worry," he sniffs, picking up on my vibe, "I haven't got a cold."

"I truly hope not. The last thing we want to do is give Nick an infection." I was Googling comas and recovery last night. It said that comatose patients had to be protected from viruses as they could lead to serious infections such as pneumonia. That can't happen. Nick needs to be kept free of germs. He must get better – he must wake up.

"It's just these places." More jacket adjusting. "They make my eyes run. I think I'm allergic to something."

"Yes, sick people, perhaps?"

He grins at me, then springs to his feet. "I'll be back in a minute. I'm bursting for a pee. Save my seat, will you?" I shake my head and laugh as I watch him hurry down the ward, feet squeaking noisily against the navy vinyl flooring. Ronan always looks like he's in a hurry. I don't know anyone who walks as fast as he does. When he disappears from view I get to my feet.

"Jesus, Nick, what's happened to you?" I entwine my fingers with his. His skin feels warm, soft…familiar. I kiss the back of his hand gently but he doesn't flinch. I wonder if he can hear me. I read that a lot of people in comas can hear but they can't respond. That must be so awful, trapped in your body, unable to communicate. I reach over and stroke his face gently with the back of my fingers. His bristles scratch, something I hated when we were together. Nick was a bit razor phobic, but now I don't seem to care. I wonder if they'd allow me to shave him. I could ask Ronan to ask one of the nurses. He knows them all by name.

"Nick?" I shake him lightly by the arm, "Nick, can you hear me?" I loom over him. "It's me. Audrey. Foxy. You're going to get better, do you hear?" I search his face for some kind of response - a twitch, a flutter, anything. But he's lying still. I watch his chest go up and down, up and down in time to the beeping of the heart monitor by his bed. "You can squeeze my hand if you can hear me." The heart monitor beep, beep, beeps. "I'm here, Nick, and when you wake up I can help you get well again. I'll nurse you back to health. Nick?" Beep, beep, beep. "Please wake up." And just as I'm about to move away I'm sure I see a flicker of movement in his face, just for a nanosecond.

"Ahem." I jerk my head around quickly. Ronan is standing behind me holding two polystyrene cups. My cheeks tingle. Shit. Did he just hear everything I said? I focus on the aroma of coffee seeping from the lids to centre myself. "It's good to talk to him," he grins. Oh God, he did. He hands me a *Costa* cup then sinks into the chair with another loud squish. "Rosie said it helps them come round."

"Ah, you're back, Ronan," says a pretty nurse with a blonde bob, bustling onto the ward. "How was Dublin?"

"Talk of the devil." Ronan raises his eyebrows and laughs. This must be Rosie, then. "Dublin was sound, thanks." He's gone slightly red. Ronan flushes quite easily. I'm not quite sure whether that's down to his fair colouring or because he's easily flustered. He takes a sip of coffee, nodding at Nick. "How's my cousin doing?" I'm surprised he's flirting with the nurse, a happily married man and father of two, but that's men for you.

"He's still stable. I'm glad he's got company, though. Talking to him…"

"Always helps…" Ronan finishes, "See," he points his finger at me, "I told you." I throw him a twitch of a smile, cheeks stinging, he heard every word I said. The nurse looks at her pocket watch.

"I need to do his Obs now and change his catheter," she announces, screwing her face up, "not very nice. Perhaps, you'd like to wait in the relatives' room?" Ronan leaps to his feet at the mention of a catheter.

"I need a fag, actually." He turns to me, "Audrey?"

"Ronaaaaan." I elbow him lightly in the ribs and he doubles over, pretending to be in agony. "I gave up ages ago, you know that, you doughnut." I glance at the nurse and roll my eyes and we share a conspiratory girly grin. I think she quite fancies him, actually.

"Don't forget to have one for me, Ronan," she calls out as we head off down the ward. Ronan was right, though, she is lovely.

I thought Rosie was joking about the smoking but there's a pool of doctors and nurses dragging hard on cigarettes outside. I wish I still smoked. I could do with a fag to take the edge off.

I shuffle from foot to foot to keep warm. The sun has disappeared and it's much colder than I expected. What on earth possessed me to wear my mac? I should've worn my black puffa coat. I think I'm still in holiday mode.

I shiver and Ronan offers me his stylish brown, herringbone blazer, but I shake my head, tell him I'm fine. He gives me a lopsided grin as he takes it off anyway and drapes it around my shoulders, cigarette hanging loosely from his mouth like a Hollywood movie star. It feels heavy and warm, fully lined in silky red satin. It also stinks of tobacco but I don't say anything.

"You okay?" Ronan touches my back gently, "Do you want to go back inside?" I stare at my feet. Seeing Nick again has stirred all sorts of emotions, got my mind ticking. My brain feels like knotted cables. My thoughts a tangled mess.

"I'm not sure if I should be here, Ro. Everyone keeps telling me I'm mad. That Nick's not my problem anymore." I step out of the way as a doctor slides past us, stethoscope swinging around his neck. "Surely they can't all be wrong? I just feel so confused. A part of me wants to be here for him but another part…" I look up at the sky. Dark clouds are rolling. It looks like we might be in for a storm. "I'm supposed to be moving forward, but I feel as if I'm going up an escalator the wrong way, that if I stop I'll roll back and fall – hard."

Ronan takes a drag from his cigarette and blows the smoke out of the side of his mouth all the while regarding me carefully. "I told him he was a bloody fool to leave you," he confesses. I fold my arms tightly across my chest and sink further into Ronan's oversized jacket. "I said he'd never find another woman like you. Jesus, I should know." I furrow my brows and look at him properly for the first time. His skin is dry and patchy. His blue eyes, red and lacklustre, missing their usual mischievous sparkle. I thought it was due to the strain of Nick but now I'm not so sure.

"Is everything all right at home?" I touch his elbow gently, his jacket slides off my shoulder. I catch it with my free hand and pull it close to my chest.

"Nah, not really." The orange tip of his cigarette glows and crackles as he takes another long drag. "Catherine's been having an affair." He blows out the smoke hard and fast through his nose and mouth.

"Oh, Ro." I wrap my fingers around his cold forearm tightly, poor man must be freezing in that flimsy white cotton shirt. "I'm so sorry." Ronan adores his family, they're his world. "When did this happen?" I ask softly, "Is it serious?" He shrugs his shoulders and stares at his brown Chelsea boots. They look expensive, soft leather, tailored with a brogue style stitching; even the elastic support at the sides have a diamond shaped leather emblem neatly stitched onto the fabric. I noticed that when we were sitting upstairs. "What are you going to do? I mean? Is it still going on? Is she in love with this guy, or what?"

"I dunno." He takes a final drag and chucks his cigarette on the floor, twisting his foot over it. Behind him I spy a square metal public ashtray overflowing with fag ends. I keep quiet. I'll pick it up before we go in. "She says it's over but…I don't know what to believe anymore. I mean, it's not that simple for us, is it? We've got the kids to consider." I'm taken aback. It wasn't that simple for me and Nick either. It was agony. I still feel bereft. "I'll never leave my kids, Audrey. Never." Then he looks at me, "I just wish Catherine was more like you, that's all." He holds my gaze, just a fraction longer than comfortably acceptable. "But I guess we both ended up with the wrong people, didn't we?" Oh my, God, are Ronan and I having a moment?

I blink hurriedly, squat, pick up the butt end and chuck it in the ashtray. "Stub bin behind you," I say, breaking the spell. I know it's pathetic but I can't think of anything else to say after that look.

He turns stiffly and looks at it. "Oh. Sorry, didn't see that. Thanks." We're silent for a few moments, and then, "You'd have made a great wife. Audrey. Nick's an idiot." My cheeks are on fire. I don't know where to look. A woman is walking towards me, smiling, tight curly hair bouncing on her shoulders. She looks at Ronan suggestively as she strolls by but he doesn't respond. "Oh, come here," he says, pulling me close and dropping a kiss on my forehead in a brotherly fashion. I let out a long sigh of relief. I must've read it wrong. Phew. "Come on, trouble, let's go inside."

We're back in the comfortable, squishy chairs. "Here, do you want one?" Ronan whispers, extending a tube of mints. "It's a bit eerie in here, isn't it?"

"Yeah…it is a bit." I ease the white sweet out of the packet and pop it into my mouth. "But most patients are heavily sedated, or in a coma."

"You'd think they'd have some visitors, though, wouldn't you?" We both look around the ward, most bays are empty. "Just the sound of movement would be nice. Oooh, there, look." He points at a little, frail old man sitting by an elderly woman's bed across the ward, a slight tremor in his hands. "But is he real or is he a ghost?…Whooooo." Ronan throws his arms up over me and widens his eyes like a phantom.

"Ronan, shhhh…" A couple of the nurses glance up at us from their worksheets. "You're going to get us kicked out," I hiss, slapping his arm.

"Sorry." He hunches his shoulders and sucks loudly on his sweet. I shake my head, smiling incredulously. "Do you believe in an afterlife, Audrey?" he asks, crunching the mint. It seems that he's determined to make as much noise as possible.

"No, I don't. This is it." Nick and I agreed that we'd enjoy every drop of life before it ran out. We're both sceptics. "I mean, I'd like to…but, well, it's not feasible, is it." Ronan nods, lips turned downward. "What about you?"

"Same here, really." The monitor bleep, bleep, bleeps. "What you said before," Ronan says, his voice now serious. "That you don't think you should be here." I don't take my eyes off Nick. "I know your family and friends are looking out for you, and they have got a point. Jeez, what he did to you was unforgivable." My stomach clenches. "I do understand, you know." He leans forward, elbow on knee, face in hand, "and I don't blame you if you just get up now and walk out those doors." He nods towards the exit. "But whatever happened between you two, well, you can still support him as a friend, can't you? You had eight great years together." Silence. "I know he still loves you, Audrey. Maybe I shouldn't say this but it was the last thing he said to me before he left the flat." My heart does an unexpected, an unwanted, an unwelcome jig in my chest. "You will come and see him again, won't you?" he asks.

I stare at him silently, watching his long, white blonde eyelashes dancing as he blinks repeatedly. "Yes," I say finally to more beeping from the monitor. "Of course, I will. At least until he wakes up." I swallow hard. "I'll pop round with you tomorrow morning before I go to check on my mum and dad's house."

CHAPTER 10

NOSTALGIA CREEPS INTO EVERY FIBRE OF MY BODY as I push the key into the lock and quietly let myself in. I always feel like this when my parents are away. I grew up here. In this neighbourhood. In this four-bedroom semi in Whetstone, with George's Fish and Chip shop around the corner and The Queen's Head down the road - Mum and Dad's local. I lean my back against the heavy oak door and it closes with a heavy thud, filling the silence.

On the hall table, a vase of dried-up roses haunts the large, square hallway. The frayed yellowing buds once bright, young and bursting with vitality, now wilted and arched over like candle snuffers – a fate that awaits us all, if we live long enough, I suppose. Apart from Mum, that is, she'll be flexible and nimble forever with all that walking and yoga she does. "Maria and I went to our first Bikram class today, Audrey," she boasted last night when she called to see how I was. "No, darling, yoga isn't all the same. This is HOT yoga. The room alone was 38ºC. You get all sweaty, burn off lots of fat and sleep like a baby. It's fabulous. You should try it."

I bend down and scoop up a pile of letters and leaflets from the original black and white tiled floor, inhaling the musty air. I'm guessing George hasn't been around for a while.

In the lounge, my eyes are instantly drawn to the Audrey Hepburn canvas on the wall. Mum's pride and joy. Her pièce de résistance. It's bang on in the centre, you can't miss it. Dad bought it for her for her sixty-fifth. We chose it together from Camden Market. I had to hide it in my bedroom wardrobe for three weeks because Dad wanted to surprise her with it on the day. Despite his alpha male demeanour, he's an old softy at heart. She was overjoyed, to say the least. She had Nick up there with a drill, screws, and rawlplugs the moment he walked through the door. I can still picture the scene in my mind's eye.

"A bit more to the left, Nicholas," Mum always called him by his full name, "no, no you've gone too far now. To the right… the right I said!"

"I AM going to the right. Goodness, Mrs F, I wouldn't like to be stuck in a car with you navigating." Mum and Nick always enjoyed a good old banter. They didn't mean anything by it. I think they actually quite enjoyed outwitting each other. Dad and I just sat there in companionable silence, watching the floorshow, tongue in cheek.

I move closer towards the picture, admiring its artistry. It is quite stunning, beautifully crafted in gold leaf and finished with a sprinkling of diamantes on the earring and necklace, bringing the image to life. Mum's a huge Hepburn fan, hence my name. She loves all her old movies; Breakfast at Tiffany's in particular, hence both our names.

I've always hated my name. Audrey Fox – so dowdy, so old-fashioned. I'd much rather have been called something glamorous and stylish like Maia or Zara, or even Louise.

Light floods the room as I pull on the curtain lead. I climb onto the armchair and reach for the top latch. The house is gasping for some fresh air. Stumbling back down, I gaze around me, hands on hips. What else needs doing? I don't want them coming back to an untidy home. Clearly, George and Vicky were more interested in spring cleaning my place than taking care of this one.

Mum's so house proud, another attribute she's bestowed on me. She likes everything to be in its place. Books returned to the shelf, drawers closed, lids put back on jars, wilted flowers BINNED! As I go towards the hallway, I catch sight of her cardigan, laid on the armrest of the floral sofa. I wonder if she forgot to take it with her. It's her favourite black cashmere.

I pick it up and draw it to my face, closing my eyes. It smells of Chanel Nº5. Inhaling deeply I'm whisked back to when I was a little girl. I'm running in from the garden, hot and sweaty from playing in the sunshine. Mum swoops me up in her arms and swings me around planting kisses all over my face, asking me if I've had a nice day, telling me how much she missed me. Dad pulling me out of her embrace as George makes a beeline for her, worm in each hand. Happy days. I'm going to miss them so much when they move to Cyprus. The shrill of the telephone makes me jump.

"Audrey!" It's George. "Where've you been? I've been calling you all morning; didn't you get any of my messages? Is your phone switched off? I've been worried sick. I thought something might've happened." Like what? Jumping off the Archway Bridge? Swallowing a handful of pills? What do they all take me for, for goodness sake?

"My battery died," I lie. I cradle the handset between my jaw and shoulder and head into the kitchen carrying the large, square, vase of dead flowers. I rejected all George's calls earlier because I was at the hospital visiting Nick, then when he persevered I was forced to switch it off.

"What about at home, then?" he persists, "I've been calling since nine this morning."

"I had a blood test at the doctor's this morning." This is true. I popped into the surgery before picking Ronan up from Nick's

NO WAY BACK

flat. I tug at the white tape on my arm holding a big blob of cotton wool in place.

"What for?" George snaps inquisitively.

"Just routine, George." I can't hide the irritation in my voice. "I was feeling a bit tired and Dr Harper suggested I have my bloods checked." Actually, I've been having funny periods but I don't want to relay that to George. Dr Harper thinks it might be stress related, so it's best we find out. "Then I popped into Sainsbury's for a few bits, then the bank." I rub my forehead. Why do I have to explain my every move to George? I squeeze a splash of washing-up liquid into the empty vase and fill it with warm water at the sink to the backdrop of a very moany George. What on earth has got into him today?

I turn the vase onto the drying rack. A flutter outside makes me jump, then I spot a Jaybird hopping along on the roof of the garage. The garage is built adjacent to the kitchen at the back of the house, accessed via a driveway that is shared with June next door. And yes, all the rumours are true; shared driveways *are* a nightmare. Cindy, June's daughter, had a terrible habit of leaving her white BMW Z4 bang in the middle of the drive, blocking Mum and Dad in. They fell out over it last year. I hadn't seen Mum lose her rag like that in years.

"Get that car off now!" she screamed, veins in her neck bulging in anger. "I'm sick to death of asking you to move it, Cindy. This is a driveway, not a car park!"

"Okay, okay keep your hair on," Cindy whined as she trotted towards her car in six-inch heels, tugging at her fitted, skimpy white mini-dress. "I told you to just knock for me if you want to get out, Ruby."

"Why should I have to knock for you every five minutes, hmm? Oh, just get a move on, will you?"

"How dare you! This is my mum's house."

"I don't give a mile-high-club whose house it is!"

Cindy screwed up her face in confusion. "A what?"

"A flying fuck," I explained, desperately trying to restrain Mum.

Mum swivelled her head towards me, hair flying, mouth foaming. "Don't swear, Audrey. I own half of this drive, Cindy, and YOU'RE trespassing."

Cindy begrudgingly climbed into her car and reversed onto the street, all the while complaining and threatening litigation. Satisfied, Mum dusted herself down and marched back into the house, slamming the door behind her. They haven't spoken since.

The Jaybird nips at the twigs in the gutter. I flick the kettle on and open the cabinet door. Mum always has some dried milk for emergencies.

"And then where did you go?" George demands.

"And then I came straight round here to check on the house," I hiss. An aroma of fragrant seasoning wafts into my face as I reach for the jar of powdered milk behind the little spice bottles. "Those were your instructions, weren't they?"

"Well, you don't have to be like that." George is offended. "If it's putting you out…"

I soften. I mustn't take my frustrations out on my brother. It isn't his fault that Nick is in a coma. It's mine. "No, no, it's not a problem, George. Look, I'm having a crap day. I'm sorry."

"Anyway." George never holds onto resentment for long. "Vicky's cooking supper for you tonight. 7 o'clock okay?" Oh no, not tonight. I wanted to go back to the hospital. I promised Ronan.

"Actually, George, I did have plans for tonight." I cringe as I pour hot water into the mug.

"What plans?" he asks accusingly as if I've no life of my own.

"I'm meeting Fearne from work," I lie, "she wants to run over

NO WAY BACK

some ideas with me for a new client's website." I stir the tea vigorously, praying he's taken the bait.

"I didn't know you were back at work," he says, munching.

"George, are you eating?" I feel my muscles relax. If George is busy eating then it means he's probably lost interest in my whereabouts of this morning and has fallen for my excuse. I pad into the lounge, sipping on the way.

"Yeah, only a Mars Bar, though," he grumbles, "I'm flipping starving. So, when did you go back to work, then? I thought you were going to take the rest of the week off." I'm not going to get away with this as lightly as I thought.

"I'm back in the office on Monday officially." I thread my fingers through my hair and stare at my reflection in the mirror above the fireplace. A sunken-eyed creature glares back at me. I really ought to get some rest. Seeing Nick yesterday has really knocked the stuffing out of me. "Fearne's got a meeting first thing," I go on, wiping mascara from the corner of my eye, "and wants to get a few ideas flowing. Sorry, George, can we do dinner another night? Is that okay?" I cross my fingers.

"S'pose." He sounds disappointed and I feel dreadful. I hate lying to my family and friends but what else am I supposed to do? They'd never approve of me visiting Nick. "What about tomorrow, then? Is that convenient?"

My heart sinks. "Oh, George, I'm seeing Louise, we've already arranged it." I'm not lying. We're meeting for an afternoon of coffee, cakes, and a gossip, but I'm sure it'll run into the evening, we've so much to talk about. "But how about Saturday?" I offer, "I'm all yours then."

"Now, that sounds like a plan." Phew. "Bring a bottle."

The doorbell shrills loudly as I return the phone into its cradle. Shit. I catch a glimpse of June's silhouette through the window as I lunge out of view. I can't handle any of mum's friends today.

I crawl in combat style out of the lounge and head for the kitchen. If I can get in there quickly and close the door behind me she'll think no one's home.

The bell rings again furiously followed by a loud knock at the door. I freeze, half-way down the corridor and turn my head slowly, eyes wide with fear, pulse hammering in my ears. Why is she so persistent? She knows that Mum and Dad are away. It's not that I don't like June, quite the contrary, actually, but I just can't deal with her inquisitiveness, not today. I'm not ready.

There's a hand poking through the letterbox. Shit, shit, shit. Any moment now June will peer through it and see me on all fours. In a moment of pure panic, I leap to my feet and back myself up against the wall. What am I doing, for goodness sake? Creeping around my parents' house like a burglar. I press my body hard against the wall, sucking in my stomach as if I'll somehow melt into the brickwork. The coolness of the wallpaper soothes my flushed cheek. I slowly edge towards the kitchen as if I'm on a tightrope. It's pretty dark in the corridor, with any luck June won't spot me.

"Audrey, I can see you." June's voice booms through the letterbox. "Open the door," she says dryly. Oh my God. I want the ground to open up and swallow me whole. I've known June since I was six-years-old. SIX. She's been a good and loyal neighbour to my parents. What on earth was I thinking? How embarrassing. What am I supposed to say to her now? With a thumping heart, I take small steps towards the front door. My eyes sting. I think I'm going to wet myself.

"Just a minute, June," I croak, waiting for my shallow breathing to return to its symmetry, all the time racking my brains for a good

NO WAY BACK

excuse. Then as I roll up my sleeves I catch sight of the cotton wool taped on the inside of my elbow. Result.

A gust of light wind breezes over me as I wrench the door open. June is standing there tapping her foot against the welcome mat, lips twisted into a pout, a large parcel in her arms.

"I saw your car parked outside." Shit, I forgot about that. Her thin lips wobble. I know I've upset her and I feel awful. "And the top window is open." She gives a quick, sharp nod to the right, almost in disgust. I lick my dry lips as she eyes me suspiciously. She's had her hair cut and coloured a warm red. It's short at the back with a high, backcombed white tufted fringe. June's in her eighties but you'd never think so. She pushes her rectangle shaped spectacles up the bridge of her nose with her finger, and I notice that it's missing a nail. "The postman left this for you over a week ago. I only wanted to drop it off."

"Oh June, come in, please." I step aside as she hands me the parcel sulkily. It's addressed to Mr and Mrs Byrne and the postmark is Scotland. It's probably a wedding gift from my uncle Jack. He always sends my Christmas cards here, too, even though I've given him my address umpteen times. I crossed him off the list I gave to Louise because he said he couldn't make it so he probably wasn't notified that the wedding was off.

"If you're busy." June takes a step back, glancing at her red pumps. "I don't want to intrude."

"No, really, June, please, I'm sorry. It's just that…" I swallow hard. "Well, I'm not well, you see." I point at the cotton wool plastered in the crook of my elbow. June arches a painted eyebrow and moves a little closer to inspect my arm. "Look," I say helplessly, "I've just come back from the hospital. I had all sorts of blood tests done. I'm sure they must've taken a pint for samples." June frowns, her eyes not leaving my arm as she steps into the hall. "When you looked through the letterbox I was just on my way to let you in," I explain, closing the door behind me, "when suddenly the room started spinning. I had to balance myself against the wall. I thought I was going to faint. Thank God you came when you did," I gasp.

"Oh, you poor, poor love, vertigo is simply awful." June folds me in her arms and I let out a sigh of relief. Christ, when did I get so good at lying? "I heard what that swine did to you," she snarls, releasing me from her tight grip and holding me at arm's length. "I got a phone call from that snotty- nosed kid you used to knock around with when you were little."

"Louise," I remind her with a smile. Poor Loulou, she was always prone to getting colds as a child. "Yes, that's the one. She said the wedding was off." She taps at her glasses again and looks at me intently. "That he'd had *a change of heart*," she says in a high rhythmical tone. Pushing past me, she heads for the kitchen, all the while slating Nick for leaving me. I don't like her speaking badly of Nick, not when he's lying in hospital fighting for his life. Maria told me that negative energy is potent. Her home is stacked with evil eye charms. She even gave me one as a leaving present. A blue glass keyring with an eye in the middle. I'm going to hang it on Nick's bedstead when I visit him later.

"It wasn't his entire fault," I hear myself say, following swiftly behind her.

"What?" June stops mid-track and looks at me, horrified.

"What I mean is…" I roll down my sleeve hurriedly, avoiding her glare.

"My girl, you can't go round defending a coward like that. You're too kind for your own good, that's your trouble, just like my Cindy." She shakes her head. "But he'll get his just desserts, you'll see. What goes around, comes ar…"

"No!" I cut in quickly, wrapping my arms around me. "I don't want anyone jinxing him." Oh Jesus, did I just say that out loud?

June unbuttons her red coat slowly as she takes a seat at the kitchen table, eyes not leaving me, painted eyebrows furrowed.

"You still have feelings for him, don't you?" I turn away and busy myself filling the kettle at the sink.

"Tea or coffee? There's only dried milk but …"

"Leave that." Her hand is on my wrist, "Come and sit down here with me." She pulls out a chair and I do as I'm told. Then before I know it I'm telling her everything, the words spilling from my mouth like an overflowing stream, and she listens in silence, nodding and smiling at the right places, hmming and errring when not so sure.

"But no one understands, June," I sniff, pulling my sleeve over my hand like an awkward teenager. "They all think that I shouldn't have anything to do with him, and I know they've got a point but if I'd just agreed to postpone our wedding like he wanted, none of this would've happened. Because everything is a chain of events, isn't it? I wouldn't have gone to Cyprus, he would've been at home with me. And…"

"Do you still love him?" June interjects softly, touching my knee.

"No…Yes. I mean no I…" I hold my head in my hands.

"Put it this way." June lays her hand flat on the table. Her skin is creased and sprinkled with age marks. "If he woke up today and said that he loved you and wanted to try again, would you take him back?" I scan June's grey eyes silently – because we both know the answer to that question.

It's six-thirty in the evening when I pull on the handbrake of my black Golf outside the hospital. I made sure I was a bit late to avoid parking fees. I paid over ten quid this morning, extortionate. Ronan isn't coming tonight. He's Skyping Catherine, the kids are missing him. So, it'll just be me and Nick – just like old times.

I'll stay a while, I think, as I step into the lift. An hour or so, then I'll visit again tomorrow morning before I meet up with Louise. I'm going to tell her everything. I'm going to take June's advice and stop lying to my family and friends, and, most importantly, stop lying to myself. If Nick agrees when he wakes up, I want us to try again.

I glance at my reflection in the lift's mirror. I made a bit of an effort tonight, put on a bit of mascara, a few strokes of blusher, a splash of lipstick. I'm not quite sure why. It's not as if Nick will be able to see me or anything. Maybe it had something to do with June asking me if the blood test I had was for anaemia as I saw her out this afternoon. I have let myself go a bit recently, that's got to change. June's orders.

The lift doors open with a ping. My feet squeak against the floor, echoing in the foyer as I walk towards the ward. It's even quieter in here at night. One of the nurses recognises me as I press the buzzer and smiles.

"Mr Byrne is popular tonight," she says in a Welsh accent.

"Oh?" I say, surprised.

"He's already got a visitor," she smiles, "but it's okay if you keep it quiet."

"Thank you," I say, "I will do." So, Ronan turned up, after all. He must've finished Skyping his kids earlier than expected. It is a school night, Catherine must've wanted to tuck them up in bed. I stride down the ward. Why on earth has Ronan pulled the curtains around Nick's bed? I suppose any moment now he's going to leap out at me from behind them and surprise me. Typical Ronan.

I tiptoe around Nick's bay. "So you couldn't keep away." I whip

NO WAY BACK

back the curtain, grinning from ear to ear. "Oh…" I falter, heat spreading through me.

The fair-haired woman looks up at me, startled. I notice immediately that she's holding Nick's hand. She flicks her long blonde fringe off her oval face and fixes me with a long, hard stare. She looks familiar but I can't quite place her. Perhaps she's a cousin I met in Malahide. Ronan must've told her about Nick and she's come to visit. How sweet. Her blue eyes are red raw, thick eyeliner is smudged above her fake eyelashes, and her lipstick looks dull and worn. She's zipped into a smart white coat; bare, shimmery tights cover her long, slender limbs.

"Hi," I say cheerfully. "Is Ronan here?"

"Huh?" She plucks a tissue from the box on Nick's bedside table and blows her nose. "Ronan?" I start to feel a little panicky. If she doesn't know Ronan then she can't be a relative.

"Oh…" I move a little closer, unbuttoning my mackintosh, trying to remember where I'd seen her before. I look at her carefully. Her features are symmetrical, her tanned skin evenly toned. She looks tall, even though she's sitting down. She must be a model. That's it! I've seen her in Nick's portfolio.

"I think I know you," I say, smiling. She narrows her eyes and frowns, "Are you a model?"

"Yeah." She smoothes down her blonde hair, a smile playing on her full lips. "You've probably seen me in magazines." I knew it, I never forget a face. Nick used to bring home fashion magazines all the time, especially if he had a feature in it. "I've been in Vogue a few times." I'm impressed but not surprised, she is quite stunning.

"Anyway, nice to meet you." I extend my hand but she doesn't take it. I hate it when that happens; it makes me feel silly and awkward. I don't know what to do with my hands so I plunge them into my pockets. Nick had always said that most models were tetchy and indifferent but I never believed him. I wrap my hand around the smoothness of the evil eye keyring. "Ronan called and asked me to visit," I go on, "he's…"

"Listen." She raises her palm, her face tightens. "I told you, I don't know anyone called Ronan." I'm taken aback by her brusqueness.

"So who are you, then?" I say, a little coldly.

"I'm Nick's girlfriend," she snaps, her hand resting on her protruding belly. "Who the hell are you?"

CHAPTER 11

"WE'LL BE EATING AT EIGHT, Audrey, perhaps you can pop round a little earlier, darling, help me get everything ready." Mum's only been back on British soil a week and already she's bossing me around. I don't even know how she coaxed me into this dinner with their Cypriot property developer. I really can't think how I'll fit in. I don't even want them to move to Cyprus let alone join them in a celebratory meal. But she cornered me the other day when I went round to see them – said George and Vicky would be there too, that I'd be doing them a massive favour by making up the numbers. I agreed, of course, anything for a quiet life, but I'm not sure if I can face it now. I wonder if I can spin her a line, tell her I'm ill or something. She hates being around people with germs, even her grandchildren are barred from her house when they're ill.

"Oh, Mum." I give a little cough, "I'm feeling drained. I think I might be coming down with something," cough, cough, cough.

"Audrey," she says firmly, "You can't lock yourself away in that flat forever. Come on now. It's been almost two weeks since you found that pregnant slut at that swine's bedside. Now, dry your tears and come and join the land of the living." My shoulders sag. She's right. I should pull myself together and get on with my life. But as each day folds into the next I just feel worse. "It'll be good to get out," she continues, "meet new people. Mingle. Besides, the children are looking forward to seeing you."

"Okay, Mum," I sigh. It'll be nice to see the kids. My nephews always cheer me up. "What time do you want me?"

"Well, don't overdo it with the enthusiasm, will you."

"Mum," I warn.

"Oh, all right, all right. I know you've got your father's temper." Oh, here we go. Mum always blames my shortcomings on Dad's genes, all my good traits I inherited from her, of course. "Let's say four-ish…that'll give us plenty of time to…" Fourish? That's three hours before their guest arrives.

"Muuuum," I whine, cutting across her. "What are we cooking him, a five-course meal?"

"Audrey, he's gone to a lot of trouble to find us several ideal properties, all at very good prices too. The very least we could do is cook him a lovely supper."

"Why can't you and Dad just take him out somewhere," I groan, punching my passcode into my mobile phone. There's a text message from Tina and a missed call from Louise, nothing from Ronan.

"Look, if you're going to be like that I'll ask your father to help me," she says, indignantly. And I agree to be there at four. Mum knows exactly how to work me. "That's marvellous, darling, I'll see you then…oh, oh, and wait…before you go."

"Yes, Mum?" I breathe heavily down the phone, hand on hip.

"Wear that lovely silk lilac top I bought you last Christmas, it's very flattering, suits you." This is a low-cut little number she bought me from *Whistles*. Why on earth does she want me to wear that?

"Muuuum," I drone, "I hope you're not trying to match-make me with this, this…"

"Daniel Taylor, darling," she finishes in a cheery tone, "and of course not, he's a happily married man. They've a daughter, didn't

NO WAY BACK

your dad tell you? Lionel," she calls out, "didn't you fill Audrey in about our guest of honour?" There's a crashing sound and then Dad's voice screaming a string of expletives in the background. "Oh, your father's fishing something out from the understairs cupboard. Four, then...and don't forget that top." And with this, she hangs up abruptly.

I look at my watch, it's one-thirty. I suppose I'd better get a move on if I'm to be there by four. The phone is still in my hand. I look at it pensively, thumb stroking the screen. Scrolling through my contacts, I quickly find Ronan's number. All I've got to do is press call. Then I can explain that I only behaved the way that I did because I was shell-shocked. I mean, the last thing I expected was to find a pregnant girlfriend by Nick's bedside. Surely, he'll understand that, won't he? Ronan's a decent bloke. He'll be fine once I apologise. Won't he?

My mind spirals back to Thursday before last. I raced out of the hospital like a woman possessed, legs like lead. I'm not even sure how I made it to my car, it's all such a blur. I sat in the driver's seat and cried and cried and cried, banging my fist against the steering wheel as if it were Nick's face and screaming, "You bastard, you liar. I hate you. How could you do this to me?' A couple walking past tapped on my steamy window, asked if I was okay, if I needed any help. I did need help. I was in no fit state to drive. I couldn't think of anyone else to call. Ronan answered on the second ring.

"Audrey? His voice was a bit hoarse. I wondered if I'd woken him. "Audrey is that you?"

"Oh, Ro...I...please," I blubbed. "I he...she...I can't..." I wasn't making any sense at all.

"Where are you, for God's sake? Just tell me and I'll be there."

"I'm at..." More snotty sobs, "please, Ro, help me, please come...I can't...he's..."

"Are you still at the hospital?" Ronan sounded terrified. "Is it Nick? Has he taken a turn for the worse?"

"Yes," I managed, between gulps. "I mean no, no! Nick's the same but I'm still here…I've…"

"Just stay where you are, I'll be there as soon as I can. I'm leaving right now. Okay?" he said firmly. "STAY WHERE YOU ARE."

"Okay, Ronan, thanks," I sniffed. "I'm in the car park."

Fifteen minutes later I saw Ronan climbing out a black cab through my rear-view mirror. I bustled out of my car as quickly as I could and stood beside it waving at him frantically. When he spotted me he raced over and I flung my arms around his neck, sobbing onto his white t-shirt, all the time telling him how stupid and let down I felt. And he held me tight, stroked my hair, soothed me with calming platitudes as I droned on and on – how could he? He promised me there was no one else. You said he loved me. Everyone was right about him. Why didn't I listen? I'm such an idiot.

"Come on," he said, when the tears finally stopped. "I'll take you home."

"But what about you?" I sniffled, searching my pockets for another tissue.

"Don't worry about me." He dabbed at my eyes with his handkerchief gently, "I'll jump on a W7 bus. It's only a short ride away."

We drove home in silence, punctured only by Ronan asking me if I'd eaten, if I wanted him to stop off for a takeaway. But I was in no mood for food. I felt as if someone had plunged their hand into my chest and wrenched out my heart. Like a fool, I believed Nick when he swore on Coleen's life that there was no one else. My mind was racing, ticking away like a time-bomb - how long had he been shagging her? Why did he lie to me? When did he meet her?

NO WAY BACK

Then as we reached Highgate, a sudden feeling of dread washed over me like a huge, angry wave.

"You knew," I said accusingly.

"What?"

"You knew and you didn't tell me. You just let me go and visit him day after day."

"No!" Ronan insisted, raising a hand. "I didn't know a thing. I swear."

"Don't lie to me, Ronan," I screamed, "we all know that you and Nick are joined at the hip. You didn't even seem surprised when I told you." I swivelled in my seat and glared at him as he switched lanes. His face was red, ginger brows knotted, eyes wide and moist. I knew I was right. He just strung me along with all his charming comments so that he wouldn't have to face this alone. So good old gullible Audrey can do a few hospital shifts.

I undid my seatbelt, the warning bell chimed and chimed. I'd always found that noise incredibly annoying, but at that moment I wanted to rip it out of the panel and hurl it out of the window at a passer-by. I was livid.

"Audrey, what are you doing?" Ronan glanced at me quickly then his eyes darted back to the road.

"I'm getting out, that's what. I don't want to spend another moment in this car with a lying, cheating scumbag like you. Stop the car!"

"Audrey, calm down, will you." A sheen of sweat glistened at his hairline. He glanced at me again, swallowing hard, a car overtook us.

"Stop the car right now or else I'm going to jump out."

"This is your car, for fuck's sake. I'm taking you home."

And then I don't know what came over me but I leant over, grabbed the steering wheel and started turning it towards me. We swerved along the road, wheels screeching, our voices blaring. Ronan, being much stronger than me, managed to keep control of the car, and I lost my grip. I fell back into my seat, hair wild, heart pumping hard and fast in my chest, my ears. "Let me out," I cried.

"Calm down, Audrey. We're almost home."

He put his foot down on the pedal. Angry drivers beeped their horns and swore at us from their rolled down windows as they sped past, faces twisted in fury. But I was having none of it. I had to get out. I felt claustrophobic, breathless. The indicator clanged as we turned into a side road. I straightened up and managed to get my hand back on the wheel, forcing it again to the left. Ronan hit the brakes as a car veered past us, horn blasting, wheels screaming, and then we were still.

The road was quiet. I was halfway down the passenger seat. For a moment I was frozen, terrified I'd broken something, and then I felt blood trickling from my nose. Ronan looked at me, face ashen, chest heaving, hands still curled around the steering wheel tightly.

He spoke first. "Are you okay?" I shifted back up the seat and wiped my nose with my fingers, no blood; just watery mucus. I nodded. "Are you sure? Do you want me to drive you back to the hospital to get a once over?"

"No," I barked, logic kicking in. "I'm fine now. I just had a moment. Please take me home."

"Are you sure?"

"Yes," I hissed, straightening my mac. "I'm sure."

"Thank Christ." The engine rumbled.

We drove the rest of the short journey in stony silence. Outside my front door Ronan turned to me and said, "I swear on my girls, Audrey, I didn't know about this other woman, or the baby." Ronan's a devout Catholic. He'd never swear on his children's lives if he was lying. I felt awful, ashamed, destroyed. "I'm really sorry, Audrey, I

NO WAY BACK

can't believe he's…" And then I don't know what came over me, but as he was still speaking I moved forward and kissed him hard on the mouth. For a moment he stood like a mannequin, arms wide by his side, and then his lips parted and I felt his warm tongue entwined with mine. He tasted of cigarettes and whiskey and peppermint.

"Let's go inside," I urged, opening the front door and pulling him by the belt of his trousers. My lips found his again and we kissed wildly, his stubble scratched my skin as our bodies locked against the doorframe and then suddenly he pulled away.

"I'm sorry, Audrey," Ronan said breathlessly. "I can't do this… I'm married, you're upset…Nick's in a coma for fucks sake. This just isn't right."

"Well, they haven't exactly been faithful to us, Ronan, have they?" I panted, straightening my knee length purple dress, Nick's favourite, by the way.

"Yeah, well two wrongs don't make a right, do they?" There was a painful silence during which his breathing steadied and we both gathered our thoughts, and then he said, "I'd better get going." I nodded silently. "I'll call you tomorrow." But he never did.

I don't even know why I snogged Ronan, it's not as if I fancy him or anything. The truth is I just wanted to get back at Nick. I feel bloody awful now. I take a deep breath and press call. Ronan answers much quicker than I expect him to.

"Hi Ronan, it's me," I say brightly, heart thrashing against my ribcage. Jeez, I don't know what to say. I want to put the phone down but I know it's too late. "I just…"

"But leave your name and number and I'll get back to you as soon as. Ciao." Voicemail - Damn. I hate it when that happens, why can't people just use a standard recorded message instead of confusing us with their personalised ones. I wait for the long beeps to end.

"Ronan, hi, it's Audrey. I…erm…just wanted to say…well, hello. Hope you're okay." I pause. Oh Godddd, help me. I should've written something down, like they do at award ceremonies. "Erm… I'm just so sorry about what happened that night. You were right I was very upset…and I er…don't usually attack men on my doorstep," I cackle nervously, "Look, can we just forget it? I'm really, really sorry." I say hurriedly, "Hope everything's okay with you and Catherine. Bye." I end the call with a loud sigh. So, that's it. Done. I feel a lot better now. Now, where did I put that lilac silk *Whistles* top?

CHAPTER 12

"AUNTIE," YELLS FLORIAN, hanging over the banister at the top of the staircase. "I can see your boobs from here. Are they real?"

"Get down those stairs right now," Vicky cries, shaking her head, annoyed, "Honestly, Audrey." I smile into my wine glass as Florian takes exaggerated, slow leaps down the steps. As soon as he's within Vicky's reach she grabs his arm and pulls him down the last step. "He's become a right *handful* these days."

I almost choke on my wine as it splatters from my mouth, spraying Vicky's black knee-length belted dress and the twins, who are clinging to her knees. Nathan rubs drops of wine into his mousy curls and whines while Vicky looks at me blankly, wet hands outstretched. She looks tired, dark circles bulge beneath her sultry, brown eyes, despite an attempt to disguise them with concealer. Her dark hair hangs limply against her shoulders. It takes a while for her to cotton-on but when she does we dissolve into a fit of giggles.

"What's the matter with you two?" George appears, beer in hand. Josh tugs at his taupe chinos, and he heaves him up, balancing him on his hip.

"Ask your wife," I say, scooping Nathan up into my arms and wiping the liquid from his hair with my fingers, "Mummy had a Freudian slip, didn't she?" I coo, pinching his button nose. "But she's right, I have got a handful, haven't I?"

"Yeah, yeah," cries Nathan, waving his arms in the air, "Mummy had Florian shit, Dadda." This only adds fuel to the fire. Tears of mirth are sliding down our faces. I point at Vicky.

"You look like a Black Sabbath groupie."

"So do you," she says, barely able to breathe from laughter. It's so good to see her cheerful again.

"Come on." I pull her by the sleeve, "Let's give the twins to George and sort our faces out upstairs. We don't want to scare off our guest of honour."

We're side by side in front of Mum and Dad's double marble basins in their black and white French-style bathroom with matching illuminated mirrors. Vicky dabs at her eyes with her index finger while I unzip my makeup pouch.

"How're you feeling now, Vicks?" I twist the body of my lipstick and begin to reapply.

"Oh, you know, the usual, knackered."

"Have you seen your GP?" I press my lips together, "He may be able to give you something to perk you up a bit." I offer casually, pouting at my reflection in the mirror.

"Nah, there's no point. My GP's bloody useless." She brushes her cheeks with a pinkish powder, throwing me a glance in the mirror. "Besides, I can handle this. It's not as if I haven't been here before, is it?"

"Yes, but it's different now, isn't it? You've got two. I don't know how you cope." I scoop my hair back into a ponytail, it's much warmer in here than I expected. Mum must have the heating on full blast again. "I had my bloods done recently," I confess, "I was having weird periods and feeling a bit urgh. They've all come back normal, though. Dr Harper reckons it might be stress related. I can have a word with her for you if you like, she's really very good, I'll..." Vicky suddenly stops applying eyeliner, pencil in hand, mouth slightly ajar. Our eyes meet in the mirror. Her face is deadpan. Oh shit.

"Are you saying that I can't cope? That I can't look after my own children?"

"No, of course not. It's just that…"

"Did George put you up to this?" she cuts in furiously.

I twist my hair in one hand and wipe the sweat off the back of my neck, staring ahead at my reflection, avoiding her gaze. George did have a private word with me last Saturday when I went round for dinner. I don't want to lie to Vicky but I don't want to land George in it either.

"He did, didn't he?" she huffs as the doorbell goes off in the background, "I knew it. Right!" She tosses her eyeliner into her makeup bag angrily.

"Vicky, please, don't." I put a hand on her arm, "He's worried about you, that's all. We all are."

"There's nothing wrong with me, Audrey! I'm fine. Look." She stretches her arms out. "I'm still in one piece. Why does he insist on making me out to be some kind of nutter?" There's a knock at the door.

"Girls?" It's George. "Everything okay in there?" He rattles the doorknob. Vicky opens her mouth to speak but I quickly cover it with my hand, my eyes pleading with her tight, livid face.

"Yes, George, we're just freshening up." I stand in front of the door like a bodyguard. "Please, Vicky," I whisper, "don't." She's close to tears and I'm not sure what to do.

"Our dinner guest has arrived," George says brightly, "Mum wants you two gorgeous girls downstairs pronto." Vicky pushes past me, silently fuming, opens the door, glares at George then stomps off down the stairs. "Vicks," George calls out after her, "Vicky? What's wrong with her?" George looks at me, confused.

"Not now, George," I warn, brushing past him and following Vicky briskly down the stairs.

"Ahh, there you all are," Mum says joyfully. "I was about to send out a search party. I duck behind Vicky and George, straightening my top. "Daniel, this is my son, George, and his wife, Vicky, their children, Florian, Josh and Nathan, and...where's Audrey?" Mum scans the room.

"I'm here," I say in a little voice.

"And my daughter, Audrey." And as Daniel turns to greet me I stare into the depths of familiar blue eyes.

"Cinderella?" He wags his finger at me, grinning. "I almost didn't recognise you with your clothes on." Mum's eyes widen. "Oh, no, no, it's not what you think, Mrs Fox. Audrey and I met on the beach in Cyprus several weeks ago, didn't we, Cindy?" He winks at me and I give him a coy smile.

"Well, what a bloody coincidence," George offers Daniel his hand and they shake heartily.

"Yes," I smile, feeling my cheeks tingle.

"I call it serendipity." Daniel smiles, holding my gaze. Clearly, he's a natural flirt. Probably comes with the job. I know his type, happily married with a mistress on the side. But if he thinks I'm going to fall for his charm, he's got another thing coming. He averts his gaze to Mum. "Dinner smells lovely, Mrs Fox."

"Oh, drop the Mrs Fox, you can call me Ruby. Come along, everyone." She claps her hands, "Let's eat."

Vicky ignores George for the most part of the meal, only conversing with him over the children in dark, sharp tones.

"So how long have you two been married?" Daniel asks them politely. I spy him from the corner of my eye. He is quite handsome in a clean-cut sort of way, freshly shaven, well-groomed, and all

NO WAY BACK

smiles and teeth. He has a slight kink in his nose, which is quite attractive, and his charisma has illuminated the table, even Vicky seems taken by him, not quite sure whether that's a good thing, though.

"Ten years next February." George reaches for Vicky's hand but she snatches it away and busies herself with Florian, urging him to eat his vegetables. George draws his hand away, curling his fingers into a limp fist, and glances at me, hurt.

"Great thing marriage," Daniel says, buoyantly. "If you find the right person, that is."

"If, being the operative word," Vicky mutters under her breath and my heart plummets. "Oh, George, please tell Florian he has to finish his supper," she snaps irritably, "or no iPad." Daniel, sensing the tension, moves on to me.

"What about you, Audrey. Married? Kids?" There's a sudden hush at the table, eclipsing the mood. Cutlery clutters against plates, the twins whine, Florian announces that green beans make him fart, and I don't know what I'm doing or where to look.

Dad speaks first. "Top-up, Daniel?" And before he can answer, Dad's pouring red wine into his glass.

"Oh, God," Daniel stops eating and looks at me, "Have I said the wrong thing?"

"Well," Mum begins.

"Auntie got ditched by that shi…" Florian blurts out. Vicky berates him quickly, and he sinks sulkily into his chair, folding his arms. But it's too late. The truth is out.

"It's okay, Vicky." I put my cutlery down and brace myself. I've got nothing to hide and nothing to be ashamed of. "I was going to get married early September but it didn't work out." I take a large glug of wine, exchanging glances with Dad. His face is tight and dark, I know he can feel my pain.

"Ah, so you're still a Foxy, then," Daniel grins. The tension loosens and everyone returns to their food, slumping with relief.

"Don't call me that," I say in a clipped tone, and he apologises immediately. Poor old Dan, he can't seem to get anything right with us neurotic lot tonight. I bet he can't wait to leave. Perhaps I was a little hasty earlier, misconstruing his gregarious nature for flirting. "But, yes, I am definitely still a Fox," I reply. "And you? How long have you been married?"

"Divorced," he says, taking a mouthful of dauphinoise potatoes, and I almost choke on my lamb. "It's been almost..." He holds up three fingers as he chews. Mum shoots me one of her looks. Her face taking on a new, fresh glow.

"Three months?" Vicky guesses as Nathan climbs onto her lap and pulls her hair.

"Years," he says, swallowing.

Mum's mouth twitches as she leans forward, fingers brushing her chin, one eyebrow raised. I can sense her antennae slowly emerging, not a good sign. "*Really*, Daniel, I thought you were happily married. Aww, that's such a shame," she croons. "I'm so sorry." And if you believe that then you'll believe anything. Mum's got it into her head lately that I need a new love interest and I think she's just found her latest victim.

"Nah, it's fine." He forks green beans. "It was all very amicable. We're still great friends. Business partners, actually. Aliki's still in Cyprus, working on your project, in fact." Which is why, I suppose, they were all playing happy families on the beach that day. Aliki didn't look like a woman who'd let go to me. There was an air of possessiveness about her that sent a chill through the scorching heat from a hundred-and-fifty-yards away. I wonder why he walked out on such a beautiful, young woman. The mother of his child. He must be a player. Or maybe she had an affair.

NO WAY BACK

"Oh, that's interesting," Dad pauses, resting his arms on the table, "is Aliki a Cypriot girl?"

Daniel nods as he fills a tall glass with water from the jug. "She's the reason why I started this business in Cyprus, Aliki had all the contacts. And she speaks fluent Greek, which helps. A lot."

"Any chance of a reconciliation?" George asks, pushing his empty plate away as Josh drones by his side, "Dada, Dada, sit on lap." He picks him up and settles him onto his knees.

"George." Vicky gives him a daggered look. "Don't be so inquisitive."

"It's okay, Vicky," Daniel says reassuringly, "I don't mind, and, no, that chapter has definitely ended."

"Dan," I clear my dry throat, "can you pass me that jug of water please."

"Daniel," he corrects, reaching for the jug, "Don't really like Dan." He wrinkles his nose, holding my gaze. Touché. I hate vindictive men.

I think I've gone pink. "Oh, it's just that I thought I hea…" I falter, and he frowns, his eyes on my lips. I wonder if I should tell him that I heard Aliki calling him Dan on the beach that day. But no, that would make me sound interested and I'm not. I'm definitely not. Clearly, that pet name is reserved for Aliki. As Foxy was for Nick, naturally.

"You thought?" His glance drops, fleeting to my cleavage then back to my lips and I feel my cheeks burn. I knew I shouldn't have worn this top. I'm going to kill Mum. I bet she knew he was divorced. She's like the Gestapo. Nothing gets past her.

"And you've got your daughter to consider, too," Dad intervenes, picking up on my discomfort. Dad is good at diffusing awkward situations, always has been.

"Oh, absolutely, yes." Daniel's eyes light up at the mention of his daughter. "Connie always comes first. We're both very involved in her life. She's our world." I glance at Dad and he winks, he knows me so well, and right now I love him all the more for it.

Mum waves off her last dinner guest at ten-thirty. She asks me to stay the night and help her clear up and I agree. I always enjoy sleepovers, and this may even be my last one here ever.

"Well," Mum gives me a sideward glance at the kitchen sink, "I do believe Daniel Taylor is quite taken by you."

"Oh, Mum, for goodness sake, he's not interested in me," I groan. She scrapes food off a plate, hands it to me and I load it into the dishwasher. "Have you seen his ex-wife? She's bloody gorgeous. And YOUNG!"

"Ex, being the operative word, darling, and where on earth did *you* see her?" I tell her all about the incident at the beach and the restaurant.

"Oh my God, was that him? The man who found your shoe?" Mum is astounded, "Small world." Then she chews the inside of her bottom lip, a twinkle in her eye.

"What?" I say, "I know that look."

"It's kismet, that's what. Your real-life Prince Charming. Oh, don't roll your eyes! Did you see the way he was looking at you? I told you that top was a good idea."

"MUM," I complain, shocked, and I'm saved by the ringing of my mobile phone, "I'll just take this outside," I say briskly. I don't care who it is, I'll talk to a PPI agent for hours if I must. "The reception in here is crap."

"Hi Audrey, it's me." I close the kitchen door behind me, the autumn chill bites at my bare legs and chest.

"Ronan. Hi!" I wrap my cardigan around me tightly, "It's good to hear your voice." I walk to a secluded spot behind the shed

NO WAY BACK

where Louise and I used to smoke as teenagers.

"Yeah, same here." He sounds breathless. I can hear the swish of traffic in the background. "So, how've you been?" We exchange a few pleasantries and then I apologise again for how inappropriately I behaved the last time we met, how sorry I was for almost getting us both killed.

"It was my fault too, just forget it, I have." I close my eyes, a mist of relief sweeps over me. He tells me he's back in Dublin and trying to make a go of it with Catherine.

"I'm really glad to hear that," I say truthfully. At least someone is prepared to work hard to save their relationship. I peer around the garage, Mum is by the sink, face like thunder. "Anyway, I'd better get back to helping Mum with the dishes, she's giving me daggers from the kitchen window." We both laugh. "You take care, Ronan."

"And you too, sweetheart."

"Okay, thanks for calling. Bye."

"Bye, and oh, errr… wait, erm…" he hesitates, "Look, I know you probably don't give a damn, and I don't blame you, but Nick's out of his coma. I just thought you should know, that's all. He's going to be okay. He'll be going home soon."

My stomach fizzes. The hairs on my arms spring to attention. I'm silent for what seems like forever, and then I say. "Ronan, I'm glad to hear that." And I am. I know he treated me really badly but I don't want him to die. "I'm glad he's feeling better and out of danger but…" I breathe in the smell of freshly cut grass mingled with the remnants of burning coal from next door's barbeque. "Look, the thing is, I haven't told anyone that I visited Nick in hospital." Apart from Mum and June, that is, but they've both been sworn to secrecy. There's a few seconds of silence.

"Okaaay."

"It's just that I've been humiliated enough and if everyone

finds out about his other woman and everything…" There's a loud thrash and I jump as Flossy, next-door's cat, leaps over the fence. "Look, just promise me you won't tell anyone I was there." My heart knocks hard against my chest – thud, thud, thud. Flipping Flossy. I glance up. June's silhouette is at the window. I move out of sight just as she yanks the curtain back.

"Yeah, yeah, I hear ya."

"Not even Nick." Silence. Shit. I bet he's already bloody told him. "Ronan!"

"Okay, okay, I promise. Cross my heart and hope to die."

Phew. Thank you, God.

CHAPTER 13

"YOU'VE GOT TO GO," Louise says excitedly when I explain about the dinner date I received this morning attached to a parcel on my doorstep.

"If she doesn't go, then I will," Tina chips in, snorting incredulously. The trouble with taking relationship advice from Tina is, well, how I can put this subtly – useless. She'll more or less date anyone with a pulse. "I don't even have to see him," she continues, my point proven, "he could have a face like Godzilla for all I care. That romantic gesture is good enough for me – a proper fairy-tale." She drains her glass and asks us all for another round.

We're at *The Flask* in Highgate, cosied up on a red, squishy seat in one of their snug, dark rooms. I even managed to persuade Vicky to come along, having been forgiven for what she interpreted as an accusation of being "a fucking useless mother" - her words, not mine. But it did take three days of grovelling. I look at my watch. It's almost nine-thirty.

"Oh, go on, then," I say, "I'll have another white wine in case Jess turns up." Jess has promised to make an appearance before meeting up with Sky, her new boyfriend, but she's yet to show. "But make it a small one this time." Tina laughs and calls me a lightweight, but I've already had two large glasses and I've got an early start tomorrow. Raymond has won a new client and is holding a morning conference to discuss their requirements, and he specifically said he wants *my* input. Mine! How amazing is that?

Fearne has been praising my work to him for weeks and it's finally sunk in. I don't want to let her down.

"He was really impressed by what I showed him, Audrey," she told me yesterday afternoon over a latte at Café Nero. "It'll be a great opportunity for you to learn and grow within the company." At least one thing in my life is going right and I can't afford to muck it up with a hangover.

"I s'pose I'll have another juice," Louise groans, swirling the orange liquid at the bottom of her glass unenthusiastically.

"Surely, you can have one proper drink." Tina stands up, grabs her purse from her Louis Vuitton bag and looks at Louise pointedly, hand on hip. I hope Louise is going to decline. She tilts her head thoughtfully, biting her bottom lip. I can see she's tempted.

"Maybe not, Loulou," I interject. "It might make you feel ill."

"You're allowed one, aren't you?" Tina addresses this question to Vicky, who, stimulated by the effects of booze, gives us a full and detailed run down on the dangers of drinking alcohol whilst pregnant in a very shouty voice. A bald man with a round, bright red face at an adjacent table gives Vicky an annoyed sideward glance, but this only spurs her on.

"And the more you drink the greater the risks." Vicky takes a swig from her Peroni bottle and throws red-faced man an annoying look. Now if that was me I'd have asked for a glass with that beer, afraid that it might smudge my lipstick or make me look unladylike, but not Vicky. Vicky has an invincible air of femininity about her, despite her tomboyish demeanour. She's one of those lucky women who are slim but full in the right places, you know the type. "It reaches your baby through your placenta," she explains, moving her hands randomly over her flat tummy. Red-face man huffs in exasperation, then with a tight expression mutters something to his companion before grabbing the waitress's attention and loudly asking for the bill.

"Really? What about those women who get pregnant after a drunken one-night stand, then?" Tina protests, flicking back her freshly blow-dried hair, "Or the ones who don't know they're pregnant and carry on drinking heavily throughout their pregnancies. They still have normal, healthy babies, don't they? In fact, I read about a woman recently who didn't know she was pregnant until she dropped it in the toilet."

I stare at my nails as they babble on about alcohol and pregnancy. I wish they'd shut up about babies. Nick's should be due soon, judging by the size of his girlfriend's belly. But they're not to know, are they? Not only would they be more sympathetic if they did, they'd hunt them both down, gag them and tie them up in my parents' shed for a week – at least.

"Well, they've just been lucky," Vicky muses. "You see, the baby can't process the drink as quickly as we can and so it stays in their system for longer, can you imagine their tiny little hearts and…"

"Stop! Enough!" Louise raises a hand, placing the other protectively over her tummy. "I'll just have another juice please, Tina." And with a "suit yourself" expression, Tina saunters off to the bar, her tall, slim body snaking through the small, noisy crowd that's just arrived.

"Sooooo, a pair of *Jimmy Choos*!" Louise says conspiratorially going back to the subject of this morning's parcel. "How exciting!"

"Well, not exactly a pair," I say.

Louise and Vicky listen transfixed, arms crossed in front of them, shoulders touching, as I recount this morning's events. The doorbell rang at about nineish. Luckily, I was working from home today but was still in my jimjams. By the time I threw on a dressing gown and got to the door, the driver had gone. I just caught a glimpse of a white van speeding into the distance. My first thought was that it was another belated wedding gift. I felt sick with unease as I carried it through to the lounge expecting a set of twin bath towels or a shiny kitchen implement to burst out of the package. But as I tore off the brown paper wrapping, I was greeted with a *Jimmy Choo* shoe box. I thought it was a mistake, to begin with. I couldn't remember ordering anything, especially not from such an expensive shop.

"You can imagine my reaction when I saw the red stiletto nestled against a tan dust bag, can't you?" I enthuse, and they both shake their heads in agreement, I'm well known for my shoe obsession. I've got over two hundred pairs. Nick used to call me *Imelda Marcos*. "Honestly, girls, it looked absolutely stunning, like a priceless jewel. It must have cost a bloody fortune." I close my eyes briefly. I can almost smell the waft of new leather seeping from the box as I opened the lid. "It was only when I read the card that I knew it wasn't a mistake."

"What did the card say?" Louise and Vicky ask in unison, eyes twinkling, mouths slightly open.

"It said, *Join me for dinner, Cinderella, and I'll bring the other one. Daniel.* And his phone number." I gaze up as Tina shoulders her way through the crowd with a tray. "Oh, and a kiss."

"Ooooh, a kiss." Vicky takes a quick intake of breath. "He's SO into you."

"But how did he know your shoe size for Christ's sake?" Louise asks curiously.

I shove up, making room for Tina, then explain how I'd lost my shoe at the Taverna in Cyprus during a drunken Greek group dance. They all roar with laughter when I recount how I landed in Daniel's lap when my shoe went flying. And go all mushy when I tell them how he found it under his table after I'd gone and handed it in to the manager.

NO WAY BACK

"He must've made a mental note of my shoe size then, I suppose." I pick up my wine glass from the tray, my attention momentarily snatched by a group of young people at a nearby table who've just erupted in laughter. "But I'm not going out with him, of course. I'm going to text him tomorrow and politely say no."

"Why not?" Tina says in a high-pitched voice, "Seriously, Audrey, is he a real minger?"

"No!" Vicky jumps in, "He's bloody gorgeous. And charming. And successful. If only I were single," she sighs, gazing forlornly at a sea of patrons at the bar, beer clutched to her chest. I feel a little miffed by that remark, has she forgotten that George is my brother? "Forget Nick, it's over," she insists with a slight slur. "I mean, don't get me wrong, I really did like him, he always made me laugh, actually." I suck my lips in. Tina and Louise exchange glances. "But, anyway, he's history now." She takes a swig of beer. "You should go, Audrey, you're bloody mad if you don't."

"Go where?" comes a familiar voice from behind me mingled with laughter from the noisy group.

"Jess," I squeal. "You made it." Numerous silver bangles chime near my face as she stretches her arms across my chest; a bottle of *Sol* and her mobile phone wedged between her gem-adorned fingers. It's always good to see Jess, but the heady smell of spicy musk and the whiff of stale cigarettes almost knocks me out as she presses her cold cheek against mine and blows several noisy kisses into the air.

I look over at Louise who's smiling dotingly at her daughter. No doubt she isn't aware of Jess's new cigarette habit. She'd have a fit if she knew, what with being so anti-smoking. Which is why, I presume, Jess has drenched herself in a gallon of cheap perfume. Something I did as a teenager to mask the smell of tobacco, only I used Mum's expensive Chanel N°5.

"What time do you call this, young lady?" Louise points at her watch.

"I found her lurking by the bar. *Texting*, would you believe." Tina throws Jess a wry smile, whirling the ice in her vodka and tonic clockwise. Jess's hand is permanently glued to her phone, her fingers expertly whizzing over the keypad. She's the only person I know who can hold a conversation and text at the same time.

Jess pulls a face at Tina. "I was on Snapchat, actually." There's an exchange of playful tongue poking then she places her beer bottle on the dark wooden table in front of us, sticky with ring marks and crumbs from our earlier feast of crisps.

"I thought you lot would be outside," Jess groans, pulling up a chair. "What're you doing cooped up in here like a bunch of oldies? And I hope there's no vodka in that, Mum."

Louise gives Jess a quick, tight smile then says, "Er, it is October, Jessica." She leans forward, arms on table. Red-face and his girlfriend have gone. Three young men have taken their place, sipping from their pints and intermittently glancing in our direction. I'm not interested whatsoever but I can see Tina eyeing the bait.

"Never mind that, Jess," I exclaim, "What've you done to your hair?" It's transformed from long, golden, soft curls to a black shoulder length bob with a bold statement fringe. She looks like she's just stepped off the set of *Cabaret* the Musical.

"I know." She strokes her glossy hair, her oversized silver hooped earrings lost in the dark mass. "Do you like it? Sky thinks it's sexy." I'm not quite sure if I do, to be honest. The new style makes her look older; and with those heavily made up eyes and red, glossy lipstick, a bit burlesque. In fact, I wouldn't be surprised if all she's wearing beneath that biker leather jacket, black winter shorts and opaque tights, is nipple tassels and a pair of French knickers. This

Sky person seems to have a lot of influence over Jess - the new look, the smoking. He sounds like a bit of a renegade to me. I'm going to have to have a quiet word.

Louise and Vicky spend the rest of the evening in a heated discussion about pregnancy and child rearing, while Tina, having edged herself closer to the three men at the adjacent table, laughs and does lots of hair flicking whenever one of them speaks.

Jess and I leave them to it and huddle together on the red squishy seating for a good old catch-up. She tells me about her life at university, she's made new friends, may even leave home and share digs with them at some point to save on travel expenses and lap up the experience; then maybe take a year off once she's finished her exams and go travelling. It isn't long before we get round to the subject of men and my new admirer.

"The shoe gesture is very romantic and everything but I'm not ready to start dating again, Jess. I'll just text him," I say lightly, smiling up at a young barmaid, arms stacked with empties. "I'll return the shoe, of course."

Jess protests at first, says I should give him a chance, that he might just be my Prince Charming. But I'm too cynical for romance and eventually she backs down, telling me not to delay replying, though, that it'd be unkind. Jess is such a lovely, thoughtful girl.

"So, have you heard from that wanker?" she snarls. Oh, and did I say, she's also very loyal.

"No," I reply, grabbing a strand of my hair and winding it around my finger, "Thank God."

"Good. Fucking tosser. At least he's done one thing right and stayed away." Jess takes a swig from her beer bottle. "Bloody twat." She shakes her head and her earrings swing against her shiny black hair. "Mum was right about him all along, wasn't she?" Louise had warned me about Nick shortly after she and Gerry started dating.

Apparently, Gerry had slipped and told her that Nick was having after-work drinks with some of the models. I didn't mind him socialising with his colleagues, but Loulou said there was one girl in particular. Her name was Steph.

I plucked up the courage and confronted him about it shortly after Louise's tip-off and we had our first major row. After I accused him of sleeping with half the female population behind my back, he threw his arms up in despair, told me that if I didn't trust him then we may as well call it a day. In the end, he managed to convince me that Louise was being jealous and overprotective. "Can't you see how controlling she is?" he said. "She doesn't like you being close to anyone else. She's trying to break us up." And because Louise has always been a bit overprotective, because she complained only a week before that I'd changed since I started going out with him, that he was taking me away from my friends, I believed him. Louise and I didn't speak for six months after that.

"Yes, Jess, your mum was right," I sigh, "As always. But anyway, that's all in the past now."

"That arsehole is so lame." Jess shakes her head in disgust, staring through Tina and the three men. One of them clocks her, gives her the eye, but she completely blanks him and returns her attention to me. "Oh, and OMG." She grabs my forearm tightly, her blue eyes widen. "You do know that Gerry's seen him, don't you? The bloody Judas." My heart almost stands still. I didn't know. Louise hadn't mentioned it. I look over at her but she's heavily engrossed in conversation with Vicky, shaking her head furiously in agreement with whatever Vicky's saying. My lips twitch. Has he been round to her house? Do they know about the baby? Have they been having cosy dinners with his new girlfriend? I want to scream.

"Yeah, he's out of hospital. Gerry's been round to visit him a few times," Jess clarifies, and I let out a small sigh of relief. "Mum doesn't want him in the house, though. She was like, *if you want to carry on seeing him then do it in your own fucking time. I don't want him round here.* Well, she didn't say fucking, but you know what I mean." My eyes moisten. I throw Louise an affectionate, grateful smile. She clocks me in mid-flow of her conversation and grins warmly before averting her eyes to Vicky. I suppose she didn't tell me Gerry had seen Nick because she wanted to spare my feelings, didn't want to hurt me. I'm so lucky to have such wonderful friends who look out for me.

"Well," I sigh, gathering my bag and coat. It's ten-thirty. I have to get home, and besides, much as I love Jess, I'm not in the mood to talk about Nick. "I can't stop Gerry from being his friend," I lay a hand on Jess's shoulder, "but I don't ever want to see or hear from him again."

And later that night, before I switch off my bedside light, I take Jess's advice and text Daniel: **"Thanks 4 lovely thought. Sorry can't do dinner. Pls let me know how 2 return shoe. Audrey."** I hesitate for a moment, biting the inside of my lip, and then firmly press 'send'.

CHAPTER 14

THE NEXT MORNING I DASH into the office meeting late and slightly dishevelled. Having slept through my alarm, thanks to that extra glass of wine I knocked back last night, I didn't even manage to have breakfast let alone comb my hair. I almost cry out in delight when I spot the croissants and freshly brewed coffee laid out on the frosted aqua glass table. A rare treat. Raymond must be in a good mood.

"Morning, Audrey," he smiles, all bright-eyed and bushy-tailed as I clumsily sit in the empty seat next to Callum, our SEO expert. I don't know where Raymond gets his energy from but I wish he'd give some to me.

"Sorry, I'm late, everyone," I murmur, dropping my handbag by my feet and pushing my dark shades onto my head. Callum raises an eyebrow, tapping his pen lightly against the yellow file in front of him. "Bus was late," I lie, glancing at Fearne's friendly face. She always has my back.

Raymond pulls at the cuffs of his chequered grey flannel jacket in readiness, smile fixed on his face. "Right, now that we're all present," he begins.

His voice hums in my ears as the brilliant sunshine streams through the tall, glass window of the fourth-floor building making my sore head feel ten times worse. I rub my right temple which is throbbing like an annoying low base beat. I hate facing the window during our board meetings on sunny days, but, having turned up twenty minutes late, the good, shady seats were already snapped up.

"Do you mind if I lower the blinds, boss." Callum stands up, using his hand as a sun visor, "That sunlight is blinding us two over here, and poor old Audrey looks as if she's nursing some kind of hangover from hell." He gives me a feeble smirk, "So I can imagine how she must be feeling." Goodness, do I look that bad? I desperately need a shot of caffeine. I help myself to a cup from the silver jug on the table with a slight tremor, resisting the urge to lower my sunglasses. I must look hideous.

"So," Raymond goes on to the hiss of the blinds unfurling. "We've got a new client on board, and it's a biggie too." He rubs his hands together. "Multiple pages, images, logo illustration and full whack SEO contracted for three years. Stacey, are you taking notes?"

"Yes, Raymond," Stacey beams, crossing one long limb over the other, her black mini-dress riding up her thigh. Stacey has a thing for Raymond, everyone knows it, even though she's got a fit security guard boyfriend who works the door at one of London's top celebrity nightclubs. But Raymond doesn't seem interested in her, or anyone else for that matter. Raymond is married to his job. *Blue Media* always comes first.

"He's a big noise in the market." Raymond turns a page noisily, "And has promised more work and referrals if we deliver. So let's make sure we do a fantastic job, yes?" We all nod and murmur in agreement.

"What line of business, Ray?" Fearne asks, scribbling onto her notepad like a top secret agent.

"International Property and investments. But not only residential, these guys also cover retail, offices, and leisure complexes. I had a meeting yesterday lunchtime with one of the partners, discussed requirements and…" At this point of the briefing, I lose interest and start thinking about what I'm going to have for dinner tonight. It occurs to me that I've forgotten to do a weekly shop. I wonder if I should pick something up from Sainsbury's on my way home tonight. I could grab one of their ready-made meals and stick it in the microwave. Vicky said that their chicken tikka is to die for.

"And this is all thanks to Audrey." The mention of my name whisks me back to the board meeting.

I start shuffling papers. "Oh, really…" I mutter. I look at Fearne for guidance but she's busy tapping away on her iPad. Oh God, what's he on about? What've I done that's so wonderful? "I…er…" I clear my throat. It must be the project I worked on with Fearne. Raymond must've included it in his PowerPoint presentation. Perhaps the client was so impressed that he signed on the dotted line. Farfetched, I know, but I'm panicking.

"Come on, Audrey, don't be shy." Raymond holds his chin and looks at me above his large, square, black rimmed glasses, a lopsided grin on his face. "Your referral?"

"Referral?" I croak, leafing through the papers in the file in front of me like a bank cashier counting notes. That'll teach me to daydream about food during a staff meeting. "Erm, what referral was that, Raymond?" I curl my hair behind my ear nervously.

"The Theodore Group," he says gleefully. I look at him with a blank expression, face tingling. "Ms Theodorou?" He squints at me quizzically, trying to nudge my memory. But I've no bloody idea who he's talking about. He must've made a mistake. This is probably someone else's referral.

My pulse quickens, my face is on fire. Jesus, I'm never going to get out of this one. Raymond will never let me near another new client again. Shit, shit! Why wasn't I listening?

Raymond thumbs through his paperwork and pulls out a sheet of paper. "And her partner. Mr Taylor." He glances at the contract on the table, then looks up at me again. "Nice chap, said he's a family friend." It takes a while for my mind to process this new piece of information. Taylor…Taylor. The name definitely rings a bell. And then my mother's words shrill in my ears, *'Daniel Taylor, darling, and of course not, he's a happily married man'.*

Every hair on my body stands on end. "Ooooh, DANIEL." I wave a hand. So, he really was interested in setting up a website, then. I thought he was just making polite dinner conversation. "Yes, the Theodopoulos Group," I nod eagerly, pushing my sliding spectacles back into position. This contract's probably worth thousands of pounds. I can't believe he gave us the gig so quickly. Securing a client usually takes weeks of buttering up and pampering, sometimes months. "They're old friends of my parents."

"Theodore Group," Raymond corrects, glancing at his file.

"Yes, that's what I said." A little barky sound slips from my lips and the room falls silent. Four faces stare at me. I want to curl into a ball and crawl under the table.

"Theodore, Theodopoulous, what does it matter," Fearne says reassuringly, "It's a brilliant gig." A collective buzz of approval ripples around the table and I sit upright, bold and proud.

I mouth 'thank you' at Fearne and she winks at me. I owe her – big time.

Raymond gives me a miniscule frown then says, "Well, congratulations, Audrey. Nice work."

"Yeah, well done, mate." Callum taps his fingers lightly against his palm.

"So, Audrey is employee of the month," Raymond announces briskly, adjusting his jacket.

"What? You've gotta be kidding me." Callum's jaw almost hits the floor as the rest of the crew congratulate me. "What about all that work I did on the Collins and…"

"Well, if you stop pissing about on Twitter," Raymond snaps, "and get some proper, decent leads for us you might be in with a chance." Callum's face reddens as he shoots me an angry, suspicious look.

"Thank you, Raymond," I say awkwardly, feeling like a bit of a fraud. Apart from mentioning *Blue Media* to Daniel during polite dinner conversation, I really haven't done anything to win this lucrative deal.

"Choose which day you'd like to take off as a reward, Audrey, and let Stacey know so she can mark it in the diary. Right. I'll set up some meetings." Raymond smooths down his black, narrow tie, he always does this when he's ready to wrap things up, "Fearne and Audrey, you can work on this one together. We'll tackle SEO, Callum, and I'll get onto the agency for graphics. Does anyone have any questions?" We all murmur no in unison. "Good. Job done." Our seats screech against the floor as we all scramble to our feet and make for our desks. "Oh, and, Audrey, before I forget."

"Yes, Raymond?" I hold the door open, Fearne and Stacey slip by, a smile dances on my lips.

"This is for you." He reaches under his seat and pulls out a plastic Waitrose bag.

"What's this?" I ask, surprised. I let the door close and walk towards him. Surely not another company gift?

Raymond shrugs his shoulders. "I've no idea." I take the bag from his outstretched arm. It feels light and fluffy. There's a card stapled at the top with my name and company address written in thick black marker. "It arrived for you by courier this morning." He rolls up the blind and squints as the sunlight pours into the room.

NO WAY BACK

"Seems you're very popular today. Thanks again for the referral, this means we'll top our target this quarter. I'll make sure you get a good bonus in your pay packet next month too." He guides me out of the boardroom, arm hovering over my back, then heads off down the corridor to his office barking orders at Stacey who's trotting behind him in five-inch heels. I scurry back to my PC, Waitrose bag in hand.

"Lunch already?" Fearne asks lightly, gesturing at the Waitrose bag. I look at her in a daze, still trying to absorb everything that just happened in that boardroom. She gets to her feet, grabs a pen from my desk tidy, then straightens her black knee-length skirt, which she's teamed up with a cream blouse covered in whimsical squiggles. My eyes focus on her dark, ash blonde hair hanging stiffly against her shoulders like straw as she sits back down and starts babbling on about the new project. Her roots are dark but the tips are broken and have turned a shade lighter since returning from a holiday in Seville with her husband and step-daughter; clearly, she's spent too much time in the sun. "Audrey?" she frowns, "You okay, love? You look a bit pasty."

"Erm," I croak, clearing my throat. "I am feeling a bit lightheaded, actually. I think it might be the start of a cold." And nothing to do with last night's alcohol consumption, of course. I avert my eyes to the bag, tearing off the stapled card as Fearne wades through The Theodore Group's notes.

"I love this client already," she says, as I rummage inside the bag removing layer upon layer of old newspaper. "They've left most of the design decisions to us, so no lengthy meetings. Only requirements are Flash on the Home page, and a corporate feel, preferably using blues and blacks. All images are on this." She waves a USB stick at me. "In JPG. Brilliant." I can still hear Fearne's voice but I'm not listening anymore. Instead, I'm staring aghast at the item in front of me. "So what do you think, Audrey?" Fearne looks up from her desk and her eyes widen. "Wow."

I gape silently at the red *Jimmy Choo* shoe perched on my desk, surrounded by pages of last Saturday's Financial Times. There's a gift card attached:

Keep them anyway, Audrey, I'd like you to. No strings. I promise. Take Care. D. No kiss this time.

NO WAY BACK

CHAPTER 15

DANIEL PEEKS AT ME from above the menu, his smile reaching his eyes, crinkling at the corners – warm, friendly, cheeky.

"This down to earth enough for you?" He whips the menu away, flashing a smile. We're at a pizza bar in Marylebone, sitting at a table for two by the French window - great for people watching if things get a bit tense or boring. One of the conditions I had when I agreed to this business dinner was that it'd be somewhere ordinary. I wanted the venue to be as unromantic as possible, no soppy background music, no dim lighting, and no candles! This fits the bill perfectly.

"Yes," I reply. "It's perfect." A moody waiter rearranges the chairs at a nearby table that have just been vacated by a bunch of student-looking tourists. He's scraping them loudly and annoyingly against the wooden floor, making my hairs stand on end. "Well, almost." I add, raising my eyebrows at the table-rearranger.

I dip my head over the menu, all the while feeling Daniel's eyes on me. What on earth am I doing? I haven't been alone like this with another man in over eight years. What are we supposed to talk about once we've finished talking shop? What am I supposed to say? And more importantly, what am I supposed to order? I can't see a thing without my glasses on. I don't want to put them on, though. I don't want him to think I've got age-related sight problems, especially if he turns out to be a bit younger than me, which I suspect he is.

Pretending to read the menu, I twiddle with my left earring nervously. I wonder if I'm underdressed. I can see he's made an effort. Cleanly shaved and smelling gorgeous, he's looking quite smart in his dark, tailored suit. I, on the other hand, am still in my office gear - black trousers and a deep red H&M short sleeved knit top - and looking a bit worse for wear. It's been a busy day. Perhaps I should've listened to Mum, after all.

"Wear that lacy black top, Audrey," she demanded when I told her that Raymond had set up a business meeting for me with Daniel to discuss the particulars of his website, "It shows off all your curves."

"Oh, Mum," I groaned, "we're just business associates for God's sake. I don't want to give him the wrong idea."

"Well, do make an effort, darling, you don't want him thinking you're scruffy, do you?" In my defence, I did try to get into that black lacy number this morning but having gained several pounds since returning from Cyprus, couldn't. It ended up being yanked over my head in a frenzy and hurled across the room, landing on my bedside lampshade – where it still resides.

I am, of course, wearing the red *Jimmy Choos*. Well, it would've been rude not to, wouldn't it? Daniel refused point blank to take them back, even threatened to cancel the contract if I declined to keep them. I've fallen in love with them, anyway. The three and a half inch stilettos feel like lovely, soft slippers.

A waitress looms over our table, slim hips tied into a tiny black apron. "Can I get you any drinks?" she says in a foreign accent. She looks hot and bothered. Her dark hair is scrunched into a large hair clamp, long fringe falling over her dark, heavily made up eyes.

"A bottle of your house wine would be nice." Daniel pivots in his chair, smiling up at the young, sultry waitress. She flicks her fringe back and flutters her long, fake eyelashes at him. I sneak a peek at

NO WAY BACK

him as he chats to the waitress, first about the wine and then about how busy the restaurant is this evening. He is very attractive.

My eyes fall onto his full, bow-shaped lips. I wonder if he's a good kisser. Oh, God, no! I quickly look back down at the menu, the words a hazy blur. I mustn't think about kissing him. I don't want another relationship. This is just business, that's all. Business.

"Red okay with you, Audrey?" he asks. I'm not a big fan of red wine. It always goes straight to my head and I end up with a stinking hangover. I'd really prefer something lighter and cooler like a bottle of Frascati or something. But, clearly, he'd prefer red, and I dare not make any more demands, he's going to think I'm fastidious.

"Yeah," I say lightly. I'll just have to make sure I pace myself, "sounds great." I smile up at the waitress. She has a pin through her arched eyebrow, which looks sore and red.

"And a bottle of sparkling mineral water, yeah? Give us a few more minutes for our food, though." I like his confidence. It's quite refreshing, actually. I used to have to pick Nick's dishes for him whenever we went out for a meal, he was so indecisive.

Daniel leans forward, the crisp, white fabric of his shirt stretches over his well-toned arms. I wonder how many hours he spends in the gym refining that body. Obviously not a daily grind, he's not bulky enough for that but he's definitely a man who takes care of his appearance. His shirt is open at the neck but not enough to look tacky, there's no dangling medallion or hairy chest in view. I suppose he removed his tie before he got here. I bet it's stuffed in the pocket of his navy jacket that's draped behind the wooden chair.

"What're you having?" he asks, rubbing his chin. I catch sight of his square silver, blingy-edged cufflinks glimmering under the spotlight.

"Nice cufflinks," I say, playing for time.

"Oh, these old things," he laughs, and I laugh too. "Seriously, though, they were a father's day gift from Connie last year." It's sure nice of Aliki to buy him such expensive looking gifts on behalf of their daughter, another sign that she hasn't let go.

"So?" He fixes me with a close-range stare. "What'll it be?"

He unnerves me. I glance quickly at the menu, anything to avoid eye contact. Flirting isn't on my agenda tonight. He's just a client, that's all. A client. I smooth down my hair, my phone bleeps on the table, lighting up with a new message. Daniel looks at it briefly then back at me.

"I'll just have a Margherita pizza, I think." I glance at my handset flashing with another message. But given that I'll need to hold the phone at least two feet away to read the texts there's really no point in retrieving them now. Daniel frowns as he stretches his arm behind him, all the time regarding me dubiously.

"Are you sure?" he asks carefully, "I fancy something a bit hot and spicy myself. Let's have a look." And with this, he whips out a pair of spectacles from his jacket pocket and slides them on. "Can't see a damn thing without these," he groans. Damn, I could've worn mine. But it's too late to admit to being long sighted now. "You young people don't know how lucky you are." My limbs jolt into action and I sit upright in my chair. He must think I'm younger than him, which is rather lovely. Perhaps Daniel Taylor should come with a health slogan emblazoned along his forehead - "Great for your ego." I've only been in his company for thirty-five minutes and already he's boosted my self-esteem.

We talk "shop" as we sip our wine, not a bad red actually, quite smooth and fruity. I give him an update on the development of his website and describe what plans we have for it. I explain the basics of setting up a site and the importance of search engine

NO WAY BACK

optimisation, which will be expertly implemented by Raymond and Callum. I assure him that his project is in good hands and that we'll get him placement on page one of Google for his chosen keywords and phrases in no time at all, and with this assurance, he's happy to move onto another topic of conversation. Me.

He quizzes me about my role at *Blue Media* and seems genuinely interested in what I do, which is a bit of a first really as most people find my occupation complicated and boring. We then get into a heated discussion about politics and Brexit and my parents' plans to move to Cyprus. Fuelled by alcohol, I make no secret of my objections. "I really think they're making a big mistake," I explain. "A holiday is one thing but emigrating?" I shake my head. "They'll regret it. I don't want them to go."

He throws his head back and laughs loudly, "What are you, five?" he says. His flippancy annoys me. What's so funny about wanting my parents to live in England? But eventually, he convinces me they're doing the right thing – I've got to let go and leave them to it. I'm lucky to have my brother, nephews and sister-in-law close by. "I wish I had family who thought that highly of me," he says, straightening the cutlery on his napkin, and I'm sure I detect a touch of sourness in his voice, but I don't say anything.

Half an hour later as we tuck into our pizzas we move onto the subject of failed relationships. I knew we'd get here eventually. I'm not usually intrusive but the red wine has loosened my conscience and revved up my curiosity, so I ask him about Aliki and why they split up. He goes quiet at first and a bit red, seems edgy, cagey even, then quickly explains that they grew apart, wanted different things. Their marriage died years ago but, like many couples with children, it was Connie that had kept them together.

"And what about you?" He pours sparkling water into my glass. I watch as the bubbles fizz and whirl around in a frenzy. Shall I tell him the truth? Tell him that the man I adored for eight years crushed my heart beyond repair and trampled all over my dignity? That I still lie in bed at night trying to work out what I did wrong, why I wasn't enough for him? That I still sometimes cry myself to sleep? That, despite everything, I still miss him.

"Same as." I take a sip of wine, he's not the only one who can fob people off with clichés. "We wanted different things." This isn't a lie. I wanted marriage, he didn't.

"Oh, I see." He shovels pizza into his mouth. "So you weren't that close then?" He chews his food, "Towards the end, I mean." Close? I want to laugh. I've never felt closer to anyone else in my entire life. It was as if Nick passed through me and our souls touched.

I cut into my pizza heavily, my eyes sting, "Why are these knives so damned blunt?" I tug at it hard with my duff cutlery. A piece breaks away, flies off my plate and lands in the middle of the table, just missing the little vase holding a single yellow Gerbera. Shit.

"I'm sorry." His hand closes over my fist, it's warm, soft. "I shouldn't have brought it up." He mops up the mess and gestures at a waiter for more napkins. "I know it's still very raw for you. It takes time to get over a relationship, especially if you've been together for a long time."

I drop my cutlery by my plate and suck my lips in, kerbing in my fury. I want to tell him to shut-the-hell-up. I want to say that my private life is none of his damned business. I'm only here because Raymond insisted. I don't need his bloody sympathy. I'm fine, and I'd cope a lot better if people stopped reminding me every five fucking minutes. But Raymond would fire me if I mess up this meeting.

"It's okay." I continue attacking my pizza, all the time complaining about the blunt knife. I can see him gearing up to apologise again

NO WAY BACK

but I'm saved by my phone chiming on the table with a call. Can't Louise or Tina wait until I get home before giving me the third degree? It stops ringing then starts again almost immediately.

"Aren't you going to get that?" he asks, as a faceless waiter places several napkins on our table. "It's been going off with messages all night." Is he always this condescending?

I snatch my handset off the table, slide the ringer onto silent, then slip it smoothly into my handbag, telling him I'll deal with them later, that I get dozens of text messages and voicemails from clients all the time.

After dessert, which I must point out was forced upon me because I am supposed to be on a diet, his mobile phone starts chiming with a string of texts messages followed by an incoming call.

"Sorry," he says abruptly, glancing at the screen, "I've got to get this." And to my surprise, he leaves the table and nips outside.

"Your cappuccino, Madam." The waitress's voice averts my attention away from Daniel on the street. I look up at her quickly with a small reflex smile, still a bit dazzled by his abrupt departure.

The hum of voices and clatter of plates fill my ears as I watch him curiously through the French doors. He's pacing up and down the pavement like an expectant father, frowning and talking hurriedly into his handset. He doesn't seem happy. I wonder if he's talking to Aliki, if she's checking up on him. I bet he'll be snuggled up in bed with her by the end of the evening. I smile and shake my head, elbows resting on the round grey marbled table, cup in hand. Why should I even care? I blow onto my coffee. This is just business. I take a sip from my huge, white cup. The hot liquid burns my lips and I wince.

"Sorry, about that." Daniel's back looking flustered and on edge. There's a bit of rain on his shirt and hair. "Is it okay if we get the bill?" he asks quickly, and before I can answer he's pushing his arm into the sleeve of his jacket and signalling to the waitress for the bill. I look at my full cup of coffee.

"Is everything all right?"

"Yeah, yeah, well, kind of. It's…it's Connie…she's just…Thanks," The waitress places the bill onto the table and he throws three twenty pounds notes onto the plate, tells her to keep the change.

"Oh God, is she okay?" I get to my feet quickly. I hope nothing has happened to her.

"She's just really upset, Audrey, she's crying, I really…"

"No, no…" I grab my mac from behind my chair urgently, "you don't have to explain, your daughter comes first. I completely understand." I shoulder my bag as we head for the door. "We're done here, anyway."

Outside he hails a black cab for me and pays the driver the fare to Muswell Hill.

"Thanks for being so understanding, Audrey. It's been great. I've really enjoyed your company." I smile and nod. "We'll do it again, yeah?" He kisses me lightly on the cheek, so close that I can smell his aftershave.

"Yes, of course," I say, suddenly feeling that I would like to see him again, because despite my earlier reservations, he's kind of grown on me. "Especially now we're working together."

And as the cab zooms off into the night, I realise that I don't even know where he lives. In fact, I don't know that much about Daniel Taylor at all, other than he's divorced, has one daughter, and is a partner in the Theodore Group. However, I do recall him saying at Mum and Dad's dinner party that Aliki lives in Crouch End, which I presume is their family home and where his daughter resides. So why, then, didn't he just share a cab with me to north London? Why are men so complicated?

CHAPTER 16

THE CAB BOUNCES OVER SPEED BUMPS and I open my eyes. We're in Muswell Hill. I must've fallen asleep. My phone buzzes in my handbag with a call. I rummage around for it in the semi-darkness. By the time I find it, it stops ringing. Five missed calls, two voicemails – all from Tina. Seven text messages, four from Tina and three from NICK. My heart bounces in my chest like a basketball.

What the hell does he want? I bypass Tina's messages and voicemail and go straight to Nick's first text.

Hello, Audrey – how r things? Need to speak to u. Can you call me?

Text 2: **Pls call. Important.**

And finally text 3: **Foxy, pls call me asap. It's urgent xx.**

Foxy? Kisses? Is he having a flipping laugh?

Outside my flat, I fumble with my door key, why won't it fit into the lock for crying out loud? My hands are shaking and I realise that I'm forcing the back door key into the lock. The keys jangle in my hands as I try to find the right one. How could he? How dare he! After everything he's done. My breath quickens. I need to get inside – fast. I finally find the key but my hands are like jelly. The keys rattle unsteadily in my hand then hit the floor. "Oh, for fuck's sake!" I'm about to cry, then as I bend down to pick up the keys I spot the red buds, hidden behind my pot plant on the stone porch. He's been round. He came to my flat while I was out.

I fly through the front door and march into the kitchen, bunch of tulips under arm. I don't even bother to read the card as I force the bouquet into the dustbin, crushing the stems in half. I know they're from him, I recognised his writing on the card, 'For Audrey' in - big, bold, swirls. I always thought his handwriting was like a girl's. I text him back furiously.

Don't text. Don't call. Don't come round again. EVER!! Leave me alone!

The cooler backlight illuminates the kitchen as I open the fridge door and I realise that I haven't even put the lights on yet. I can't believe I'm letting him get to me. What the hell does he want? I yank out a bottle of wine, hot with rage, and flick the lights on.

Leaning against the worktop, I close my eyes, savouring the cool, tangy liquid sliding down my throat. Then just as I regain my equilibrium the landline goes off. It's him. He's received my text. I march into the lounge, determined, wine spilling from my glass. I'm going to give him a piece of my mind, tell him to leave me alone or I'll call the police, report him for harassment. I'll even get a restraining order out on him if I have to. I answer on the fifth ring.

"What?" I demand furiously.

"Audrey?" says a muffled woman's voice.

"Yes, who is this?" I put the drink down on the coffee table, fingers wet with wine. I wipe them on the edge of my knit top.

"Where've you been?"

"Tina, is that you?" I push a hand through my hair and realise that I've broken a nail, must've been when I forced the bouquet savagely into the dustbin.

"Yes, of course, it's me." She takes huge gulps between sentences. I can barely make out what she's saying. "I've been calling you all night," she cries, "And texting." More gulps, "Where were you?"

"I was out with Daniel, remember?" I grind my broken nail against my teeth. "I told you I was seeing him tonight."

"Oh, yeah," she sniffs, "I remember now. I left so many messages, though, didn't you get them?"

"Tina, it was work." I play for time, clearly, she's very upset so there's no point in telling her that I couldn't read her messages earlier because I was too embarrassed to wear my glasses in front of Daniel, an anecdote she'd have found hilarious under normal circumstances.

"So? It was out of hours. Surely, you can answer your phone."

Damn. I'm not going to get away with this lightly. In the bathroom, I grab a towel and rub the sweat off my face. "Well, the thing is, Tina," I begin, then catch my reflection in the mirrored cabinet above the sink. I almost cry out in shock as a pair of panda eyes stare back at me in horror. My hair has doubled in size. My teeth are tinged with red wine and there's a thin purple line along my lips. Oh, God, no wonder the cabbie was giving me strange looks as I climbed out of his taxi. I walk back into the lounge, wearing the white towel around my neck like a heavy-weight boxer. "My battery died," I lie as casually as I can. "Are you okay?"

"What do you think?" My mind immediately shifts to her druggie ex-husband, setting off alarm bells.

"You haven't seen Micky, have you?"

"Are you fucking mad?" Tina's been drinking. I can tell when she's had one too many, she gets all sweary and defensive. Arguing with a drunk Tina isn't a good idea.

"Look, just calm down, will you, and tell me what's wrong." I look at my watch. It's only eight-thirty. "Do you want me to come round?" She only lives in Palmers Green, I could be there in fifteen minutes.

"No." I can hear her sniffling, "S'okay." Her tears must be drying

– result. "I just wanted to tell you that…" And then the tears start again.

"What? You're scaring me, Tean." My heart feels as if it's climbing into my mouth. What's happened to her? I've never known Tina to be this upset before.

"Oh, Goddddd." There's a retching sound. "I think I'm going to be sick." Shit. She must be hammered. "Audrey, I'm going to die." I can hear her shuffling now, blowing her nose. At least she hasn't vomited.

"Die?" I collapse onto the sofa, letting out a sigh of relief. She must be *very* drunk. "Tina, you're not going to die, Hun. Just drink plenty of water." I kick off my shoes and tip my head back on the headrest, "Sleep it off, everything will seem much better in the…" But she doesn't let me finish.

"I've found a lump," she cries in a little voice.

"A lump?" I leap to the edge of my seat. "Where?" Silence. "Tina!"

"In my breast," she sobs. "Audrey, I've got cancer."

"What?" My hand closes over my mouth, sealing in a silent scream.

"And there's more…"

"More?" I exclaim. Oh, God, please don't let her tell me that she's known for ages, that it's spread. That there's no treatment. Oh, God, oh God. No, no, no.

"I'm so sorry, Audrey…"

"Sorry?" I cry, my eyes bulging with fear. "You're not making any sense."

"I did something stupid." She pauses, blows her nose. "It's just that I was desperate, and I couldn't find you, and I tried calling your mum and Louise but there weren't picking up…and I had no one else to turn to and I…"

NO WAY BACK

"What did you do?" Oh my God, she's taken an overdose. I've got to get off the line, call 999, and get round there fast. I push my feet into my shoes, staring around the room wildly. Where're my bloody car keys?

"I rang Nick," she says in a teary voice, "and I begged him to find you for me."

CHAPTER 17

"NINE OUT OF TEN BREAST LUMPS ARE BENIGN." The nurse is small and round with short blonde hair – late fifties, mumsy. "Try not to worry, love," she says softly. But Tina is a whimpering wreck. "If you can just pop into the changing room over there and slip into this, someone will see you shortly." Tina snatches the patterned gown from the nurse's hand, swallowing hard. I give the nurse a knowing look depicting "she doesn't mean to be rude, it's just her nerves." and she smiles at me warmly, eyes soft, kind. I expect she's used to anxious patients.

"Go on, Tina," I urge, squeezing her arm, "you'll be fine." Although I'm not quite sure who I'm trying to convince, her or me. "I'll be waiting for you right here." Her eyes search mine anxiously, gown in hand. I don't know how she got through the last eleven days, to be honest, let alone this morning. It took a lot of coaxing and pleading to get her to see a specialist. For although initially frantic with worry, she then went into denial, hoping the lump would just go away. It was Nick who persuaded her to see a doctor in the end. He's very good with words, gentle and calming, and she's always trusted him.

"Okay," she says after a few moments, nodding quickly. "Look after my stuff, will you." And she's gone.

I take a deep breath and glance around the posh waiting room. We're at a clinic in Chelsea. Tina's PR job comes with private medical insurance, thank goodness, because I hate to think how much they charge here. Everyone looks tanned and unlined, and rich!

We arrived bright and early and were seen almost immediately, which was a godsend as a long wait might've caused Tina to leg it through their automatic sliding doors. I did see her eyeing them longingly when we first sat down, but were saved just in the nick of time by her consultant, Mr Roberts, a middle-aged man in a lilac wrinkled shirt with gentle brown eyes and a warm smile.

We sat in front of his large, oak desk like two misbehaving school girls stealing glances at each other while he leafed through some paperwork and explained what was going to happen today. A painting of *The Sunflower* hung slightly lopsided on the otherwise bare magnolia wall behind him. A medical couch with a blue and white curtain loomed in the far corner, but, weirdly, all I could think about was why he left the house in an unironed shirt.

"How do I look?" Tina's back looking small and vulnerable in her patterned gown, white fluffy robe and slippers. I'm still holding her hand when the radiologist calls out her name. I stand up, like a worried parent, mouth dry. "Can I come in with her please?" I croak, bile swarming my stomach.

"I'm afraid not." The radiologist crinkles her nose, hand resting on Tina's back lightly, "No one is allowed in the x-ray room. But don't worry." She leans forward on the sole of her white plastic clog peeking from her blue scrubs. "I'll look after her," she whispers, clutching Tina's file close to her chest and giving my arm a light squeeze. "I promise."

Within fifteen minutes Tina's back in the waiting room, pale and anxious.

"How was it, Tean?" I wrap my arm around her shoulders. "You look exhausted."

"So would you be if you had your boobs squeezed between two plates from all directions, it was bloody painful." She tightens the belt of her dressing gown angrily. A mature lady sitting opposite gives us a thin smile, drawing her black oversized bag close to her chest.

"So what happens now?" I ask.

"Oh, I dunno," Tina huffs. "A doctor has to read the mammogram or something." A scent of mango infused shampoo dances under my nose as she loosens her hair. "Then I've got to have an ultrasound," she mumbles, clamping the hairband between her teeth as she gathers her red tresses in her hands. "So, it's not over yet."

Tina has nearly worn out the carpet with her foot tapping. We've only been waiting thirteen minutes, but each minute seems like an hour. I inhale deeply, stomach clenching. It'll all be fine, I tell myself. I've got to stay strong for Tina.

"Why are they taking so long?" I can see her heart beating through her patterned gown. She stands up and scans the narrow, long corridor, twisting a pretty silver weave ring around her finger. "They must've found something." Her eyes fill. "It must be bad. Oh God, what's going to happen to me?"

"Just stay positive, Tina." I pull her down by the sleeve of her robe, "You heard what the nurse said – most breast lumps are benign and they deal with this kind of stuff every day, so they should know." I stroke her soft cheek with the back of my fingers as her mobile phone goes off in her bag. She stands up as she reads the message, then rushes to the window, waving frantically. "Who is it?" I ask, peering over her shoulder. The morning has turned grey and dull, despite a promising start.

"Look." She points down at the street. I can feel the warmth of her cheek, the smell of mango shampoo. "Just there by that blue car."

I steady myself against the ledge as a sudden wave of vertigo washes over me. "Oh, bloody hell, Tean." I glance at her quickly. "What the hell is he doing here?" Nick looks frail and slight in his loose clothing. He's lost weight, looks gaunt, humble. I look away quickly. I can't do this.

Tina's phone tinkles with another text. She reads it quickly, a small grin on her lips. "He is quite sweet, isn't he? He says he just wants to make sure that I'm all right." Really? Or does he have an ulterior motive? Get to me through Tina, perhaps? He sent me two remorseful texts since I fired off that angry message to him last week; pleading with me to meet him so we can talk, so he can explain. I've ignored them all, of course. Louise has suggested I block him, which I will do if he continues to harass me. "I can't believe how stupid he's been," Tina goes on, "You know, with you I mean." And just at that moment, the phone rings in her hand. "It's him!" Oh, no. I can't believe this is happening. "Just a mo." Tina slips into the corridor with her phone. Within seconds, she's back at the window – waving.

"Well?" I say, leaning against the pillar, anything to avoid looking at him. The heavy, dark clouds have erupted; streaks of rain like two-inch needles are raging against the pane.

"He said he just wants to hang around until I get my results." She smiles down at him sadly, face pressed against the window, breath steaming up the glass.

I throw a glance at him over my shoulder. "In the rain? He'll catch his death, daft man."

"I know. I didn't think you'd want him up here." She pauses. A phone goes off, the sound of a keyboard tap, tap, taps in the distance. "You don't mind him waiting outside, though, do you? They won't allow him in the foyer, not without a permit, something to do with security."

"Well, it doesn't seem like I've got much of a choice, does it?" I stare at my nails.

We're silent for a few moments, then Tina says, "He is very caring and generous, though, isn't he?" I sigh loudly. I'd often tease him about being a lightweight whenever he complained about feeling faint after donating blood, and he's the only person I know who carries a donor card with him at all times. Yes, he is very kind and helpful. It's one of the attributes I loved about him, but that doesn't change the fact that he cheated on me. She's no idea what he's capable of. The extent of what he's done. If she knew he had impregnated another woman, she'd be throwing bricks down at him from the window not waving and cooing. She'd be furious. She'd never forgive him. Ever.

"I know about the baby," she says suddenly.

"What?" My stomach twists. I stare at her in disbelief. She's got to be kidding me.

"Yeah, sorry, Hun. He told me a couple of days ago." She pauses, chews her bottom lip as she regards me carefully. "He seems to think that you know about it too." Damn Ronan. He promised me he wouldn't say anything. "Why didn't you tell us, Audrey? We could've helped you through this. You must feel terrible."

I finally find my voice. "Oh, Tina, I don't know. I just felt so embarrassed, humiliated. I didn't want anyone to know how stupid I'd been," I admit. A feeling of relief sluices through me. At least I won't have lie to my family and friends anymore. "Please tell me that you're just as furious as I am." Silence. "I mean, I know you've been friends with him for years, and he's helped you through this, but surely you can't accept what he's done to me?" I look down at Nick. He's standing at the edge of a café, hands in pockets, rain dripping off his navy PVC hooded raincoat.

"Audrey, I was bloody livid when he left you. But now I've had a chance to speak to him…" she falters, "What I mean is, now he's explained it all makes sense."

"You can't be serious." I rake a hand through my hair. "You do realise that he was shagging another woman behind my back, don't you?"

"Yes, of course, I do, but he said it was a one-off." I look at her in horror. Is that supposed to make everything all right, then? "He's not in love with her, Audrey. They're not together. He said it happened when…"

But I just talk over her. "Can't you see he's just using you to get to me?"

Tina touches my hand and I flinch, her fingers are icy. "Look, why don't you give him a chance to explain? I think he just wants to apologise."

"Ease his conscience, you mean?" Silence. I look down at him; he's now standing under the shop canopy. "It's too late for apologies, Tina. Anyway, why should I lessen his guilt? I'm not interested. Tell him to just leave me alone and get on with his life with his new girlfriend and baby."

"But aren't you just a teensy-weensy bit curious?" She holds her thumb and index finger an inch apart.

"No," I bark, and Tina jumps. I've startled her. "Oh, Tina, I'm sorry." I run a hand over my face. Poor thing, she doesn't need all this, today is supposed to be about her. "Look, we're here for you today, I don't want to stress you out with my problems."

"It's okay," she sighs, "the distraction is helping. A bit." She leans into me, arms folded, nudging me lightly with her shoulder. "I told him you're seeing someone else, anyway." I'm sure he was delighted. That's probably what all this is about. He doesn't want me, but he doesn't want anyone else to have me either. "He said he still loves you, Audrey."

"Love? Ha."

"I think you two just need to talk. Clear the air."

I rub my forehead. Tina's persistence is doing my head in. "Tina, please." I pause. "Look, I love you dearly, and I know you mean well, but don't push me on this one, okay?"

She shakes her head in agreement, and we return to our seats leaving Nick in the rain.

"So, how's it going with Daniel?" Tina asks, the moment we sit down.

"Okay," I reply, pleased that she finally wants to talk about something else. I tell her that we've had a couple of dates since the pizza bar meeting. And that I like him. A lot. "He is a bit full-on, though," I admit. Tina nods, beckoning me to go on. "I mean, he wants me to meet his daughter."

"Already?" she says a little loudly. The receptionist looks up at us briefly, face tight. "It's only been two weeks."

"Eleven days, actually." I chew my fingernail. "Do you see what I mean?"

"When does he want you to meet her?" she whispers eagerly, throwing a quick glance at the receptionist.

"Tomorrow." I twist my lips, cringing. "I said yes because, well, he kind of cornered me." It was during our second bottle of *Laurent-Perrier Rosé* at *The Flask* last Tuesday. I'd have agreed to marry him naked on Brighton Pier if he'd asked. "It was a spur of the moment thing, but I'm having second thoughts now. It just all seems to be happening a bit too fast."

Tina raises her eyebrows. "Well, he must really like you, then. Maybe he just wants to make sure you and his little girl get along before, you know, anything develops."

"Hmm…" Perhaps Tina's right. I hadn't thought of that. Although there's no way I want another serious relationship. It's too soon for that. "Anyway, I'm child-minding Florian tomorrow – a last minute thing. I promised Vicky." A nurse bustles past us and we both draw our legs in. "So, I'll have to ask him for a rain check."

"How old is his Princess?"

"About four, five?" I stare at the window blithely. The rain is unforgiving. I wonder if Nick had the sense to wait inside the café.

"Oh, you don't know, then?"

"Not exactly, no. I never thought to ask. Daniel doesn't really talk about his family." I incline my head thoughtfully. "But when I saw her on the beach in Cyprus she looked about that age."

"So, take Florian with."

"Nah, he'll probably get bored. He's going through that 'all girls smell' period."

"Or are you just making excuses?" She pivots in her chair and grabs my hands. "Audrey. Look at me, look at where we are." She gazes around her. "Life is short, damn it, don't let chances pass you by. Daniel sounds like a lovely bloke. I wouldn't push him away if I were you. I mean, look what happened with me and Ronan." I feel my face redden. Does she still have feelings for Ronan? I run my tongue against my bottom lip. I wonder if I should confess about the kiss. Surely, it wouldn't bother her. She'd understand that it was a moment of madness when I explain. I bet she'd even find it funny. I mean, it's not as if she was going out with him when I threw myself at him on my doorstep. I open my mouth to speak but the radiologist appears with another file clutched to her chest and we both look up at her expectantly.

"Rosemary Frost?" The lady opposite with the black oversized bag raises her eyebrows at me as if to say "here goes". I mouth "good luck" and she smiles as she gets to her feet. Tina and I deflate back into our seats and the moment has gone.

"So, are you going to shag him tomorrow?" Tina says after a while, tapping my foot with her white slipper playfully.

"Tina!"

"What?"

"No! We'll have the kids, remember." I shake my head. "That's if I go."

"Not all night you won't." Tina looks at the window. "It's bucketing down. Do you think Nick's still there?"

And before I can answer a voice calls out, "Tina Hunt?" We both shoot to our feet. We trot behind the nurse along the dark corridor, veering off to the left at the end.

Dr Hill is a quirky, well-spoken woman in her late forties who uses short, snappy sentences to get her point across quickly. Of course, I can sit in, she tells me, waving a hand. Her thick, dark bob bounces around her shoulders as she moves around the room, "It's no problem at all." She smells of luxurious perfume but I'm not quite sure about the grey pinafore dress she's wearing, very officey, I was expecting her to turn up in scrubs.

I sit stiffly in the corner, facing Tina, my fingers and legs tightly crossed for her, my heart pounding in my chest, stomach, ears. The dark room, illuminated by the glare of the computer screen, is thick with tension.

"Right," she trills as if we're all going on an adventure, "let's see what's happening." Her thin eyebrows knot in concentration as she slides the scanner vertically, then horizontally over Tina's skin, eyes glued to the screen.

"Just as I thought," she says after a while. My bum finds the edge of the seat, my eyes widen. "You've got cysts," she announces triumphantly.

"What? You mean more than one?" Tina is staring at Dr Hill in horror. "Am I going to die?"

"No, of course not," she laughs, "They're perfectly harmless." We all breathe a loud sigh of relief. It takes all the strength I have to stop myself from getting up and kissing Dr Hill. Hard on the lips. "How old are you, Tina?" She glances at her notes, "Oh, thirty-six." She shakes her head and her brown bob dances around her face, "Yes, they're very common in women your age. And the mammogram looks clear too. Right. Do you want me to aspirate them for you?"

Tina is dressed and we're ready to go. The rain has stopped and the sun is streaming through the windows.

"Come on," I say, with glee, "I'm buying."

"It'd better be a bottle of prosecco," she warns, as she slides an arm into her brown leather jacket, "Each." We both laugh, although I'm sure she means it. "Thanks for today, Audrey." She yanks her long, auburn curls out of her jacket then pulls me into her arms. "You're the best friend in the world." We rock from side to side in a tight bear hug, then suddenly she pulls away. "Oh, shit, I almost forgot." We disentangle quickly and she rushes to the window. I watch as she frowns down at the street, craning her neck, hands on the ledge, then suddenly she grins widely and holds up her thumbs.

I shake my head as I make my way towards her. Nick's still here. I knew it. Stubborn as ever. But if he thinks he's going to catch me off guard as I walk out of the hospital, force me into the pub for a drink and a chat, then he's more deluded than I thought.

And as I look out of the window I catch a glimpse of Nick throwing his rucksack over his shoulder and melting into a crowd of people.

CHAPTER 18

I WHIP BACK THE CURTAINS and the sun splashes through the window, illuminating my bedroom, its enthusiasm and vitality seeping into the pores of my skin. I love the autumn sunshine. It reminds me of rare family visits to Highgate Woods when I was little; of me and George playing hide and seek, of my parents chasing us around the green then tickling us until we cried out for mercy.

Opening the window, I fill my lungs with the cool, crisp air. Isn't life great? Tina got the all clear yesterday, not a peep out of Nick, and I have a fabulous new man in my life. I close my eyes, savouring the moment as the phone trills in the background. I glance at my alarm clock quickly - five seconds past ten. Daniel said he'd call me at ten o'clock. I bound into the lounge and grab the phone before the answering machine kicks in.

"Great news about Tina," Daniel says a little breathlessly after we get the preambles out of the way. I was so excited about Tina's good news that I texted him yesterday afternoon. "We are still on for today, aren't we?"

"Yes, yes, of course." Yesterday in the pub, Tina persuaded me to keep my date with Daniel but suggest a cosy night in instead of lunch with his daughter. I could invite him round once Vicky picks up Florian, and that way I'll avoid meeting Connie today but still see him. Good thinking. I pad into the kitchen and grab the semi-skimmed milk from the fridge. "You okay? You sound out of breath," I laugh, closing the fridge door with my elbow.

"Yeah, sorry, just got back from my run." Run? I knew he was fit but didn't have him down for pounding the streets of north-west London.

"Really? I thought you were more of a gym man," I say a little loudly over the rumble of the kettle.

"Nah, nothing like running in the fresh air." I can almost hear him smiling down the phone. "You should join me next time?"

"Yeah, might just do that." I could do with losing a bit of weight. "A jog around the park sounds like fun." He laughs and tells me that he ran ten miles today. "What?" I exclaim, "Without stopping?" I'm gobsmacked and slightly in awe. I get breathless running for the 134 bus. "Well, in that case, you'll need the paramedics on speed dial if I come along."

We share a moment of laughter as I shuffle into the lounge with my coffee and bowl of Weetabix, phone jammed between my shoulder and jaw. He sounds excited, happy, the endorphins must be tearing through his body. I'm glad I've got him in a good mood, it'll make telling him about my change of plans much easier. I'm sure he'll be fine about it all, especially when I suggest a quiet night in with a bottle of wine, a takeaway and a soppy movie on Netflix. He's a reasonable man. He'll understand.

"So, what time do you want to meet up?" he asks brightly. "We said about lunchtime, didn't we? I could pick you up or –"

But I don't let him finish. "Well, I was going to say could we do Connie another day, actually." I pause for a response but am met with a cold silence. Shit. I hope he hasn't taken this the wrong way. "I mean, it's not that I don't want to meet her or anything, but I promised Vicky I'd have Florian today, a last minute thing and…"

"But she's been looking forward to it all week," he cuts in crisply. I'm slightly taken aback by his sharp tone.

"Well, I'll have Florian until about fiveish." I push the cereal bowl away from me, my appetite suddenly depleted.

"Bring him along," he says cheerfully. I can hear him shuffling around, banging cupboard doors, then the hiss of a can being opened, "The more the merrier. Connie won't mind."

"Yes, I know…but the thing is…" I rack my brains for a reasonable excuse. Oh, God, why can't I just be honest? Why can't I just say *"I'd like to get to know you a little bit better before we do the family stuff. What's the rush?"*

"Oh, come on, Audrey, please." He breathes heavily down the phone. "I can't cancel on her now. She's so excited. Is two o'clock okay with you?" It doesn't look like he's going to take no for an answer. I spoon the gloopy Weetabix around in the bowl in front of me. I suppose it can't hurt to meet his little girl, and I don't want to be a spoilsport, especially if she's been looking forward to it all week.

"Okaaaay," I say sulkily. "Vicky should be dropping Florian off at twelve, so two should be fine. We'll come to you. There's more to do in Hampstead. Florian and I can just jump on the tube, he loves travelling on the underground. Where do you fancy eating?" I take a sip of much-needed coffee. He tells me it's up to me. "How about McDonalds, then? It's Florian's favourite treat." Vicky always lets me spoil him when I'm child-minding.

"Oh, McDonalds." He sounds disappointed with my choice of venue but agrees to meet us outside the restaurant at 2 p.m., if that's what I want. Well, where are you supposed to take kids for lunch, for Christ's sake, *The Shard*?

At twelve-thirty, Florian and I catch the 134 to Highgate then jump onto the Northern Line heading for Hampstead, I with a copy of *Marie Claire* under my arm and he with his mini iPad, which I bought him for his last birthday. And as the train thunders

NO WAY BACK

into the dark tunnel whisking me towards my latest challenge, I start wondering what on earth I've let myself in for. What am I doing messing around with a man with a family? A man whose business partner is his ex-wife? A gorgeous, young ex-wife who enjoys family holidays with him in Cyprus. And what will happen if Connie hates me? Will that be the end of our short relationship? And why, oh why, did I let him manipulate me into meeting his daughter today when clearly I'm not ready for it?

I berate myself for being such a big wimp, elbow on armrest, chin in hand. I'll never learn. A young woman opposite with blonde shoulder length hair looks up at me from her kindle and smiles, and I realise I've been giving her the-thousand-mile-stare for the last five minutes. Sitting up straight, I smile back quickly before averting my eyes to the middle-aged man next to her. He's fast asleep, arms folded, head lolling near his chest, and momentarily I'm transported to the time I fell asleep on the train after an office party and missed my stop.

I spent the entire journey with my head against a nun's shoulder, snoring. I don't think she had the heart to disturb me but when we arrived at her stop, she gently shook me awake and said, "I'm getting off here, love." I looked up at her, bleary-eyed, mouth ajar. A huge crucifix swayed close to my face, and for a brief moment, I thought I'd died and gone to heaven. "And you really shouldn't drink so much in the future, dear. It makes you snore and it's given you smelly breath. God bless."

I press my lips together, kerbing in a laugh that's bursting to escape. I've got to get the image of the nun out of my head. I gaze around the carriage, desperate for distraction. A little girl, about Connie's age, is sitting three seats away with her mother, swinging a teddy bear in the air as if it were a flag. When she catches me watching she clings to her mum, then shyly makes the bear give me a little wave. It's new, it still has the price tag hanging off its foot, must've been a treat from mum. And as I wriggle my fingers at her and mouth "hello" a feeling of dread tears through me like a Japanese bullet train. Shit. I haven't bought Connie a present.

I cover my mouth and gasp. Kindle-lady glances up at me, nutter alert etched on her face. My face feels like it's on fire. I can't turn up empty handed on our first meeting. Daniel will think I'm a cheapskate. Connie will be disappointed. She'll hate me from the word go. I pinch the skin of my neck nervously, frowning at my double reflection in the window. I suppose I could buy her something once I get there, some sweets or a cuddly toy. Surely, there's a newsagent in Hampstead. Satisfied by this brainwave, I relax and cross one leg over the other, smiling down at Florian who's looking at me sideways, lips slightly parted, as if I'm deranged.

"Almost there," I say excitedly, leafing through the pages of my magazine absentmindedly. And he rolls his eyes and goes back to his game.

Outside Hampstead Station, Florian and I walk hand in hand down the slope towards the High Street, I with a flutter of anxiety in my stomach and he with his mini iPad. We're fifteen minutes early – result. It'll give me time to buy Connie a gift.

"Remember what I said, Florian, be nice to the little girl or no iTunes top-up, okay?"

"Yes, Auntie," he drones, gazing at the screen of his iPad.

"And no playing games in McDonalds either, give me that." I snatch his iPad and stuff it into my bag. "You can play with it on the journey home." And after a little protest, he grumpily agrees.

We turn into the High Street, and my heart does an unexpected jig in my chest. Daniel and Connie are already here. They're hovering over a shop window about fifty yards past McDonalds. I'm not surprised they're early, Daniel's super-efficient, but this means I won't have time to buy Connie a present. Damn.

"Oh, look, they're already here, Florian. Come on, hurry up."

We scurry towards them. The brisk wind blows in my face, whipping my hair back like a top model on a fashion shoot. I open my mouth to call out his name, but it catches in my throat. I watch in horror as he stretches his arm across a woman's shoulders. What's going on? I halt suddenly and my *Jimmy Choo* jams in-between the paving. I wriggle my foot, trying to release it. They're laughing now and she's digging him playfully in the ribs. Oh, shit, I think it's Aliki. My heart picks up speed. He's bloody well brought his ex-wife along! I rock my shoe back and forth. Talk about being laid back and easy going. I wonder if they're a couple of swingers. No wonder he's so bloody keen. He's probably been grooming me for weeks.

"Why have we stopped, Auntie?"

"Shhh…Florian, just a minute." I crane my neck to get a better view, all the while rocking my heel. Their chatting now. Connie is skipping on the pavement next to them.

"But I'm hungry."

Connie's tugging at her mother's sleeve. Aliki looks down at her and then opens her handbag and pulls out a colourful bottle. Oh, my God, I've got to get out of here. This is a complete nightmare. I should've trusted my instincts. I knew I shouldn't have come today.

"Come on, Florian, we're going. I'll take you to a McDonalds nearer home." And with a final jerk, I dislodge my heel from the gap and spin round.

"But there's no McDonald's near your flat, Auntie," Florian whines, "you promised."

"Just hurry, Florian, please. I'll buy you lots of treats." Florian stops dragging his feet and we pick up speed.

"Audrey!" Daniel's voice bellows in my ears, a middle-aged couple sidestep as we tear up the street. My step quickens. "Audrey," he whistles loudly as we continue to power-walk up the hill, heart in my mouth. "Over here. Audrey!" His whistle is louder this time and I know he's in close range. I slow down. It's no use; he's caught up with us. "Audrey," he pants, hands on hips, catching his breath, "didn't you hear me calling?"

CHAPTER 19

"COME ON." DANIEL GRABS MY HAND QUICKLY, "They're waiting." He can't be for real? I know I told him that I'm open minded and not the jealous type but this is ridiculous. I don't know what to say. I open my mouth to speak but the words seem to be glued to my tongue.

"Yay," cries Florian, punching the air, "McDonalds!" Daniel smiles down at him as he practically frogmarches us down the road.

"Daniel," I manage breathlessly, my heels clattering against the pavement trying to keep up, "wait...I."

But he ignores me. "Come on, Audrey, look, there they are. Connie!" He waves frantically at them. They clock us and start waving back. Oh, bloody hell.

"Who's...what's..." I can't seem to string a coherent sentence together. Each step feels as if I'm descending to the bottom of a pool, everything seems blurred, out of focus. Florian is trying to wriggle free from my clasp, whining - my grip is too tight, let go, it hurts. Daniel is firing questions at me - how was your journey, are you hungry, what shall we do afterwards. I can't concentrate. It's all happening so fast.

And then I'm face to face with Aliki. I look at her in a haze, blowing a strand of hair off my hot, sweaty face. Her red lips are moving but I can't seem to take in what she's saying, something about burgers and her waistline. Having only seen her from a distance, she's even younger than I imagined. All fresh faced and unlined, how on earth can I compete with that? Her hair is short, wavy and blonde, possibly bottle blonde, with a large, wave curl at the front like a 1950's pinup girl, very *Monroe-esque*.

I can tell right away that she's bold, fearless and quirky. I can see it in her heavily made up green eyes as she regards me inquisitively, thumbs resting in the slit pockets of her retro leopard print faux fur coat. Next to her, Connie is zipped into a pink quilted jacket, shyly looking up at me. I gaze at them stupidly, wishing I could be teleported back to Dukes Avenue. Now. Daniel takes his place behind his daughter, feet wide apart, hands gently resting on her narrow shoulders.

"Right," he says in a regimental tone, "enough about weight-watchers. Introductions. Connie, this is Audrey and her nephew, Florian." Oh God, I can't believe this is happening to me. Swallowing hard, I crouch down to Connie's eye level. She has Daniel's deep blue eyes and her mother's soft, wavy, blonde hair, tumbling over her shoulders like a little cherub. Her lips are bow shaped and pink, like her dad's.

"Hi, Connie," I coo, holding out my hand, "lovely to meet you." She frowns up at Aliki and then turns her head away, burying her chin into her shoulder. Not the response I expected from a child who was dying to meet me today. I was right – she hates me. Probably because I haven't come bearing gifts. Shit.

"Ahem…" Daniel murmurs. I look up and he gestures towards Aliki with his head.

"Sorry. Where are my manners?" I stand up and straighten my dress, which has somehow managed to crawl up to the top of my thighs. I can't believe that Daniel has put me in this awkward position. I knew he was too good to be true. Wait until I tell Louise and Tina that my new boyfriend brought his ex-wife along on a

NO WAY BACK

date. They'll think he's a psycho. "Aliki." I hold out my hand, my breathing has steadied, my composure regained. "Pleased to meet you."

There's a stillness in the air, an eerie anticipation. A car horn beep, beep, beeps. A man's voice calls out in a foreign language. The knot in my stomach tightens. Why is she ignoring me? It's not as if I'm out to steal her husband. They're divorced, for goodness sake!

Aliki looks at Daniel, raising a brown, drawn-in eyebrow. A small, wry smile is starting at her scarlet lips. Great, this is all I need, an ex-wife who's out to score points. She'll be telling him I'm not good enough for him next and denying him access to Connie.

My eyes flick from Aliki to Daniel nervously and then it suddenly dawns on me - that's why she's here, to check me out, to make sure I'm good enough to be left with her daughter. Well, this is a first. I've never been out with a man who puts me through a childcare examination. My face tingles as I wait for her to respond but she's still looking at me as if I'm unhinged. I bet she's a model. She's certainly tall and pretty enough. She's probably a cordon bleu chef and runs charity marathons too. Oh, Christ. I don't need this. I knew it was too soon to get involved with another man. What am I doing here?

"Audrey," Daniel says quietly, breaking the tense silence, "*this* is Connie." He puts his arm around the young woman and she rests her head briefly on his shoulder, smiling. "And this is Lily." He rests a hand gently on the little girl's head, "Connie's daughter. We were going to leave her with Aliki but as Florian was coming we thought it'd be nice for her to come along too."

His words swim around in my head. Have I misheard or did he just say that this grown woman standing before me is his daughter? It takes a while for it to all sink in, and then all I can say is, "Oh!" I stare at the three of them in amazement. It's a few moments before I can speak again. "So." I clear my dry throat, shifting my weight on to one leg. "Let me just get this straight. She," I quite rudely, but unintentionally, point at the young woman with the 1950's hairstyle, "is your daughter Connie, and this," I point down at the little girl who's now peeking at Florian from behind her mother's waist, "is your *granddaughter*?" There's a brief moment of silence and then Connie bursts out laughing, bending over double and slapping her thigh.

"You thought that he and I ..." she can barely speak from laughter, "were an item? Ahahahaha." Connie holds her chest as tears of mirth spill from her green eyes, and then Lily joins in, jumping up and down and squealing. "Hey, Dad," she dabs at the corner of her eye with the back of her finger, "you've still got it, you old dog." She grins, pinching his cheek. Daniel's face is red, embarrassed.

"Connie," he warns, "behave."

"Oh, Daddy, you've got to admit, it is hilar." He raises his eyebrows at me helplessly, then gives her a sideward glance. "Oh, come on, you know I'm only teasing. Nice to meet you, Audrey." She does a little mock curtsy before giving me a limp handshake. "I can't believe you didn't tell her how old I was," she says, shaking her head at Daniel, "Hilarious, just hilarious." And with this, she presses her back against the glass door of McDonalds and ushers Lily into the restaurant.

Daniel, Florian and I are still outside, staring at each other, speechless. Daniel with a worried look on his face and I in wide-eyed bewilderment, still in recovery mode.

"I'm hungry too, Auntie." Florian tugs at my sleeve. "Can we go inside now? I'm cold." He rubs his arms.

"Yes, of course, Florian," Daniel murmurs, looking away first, "come on, son."

"Good. I want a Big Mac, large fries and a chocolate shake."

Inside, Daniel gives Connie a fifty-pound note and sends her to the counter with the kids. We're alone.

"I'm so sorry, Audrey," he says anxiously, searching around for a free, clean table. "I thought you knew I had a grown-up daughter."

"Well, you didn't say." I shoulder my way through a crowd of people, following him to a table by the window.

"But you heard her calling me that day on the beach in Cyprus, and then the way you spoke about her at your parent's dinner, I just assumed…" My mind goes into fast rewind. We're on the beach, chatting. The wind is whirring in my ears. He looks back at a young woman in a white bikini with a child. She's calling out to him. "*Dan, hurry up.*"

My hand flies to my mouth. "*Dad*", she was calling out "*Dad, hurry up*".

"Oh, my God, Daniel" I drop into the seat opposite him heavily. "I thought she was calling you Dan. It's just your name….and I put two and two together…and, and….well, you just don't look old enough to have a daughter in her twenties!"

"Twenty-nine, actually," he cringes. My mouth hangs open. Reaching over, he gently closes it with his fingertips.

"*She's* almost thirty?" I point in the direction of the food counter with my thumb. I can see where she gets her youthful looks from. And I'm not sure why I'm whispering, it's not as if she can hear me at fifty feet away unless she's got a spying device wedged in her ear, which is highly unlikely.

Daniel reaches for my hand across the table, and as I curl my fingers around his a huge wave of relief washes over me. This young, hot-chick whom I thought to be my potential love rival is actually his daughter. Phew, thank you, Lord, no more worries. I whip my mac off and drape it haphazardly on the back of my chair then roll up the sleeves of my black wool dress, suddenly feeling the heat. "And why didn't you tell me about Lily, for goodness sake?" I reach for his hand again. "She's just adorable."

He crinkles his nose. "It's not exactly an ice-breaker, is it? Hi, I'm Daniel and I'm a grandfather. Not very sexy." He curls his lips downwards. "Thought it might put you off."

"Yes, but a young, hot, grandfather." I lean across the table and kiss him gently on the lips, once, then again…his breath is fresh, minty, his lips part and close over my bottom lip and…

"Oh, get a room you two." Connie slams a tray of burgers and fries between us. Daniel leans back in his chair and we grin at each other like a couple of teenagers. Florian slides into the seat next to me, unsteadily holding a tray of drinks. I shake my head and smile as I sort out his meal. What have I let myself in for?

Connie talks mostly about herself throughout lunch, she tells me that she speaks Greek fluently, taught by her granny, she's a writer, an actress and a model. A woman of many talents, I see. I'm genuinely fascinated by her colourful career and ask lots of questions. What films has she been in? Has she met lots of famous people?

"Oh, loads," she says with a dismissive wave, dipping a chip into Lily's ketchup tub. My eyes are drawn to the collar of her blouse, which is sticking out of her coat awkwardly. "I've been in TV ads, soaps and I'm invited to all the celeb parties too." I nod enthusiastically, my eyes flitting to her white collar. "But I'm just waiting for that big break. Do you know what I mean?" I tell her that I do, that I'm impressed, and Daniel throws me an approving smile. It's nice to see him looking so relaxed in a black t-shirt, jeans and brown vintage leather jacket instead of a suit, although I'm sure they're all top of the range brands and very expensive.

"*And* she's got a beautiful voice," he says proudly, stretching his arm across the back of Lily's chair as she happily listens to Florian nattering on about his iPad and the latest Apps he's downloaded. "Writes all her own stuff too, don't you, Con?" Connie nods and they grin at each other lovingly. "We'll go and see her one night if you like. She's amazing. Have you got any gigs booked, darling?" He leans over and pinches one of her chips and she slaps his hand away. He polished his own meal off in less than ten minutes.

"Nah, nothing booked this year." She munches on her cheeseburger. I stare at her protruding collar. I wish she'd tuck it back in, it's incredibly distracting. "Hey, I've got a brilliant idea." She stops eating and looks at me excitedly, "Why don't you two come around to mine for dinner next week?" Ah, so she wants to show off her culinary skills too, why am I not surprised? "We can grab a takeaway from the new Indian around the corner." Or maybe not. "Then I can try out a couple of the new songs I've just written."

We agree and then she spends the next ten minutes telling me all about her lovely apartment in Bayswater. How she and Lily spend weekdays there and weekends with her mum and granny in Crouch End, or at Daniel's when they're away. When asked about Lily's father she informs me that he's an arsehole she met at a party one night and has nothing to do with Lily's upbringing. So, I assume that responsibility has been assigned to Daniel, then. His baggage seems to be getting heavier by the second.

"So, tell me, Audrey," FINALLY, a question about me, "any kids of your own?" She sucks hard on her straw. She has her father's unnerving stare. I focus on her white collar as I mull over her question. It's now seriously getting on my nerves.

"What?" she frowns, locking her jaw down towards her right shoulder for a better view.

"Nothing, it's just…"

"Fuck. Is it a stain?" She grabs a serviette and starts rubbing her lapel vigorously. "I've just got this back from the dry cleaners. Dad?"

Daniel leans over, "Can't see anything."

"No, it's…Ooooh." I stand up, reach over and tuck her collar back into her coat hurriedly. "Sorry." I give a little nervous chuckle as I sit back down. My face tingles. "I just can't stand seeing things out of place, that's all. I'm a bit of a tidy freak. My family and friends will tell you. I'm forever loading their dishwashers, clearing their tables. I even tuck their clothes back into laundry baskets and wardrobes if they're sticking out." I shiver, "I just can't stand it."

Connie looks at Daniel, a hint of a sneer on her red lips. "Uh-oh, OCD alert."

"Well, not quite OC…."

"Just tidy," Daniel says in a clipped tone. Finally, a bit of support from him. Hallelujah. "I love an organised woman."

"Okaaaay?" Connie says slowly.

"I like neatness, things to be in place," I explain, smoothing down my hair as I chew the inside of my lip. I'm not liking this interrogation. This interview.

"So…" Connie leans forward, crossing her arms over the table, "you still haven't answered my question." I frown at her. What bloody question? She's doing my head in. "Any little Audreys or Audriuses at home?"

"Oh, I see. No. Just three nephews." I stroke Florian's brown, cropped hair as he slurps on his chocolate milkshake, "And I love the bones of them."

NO WAY BACK

"Oh, dear." Connie leans back in her chair, "Tick-tock, tick-tock." She waves a finger to and fro at Daniel. "Well, you can forget about getting any off him." She shifts around in her seat and then fixes her gaze on a tall, good-looking lad walking by our table in low hung jeans, displaying the rim of grey underpants and bare flesh. He looks back at her appreciatively as he passes with a lopsided grin.

"Connie," Daniel warns.

"What?"

"You know what." She pulls a face at him. "I mean it, Con." But she completely ignores his warning and continues to grill me.

"Dad said you were with someone for years. How come you split up? Did he trade you in for a younger model?" She sucks the last drops of cola through her straw noisily and then berates Lily for taking too long to finish her meal.

I gaze down at my clasped hands on the table, fury bubbling in my chest. I can't believe Daniel told her all about me and Nick. I give him a look, and, sensing my tension, he leans forward and says, "Now, come on, Connie. Enough. I'm sorry, Audrey."

"Okay, okay." She holds up her hands in submission, "Keep your drawers on." She gives him a wry smile and for a few moments he holds onto his annoyance, his brows knotted in disdain, but then he cracks, shakes his head and laughs. She really does have him wrapped around her little finger, doesn't she?

I refuse a lift home from Daniel, tell him that I've got my Oyster, remind him that Florian enjoys travelling on public transport, but agree to meet up later for dinner. I don't think I can spend another moment with Connie, she's completely drained me. But as they walk us to the underground, she grabs my arm as if we're the best of friends and hurries me up the hill.

"Girl talk," she calls over her shoulder at Daniel, "you take care of the kids."

I glance back. Daniel is holding Florian in one hand and Lily in the other trotting several feet behind.

"Listen," Connie says, chewing on a gum eagerly, "one of the reasons I wanted to meet you today was to tell you something important." She looks back again to make sure Daniel isn't within earshot.

"Oh, yeah?" I'm intrigued. We huddle closer, "Go on."

"Well, Dad's got his fiftieth coming up shortly." Christ, he's almost fifty? "We're throwing a surprise birthday party for him at his flat up the road." She points her finger aimlessly in the air, "And I wanted you in on it, what with you being his new love interest and all, he'll be spending lots of time with you. What d'ya say?"

"Well, it sounds like a wonderful idea, Connie…."

"Great!"

"But I'm not sure how I can help with something as personal as this. We are still getting to know each other." I push my hair behind my ears. I don't tell her that I am starting to have some feelings for him, "He hasn't even met any of my friends yet."

"Yeah, so? Invite them all, he can meet them there." She stops, spits her gum into a tissue and lights up a cigarette. "So?" She blows the smoke high up into the air. We're walking up the hill again. "Come on, Audrey, don't be a spoilsport." And I agree to do all I can, within reason, if we're still seeing each other by then that is. Well, it's pretty difficult to say no to Connie.

On the journey home, Florian and I cuddle up on a two-seater chair, rocking gently in our seats as the train tears across the tracks. I think about this afternoon. It went well albeit the slight hiccup with collar-gate and her interrogation about my personal life. But as the train thunders through the dark tunnel, my mind starts ticking. I wonder what Connie meant about not getting any kids off Daniel? Has he had a vasectomy or doesn't he want any more children? Certainly, Connie is a handful. I wonder why he cut short our first date to run to a crying twenty-nine-year-old woman. I wonder why he couldn't cancel with her today even though he knew I wasn't up to it. I wonder if Connie is a threat after all.

CHAPTER 20

PULLING UP OUTSIDE LOUISE'S HOUSE, I glance at the dashboard. The red LCD flashes: 11.30. I'm half an hour early. She'll not be back from the town centre yet. A young couple with a brawny dog shuffle past, laughing loudly; she's got her arm threaded through his, he's gripping the lead with resistance as the dog drags them down the road, sniffing and peeing against a lamp post on the way. I switch off the ignition and watch as they shrink into the distance. I wonder if they're happy or if their lives are just as confusing as mine is.

I drum my fingers on the steering wheel, anxiety swishing around in my stomach. I just hope I'm doing the right thing, that's all, and not digging myself into a bigger hole. I reach over and grab a bottle of mineral water from the glove compartment and take a quick swig. Of course if I'd stayed in bed with Daniel this morning instead of sneaking off with my mobile phone to check for any messages, this never would've happened. But is it my fault that gorgeous as he is, he snores?

I barely slept a wink last night. Although to give him credit, there were short periods when lying on his side, he was blissfully silent and I did start to drift off, only to be startled awake by loud snorts and gasps as he rolled onto his back and resumed snoring for England. In the end I just gave up, threw the sheets back and huffily got dressed.

NO WAY BACK

I press my forehead against the steering wheel and stare into the darkness. It's just that I wasn't expecting to hear from Nick again, that's all. He took me by surprise. I thought that after what happened with Tina he'd got the message. Damn, why does he have to be so stubborn? Why can't he just leave me alone?

I take another swig of water. I mustn't let him get to me. I've got to pull myself together. Louise will know what to do. I wish she'd bloody well hurry up. I glance at the clock again, still fifteen minutes to go. Deflated, I unbuckle my seatbelt and just then I catch sight of a figure at the front door. It's Gerry. I buzz my window down quickly.

"Gerry," I holler, "wait."

"Audrey." He waves me over. I climb out of my car and with two high pitched bleeps from my remote-control fob, I'm at the door. His goatee beard scratches my skin as he pecks my cheek quickly. We exchange a few preambles on the doorstep. He looks different somehow, younger, fresher. At 42, Gerry's only a year older than Louise but he's always looked much older than her. However, today he doesn't look a day over thirty-five. His pale blue eyes seem brighter, and he's lost a bit of weight too since I last saw him. Although still quite chunky, his tummy seems to have shrunk, giving his navy suit a looser fit. It must be the excitement of expecting a baby.

"You just caught me," he says, "Lou's not back yet, had some errands to run." He holds the door open for me and I step inside, all the time staring at his curly, dark hair. Where have all the greys gone?

"Yes, I know, she said. I'm early, actually, didn't think anyone was in. What're you doing home?"

"Just popped in to pick up some paperwork." He waves a yellow folder at me. "Listen, help yourself to tea or coffee, you know where everything is. She shouldn't be long. Anyway, gotta dash, lovely to see you." And he's gone.

I close the door behind me, shrug out of my mac and drape it over the banister. A ritual of mine and Nick's whenever we visited. My mac would go on first then he'd hang his denim jacket over it. Nick only ever wore a blue denim jacket, even during winter. I close my eyes. I can almost hear our voices, the clatter of plates in the kitchen, the laughter from the lounge, the hum of music drifting down the stairs from Jess's room. There's a thrash at the door. I open my eyes wide, snapping out of my reverie. It's the postman. Oh, God, why am I daydreaming about the past? I need to speak to Daniel. Fast. He answers on the second ring.

"Hey, sexy," he murmurs.

"Hi." I sit on the stairs grinning down the phone. "How are you?"

"Great. Where are you? At the office? I thought you had the day off."

"No, I'm at Louise's." I stand up and walk along the corridor into the kitchen, closing the door behind me, drowning out some of the street noise. "Listen," I say hesitantly, I'm not usually spontaneous with men but here goes, "I was just wondering if you were free this afternoon." I pause for a response but he doesn't answer. "You could come over or I could come to you. We could go out for a coffee or a walk, perhaps." I'm blabbering, but I can't seem to stop myself. "Or catch a movie if you prefer, that's if…."

"Audrey, I'd love to."

"Excellent!"

"But I can't." My shoulders slump and my bag slides onto my forearm. "I'm running with Connie after work."

"Oh, Daniel," I plead, "I really want to see you." I flop onto a kitchen chair, chucking my bag by my feet.

"Aw, Cinders." His new pet name for me, because of the shoe incident, which is quite romantic, I suppose. "Connie and I always run together once a week in Hyde Park, it's a regular thing. I'm sure I told you."

He didn't but I don't argue the point. "I could jog alongside you," I suggest, hopefully, "get to know her a little better?"

"Well, the thing is, we're training for a charity half marathon. You'd never be able to keep up with us. We need to do a PB." There's a moment of silence. "Audrey? Are you still there? Hello."

"Yes, I'm still here," I groan.

"Aw, I feel awful now. You do understand, don't you?" In a huff, I tell him that I do but that I'm disappointed, and he promises to make it up to me later this evening. "Get your gorgeous self around here at eight o' clock, and I'll have dinner ready and a bottle of fizz on ice." I smile into the phone. He's got such a sexy voice. "Oh, and Audrey, Audrey, wait, before you go…you left your purse at my flat this morning."

"Oh no, did I?" I thought my bag felt lighter. It must've been when I paid for the takeaway last night. Daniel and I fought at the door but I managed to persuade the delivery man to take my money. "I've got all my cards in there, Daniel." I say, panicking, "I've got no access to any money now." I hold my head worriedly, get to my feet and start circling the kitchen. "What if there's an emergency?"

"Hey, hey, calm down. You're at Louise's, aren't you?" he says coolly. "I'm sure she'll lend you a fiver if you need it and you can pick your purse up tonight." Great, I'm now penniless as well as dateless. But he manages to calm me and we end the call on the promise of dinner at eight.

There's a jangle at the front door.

"Hello," Louise calls out. "Anyone home?"

"In here," I yell.

"Oh, hi Audrey. Did Jess let you in before she left for uni?" Louise plonks several shopping bags onto the huge rustic table, looking frazzled. "I'm not late am I?" Her eyes flick to the clock above the door. The aroma of the fresh baguette poking out of one of the grocery bags wafts under my nose, reminding me that I missed breakfast.

"No. I was early. Gerry let me in." Louise frowns as she slides off her black wool coat and bends down to kiss me. Her cheek is rosy and warm despite the chill outside. "Said he had some paperwork to pick up."

"Oh, right," she says in a short tone, pulling the baguette out of the bag, and I get the feeling things are a bit tense between them.

She fills a tall glass from the filter jug, downs it in one, then turns to me with a wide grin. I know that look, it means she's been up to mischief. I brace myself and within a blink of an eye, she whisks out a woolly garment from a colourful paper carrier bag with the words *Mamababa* strewn across it in the colours of the rainbow.

"Look," she enthuses, holding up a tiny baby's cardigan, "isn't it adorable?"

"It's lovely," I smile, standing up to examine the lilac cardi. "But what if it's a boy?" It feels incredibly soft, well made, expensive. It's probably cashmere. I glance at the price tag and the room spins.

"A hundred and twenty quid? For this tiny thing?"

"It's designer!"

"Oh, well, that's all right then."

"Oh, shut up, you." She snatches it out of my hands hastily, "You're beginning to sound like Gerry. And anyway, boys can wear bright colours. Gerry's got a pink shirt that he wears all the time."

I raise my eyebrows as she gently folds the sweater and places it back into the bag.

"So, come on." She's on her knees, stuffing the *Mamababa* bag behind some saucepans in the bottom cupboard, "Tell me about your weekend with Daniel." I stare in silence as she fumbles around wildly, pots and pans clank against each other, spilling out onto the grey slate kitchen tiles. "Well?" she demands, with a quick glance over her shoulder. "Oh, don't look at me like that. Gerry doesn't like me buying baby things, says we should wait until he/ she arrives, but I just can't resist sometimes."

"Well, he does have a point, Lou."

She stands up, red-faced and looking like she's been tied to the back of a truck and dragged through the Sahara desert. "Er… excuse me, who's side are you on?"

"Yours," I groan, folding my arms.

"Good." She blows her blonde fringe off her face, some of which has stuck to her forehead during her hiding rampage, rolls up her sleeves and starts unpacking the groceries. "Now, tell me about Daniel before I explode. And no filtering. I want the full fat version."

"Well, I came here straight from his flat this morning," I brag, grinning at her stupidly. She stops unpacking.

"You didn't do it?"

"We did!"

"You old tart. What was he like?"

"I'm not telling you, you perv." We both dissolve into a fit of giggles. I haven't seen Louise this happy in years.

"So when are we going to meet him, then?" She slides an overloaded blue plastic laundry basket across the kitchen floor with the side of her red Converse shoe.

I tell her that he works hard, that his hours are unpredictable and, to my complete dismay, he spends a lot of his free time tending to Connie and Lily's needs.

"Honestly, Lou, I'm getting a bit peeved by it all, to be honest." I get to my feet, "Let me do that," I crouch down next to her at the washing machine, elbowing her out of the way. She protests at first but then allows me to help. "Take last night, for instance," I say, stuffing clothes into the machine, "we had to plan our evening around picking Connie and Lily up from Aliki's house, around the corner from here, actually, Wolseley Road?" Louise nods, says she drives past that road several times a day, nice houses, big. "And chauffeur them home to flipping Bayswater. So, that was most of our evening gone."

"Doesn't his daughter drive?"

"Yes, but she likes a drink!"

"Why don't you download the Uber app onto her phone when she's not looking?" We both laugh. If only it were that simple. "And I still can't believe how old she is. Shit! So, what's she like, then, apart from a drunken attention seeking diva?"

"Okay. Ish. Quite spoilt and loud, but that's to be expected, I suppose, with Daniel as a father. Does this go in with the coloureds?" I hold a white lacy bra over my head, clearly Jess's judging by the cup size; Louise is tiny, even now she's expecting. She grabs it out of my hand and tosses it into the whites by the table.

"And the ex-wife?"

"I haven't met her yet, although she did wave from the doorway when we picked them up yesterday. She seems quite friendly."

"Well, don't rush into anything, Audrey, he does seem to have quite a bit of baggage. Just be careful." Louise stretches her back and grimaces. "You don't want to get hurt again."

"Yeah, I know what you mean. I really do like him, though. He makes me feel…I dunno…safe. I didn't…" I glance up. "You okay?"

"Yes, just a bit of back pain, GP said it's quite normal, although I can't remember feeling like this with Jess during the first trimester. But that was over nineteen years ago."

"The what?"

"Oh, never mind." She smiles as she wipes down her gleaming, spotless worktop, one hand supporting the small of her back. "You were saying…"

"I was about to say that at least I didn't have this trouble with Nick." A heavy silence hangs in the air. A dog barks crazily in the distance followed by a hiss from the table as one of the supermarket bags unfurls. I look up at her "Because he didn't have a family, I mean. I'm just not used to it."

"Well, he's history, isn't he?" she says crisply, unloading the contents of a large bag for life.

"Actually, that's what I wanted to talk to you about today." I open the dispenser drawer and pour in the fabric conditioner, the smell of jasmine wafting under my nose, "I had a chat with him on Messenger this morning. I've arranged to meet up with him, although now I'm…"

The sound of a tin hitting the kitchen floor startles me. "Please tell me you're joking."

I close the drawer and start fiddling with the controls. "Good job that wasn't a bottle of olive oil. Or worse still, wine!" I laugh, trying to defuse the tension.

"I seriously can't believe you're giving him the time of day." She throws her hands up in the air. "A man who cheated on you, jilted you. Fathered another woman's child, for fuck's sake. You said you never wanted to see him again." I know Nick isn't flavour of the month at the moment but I wasn't expecting her to be this angry. It must be her hormones. She picks the can of baked beans off the floor and then starts loading the fridge fast and furious, stuffing cucumbers, tomatoes, carrots and mushrooms into the salad box.

"We only exchanged a few words," I say, a bit miffed by her headmistress tone. "He says he just wants a quick word to explain, just so that we can put it all behind us and move on. I mean, Gerry and Tina are still his friends, aren't they? We might bump into each other now and again. Surely, it'd be better if we clear the air, if we're on speaking terms, at least." Her silence and the murderous look on her face tells me that she disagrees. "Look, he keeps hounding me, Louise. Maybe if I just speak to him once, let him explain. Let him get it out of his system. Perhaps then he'll leave me alone."

"You're making a big mistake if you see him, Audrey." She slams the fridge door, grabs a tea towel and starts folding it quickly, angrily. "I'd let sleeping dogs lie if I were you."

"Well, he knows I'm seeing someone new and he's busy with what's-her-face."

"With who?" She stops folding and looks at me, lips slightly parted. "What's her name? Do we know her?"

"No, of course not," I yell, returning my attention to the washing machine. "I don't care who she is. I just want to get on with the rest of my life." Even if I knew who she was I wouldn't tell Louise. She'd hunt her down and commit a crime.

"That's a shame. We could've Googled her. Find out what the hell she's playing at." See what I mean? She puts the folded tea towel down on the worktop and walks over to me, her blonde brows knitted, forehead lined with concern. Then her face softens. "Here," she says kindly. "You need to turn the dial to thirty degrees, then press this button." The machine whirs into action. She places a hand on my arm gently.

"Look, Audrey…" We're face to face. I can see a few crows' feet around her eyes. My poor friend is so tired, she doesn't need this.

"I'm just looking out for you, that's all." She rubs my arm. "I don't want him to hurt you again. It's taken us ages to get you back on your feet." I tell her that Gerry's still friends with him and she doesn't seem to mind that. "That's different. You know what men are like. Look, you've found a lovely, decent bloke, what more do you want?" I thought she just told me to take it slowly with Daniel? Does she really hate Nick that much?

I run a hand over my face. I can't blame her for hating him. She's right, I know she is. What was I thinking? Nick's a shit. Seeing him again would only open old wounds. And whatever explanation he gives me, still won't change the fact that he got another woman up the duff behind my back.

"Yes, you're right," I exhale loudly. "I'll text him and cancel."

"That's my girl. I'll ask Gerry to have a word too, tell him to leave you alone." I'm so lucky to have such caring, supportive friends. I really don't know what I'd do without them in my life.

"Thanks, Louise. There's so much shit going on in my head at the moment. I can't think straight."

"No problem. That's what friends are for. Right," she says briskly. "I'm bursting for the loo. I made us a veg soup this morning, your favourite. It's in the fridge, stick it on the hob and I'll be right back. You know where everything is."

I grab a large saucepan from the rack at the sink by the window. Louise's garden is looking great, lovely green shrubs, neat lawn. It was wild and unkempt the last time I saw it.

"Gerry's done a great job with the garden," I yell.

"Yeah," she shouts back from the downstairs toilet, "he took two weeks off work and did the lot."

"Did he lay the patio slabs himself?" I turn on one of the rings at the hob. The orange liquid starts to bubble, spitting at the sides of the pan. It smells divine with lots of fresh, thick cut carrots, potatoes, leeks, and peas. "Loulou? Did you hear?" I stir the soup, my stomach grumbles. "Lou?" I lower the heat to simmer and walk towards the toilet. "Louise?" I tap lightly on the door. It's deadly quiet. "You okay in there?" I rattle the door knob, it's locked. My heart starts to thump a little faster. I hope she hasn't passed out. She did look a bit pasty. "Louise? Open the door." I cry, banging hard with my fist.

And then there's a click. The door opens. She's standing before me, white as a sheet, stained toilet paper scrunched in her hand. I slowly glance down at the toilet bowl, streaked with blood. Oh no, oh God, please no.

CHAPTER 21

"I DON'T KNOW WHAT TO SAY, GERRY." I'm drained of energy. He's sitting on the leather sofa, elbows resting on his knees, hands covering his face. The shutters are closed, even though it's still daylight outside. I dare not open them, dare not let in normality. "The doctor said that it's very common, one in five, apparently. It's no one's fault." I place a mug of coffee in front of him but he doesn't even look up.

"I know. I read the leaflet," he says after a few moments between a gap through his fingers, "She was being so careful with everything."

"I know she was." The sudden sound of loud foreign voices catches our attention and we both glance towards the cream coloured shutters.

"Probably next door." He rubs his chin. "Landlord said new tenants were moving in. Two couples. And a dog. I think." I acknowledge this piece of useless information with a sharp, small nod. We listen to the foreign voices for a while in silence and then, "I think she's blaming me for the miscarriage."

I lay a hand on his shoulder. "No, no, that is NOT true." Actually, it is. She was complaining to me earlier in A&E that he wasn't there enough for her, he was always working late, on purpose, and kept nagging her about her spending. She even suggested that he jinxed the pregnancy because he wasn't as excited about it as she was. I pat his back gently. "You'll get through this, Gerry, don't worry." And then to my dismay, his shoulders start shaking. I don't think I've ever seen him cry. I'm not sure what to do; shouldn't he be upstairs sharing this grief with Louise? I put my arm around his trembling frame and lean my head against his. I try to keep him still but his body is too big in my embrace. "Shhhh, it's going to be all right." He reaches up and grasps my hand, his other hand shielding his face like a shy schoolboy. "Come on now, you've got to be strong for Louise, she needs you."

He stops crying and wipes his wet, red face with the cuff of his pale blue shirt. "She doesn't need me," he snivels, rubbing his palms together, "she's got Jess." He flicks his head back towards the stairs. "You saw how she was with me in the car earlier." It's true. Louise almost bit his head off when he tried to comfort her in the back seat of my VW on the journey home. I even caught her shrugging him off furiously in my rear view mirror a couple of times when he tried to put his arm around her. But I know that was because he wasn't there to support her at the hospital. Five hours we were in the mayhem of A&E. Five. And where was Gerry? Nowhere to be found. Half a dozen voicemails, several texts and about twenty missed calls later he appeared in the Casualty Department looking weary and distraught and smelling like a brewery. But it was too late.

"Gerry, she's just lost your baby. She's upset. She didn't mean any of those things she said in the car. She loves you." I pause. "Look, go up and talk to her," I say gently, "You two need to be together now." I stand up and pull him by the hand. "Come on." He shuffles to his feet and follows me sadly up the stairs. And once they're in each other's arms, I close the door behind me and slip away quietly.

Why can't I ever find any frigging parking on Dukes Avenue? WHY? I've had to park half a mile down the road. Again. As

NO WAY BACK

expected, dinner with Daniel is off. I rang him from A&E and told him the news. He was sympathetic enough, even though he's never met Gerry and Louise. "I suppose you won't be coming over later, then?" he said. "Oh no, don't apologise, of course, I understand. Look, Connie and I have just got in from our run. I'm about to cook us something to refuel. I'll give you a call later this evening, say seven, yeah?"

Was it too much to expect him to leave Connie to her own devices and come to me? He could hear how distressed I was. I shoulder my bag and head for my flat. Oh, I don't know, maybe it was too much to ask. Maybe I'm overreacting.

My black *Manolos* click along the pavement. A motorbike roars past me, charges up the road swerving through the traffic then disappears into the evening. I root around for my door keys in my bag. I can't wait to get home, freshen up, and have something to eat. I'm flipping starving. I've been living on coffee all day. I'm sure I've got a slice of leftover pizza in the fridge, then as I look up I squint at two figures in the distance. They're leaning against a familiar black Audi Q7 outside my front door. The woman is in a luminous pink top and black Lycra sports pants with a thick pink stripe running down the side, the man casual in jeans and a white shirt. They're chatting, laughing. I narrow my eyes as I get closer. I recognise them immediately; a bolt of acid hits my stomach.

"Hey," Connie rushes over to me. "How are you? Is everything okay? Sorry about your friend." She pauses while I nod in gratitude, staring at the pavement. "Dad asked me to drop this off on my way to Mum's." She holds my purse up over her head. I'd forgotten about that. She barely looks twenty with her hair pulled back into a tight ponytail. "Said it was really important you got it." At least Daniel was thoughtful enough to get my purse back to me. "I tried pushing it through your letter box but it wouldn't fit."

My purple patent purse is so big it could double up as a clutch bag. "So, thought I'd just hang around a while. Good job I had your friend here to keep me company."

"Thanks," I manage, trying to ignore the out of focus figure behind her.

"Anyway, excuse my attire. I haven't had a chance to shower or change yet. I probably stink so don't come too close." She laughs loudly and glances at Nick, who gives her a small smile in return. I look at him and for the first time, I don't feel a thing.

"Audrey?" He moves closer, despite a few visible cuts and bruises, he's still flipping good looking, in a dishevelled, rugged kind of way - no patch on Daniel, of course. "Gerry told me about the baby. I tried calling you at the hospital but it went straight to voicemail."

"Thanks for bringing this over, Connie," I say, ignoring him. "Would you like to come in for a cuppa?" I push the dwarf gate open and it shrieks annoyingly. I must get it oiled.

"Errrrm…no." She looks at us dubiously, backing away, probably sensing the tension. "Gotta pick Lily up from Mum's and then drop the car back at Dad's, so better dash. Thanks, though. Are we still on for Thursday?" Connie and I had agreed to meet for coffee, discuss the details for Daniel's surprise birthday party. I nod, wordless. "Great, I'll text you to arrange time, etc. And, hey, Nick, don't forget what I said."

"Oh no, I won't," he says, taking a tentative step towards her, and I'm not sure if I imagine it, but I'm sure I see a dash of interest in her eyes.

"Fab." She squeezes the key fob and the central locking responds with a thud, "Ciao, then." She buzzes down the window, music blares into the street. "Speak soon," she yells as she buckles in. Nick and I stand together, side by side, and watch as she speeds off into the evening, orange and red lights flashing in the distance.

NO WAY BACK

"Nice girl," he says, gesturing towards the departed car, "said she's a model."

"Yes, that's right."

"Your new bloke's daughter, eh?"

I nod quickly, twisting my lips into a pout, staring at my feet and feeling awkward. Talking about my new boyfriend with Nick just feels weird. "What did she mean back then?" I ask cautiously, glancing at him briefly. "About you not forgetting?"

"Er…" He scratches his head, "I told her I was a photographer, and she just gave me her number in case any gigs come up."

My stomach twists. There's a moment of silence, and then, "I don't want you to call her, Nick."

He regards me for a moment and then whips out his mobile phone from his back pocket. "I won't. I promise." He runs his thumb over the screen, finds her details. "Look, I'll delete her number now." He shows me the screen `Connie Taylor -` `Delete Contact`. He taps on `Delete` and her details vanish. Slipping his phone into his shirt pocket, he looks at me hopefully. Am I supposed to be grateful for that?

"It's good to see you," he says lightly. Well, it's not good to see you, I want to say. In fact, he's the last person I wanted to see after the day I've had.

"Look, what do you want, Nick?"

He sighs, hands loosely on hips. "I wanted to make sure you were okay. Gerry said Louise is in a bad way. That you were upset too." I nod, fold my arms, and he shakes his head. "I got your text cancelling tomorrow, by the way, and I completely understand." I fired it off to him while I was waiting for Louise in A&E.

"It's tough, but at least they've got each other. They'll get through it." I turn away and start walking down the path.

"Audrey, wait." I feel his hand on my back. "Can I come in?

Just for a while?"

We're face to face on my doorstep. "No. I think you should just go. In fact, I don't want you to contact me again – no calls, emails or texts, and no DMs on Messenger either. Nothing."

"What?" he says incredulously. "You don't mean that. Only this morning on Messenger you said you'd give me a chance to…"

"That was this morning," I cut in, raising a hand, "things are different now. I've changed my mind."

"Look, you're just stressed because of today. I know you. Please, I only want a few minutes of your time, that's all." I push the key in my lock, ignoring him, and rush inside. "Audrey, wait." He pushes his hand on the door before I can close it. "I'll cut to the chase. I didn't cheat on you, okay." I raise an eyebrow at him depicting "I think you'll find you did". "Well, technically I did but…"

"I don't want to hear it, Nick." I raise my hands to fend off his words, blocking the doorway, but he's on his knees.

"Please, Audrey, I'm begging you. Give me a chance to explain and then I promise I'll leave you alone, you won't hear from me again. Ever. I swear on my mother's life." I huff in exasperation as I step aside and he gets to his feet.

"Five minutes," I say firmly, closing the door behind me, "and then I want you out."

CHAPTER 22

I TURN THE LIGHTS ON and drop my bag by the coat stand. The flat is cold. Nick rubs his hands together to keep warm. He left his jacket at home, wasn't expecting it to be so chilly. There's a rumble from the boiler in the kitchen as I flick the heating on. He used to programme the thermostat for me when we were together so that I could always come home to a warm flat. But I don't know how to do it. I ought to learn really. How hard can it be?

"I suppose you want a coffee?" I unbutton my trench coat as I head into the kitchen.

"Actually, got anything stronger?"

"There's a bottle of white in the fridge, I think," I say over my shoulder as I pour myself a glass of water. Wine will go straight to my head on an empty stomach, but I'm glad of the suggestion. It's been a long day.

"Louise and Gerry are so lucky to have you. Gerry said you've been a rock."

I shrug, necking the water. "That's what friends are for."

We move around the kitchen in synchronisation. I pull out a bottle of wine from the fridge, he grabs two glasses from the cabinet and plonks them onto the worktop, just like old times. "Is that a screw cap or a cork? Here give it to me." He takes the bottle from my hand, opens the middle drawer and roots around for the corkscrew.

At the dining table, we sip our drinks like two lonely strangers in a bar. The sombre mood seeps into my bones, awakening thoughts that were buried years ago. I shake them away. I wonder how Louise is. I should call; find out if they're okay, if they need anything, if Tina's shown up yet? I hope she pops round to see her after work like she promised. Louise needs all the support she can get.

"They'll be okay," Nick says as if he's telepathic. He reaches out and touches my hand lightly. I draw it away and curl it into a fist, and his face drops. Well, what does he expect? Hand-holding across the table?

"So, how've you been?" He stares into his glass, swishing the pale liquid around uneasily.

"Good. I've been good." I force a smile. "You?"

"Not so good," he admits, pointing at the yellow bruising under his eyes. "Almost didn't make it." He studies my face but I don't flinch.

"Yes, I heard." I rub my forehead vigorously as if my fingers will magically rub out the last eight years of my life; then suddenly I feel agitated. The chair scratches against the wooden floor as I get to my feet. I've had enough. I can't be affable with a man whom I thought I'd be spending the rest of my life with, a man who was shagging another woman while I was happily planning our wedding, who's having a baby WITH said woman. I want him to leave. "Listen, it's getting late. I've had a hell of a day."

"Please, just let me say my piece." He half-stands and pulls me back down by the hand and I drop into my seat. "I didn't cheat on you, Audrey." Here we go, more lies. I sigh loudly, gazing at my nails. "Surely, you know that I'd never do anything to hurt you, not on purpose. And you weren't meant to find out the way you did either, that was a low blow." Finally, a bit self-reproach.

"I wanted to tell you. I WAS going to tell you." I throw a glance at his hands, pressed together on the table as if in prayer. "And this…this accident. Well, it's changed me. I'm different now." He hesitates, rubs his chin, eyes fixed on me. I know that look, he's bracing himself. "I want you back."

"What?" I say incredulously. He can't be for real. "Are you having a laugh?"

"No," he gives a nervous little chuckle. "I'm deadly serious. I want you back, Foxy. I should never have ended it with you." I shake my head, tell him he's mad, that I'd never go back with him, not in a million years, especially after the way he's behaved. But my rejection only spurs him on. "But things will be different now," he swears. "Now it's all out in the open, we can get married right away. I'll arrange everything, you won't have to lift a finger, and then…"

"No! Stop," I cut in, raising my hand. His audacity is almost laughable. "I'm with Daniel now."

He pulls a puzzled expression and bobs his head back as if I'm talking total bollocks. I've always hated that gesture. "You barely know him." See what I mean?

"I know him better than you think," I hiss, "and he's twice the man you'll ever be."

Leaning forward, he grabs my hands. "I know you still love me." His grey eyes search mine, hungry, determined, insistent, and for a moment, I feel myself sinking.

We stare at each other, wordless, and then, "Get over yourself, Nick," I bark, snatching my hands away.

"I know you came to see me at the hospital." Bloody Ronan. I knew I couldn't trust him. "You said you'd nurse me back to health." So, Ronan did hear everything I said, after all. Bloody brilliant. "I know you still care."

"For Christ's sake, Nick, you pissed off and left me to pick up the pieces! Another woman is expecting your child." I comb a hand through my hair, which feels like it's been sprayed with a mist of treacle. "What do you want from me?"

"That was a mistake. SHE was a mistake," he insists, "It was a one-night stand, that's all. It didn't mean anything." If this is supposed to make me feel better, it isn't working. "You and I weren't even together at the time. It happened during our few weeks apart." I look up at him then, narrowing my eyes. "The time you threw me out of your flat and told me to do one, remember?" I shake my head, pretending that I can't, trying to dismiss the sliver of relief that swims in my stomach. "Come on, you must remember. It was the time we argued over whose turn it was to order the takeaway, and you went flipping mental. How could you forget that?"

"Oh really?" I say, my annoyance returning. Just because it happened while we were on a break doesn't wipe the slate clean. "You didn't waste much time, then."

"Don't be like that." He cocks his head and knits his brows together. "I was drunk. Ask Gerry, he'll tell you what happened."

"Gerry?" I'm startled. The Judas. "Don't tell me he's known all along?" I wonder if Gerry told Louise too. But no, she'd have said, we tell each other everything. I trust her with my life. "What about Ronan?" I snap.

"Ronan didn't find out until I woke up. I only confided in Gerry and he promised to keep schtum. He's my best mate. I had to tell someone, it was doing my head in." He rubs his mouth nervously. His lips are dry and a bit cracked. "Look," he sighs. "I was screwed up. I panicked for heaven's sake. I was terrified you'd find out and hate me." Well, he's right about one thing. He rakes a hand through his hair. It's grown longer, it suits him.

"So, go on then, if you've taken a truth pill. Who is she? Where did you meet her?" I take a swig of wine angrily.

"Does it matter?" I tell him that it does to me. "Just some woman I met down The Bald Faced Stag." He stands up and starts pacing the room, a sure sign that he's lying. I bet it's one of the models he's worked with. She told me herself she's been in Vogue. They've probably been at it for months. "I was upset about us breaking up so I went out and got smashed. You dumping me like that really got to me, you know." He sounds hurt. Good! "Anyway, I asked her back to mine, poured out my heart to her and one thing led to another."

"Well, guess what, Nick? I spoke to her myself at the hospital and she told me she was your girlfriend."

"She was lying…or maybe she's a fantasist." He throws his hands up. "I dunno!"

I get to my feet and walk towards him, applauding along the way. "You should get a BAFTA for that, great performance."

"I'm telling you the truth," he protests. I shake my head and give a little laugh that comes out like borderline hysteria. He really must take me for a complete mug.

"You never wanted to marry me," I snap, puffing my chest out. "You were just looking for a good excuse to get out of it." Tears sting my eyes. I don't want them to. I don't want him to see my cry. "And now you've changed your mind. Well, tough!"

"Come on, that's not fair. I loved you. I wanted to make you happy. I still do!! Yes, I admit, I did drag my feet a bit to begin with, but then once it was all settled…I was happy, I was looking forward to it…I…" I roll my eyes and he falters. He knows he's fighting a losing battle.

I look at my watch, it's ten to seven. Daniel should be calling shortly. "Look, you've had your say, now I want you to get out.

Your five minutes are up."

He stares at the floor, hands loosely on hips. I watch his chest go up and down, up and down, hard and fast, and then he says, "You don't believe me, do you?" I don't reply. We both know the answer to that one. "Look," he drops back into his chair and runs a hand over his face. "Please," he says. "There's more... I want to tell you everything." More? I'm not sure I can take any more surprises today.

"Go on, then," I drone. "Five more minutes." I know he won't go until he's had his say. I top up our glasses and take a large sip. I know I'm going to need it.

"When she first told me she was pregnant I was completely floored. I asked her what she was planning to do, explained that we were back together, getting married." He closes his eyes briefly and takes a deep breath through his nose. "I said that if she decided to keep the baby, I'd do all I could, help out with money and everything, but I couldn't promise anything else. I made it crystal clear that I was in love with YOU, that you were my future. Obviously, I knew you'd freak out about the pregnancy when you found out, and I was going to tell you, Foxy. I promise." My stomach lurches. I wish he'd stop calling me that. "Anyway, I left the decision to her, and she said she wanted a termination."

"Well, I'm glad you were supportive. It can't have been easy for her." He scoffs when I say this and shakes his head, twirling the stem of his wine glass. I think he's about to cry. "So, obviously, she changed her mind, then."

"No, that's just it, as far as I was concerned she'd gone ahead with it." He sucks his lips in. "She sorted out a clinic, we met up for a coffee, and I gave her the money."

"Money? Why didn't she go on the NHS?"

"Couldn't wait that long..." he sighs. "Anyway, I didn't hear

NO WAY BACK

from her again. And that was that. It was over, there was no point in telling you." He pauses, knocks the wine back in one. I hope he's not driving. "Then, a few weeks before our wedding she turns up on my doorstep bloody pregnant!"

I think about what he's saying, it is starting to make sense – his irritability, mood swings, distance. I thought it was because he was feeling trapped by the prospect of marrying me, but perhaps he was already tangled in a trap of a completely different kind.

"I asked you to postpone our wedding just to buy me some time, to find a solution, find a way of telling you. I didn't want our marriage to start off with secrets and lies." I raise my eyebrows, folding my arms. I suppose that's true – he could've just married me and hurt me even more. "I swear on my mother's grave, Foxy, I'm not lying. You've got to believe me." I nod. I think he's telling me the truth.

"So, let me just get this straight." I lean forward against the table. "You gave a stranger, whom you met in a pub for casual sex, cash to have a termination?"

"Yes," he says, pulling that annoying puzzled expression again. "Quite a bit of cash, actually."

"And you trusted her?"

"Why wouldn't I? She said she didn't want my sprog if there was no future for us. And when I told her that I may be carrying a dodgy gene she bolted out the door. Couldn't get away fast enough."

"Well, how can you be sure it's yours?"

"I can't, but she swore she hadn't been with anyone else in over six months." An image of her at the hospital holding his hand flashes in my mind. Those tears did look very real to me – she's probably in love with him, that's why she kept it. "There's a good chance that I'm the father, and, at the time, it was easier to just give in to her than risk you finding out what a knob I'd been." Typical Nick, always taking the easy way out.

"Did it not occur to you for one moment that she'd change her mind?" He stares at his clenched hands on the table. "You didn't think she was hormonal, unsure? You didn't think to go with her, to make sure she was all right, to see if it's what she really wanted? Hell." I throw my hands up, "What you both wanted? Because, clearly she wanted to keep her baby, didn't she?"

"God, you make it sound as if we were in a relationship." He leaps to his feet. "We only had sex once, for goodness sake, and even that's a complete blur. Look, I think she was just as shocked as I was to begin with. But then, once we talked it though, she got a clearer picture. She said bringing up a child on her own was out of the question – she'd just started a new job, had commitments, stuff going on in her life. I don't think I could've stopped her if I wanted to. So yes, I took her word for it. I'm a mug, what can I say?"

"But you weren't such a careless mug with me, were you?" I scream into his back. My hand comes down hard and fast on the table, the glasses rattle. He spins around, startled, and a cold shiver tears through me.

CHAPTER 23

"I CAN'T BELIEVE YOU'VE BROUGHT THAT UP," Nick says quietly. "It…it was an accident. We agreed it was for the best. We'd only been together a few weeks." His eyes search mine worriedly. He's right. I'm being unfair. I want to blame him for everything. I cover my face with my hands. It's been a shit day. "You're angry," he says gently, "and you've every right to be." He's kneeling by my side, hand on my knee.

"Look, Nick." I massage my throbbing temple. "It's late, I'm tired."

"I only said I couldn't marry you because she started threatening me," he goes on, ignoring me. "She's a nasty piece of work, Audrey. I wish I'd never clapped eyes on her. I wish I'd just stayed home that night with a few cans and *Match of The Day*." His skin stretches over his Adam's apple as he tilts his head back and stares at the ceiling, neck full of abrasions. I wonder if they're from the accident or from a blunt razor.

"She found your number on my phone," he says wearily, "must've been when she stayed over – said she'd phone you and tell you everything herself if I didn't call off our wedding, lie that we'd been having an affair for months. She even dialled your number in front of me once; put you on loudspeaker, then hung up when you answered. So I knew she meant it."

Shit. She sounds like a psycho. I wonder if all those silent, breathy calls I kept getting from Unknown ID were from her. I thought it was Callum winding me up. I think I even shouted, "Fuck off, Callum," down the phone once.

"I told her there was no way I'd cancel our wedding, but when she threatened to turn up at the altar in protest…" Blimey, she's definitely a psycho. "Well, I had to do something to protect you. I couldn't stand by and let her humiliate you in public." I give him a daggered look. "Humiliate us," he corrects. "It was all happening so quickly. I felt like I was on a carousel. I just needed a bit of time to sort something out. But when you refused…well, you didn't leave me with much choice. I had to call it off."

"You could've come clean," I say crisply. Silence. "Okay, okay whatever," I look at my watch. "I've heard enough, now will you please just go? I'm expecting Daniel any moment now," I lie.

"I thought you were tired?"

"I am." I wave a finger at the blank T.V. screen "We're just going to watch something on Netflix."

He laughs. "Remember how long it would take us to find a film we both wanted to watch?"

"Nick, please."

"I didn't want to hurt you, Audrey." He's back in his seat, picking at a fingernail. "I thought I could handle it. But now I know I made the biggest mistake of my life, walking out on you – on us. You're right, I should've come clean. Told you everything from the start. I've regretted it every day. But when you almost die, well, everything changes, your values, your aspirations - everything."

"Nick, come on. I don't want Daniel to find you here." I get to my feet. "If you really care about me at all, you'll go."

"But what about us?"

"Nick, you're having a baby with another woman, one-night-stand or not. There is no us, not anymore."

NO WAY BACK

"You don't mean that. We're good together, you and me. I promise I'll…"

"No, Nick. Please. Stop!" I close my eyes for a moment, taking a big gulp of air. "There's no way back for us. Not now. Not ever."

He stares at his brown loafers. "Okay, okay. I'm sorry. I want you to be happy. And if that means being with *him*…" he trails off. "But I just want you to know that I do love you. I always have and I always will. You're everything to me." I feel a tug in my stomach. I wish he'd stop doing this to me. He's just making it all worse. "You saw me in Cyprus too, didn't you?" He looks at me carefully beneath furrowed brows.

"What?"

"By your bedside on the morning of our wedding. I told you then that I'd be back for you, remember?" I don't know what he's talking about. I dreamt of him, yes, but he wasn't physically there in the room with me, that I know for certain. "Then when you thought you'd woken from a dream and began to cry," he continues, his voice thick with emotion, "I climbed into bed with you, cried with you, held you in my arms but you couldn't feel me, of course."

"Nick, you're deluded or drunk, or both. It's late, come on." I look at my watch. It's almost seven – any minute now the phone is going to ring. I march into the hall, he charges after me.

"And at that restaurant in Ayia Napa." He forces himself between me and the front door, the phone shrills in the background. "You saw me at the window as well. I know you did." How could he know that? The phone trills and trills. He's spooking me out. Then I remember that I told Louise just after I'd got back, she told Gerry and he updated Nick. Simple. News travels fast. The phone stops ringing and my mobile goes off on the dining table.

"Please, just go." Dancing Queen chimes in the background.

"No, not until you admit you saw me."

"And how did you get there, hmm? By magic?" I snort, hands on hips. My mobile phone stops ringing then starts almost immediately.

"I had an out of body experience," he says uneasily, throwing a glance at the tinny tune coming from the lounge.

"Look, stop all this nonsense!" I push him out of the way and wrench the front door open. "I know Gerry and Ronan have filled you in with all my comings and goings, so stop lying."

"I knew you wouldn't believe me."

We both fall silent. I speak first, "Goodbye, Nick. And congratulations, by the way, do try to be a decent father." He looks at me, face dark, eyes full of remorse. I've never seen him this upset. I hope he's okay. I've heard that a blow to the head can cause all sorts of complications.

He steps onto the porch, then suddenly spins round, "What about on the aeroplane, then?" he says, eyes bright. The phone starts ringing again. "I know you felt my presence. I sat beside you on your journey home. I kept talking to you and then, for a moment, you heard me, didn't you? When I said, '*We'd have been on our honeymoon now*'. You flinched. And the little girl who kept washing her hands…and, and…" A bit of saliva flies from his mouth, his face is shiny with sweat. I try to filter everything he's saying. The phone is ringing, ringing, ringing in my ears. I'm sure I told Louise all this. Jeez, she must tell Gerry everything. "And the man next to you with that big, hairy mole and bad breath." Come to think of it, yes, he did have bad breath. I don't think I told anyone that.

"Look, sorry, Nick, I've got to get that. It might be Louise."

He follows me briskly into the lounge to the ring, ring, ring of the phone. "Can't you see, you and I have a spiritual bond, a connection. That's why you could see and hear me sometimes."

As I reach for the phone it goes dead. I look up at him, deadpan. "You couldn't have been anywhere near me," I say sternly, "you were lying in a hospital bed in a coma, you almost died."

"No, I didn't almost die."

"I think you'll find that you did." My mobile phone tinkles with a message on the table.

"No," he shakes his head, takes a step back. "I died, Audrey, the doctors said my heart stopped beating for about fifteen minutes. And I leapt out of my body and came straight to find you." We stare at each other silently. The wall clock tick, tick, ticks in the background like a time bomb.

"Died?" I murmur, stunned.

"I know, sounds strange, doesn't it?"

"But that's impossible; you're here…now…I…" I touch my lips and notice that my hand is trembling.

"You must've heard of it before?" he asks, pushing my long fringe off my face and gently tucking it behind my ear. "People dying for a few moments, minutes even? And then coming back to life again."

I nod as I vaguely recall an article I read on the internet recently about a little girl who'd drowned and, although pronounced dead at the scene, was resuscitated in the ambulance ten minutes later.

"Well, that's what happened to me," he goes on, stroking my cheek with the back of his hand. I close my eyes, it feels warm, familiar. I'm sinking, sinking, sinking. "When I hit the car, I flew off my bike and landed on the pavement." I open my eyes and take a step back, turning my face away. I can't be intimate with Nick. His near-death experience doesn't change anything. "My body was sprawled on the ground." He lets his arm drop by his side, "Blood was squirting everywhere and the pain in my head." He shuts his eyes tightly, "Was excruciating. I just wanted to die so that it would stop. And then…"

"And then?" I say, swallowing hard.

"And then I saw the light."

NO WAY BACK

CHAPTER 24

"YOU'RE KIDDING ME!" Tina exclaims as she charges over the road bumps on Dukes Avenue. I've had three days to mull over Nick's near-death experience and I still can't get my head around it, let alone convince Tina. "You mean he ACTUALLY died?"

"Yes!" I say, bouncing around in the passenger seat, my head almost touching the roof. "And watch it, will you?" I cry. "You're going to give me cystitis, those speed bumps are there for a reason, you know."

"Sorry." She slows down and rides the next one smoothly. "I can't believe Nick didn't tell me." Nick doesn't want many people to know, said they might think he's a nutter. But agreed that I could tell Tina. She twists her lips to the side. "So, come on, then, spill."

"Well, he said he was sprawled on the pavement in agony, and then suddenly the pain stopped and he felt himself rise above his body. When he looked down, he could see people rushing around him. He reckons he tried talking to them but they couldn't hear him. So he just stood there, next to his body, completely helpless. A passerby rang the emergency services, then about ten minutes later he was being bundled into the back of an ambulance."

"Wow, that's just amazing. I wish I could do it." I give her a worried, sideward glance, "Well, I don't mean actually die but, you know, just pop-out for a bit."

"I think you do enough of that already, love." We both look down at her cleavage. She's wearing a low-cut black ribbed vest top embellished with words *Crazy Baby* in Rhinestones. Not the most appropriate attire for visiting friends who've just lost their unborn child.

"He was actually dead for fifteen minutes," I go on, "said it was the most bizarre sensation imaginable."

Slowing down at the zebra crossing, Tina narrows her eyes, mulling it over. "Did he see a light?" Her eyes shine with excitement as she shifts into first gear.

I tell her that he did see a warm, alluring glow in the distance and it was only the thought of me that kept him from going to it. "And the moment he called out my name," I say, "he fell back into his body again. The last thing he heard before losing consciousness was a voice crying out, "*We've got him back*" And then the wail of an ambulance siren. How surreal is that?" I stare at the traffic ahead and glance at my watch. I'm never going to make it to Louise's *and* meet up with Connie in Hampstead at this rate. It's not usually this busy at this time of day. What's going on? Perhaps there's been an accident or a burst water pipe or something.

"Nicky's story is bloody awesome." Tina shakes her head. "Just, AWESOME. He could sell it to a magazine, you know. I'm sure he'd get a few hundred quid for it. I've always been interested in the paranormal."

We slow down in traffic, she puts the car in neutral, and pulls on the handbreak so hard, I'm surprised it doesn't come off in her hand.

"I thought I saw a ghost once!" Tina says suddenly. Traffic starts trickling along. "I was staying with my aunt Mary in Devon during summer term one year. She had one of those big, creepy houses, you know, those detached ones on the seafront. Very Dickensian." She gives a little shiver. "Anyway, I was hanging out of the bedroom window having a sneaky fag when I thought I heard a noise. I

NO WAY BACK

looked round and saw a woman's reflection in the dressing table mirror. Just sitting there, staring at me."

"Really?" I say in a high-pitched voice. "What did you do?"

"What do you think I did? I chucked my ciggie out of the window and frigging legged it to Aunt Mary's room. I insisted on sleeping with her for the remainder of my stay. She and Uncle Robert tried to convince me it was only the reflection of the clotheshorse, but I wouldn't have it. Poor old Uncle Robert was forced to sleep in the guest room." She laughs loudly. "Naturally, I was never invited back," she says, glancing in her rear-view mirror. "What do you make of Nick's story, then? Do you believe him?"

"The thing is, Tean. Well, Nick's always been an agnostic, so…" I trail off.

"Hmmmm…but wasn't he in a coma for weeks? He may have dreamt the whole thing. I mean, he probably believes it happened but…well, he did have a knock on the head, didn't he? And his injuries were quite serious."

I nod slowly, she's only repeating thoughts that have been bouncing around in my mind like a basketball since he told me. Yes, he was very accurate about the events on my plane journey home, but, having slept on it, I can't be a hundred per cent sure that I didn't relay my entire experience to Louise, even bad-breath-hairy-mole-man. I was a bit jetlagged the next day. My head was all over the place.

"Yes, but there's more," I continue. "He also now claims that he can astral project."

"You what?"

"He's had several OBEs," I explain, to a very confused looking Tina. "You know, out of body experiences."

"No way!" she yelps. "I saw a documentary about that on Channel 4 a few weeks ago."

"Well, he said he was able to transport himself to Cyprus. All he had to do was think of where he wanted to be and, puff, he was there. How mad is that? I told you about the times I thought I saw him in Cyprus, didn't I?"

Tina shakes her head. "You said something about dreams and voices."

"Yes, but I thought I physically saw him too, outside a restaurant one evening. My parents even called a doctor in. He said I was hallucinating, you know, from the stress."

"Oh God, Aud, you mean you actually saw him with your own eyes when he was supposed to be in hospital? Like a ghost?" I tell her that I *thought* I saw him a couple of times. Tina gawps at me. "You're seriously freaking me out now."

"Watch out!" I cry. The seatbelt digs into my ribs as Tina jams on the brakes and we come to a screeching halt, missing the white van in front of us by inches. "Flipping hell, Tina," I gasp, holding my chest, "you're going get us killed."

"It's you," she retorts, "spooking me out!"

"I'm only telling you what happened. You said you wanted to know."

"Well?" We're moving again, the hold-up has cleared; it was due to temporary lights on Park Road. Tina stares ahead, arms outstretched in front of her, gripping the wheel hard with both hands. "Do you believe him?"

"I don't know." I suck my lips in. "No, actually," I say, logic kicking in, "I don't think I do. I think Gerry told him all about my weird experiences in Cyprus, and my episodes were from severe stress." We stop at the traffic lights. "He was just trying his luck, as men do."

Tina laughs. "Nicky can tell a good story, can't he? I used to love Saturday nights in round yours when you were together," she says, and I nod, smiling. Nick can keep a crowd entertained for ages with his banter. "Well, at least you two are talking again. I knew that once he explained things you'd understand. I mean, I know you won't have him back because he got that slapper preggers, but it's nice that you're still friends, isn't it?"

"Yes, Tina, it is. I'm glad I gave him the chance to explain. You were right." Knowing that he didn't dump me for someone else has somehow lifted my morale. Yes, he did have a one-night-stand with another woman but at least it was while we were on a break. He did want to marry me, after all, but just couldn't find a way out of the hole he'd dug.

"He's lost without you, Aud. He's never been very good on his own."

"Well, he should have thought of that before he leapt into bed with another woman and got her pregnant." I stretch my back. I hate being stuck in traffic at the best of times. "Anyway, now that he knows there's no chance with us, he might give it a go with her."

"Yeah, you're right. Oh well, it's his loss. You've moved on now," she says determinedly. We drive in silence for a few moments, and then, "Will you see Nick again?"

I shake my head. "I don't know." And just at that moment, my mobile phone beeps with a message. I whip it out of my handbag.

"What are you grinning at?" Tina smiles, eyes flitting between the road and my phone, "Is it a sextext from Daniel?"

"It's from Nick, actually."

"A sextext from Nick?" Tina yells, "What the fuck?"

"Calm down, Tina, and keep your eyes on the road." I read the text again and smile.

"He just wants to say thanks for the other night."

"Don't tell me you two…"

"For listening, you muppet." I tap her head lightly with my phone. "Honestly, you've got a mind like a sewer."

"Phew." Her hand flies to her chest, "You had me worried there for a moment." Tina puts her foot down and switches lanes. "So, are you going to tell Louise about your rekindled friendship?"

I swivel in my seat and face her. "Are you mad?"

"Yeah, I know." She flicks the indicator on, "She hates him now, doesn't she? They've never really got on."

"It's not that. I just don't want to stress her out. She's got enough on her plate." I shift in my seat. "Anyway, she's only being loyal." We stop at the red lights. I glance at Tina. Her face is tight. Damn. I've offended her. "Not that you're not loyal. God, no, you two are my best friends in equal measures. She's just different from you, that's all?"

"Different how?" Tina looks hurt.

"You're more laid back, easy going, easier to talk to." Tina grins happily at this astute appraisal of her character, and we enjoy the rest of the journey listening to Magic 105.4 in companionable silence.

"OH. MY GOD," Tina squeals. "He's adorable!" Gerry's standing in the doorway holding a black puppy. The sweet aroma of freshly baked pastry drifts from the kitchen, mingling with Tina's strong perfume, which she spritzed herself with just before we got out of the car. In case Gerry had any fit friends round, she said. That girl is a born flirt.

"She," Gerry corrects, handing the puppy over.

"Gerry, she's gorgeous." I stroke her soft, shiny hair. She feels warm and fresh. Her tongue tickles my hand as I rub her floppy ears.

"What breed is she?" Tina asks.

"She's an eight-week-old Labrador," Gerry smiles, pressing his back against the door. "Go through, Louise is in the kitchen."

"I'm in here!" Louise hollers.

"Smells lovely, whatever it is," I yell back, draping my mac over banister. "Is Louise okay about the puppy?" I say to Gerry in a hushed tone as we walk behind a very besotted Tina cooing at the puppy in her arms.

"Orange and Blueberry muffins," Louise calls out, "hope you like."

"No, not really," Gerry whispers, "I thought it'd make her happy. You know, might cheer her up a bit, but she reckons I'm trying to sub it for our loss."

I click my tongue. "Oh, no."

"She wants me to take it back," Gerry hisses in my ear just as we walk into the warm kitchen. "But they won't give me a refund. Eight hundred quid she cost me."

Louise is at the double butler sink washing her hands. She's wearing a long, white chef's apron and has bits of flour in her hair.

"Get that mutt out of my kitchen," she warns, the moment she claps eyes on the puppy in Tina's arms.

"Awww," Tina coos at the puppy, "Mummy-Wummy doesn't mean it." We all fall silent. I can't believe she just said that. I know she can be a bit clumsy and thoughtless at times but this is below the belt. I glare at her, wishing that I'd stuck a large piece of parcel tape over her mouth before we came in. That strong, thick brown one that I use to pack things I've sold on eBay with. "Oh, Lou," she flounders, "I'm so sorry, I didn't mean …" Tina's eyes flit nervously from me to Louise and then at Gerry. "Gerry I'm…" She's gone red, there's a sheen of sweat at her hairline. I soften. Poor Tina, she didn't mean it.

"It's okay, Tina, you don't have to tread on eggshells around us," Gerry says kindly. "We've got to get used to it, get back to normal. We're not the only couple to lose a baby. Come on, Roxy," He takes the puppy from Tina's arms. Roxy yelps and licks his face excitedly.

"And wash your hands, Tina," Louise demands, throwing a vicious glance in Gerry's direction. "I don't want any germs contaminating my food." Tina heads to the sink and does as she's told, bangles rattling around on her wrists, face burning.

"See," Gerry hisses in my ear as he shoulders past me. "I can't do anything right." I know Louise is feeling wrecked but taking it out on Gerry isn't going to help.

The door closes. Louise and I are at the kitchen table. A huge tray of freshly baked muffins and a fresh pot of tea splayed in front of us. I only ever have tea in a pot when I'm at Louise's or Mum's. I'm more of a teabag kind of girl. I'm lazy, what can I say? So it's always a nice treat.

"I'm really sorry, Louise." Tina searches around for a tea towel and then wipes her wet palms on her white jeans, hurrying to join us at the table. "About before, I mean."

"Don't be. I'm okay." She doesn't look okay to me, she looks tense, irritated. "Milk and two sugars for you, isn't it, Tina?" She spoons sugar into a floral china tea cup. "Audrey, you still on a diet? I'm sure I've got some sweeteners somewhere." She gets to her feet and starts opening cabinet doors.

"How've you been?" I ask as she hands me a little green plastic box. "How're things? We're worried about you." I gesture at Tina.

"Oh, you know, getting there. I'll survive," she says in overdone merriment. "Help yourselves to muffins. Oh shit, I forgot to bring plates." She gets up.

"If you need any help," Tina offers, "I'm free most weekends."

"Nah, it's okay. We've got it covered but thanks anyway. And besides, Francesca's over soon, business trip, so the house will soon be bustling."

"Again?" I say. "She might as well move in."

"Tell me about it. This is the last time," she grumbles. Tina and

I exchange wry glances. She always says this. "I've already warned Gerry. It's not as if they can't afford to stay in a hotel."

"I can't believe we haven't met Gerry's sister in all this time?" Tina bites into a muffin then flaps her hand in front of her face miming "hot" at me. "Be great to hang out," she mumbles through a mouthful of scorching muffin. I know she's trying to be sociable, lighten the mood, but Francesca has never been Louise's favourite topic of conversation.

"Well, I only met her myself a few years ago, worse luck," Louise huffs, her head buried in a cupboard. My point proven. "And that was only because Gerry's father died and she had to come over for the funeral. We had a job tracking her down. She and Jean-Pierre are always moving around, something to do with him being a self-employed bank analyst. Where on earth did I put those Wedgewood dessert plates? I bet Gerry's been rearranging my kitchenware again," she mutters under her breath.

"Maybe we can have a girlie night out with her," Tina suggest. "The four of us."

"Yeah," Louise replies absently, opening a bottom cabinet. "Ha! Just as I thought." She pulls out a set of colourful ripple-edged plates. "I wish he'd bloody well leave my stuff alone." Tina and I exchange glances as we take a sip from our teacups simultaneously. There's a creak in the floorboards above followed quickly by the sound of footsteps thundering down the stairs. Roxy barks in the background, the kitchen door flies open and two giggling women fly in.

"Hi, Jess," I get to my feet.

"Hey, Audrey." Jess reaches out and gives me a bear hug, then strokes Tina's head like a pet. "All right, Tina."

"You girls off?" Louise says, stack of plates in her arms. "Those are fresh out of the oven, help yourselves. Miriam, these are my friends, Audrey and Tina."

"Hello." Miriam gives us a little curt nod, hands stuffed in the back pockets of her skinny jeans, voice barely audible. She's a pretty twenty-something girl with large, brown, sultry eyes and short, dark hair, long fringe swept to the side like blades of grass.

"Yeah, we've got a class," Jess explains, grabbing two muffins, "Ouch, they're hot, Mum. We'd better get off or we'll miss our train. Laters." And they're gone.

We spend the next hour-and-a-half talking about Tina's cancer scare, Louise's miscarriage – and Daniel. Mostly about Daniel. I tell them how generous and thoughtful he is. Just the other day he sent my parent's theatre tickets for a West End show that Mum's been dying to see, best seats in the house too. And he's found them the ideal home in Larnaca, right on the seafront at a fraction of the usual cost.

Louise and Tina tell me that I've got a good catch, that I should hold onto him tightly. And they're right, of course, they are. But - and there's always is a but, isn't there? Is it wrong to want to be with a man who has less baggage? A man who puts me first? Because wonderful as Daniel is, and there's no disputing that, I know deep down in my heart, and so does he, that I won't ever be the centre of his universe. Because that place was taken twenty-nine years ago.

CHAPTER 25

CONNIE DROPS A BUNCH OF KEYS onto the table in front of me then takes a large slurp of hot chocolate, regarding me under a grey trilby. Despite hardly any makeup today, she still looks stunning in a navy blue sweater with beige elbow patches and skinny blue jeans, ripped at the knees and thighs. Leaning back in my chair, I catch a glimpse of her red pumps. The exact red *Pradas* that Daniel bought me recently. I wonder if they chose them together.

"What's this?" I ask, throwing a glance at the *C* initial keyring.

"My spare keys to Dad's flat. You'll need them for when you go round later to collect a delivery for me." Another loud slurp.

I almost choke on my drink. "I'm going round?" I ask in horror, spritzing the table with coffee. Connie grimaces, wiping her cheek. Two women at the next table stop talking and gawp at me, white cups in mid-air. "What for?" I whisper in the manner of an M15 agent. I mop up the brown beads of liquid with a napkin in harsh, angry strokes. The women return to their conversation, one of them eyeing me curiously over her cup.

I should've known Connie had an ulterior motive for insisting we meet in Hampstead instead of Crouch End; even though I told her I could call round for her at Aliki's seeing as she'd be in the area, that it's only a ten-minute walk from Louise's.

I gaze around the patisserie, taking in the mouth-watering display of fresh cakes on the counter, which I spied hungrily as I breezed in. Big chandeliers sparkle from the high ceilings illuminating the slick, dark furniture, Parisian art hangs on the deep red walls. It is rather lovely in here, though, not to mention expensive. But money means nothing to Connie and it's her treat today.

"I've ordered some stuff for Dad's party from an online supplier," Connie says, "balloons, napkins, party bags, that sort of thing." Jesus, is this a party for a fifty-year-old or a child?

"But it's over three weeks away," I exclaim, causing a bearded hipster to look up at me from his laptop. Connie always seems to bring out the shouty person in me.

"Audrey." She nudges her trilby back, displaying an inch of brown roots against blonde hair. "I need to prepare. I don't want to leave things until the last minute." My eyes flit to her pink, plump lips. A bit of hot chocolate had lodged in the corner of her mouth, and I've a sudden urge to wipe it. "Mum promised me yesterday that she'd do it, but something's come up and now she's backed out," she says, annoyed. "I'd go myself, but they're delivering during the school run." She flicks a glance at her phone. "I wouldn't ask but I couldn't think of anyone else."

"Well, what about your Granny?"

"Oh, my yiayia can't communicate very well in English." She rests both elbows on the table, takes another sip, then runs her tongue over her lips, licking off the chocolate stain. Phew. "Besides, how'll she get there? She can't even drive. And forget about London Transport, she'll end up in Cyprus."

"Connie," I say regretfully, "when I said I'd help with your dad's surprise fiftieth, I just meant with simple things, like helping you choose the cake, arranging the catering. My friend Louise is a top chef, actually, I was going to recommend her – mates rates." She nods approvingly at this, lips curved downwards, and for a moment she morphs into Daniel, which is weird because she doesn't really look like him. Well, not much.

NO WAY BACK

"Look," I add quickly, diverting from the image in my mind. "I don't really feel comfortable being in your dad's flat on my own, not without his permission. I'm sorry, Connie, I'm going have to say no." Satisfied, I curl my fingers around the curved handle of my white designer mug and take a sip with poise.

"Oh, come on, Audrey, you'll be doing me a massive favour." She gathers her eyebrows and inclines her head, mutating into Daniel again. I look away. How can someone's gestures make you look so much like them? "Dad won't mind you being there on your own. He's not like that," she claims. "He doesn't mind people looking at his things. You know how easy going he is. Please, Audrey. It'll only be a ten-minute job - sign for the goods, hide them in the bottom draw of the closet in the lounge, he never looks in there, and then leave. You can bury the keys in the pot plant by the door and I'll pick them up later."

I take another sip of coffee as I mull over her suggestion. Helping her out would be a good thing, right? She's at a loose end and it would give me a few extra brownie points with Daniel. "Connie," I begin, thinking better of it, "how would I like it if your dad had free rein in my flat without my knowledge, hmm? The thing is…" And just at that moment, my mobile phone goes off in my handbag. "Sorry, Connie, better get this. I'm expecting a call from your dad." I said I'd cook Daniel a meal tonight. When I say cook I mean heating up M&S grub. I'm not the best cook in the world. He's probably calling just to confirm. I look at the screen "*Mum calling*".

"Hi, Mum." Connie rolls her eyes.

"Darling, I've been trying to reach you all morning, where've you been?" I bypass my overnight stay at Daniel's and go on to explain how I went round to see Louise and that now I'm now having coffee with Connie. "Oh, I won't keep you then, just wanted to let you know that George called. Vicky's been diagnosed with PND."

"What's that when it's at home?" I say, glancing at an older couple who've just arrived. When Mum learns a new word or term she uses it abundantly to show off.

"Post Natal Depression, dear, don't you read any magazines? That's what all those secret appointments were about."

"Oh, Mum." My hand flies to my head. Poor Vicky. "Is she okay?" Connie glances up briefly with a reflex frown.

"Yes, yes," Mum insists, "she's fine. It's about time she faced up to her problems instead of taking it all out on your poor brother. They've put her on something called… Lionel," she calls out to Dad, "what anti-depressants is Vicky on?"

"Zoloft," he shouts.

"Did you hear that, darling?"

"Yes, Mum. Look I'd better go, thanks for letting me know. I'll give Vicky a call later…yes…bye…bye. Love you too."

I put my phone on the table and take a gulp of lukewarm coffee. The older couple shuffle chairs at an adjacent table as they gaze around the impressive patisserie. He reminds me a bit of my dad, actually, white thinning hair, stocky, orange tan. "You sit over there," he commands to his wife, pulling out a chair and throwing a glance in our direction, and the small, mature, grey-haired woman does as she's told.

"Well?" Connie is looking at me expectantly, arms folded. "Will you do it?" My lips part but I'm saved by my phone vibrating on the table.

"Oh, for God's sake," she huffs, "you're worse than a bloody teenager."

"Sorry, Connie, this really has got to be your dad." Connie, clearly narked, snatches her phone off the table and starts texting, fingers whizzing over the keyboard furiously.

I squint at the lit up screen: *Nick calling*. Shit.

"Well?" Connie says, her eyes not leaving her phone, "Aren't you going to answer it? Don't want to keep his highness waiting." No, I don't suppose we do.

"Hi," I say in an unintended piercing tone.

"Hey, Foxy." I'm surprised at how normal it feels to hear his voice. "How're you?"

"Yes, yes…fine." My eyes don't leave Connie. "You?"

"Okaaaay," he says tentatively, "have I called at a bad time?" He knows me so well.

"Kind of," I laugh nervously, tapping my fingertips on the rim of my cup.

Connie gives me a fleeting glance, "Tell Dad that Mum wants to talk to him about some property thingy. I think it's for your oldies."

"You didn't reply to my text earlier," Nick says, "did it come through?" I murmur a response, pressing the handset so close to my ear that it hurts. I don't want Connie to hear his voice, and Nick does have quite a loud voice. "Anyway, it was just to say thank you for being so understanding last Monday. It meant a lot." I hear him taking a long lug on a cigarette. "I can't tell you how happy I am that we're friends again." He pauses for my response but I stay silent. "Look I know you can't talk but I was wondering if you were free for a drink tonight." He pauses again, "As mates," he adds quickly. "Thought we could pop into *The Flask*."

"No, I can't tonight." Actually, I don't think I can on any night. I'm sure that cosying up with my ex on one of the snug seats in *The Flask* won't go down too well with Daniel.

Connie's eyebrows knot in concentration. "Can't what?"

I wish she'd stop interfering in my telephone conversation, for goodness sake, she's putting me off. I push the coffee cup away and rest my forearm on the table, twiddling with my left earring.

"No problem," Nick says. "Look, I know you can't talk. I'll call back another time."

"That sounds great," I say, feeling relieved, 'Okay, bye…" I drop my voice to a whisper. "Yes, I will do…bye…bye." Why do people lower their tone at the end of a conversation? I can never figure it out, yet I feel completely compelled to do so every time.

"So?" Connie chucks her phone onto the table and folds her arms. "Why didn't you pass on my message?"

"Well." I rub my lips. "Because it wasn't your dad."

"ooOOoo." She raises her eyebrows and adjusts in her seat as her phone tingles with a message. "Ha, it's Dad." She taps the screen, "Just to say that we're on for tonight." Well, he's clearly blown me out, then. "Lily hasn't seen him for a few days. I texted this morning and asked if he fancied meeting up for a pizza. He says you're coming along too." Oh, does he now? Connie swirls the liquid in her cup, loosening the last dregs of chocolate then knocks it back, swishing it around in her mouth as if it were a Merlot before swallowing and licking her lips.

"So, come on." Connie gently taps my ankle with her foot under the table, "Who was the mysterious caller? I hope you're not cheating on my old man already. " She grins wickedly, but I don't miss the sudden flinch in her green eyes.

"Oh, don't be so ridiculous. It was…" I falter, "…a colleague, if you must know. Now about that delivery," I say, steering her off the subject, "just a ten-minute job, you say?"

CHAPTER 26

I LOVE DANIEL'S TWO-BEDROOM FLAT despite it being on the first floor of a house conversion with no garden. It's luxurious and plush and in a leafy part of West Hampstead. But it is very blokey – all open plan with lots of black furniture. He's even got a black floor lamp, which he said he bought from Portobello Market. He reckons it's retro but I just think it looks ugly. The pièce de résistance - as he calls it - is a fireplace that is integrated into the wall housing a two-foot gold Buddha. Clearly never used. Yes, it's very much a bachelor pad, no room for a permanent fixture, such as a wife for instance, which is just as well because I've gone right off that idea.

My first port of call is the loo. Thanks to Connie plying me with two large cups of coffee and half-a-gallon of lemon infused water, which she insisted we drank because she paid for it, I'm now bursting to go. I dash into the bathroom adjacent to the second bedroom; Connie's room, as it's known. It's the only room kitted out in pastel colours and has a few of Lily's dolls and teddy bears lying on the bed. It's sacred. We're not allowed in there.

I immediately notice that he's out of toilet paper. Brilliant. Why can't people replace an empty loo roll for crying out loud? How hard can it be? But I'm savvy nowadays when it comes to using public lavs. I am no longer that woman who glances at an empty loo roll during mid-flow in horror, the woman who has to drip-dry or hobble around a bathroom, knees clasped together, looking for spares in vanity cupboards or tissue boxes hidden in obscure corners. No, these days, I ALWAYS check first.

I leg it into Daniel's en-suite bathroom as quickly as my legs will carry me. Loo paper? Check. Hand towel? Check. Soap dispenser? Loaded. Great.

Gazing at the shiny bathroom taps, I inhale the scent of fresh pine. Daniel's flat is spotless. The sliding doors of his shower cubicle at the rear of the en-suite are gleaming. All thanks to Pranvera, his loyal cleaner, who blitzes the flat twice a week.

A babble of voices drift up from the street as I pad into Daniel's bedroom. I wonder if it's the couriers. Perhaps they've come early. I fiddle with the drawstring of the black Venetian blind as I stare down at two burly men talking loudly on the pavement; they look like builders. They step out of the way as a middle-aged jogger trudges past them. One of them glances up at the window, and I back away. It's only ten-past-four. I've got ages yet. God, I'm bored. I hate waiting around. I have been known to become a bit destructive when left alone with nothing to do, so I'd better not touch anything valuable.

I run my fingers along the frame of Daniel's bed and sigh joyfully. It's in a much neater state than when we left it this morning – bedcovers tucked in neatly, pillows plumped to perfection. Pranvera must've come around just after we left. I grin as I mosey over and sit on his side of the mattress feeling lucky, elated, excited about the future; then just as I'm about to tidy an uneven pile of paperbacks on the bedside table, my phone purrs in my handbag. I fish it out. A message from Daniel – finally.

Sorry, darling, change of plans. Con and Lily want to see us for pizza at 7.30. That ok?

Is that okay? I laugh. He's already bloody well arranged it. I shake my head as I punch in my reply. A few moments later my phone vibrates again.

NO WAY BACK

Great. Con & Lil with Aliki aft school. I'll go straight from work. Meet outside the pizza bar on Pk Rd @ 7.30. Can't wait 2 c u xxx

Yeah, yeah, yeah, that's why you swapped an intimate dinner date for a family outing for four, is it? Oh well, I shouldn't grumble, as Mum said, *"You knew he had a family, dear, you'd do the same in his shoes. At least he's showing responsibility as a father".*

I slip my phone back into my handbag, catching my reflection in the wall-to-wall mirror of the fitted wardrobes that line the far end of the room. They make the average sized bedroom look enormous, nice trick. I'm about to look away when I notice a t-shirt sticking out of the chest of drawers next to the 42 inch T.V. mounted on the wall. Oh, bloody hell! Pranvera must be slacking - no loo paper, no book tidying, clothes trapped in drawers. I'm going to have to fix it, of course. I can't spend the next fifteen minutes with that on my conscience.

The drawer slides open with a hiss. Daniel's t-shirts are stacked in military style. Why am I not surprised? He's almost as efficient as my mother. I said, almost. I tuck the t-shirt back inside, smiling to myself, and just then, I spot an A4 envelope with the words *'My Treasures'* written across it in Daniel's handwriting. Who keeps their paperwork in clothes drawers? I stroke the brown envelope. Treasures? Hmm…I wonder what's inside. Curiosity slithers through me. I slide my fingers under the seal - it's open. No, I can't invade his privacy. I'm here to do a job, that's all.

I close the drawer and walk away, but as I reach the door, I turn back. What harm could a little peek do? I am bored, and Connie did say that he doesn't mind people looking at his stuff. If it were private, it'd be sealed, right? I bet it's just memorabilia – family photos, that sort of thing. I glance at my watch again. There's still another ten minutes before the delivery arrives. I go back to the drawer.

I'm sitting on the edge of the bed, envelope in hand. Maybe I should put it back. I chew the inside of my bottom lip, then quickly flip open the envelope and pull out a bundle of papers and photographs. They're held together with a large, red elastic band. I carefully unbind them and they spill onto the bed like confetti.

A big grin spreads across my face. There's a child's drawing of a little girl in brown plaits with her parents on either side. They're all united, holding hands in one long line. In the background, there's a house with oversized windows and a big yellow sun, bigger than the house. On the top right-hand corner of the page, it's signed *Constance Taylor Class 2B Aged 4 ½*. It's pretty damned good for a four-year-old. Clearly, she was artistic from the outset.

Next, there's a strand of blonde hair taped onto a white card with the inscription '*Lily's hair at eighteen months*' in neat handwriting. Not Daniel's, must be Connie's. I sift through a few envelopes addressed to Daniel and put them at the bottom of the pile. I won't read his personal documents. Beneath the envelopes, I find several photographs. Oh my God, one is of me! It's the one we took at Hyde Park recently. It was a warmish day so we decided to pop into *Pret a Manger*, grab a couple of sandwiches and coffees and head to the park.

We walked along, hand in hand, the autumn leaves swirling around our feet. On the bench, he held me in his arms, my head on his shoulder as we gazed at the swans and ducks gliding along the pond, telling each other anecdotes about our lives. Daniel decided to take a few selfies with his phone so that we could remember how happy we felt on that day. I'm touched that he actually got them printed. Mine are all on my phone clogging up all the memory.

I giggle at a photo of the two of us pulling faces at the camera. I'm honoured that he's included me in his pile of treasures but, if I'm honest, I'm also a bit overwhelmed, and, dare I say it, creeped

NO WAY BACK

out. He hasn't really known me that long. Don't get me wrong, I really do like him but, I don't know, he is a bit full-on sometimes. I flick through a few more photos, smiling. Perhaps he just really thinks a lot of me. My phone hums with a call. It's my brother.

"Hi Aud, it's me," he says to the backdrop of yelling and the rumble of traffic. He must've just left school.

"Hey, George, you okay?"

"Yeah, not bad, you know how it is. Did Mum tell you about Vicks?"

"Yes, George, she did." I tuck my hair behind my ear, concerned. "I knew there was something wrong, she's just not been herself, has she? Poor Vicky." I pause for a moment remembering her outburst in Mum and Dad's bathroom a few weeks ago. "Anyway, I'm glad she's sorting it out. Listen, I'm at Daniel's now but I'll give her a buzz later."

"What in the middle of the afternoon? Don't you people ever work?"

"It's a long story. I'll tell you when I see you. And for your information, I'm working from home today; just launched Daniel's website, actually. You should see it, George, it's amazing. Fearne really did a great job on it. Erm…" I cluck my tongue in concentration, "Can I come round and see Vicky and the kids tomorrow? I really miss them. Would that be okay?"

"It'd be brilliant. We'd love it," he says, "Florian's been asking after his favourite aunt." I smile down the phone.

"Er, hang on. I am his only aunt!" Vicky's only got brothers.

"Speak to you tomorrow, sis," he laughs, "love yooooou."

I stand up, photos in hand, and walk towards the window, a smile dancing on my lips. George is such a lovable clown, I'm so lucky to have him. I fix my gaze on a rustling tree outside. I can't believe how things have panned out. Nick's having a child with someone else; I'm getting close to another man with a family. Not what I had planned a couple of months ago. Who'd have thought it?

I shake my head as I start sifting through the pictures again. There's one of Connie smiling happily on the beach, must be in Cyprus. I crinkle my nose, how sweet. There are a few shots of Connie on her own, a couple with Lily, one of Daniel, Aliki and Lily, and several of family holidays and outings.

But it's the last one that raises my curiosity. An oldey monochrome photo, out of focus and dog-eared. I place the rest of the pictures on the window-sill and hold onto it with both hands. A very young Daniel stares back at me, his arm slung around Aliki with baby Connie in her arms. Blimey Aliki's put on a few pounds. She's almost unrecognisable. A flicker of envy flutters in my stomach. They're all smiling at the camera, their smiles reaching their eyes, they look so happy together. I wonder what went wrong, why after so many years of marriage they chose to go their separate ways.

"What the hell do you think you're doing?" The voice slices through the silence. I spin round, startled.

"Oh my God," I gasp, "Daniel. You made me jump." My hand flies to my chest, the photograph slips from my fingers and flutters to the floor like a feather. "I didn't hear you come in." He tosses a newspaper onto the bed angrily. It lands on top of his other keepsakes. Clearly, he's cross, and who could blame him? I glance down at the photograph at my feet and then slowly bend down to pick it up.

"Leave it," he demands as if I were a dog in training. The wooden floor creaks beneath his weight as he strides towards me. I'm on my knees, I look up at him. I've never seen him angry before. His eyes have almost doubled in size, his jaw is clenched, fists balled against his sides. I get up and find myself in front of him.

"Daniel, I can explain." He folds his arms tightly against his chest. I can smell his cologne infused with perspiration.

"Well? Go on then," he says, confrontationally, "I'm waiting."

"Daniel, this isn't what you think. I -"

But he doesn't let me finish. "Oh, isn't it?" He starts pacing the room irritably. "Then can you please tell me why and how you broke into my flat and started rummaging through my personal belongings?"

"I didn't break in," I say defensively, "I used a key."

"Oh sorry, silly me." He wobbles his head incredulously. "You let yourself in, did you? What did you do, slip out of bed one morning and pop to the locksmiths around the corner? I've a good mind to call the police!"

"Daniel!" I can't believe he's talking to me like this.

"It's all you deserve," he spits. "I could have you for breaking and entering."

"I can't believe I'm hearing this. Look, I didn't break in, what do you take me for?"

"I dunno." He pinches the bridge of his nose and closes his eyes briefly, "Bunny boiler springs to mind."

"Oh, don't flatter yourself." I've heard enough. I cross the room, pushing past him and start gathering my belongings. "Connie gave me your front door keys. I'm waiting for a delivery for, for..." It's supposed to be a flipping surprise, if I tell him the truth now I'll blow it. "Oh, what the bloody hell are you doing home so early, anyway? I thought you were going straight to The Pizza Bar?"

"I wanted to freshen up! I've had a tough day. Why are you in my bedroom, anyway?"

"I had to use your loo," I huff. "If you stocked the guest cloakroom properly I'd never have come in here in the first place."

"What are you talking about? There was a full roll in there this morning."

"Well, it's not there now!"

"You're lying," he storms, "I tore off a few sheets when I cut myself shaving this morning." He touches an aberration on his chin.

"Well, maybe the cleaning fairies had a boozy party and used it all up," I scream.

"Oh, don't be so infantile," he rages, then gesticulates at the papers strewn across the bed with a sharp flick of his head. "How did you find all this, anyway?"

"Your t-shirt was sticking out of the drawer, I went to tidy it back and –"

"Oh, don't give me that –" He air quotes, "I can't stand seeing things out of place, malarkey. That envelope was buried under a stack of clothes. You were just being bloody well nosey, as usual!" I'm too shocked to answer. "So, come on, how much have you seen, hmm? He charges towards me. "Read all my bloody personal letters have you?"

"Whoa." I put my hands up, "Hang on a moment, I…"

"What gives you the right to look at my stuff, hey?" he talks over me, pointing his finger, raising his voice. "This part of my life has nothing to do with you. It's none of your damned business."

"What's bloody wrong with you? They're only a few old photos, for crying out loud. You're acting like I've read your diaries or something." I throw my hands up in anger.

"Those photos are MY property – MINE!" He taps his chest hard and I take a step back, a bit of his saliva spits from his mouth and lands on my chin. "You had no damned right, Audrey." He's scaring me. I need to get out of here before something bad happens.

I pull my sleeve across my chin. "I don't have to listen to this. I was only trying to do you lot a favour." I grab my bag and head for the door and just at that moment the intercom buzzes. Great, the courier, ten minutes too fucking late. He follows me to the door.

"Did you read my letters," he demands, his jaw muscles throbbing, "Well?"

"No, I didn't. Now just get out of my bloody way, will you!"

"Just tell me what you were doing here then, alone in my flat?" he demands as if I'm some hustler out to fleece him. Right, that's it!

"I was supposed to be receiving a delivery for your sodding surprise fiftieth birthday party that Connie's organising for you," I blurt out, pushing him out of the way, "but you've ruined the whole flipping thing now, haven't you." There I've said it. "Happy bloody birthday, Daniel. Are you happy now?"

And with this I race down the stairs and wrench the front door open, he pounds down after me. A man in a green uniform is holding a box and smiling at me.

"Afternoon, delivery for Connie Taylor." I push past him.

"Audrey wait," Daniel cries.

"Delivery for Miss Connie Taylor?" the driver says to Daniel.

"Oh, get stuffed!" I hear him say, as he rushes behind me. "Audrey," he shouts, but I'm already on the pavement hailing a black cab. "Why didn't you say for Christ's sake? Audrey."

"Please," I gasp at the driver, throwing a worried glance behind me. "Muswell Hill, and hurry." The cabbie clocks Daniel running towards us, unlocks the doors quickly and I clamber into the back. We start moving, my mouth is dry, my heart is thrashing against my chest. Daniel is at the window, drumming his knuckles against the glass.

"Audrey, wait. Please. We need to talk!" He's running alongside the cab, the indicators clang loudly, "I'm sorry," he cries. He's running faster, trying to keep up, his red tie flapping over his shoulder. "AUDREY!"

CHAPTER 27

THE CAB DRIVER GLANCES AT ME in his rear-view mirror as we approach Fortis Green Road. I feel completely drained. What the hell just happened? How could Daniel speak to me like that? Accuse me of being an obsessed freak? A thief? Our first row…so soon. I knew he was too good to be true. I lean my head back against the headrest and it occurs to me that in eight years Nick never once raised his voice to me like that. In fact, I don't think he was ever really angry with me. I close my eyes, taking a big gulp of air.

"Whereabouts in Muswell Hill, love?" asks the driver.

Right now all I want is a large gin and tonic and a long soak in the bath. I glance at my watch. It's almost five-thirty. I lean forward.

"Actually, do you mind taking me to Nelson Road in Crouch End instead?"

"You're the boss," he says, smiling.

Nick's new red Volkswagen Passat Estate is parked outside. The living room window is slightly ajar. He's in. I ring the doorbell furiously. Within seconds, he's at the door.

"Audrey." Nick looks surprised to see me. He pulls the door behind him, not quite shut but enough to keep out the cold. I study his face, the bruises are fading, his freshly cut hair has taken years off him, and he looks nice and relaxed in a long-sleeved white t-shirt and faded blue jeans. "Well, this is a surprise." He scratches his five o'clock shadow. "I thought you said you were out tonight."

NO WAY BACK

"Change of plans." I shuffle on the doorstep, feeling awkward. Oh, what the hell am I doing here? I should never have come. What was I thinking? "I've had an arse of a day," the words slip out of my mouth hurriedly, "I could really do with a drink and a friendly ear…erm… can I come in?" The wind has blown the door half open. He stands in front of it, rigid, blocking my view, then shoves his hands into his pockets.

"Actually, it's not a good time. Audrey," he grimaces. Oh God, he's got a woman in there. I wonder if it's *her*. I bet they were just getting it on.

"Oh," I stammer. A shot of jealousy comes out of nowhere and almost knocks me out. "You've got company. I'm sorry. I shouldn't have just turned up like this." Turning away, I hurry down the steps.

"No, wait," he says urgently, "don't go." I turn and slowly walk back up. He rubs the back of his neck, a sure sign that he's anxious. "Are you okay? You look upset." I tell him that I'm not really, that I could do with a stiff drink and a chat. "Look, give me half-an-hour," he whispers, glancing behind him, "we can meet up then. I can come round to your place if you like."

"That would be nice," I smile. "But there's really no need, I don't want to spoil your plans." And I don't. He's got every right to start dating again. He is, after all, a free agent now. Then just as I turn to leave, I catch sight of a woman's silhouette behind him. "Who's that?"

"No-one, it's…" He tries to pull the door shut behind him but in his haste, he loses his grip and the door flies open.

"Nick," a familiar woman's voice says, "who is it?" She's in full view now, standing before me bold as brass, a wicked grin dancing on her lips. Nick swings around and then covers his face with his hands. A half-naked Connie stands before me, a white bed sheet wrapped around her body like a Greek goddess. There's a black enchantment heart tattoo on her left shoulder that I haven't seen before, or at least never noticed. My stomach tightens.

"You bastard," I say coldly, "you promised me."

Nick looks at Connie aghast. I turn on my heel and hurry down the steps. "Audrey, wait. Come back, I can explain. AUDREY!" But I'm already rushing down the street. I look back as his front door slams, and just then I catch sight of Ronan climbing out of a black cab, overnight case in hand. I wonder what he's doing here, talk about bad timing. I don't want him to see me. I hurry down the street, tears of fury spilling from my eyes.

As I reach the bottom of the road, I feel sick. I stop running and steady myself against a street lamppost, gasping for breath. A bitter gust blows in my face. It's turned chilly but I'm too wound up to feel the cold.

Trees are raging in the wind, hissing in my ears like chips frying in hot oil. It's rush hour, commuters are heading home, hurrying by, talking into their mobile phones. A gawky teenage boy shuffles past, throwing me a confused look beneath his long fringe. A mature lady in a business suit stops, asks if I'm okay. I can't believe this is happening to me – not all in one frigging day.

I start to calm as I reach The Broadway and see the bus stop in the distance, not long now and I'll be in my warm, safe home, sipping a large gin and tonic in the bath. I wipe the cold, wet tears off my face with my fingers. Connie and Nick, I can't believe it, Daniel will be furious. Oh, my God, Daniel. My eyes swell with fresh, hot tears. Talk about Jekyll and Hyde.

My mind starts racing as my heels click against the pavement hurriedly. Daniel didn't really seem to mind me seeing the old photographs and childhood tokens. It's the letters that infuriated him. What was in those envelopes? Why was he so anxious? What

NO WAY BACK

secrets is he hiding?

The W7 approaches as I stride up to the bus stop. The doors open, people start to shuffle on. I push my long fringe off my face. I ought to go home, get some rest, have a drink, a bath - give Tina or Louise a call, tell them what happened.

But I don't board the W7 bus. I don't break my stride at all. I just carry on walking and walking and walking until I find myself outside number 6 Wolseley Road. I won't be made a fool of by a man again. I need answers and I need them now.

CHAPTER 28

I HAMMER ON THE KNOCKER, no doorbell in sight. The curtains twitch, then the hall light comes on, the door opens. I'm instantly greeted by a gust of Mediterranean cooking. A slight, elderly lady dressed in black is staring up at me. Her hair in a neat white bun, her creased, tanned face etched with bewilderment.

"I'm sorry to trouble you," I say lightly. She doesn't answer. "Is Aliki home?"

"Aliki?" she asks, confused. I nod fervently. "Who arrr you?" she demands in a heavy accent, all the time regarding me dubiously. I tell her I'm a friend of Connie's; she furrows her brows. "Constantina?" she says almost accusingly.

"Yes," I reply. Connie did say that her grandmother calls her by her full Greek name. "Constantina."

"Constantina no in." Yes, love, I want to say, I know that. She's a few blocks away fucking my ex-fiancé's brains out.

"Aliki in?" I find myself saying in an accent similar to hers.

"Aliki, yes, she in." She gives me a small, tight smile before hollering, "Aliki mou! Eineh mia fili tis Constantina's, seh theli. Ela etho." Well, all I could fathom from that sentence was Constantina. But, judging from her expression, I expect she's just told her that there's an insane looking woman at the door who wants to see you.

"Okay, Mamma," a voice yells in the distance, "I'm coming." Within moments Aliki's at the door, drying her hands on a tea towel. "Hi," she says brightly, throwing the towel onto her left

NO WAY BACK

shoulder with a miniscule reflex frown. "Can I help you?" She doesn't know who I am. There's a bit of grease on her olive skin, she wipes it with the back of her hand. She's very much as I expected, small and plump with short, dark brown layered hair, large dark eyes and a big friendly smile. Very mumsy.

"Hi, Aliki," I say a little too chirpily. My heart dances in my chest, its rhythm cascading down into my stomach. "I'm so sorry to bother you." I croak, then clear my throat. This isn't going to be as easy as I thought. "I'm Audrey." She looks at me a little hesitantly for a few moments. To give her credit she has only ever seen me from a distance and I've always been in the car. Suddenly, her expression brightens. She's recognised me, her lips part.

"Audrey!" Lily bounds towards me. I bend down and she wraps her little arms around my neck and gives me a big, tight hug. "We're not going for a pizza now; Yiayia's making me pasta with tomato sauce and halloumi cheese, mmm, my favourite. Granddad just rang and said you were ill." She pauses and knots her fine eyebrows together. "Are you all right, Audrey? You don't look ill." She touches my cheek, "You've got mascara shaped tears. Mummy has them too sometimes. Have you been crying?" I didn't think about the possibility of smudgy, teary make-up. No wonder Aliki's mum was looking at me as if I'd just crawled out of the woods.

"Come on, Lily," Aliki says, taking her hand. "Let Audrey come inside. It's chilly out there and we don't want her cold to get worse, do we?" She winks at me and waves me inside. I step into the large, square hall, cluttered with boxes of bric-a-brac and bin bags. They must be in the middle of a move.

"I've come at a bad time, haven't I?" I glance at my watch without registering the time. "I don't want to spoil your dinner."

"No, it's okay." She closes the door behind us. "Mum and I have already eaten. We had bangers and chips earlier, can't beat good old British grub, can you? Mamma," she shouts, "can you watch Lily's pasta?" The petite lady reappears at the kitchen door and nods ardently.

"Mamma, this is Audrey."

Mamma furrows her white brows. "Ah, yes," she says after a moment, "Danny's gayfriend."

"Oh no," I protest. "Does she think I'm a lesbian?"

"No," Aliki giggles, "she means girlfriend, it's just her accent."

"You hungry Oddry?" she asks, then looks at her daughter. "I makey some more soshinga and chips Aliki, mou?" I'd forgotten how hospitable the Greek Cypriots are, but the last thing I want is a plate of sausage and chips. Aliki looks at me and I shake my head.

"I've already eaten," I lie, hoping that my stomach doesn't let me down with gurgling noises. The food does smell good. "But thanks."

"I go buy you chips from the Fishatigo," Mamma insists reaching for her coat on a nearby armchair. "You very skinny, you eat and be big and strong like Aliki."

"Oooh, oooh, I love chips from the chippie!" Lily says excitedly, "Can I come with you, yiaya Despina?"

"Oh, Mamma," Aliki says, annoyed. "Stop trying to force feed people, Audrey said she's eaten."

"Ah, okay. I put the kettlon on, then, and make a nice cub o'tea," Despina announces, clasping her hands together and nodding at me cheerfully.

"Oh er…" I begin.

"No, Mamma, leave the kettle alone. I think Audrey would appreciate something stronger."

"Oh-rite," she grumbles, "Come, Lily mou, come." And with

NO WAY BACK

this, Lily happily follows her great-grandmother into the kitchen with the promise of being allowed to grate the halloumi cheese.

"Please, sit down." Aliki gesticulates at the sofa covered in a massive burnt orange throw. "I'll just get us some glasses for this." She plonks a bottle of Five Kings Brandy onto the walnut coffee table and totters off.

I stare at the tawny liquid in the familiar broad-shouldered bottle and smile sadly. It's one of Dad's favourite tipples, especially when he's in Cyprus. He was particularly impressed with its historical namesake. "It was created by the KEO Company to commemorate the banquet of the Five Kings, Audrey," he told me as he filled two tumblers on the balcony in Cyprus a few weeks ago, "and hosted in London by Sir Henry Picard in 1363 for the kings of England, Cyprus, Scotland, France and Denmark. What an honourable name for a brandy, eh? Yiamas."

I survey the room. Aliki must be a smoker, there's an ashtray full of butt ends on the table next to the bottle of brandy and a whiff of tobacco in the air. To say it feels a bit surreal being in the home that Daniel once shared with his family is an understatement. I shouldn't have turned up like this, but he left me with no other choice. Aliki is the only person who can answer my questions.

Getting to my feet, I take in the cluttered room. Two piles of old magazines and newspapers tower near the door like uneven pillars; ornaments and photo frames fill every conceivable space, and there's at least twenty shopping bags sitting on the hearth of the fireplace.

I mosey over to the photographs that line the cigarette-stained magnolia wall, and gaze at them as if they were exhibits in an art gallery. I've always found family photographs fascinating, the history, the adventures. It's such a pity that we carry all our photos on our mobile phones these days.

I peer at them closely. Some date back to the early century, undoubtedly Aliki's clan, Greeks usually have large families. A section of the wall is packed with photos of Connie – baby photos, nursery and school photos, pictures of her on holiday with mates, modelling shots. It's like some sort of shrine, if I'm honest, and slightly eerie. A recent one, taken at a Race for Life event, catches my eye. She's arm-in-arm with another girl at the finishing line. They're wearing pink costume wigs and silly grins. I'm impressed. I wonder how much they raised for the charity. I keep meaning to sign up for an event. A 5k walk or something. I'm sure Loulou and Tina would join me. If I asked nicely.

On the sideboard, more photos of Connie and Lily fill the space, none of Daniel, well they are divorced. But then right at the back, I spy a picture of a young Daniel and Aliki. I reach out for it, it bashes against another photograph, the ripple effect knocking several neighbouring frames in succession. Great. I've only been here five minutes and already I'm causing chaos. I glance over my shoulder nervously as I prop them all back up haphazardly, the centrepiece safely in my left hand.

"That was taken in our dancing days," Aliki says, returning with two tumblers and a bowl of nuts. The sofa hisses under her weight, inflating the seat next to her. I study the photograph to the backdrop of brandy glugging into tumblers. They look like a couple of *Strictly* contestants. Aliki's in a short, sparkly little number and Daniel's wearing a red satin shirt, open to the waist and tight black trousers. He actually looks pretty hot. And my God! Aliki looks bloody amazing, so slender, so fit.

"I didn't know Daniel dabbled in dancing." It seems like there's a lot about him I don't know.

"Dabbled?" Aliki laughs heartily. "We were regional champions back in the day, three years on the trot. No one could match our

NO WAY BACK

Argentine Tango." No wonder Daniel walks with such grace. She takes a swig of brandy and winces. "This is strong stuff, but good. Here." I take the tumbler from her hand and sit down next to her. "Yiamas." Our glasses clink, crystal.

I can't believe that Daniel's ex-wife and I are sitting here sharing a drink together. It does feel a bit *Fatal-Attractioney*. "Excuse the mess," she groans, grabbing a handful of nuts. "We're decorating upstairs." Ah, so that's what it is. Why didn't I think of that? "Of course," she goes on, munching on the nuts and gesturing at the photograph, "Daniel managed to keep trim by exercising, unlike me!" I follow her eyes to her round body. "Too many Koubes and Lokmathes, I'm afraid. I love my food, as you can see." She's very self- deprecating. I'm beginning to warm to her.

"You're not overweight." I throw her a nervy smile. "You have had a child. I know it was close to thirty years ago, but still."

She raises her eyebrows. It was a stupid thing to say. I don't know why I said it. I'm nervous. "Anyway," she says brightly, "what can I do for you?"

Swallowing hard, I get straight to the point. I was at Daniel's flat waiting for Connie's delivery. I had a look at some photos in an envelope, just to pass the time. He came home unexpectedly, caught me, and went into a rage. We rowed and I ran out of his flat.

"Yes," she says once I've stopped talking, "Daniel said. He rang not long ago, just to say he won't be taking the kids out for pizza, after all." Kids? Connie's nearly thirty. I can see that she's spoilt rotten by both parents. "He also mentioned the fallout." The phone trills in the background and my heart skips a beat. I hope it's not him.

"It's just that he acted so out of character, went into a complete rage and over what? A few crumpled photographs and a couple of Connie's childhood drawings. I mean, you of all people know what he's usually like. He really took me by surprise, do you know what I mean?" I pause but she doesn't say anything. "I shouldn't have gone through his things, I know, but..." I falter, deciding quickly that she doesn't need to know about my quirky tidiness, particularly as her place is so chaotic at the moment.

She takes a big glug of air; her large chest rises and falls. "He said you were reading his stuff, Audrey. His personal things." She doesn't look at me when she says this.

"No," I insist, shaking my head. "I didn't read anything personal, I promise. I just saw a few photographs and the sketches, that's all." I cluck my tongue, irritated. "I didn't even want to go there in the first place." I complain, twirling the amber liquid in my glass clockwise. I take a large sip. It burns my mouth, then slides down my throat, awakening each fibre in my body. The way I feel right now, I could down the whole frigging lot in one. But I don't want Aliki to think I'm an alcoholic. "If only you'd gone there as planned this never would've happened," I say dryly.

"Gone where?"

"To Daniel's flat." There's a hint of confusion in her eyes. "You know, to wait for the delivery?" I frown at her now. "Connie said she asked you first but you had a last-minute emergency."

"Aliki, mou." There's a gentle tap at the door and then Despina's face peers around it. She's holding the phone. "Telephono." Aliki frowns, sticks her hand out, fingers erect and gives her wrist a quick, sharp twist. I know what that hand gesture means, "*who is it or what's up*". I picked up a few Cypriot gestures from Maria, Mum's cleaner, when I was in Cyprus.

Despina covers the mouthpiece and whispers, "Ei poutana." Now, I think I stayed in Cyprus long enough to know that the word poutana means prostitute, and I do hope she's not talking about me!

Aliki gives her a puzzled look, "What poutana?" I cover my mouth, squeezing in a laugh. How many sluts does Aliki befriend?

"Afti ie shillobelli," Despina whispers.

Aliki looks at her mother blankly, then glances at me. "That means mad bitch, by the way. My mother has such a way with words."

"Ie Kalamarou," Despina hisses.

"Oh Mamma," Aliki says in exasperation, "tell Melina I'll call her back in half an hour." And with pursed lips the old lady rocks her head from side to side (something Maria would do behind her supervisor's back when she was narked with her), and walks off mumbling into the phone. "Sorry, that's my brother's wife – Mum's not that keen." She rolls her eyes, "I bet you picked up a few swear words in Cyprus." I smile and tell her that I did – poutana being one of them. "Melina had a brief affair with a colleague a few years ago. Mum can't forgive her."

"Oh, I see. I'm sorry."

"Don't be, they got through it. Besides, my brother Vas is no saint, he had it coming." She sucks her lips in. "But people are always quick to judge the woman, aren't they?" I give her a thin smile and a little nod. I'm not sure what else to say.

"Melina? That's Greek isn't it?" My stomach gives a low rumble; I reach out and help myself to some nuts. Aliki pushes the bowl closer to me, telling me that Melina is from Greece. "Same difference, isn't it? You speak the same language."

"I can't understand a bloody word she says," she grumbles. "They speak Modern Greek whereas we speak Ancient Greek. Nah, we just stick to English, much easier. Anyway," she continues briskly wiping her salty fingers on her legging-clad thighs, "where were we? Oh yes, the delivery." Her eyes close briefly. "Sorry, you caught me off-guard. I've a mind like a sieve nowadays – menopause. But, yes, I had a last-minute appointment with a client."

She's gone a bit red. I wonder if it's the brandy or if she's lying. I don't challenge her. I haven't got time for mind games.

"Look, Daniel's a good man, Audrey." She places her glass on the table and swivels towards me. My mobile rings in my bag. I let it go to answerphone. "He'd do anything to protect his family, but he really does care about you. He was in pieces when he called earlier." Clearly, she's well and truly over him. Either that or this woman is a saint. I can see now why Daniel fell in love with her, why she's still a big part of his life. The familiar ding of a message goes off in my bag, I ignore it.

"I don't think it's working out, Aliki. I –" I falter, twisting a strand of hair around my finger.

Her shoulders sag. "Do you think he's moving too fast? Is that it?" I stay silent. "I thought that too when I first met him." Rubbing her lips, she stares ahead. "Daniel's a proactive, impulsive man. How else do you think we built up our successful business? Sure I had all the contacts but he was the driving force behind it. This afternoon was a one-off. He hardly ever lost his temper during our marriage." She picks her glass up. "I presume that's why you're here…to find out why he flew off the handle. If it's a regular thing. It isn't."

I want to scream at her. I want to shake her by the shoulders and ask her why she divorced him if he's so bloody perfect. I focus on a yellowing pot plant instead. An image of Daniel's face, twisted in fury, flashes before me. "But what was it that he didn't want me to see, Aliki? Is there something I should know?"

Her hand flies up like a buckler. "Audrey, you've got to talk to Daniel about that." So there is! I was right. My phone starts throbbing with a call again. Aliki glances down at my bag. "Someone's keen to talk to you." I plunge my hand into my bag irritably, whip out the phone and switch it off without even looking at the screen.

NO WAY BACK

"Please, Aliki."

"Look." She exhales heavily, her face softening, "I won't lie, Connie's his priority – his life. They're very close. Anything else he'll have to tell you himself." Well, thank you very much, Aliki, for stating the obvious.

"So, there is something else, then?" I probe. She doesn't answer. Then suddenly it dawns on me. I lean forward, my eyes narrow. "You would tell me if there was another woman involved, wouldn't you?"

"Please, Audrey." I can hear the annoyance in her voice. She wants me to stop. "I really can't help you anymore." She leaps out of her seat. My cue to leave.

"Thanks for the drink, Aliki." Cleary, I'm wasting my time here. Aliki isn't going to spill the beans on Daniel. I drain my glass. "And for your time. Say bye to your mum and Lily for me please." I get to my feet, she follows me to the door. "Oh, and by the way, that picture I saw at his flat," I say in *Columbo* style. "You looked so different in that one compared to the one in there." I motion at the photograph of them on the sideboard. There's a long pause before she speaks again.

"People change," she says briskly, not meeting my gaze. "Time can be cruel to some of us."

And as the door closes behind me, Daniel's big, dark secret wraps itself around me like a haunting mist.

From an open car window, Ed Sheeran's *Shape of You* blasts into the street as I hurry down the slope, trying to piece the jigsaw together. That old snapshot I saw of a happy family at Daniel's apartment today wasn't of him with Aliki and Connie. It was a different family altogether. He must've been married before. Somewhere there is another wife and another child. I've been played like a *Stradivarius*. The beep of a car horn startles me. I look around and almost scream when I see Nick's red VW Passat crawling along the pavement. Oh fucking hell, how did he find me? Has he been following me? I start walking faster, face hot with fury. The horn beeps again.

"Audrey!" The car stops next to me, window half open, engine still running. I narrow my eyes at the driver. It's Ronan.

CHAPTER 29

I WALK OVER AND RONAN BUZZES DOWN HIS WINDOW. He looks different. He's shaved off all his hair and now sports a neat ginger goatee. He actually looks pretty cool.

"Ronan, what are you doing here?"

"I just dropped Nick's new girlfriend off up the road." Connie, I presume. My face tightens. "They had some kind of bust-up and he stormed off, said he had to see Gerry about something. I walked in right in the thick of it. He just threw his car keys at me and told me to sort it out. Good job I've got quick reflexes, eh?" He laughs. I think he's had his teeth whitened too. "You know what he's like," he adds, and I nod, wordless because I fear if I open my mouth to speak I'll start blubbering on the pavement. "The girl was in floods of tears. He was a bit harsh with her, actually, probably a lover's tiff." I grimace in silence. "Anyway, what are you doing in this neck of the woods? Want a ride home?" I'm cold, tired and hungry, and it's starting to drizzle. I get in.

We're on our second bottle of wine and I'm definitely feeling it. My phone rang endlessly the moment we walked through the door so I pulled it out of its socket. Tonight I just want to be left alone to moan, wail, and get sloshed with Ronan.

We're curled up on my sofa with the TV sound on low. Ronan has spent the last hour pouring his heart out to me. He's left Catherine, they've started divorce proceedings. They tried hard to make it work but couldn't. It's getting ugly. He's been sleeping in the spare room for the last three weeks – he thinks she's back with her lover, reckons she never let him go.

"She's even blocked me on Facebook," he complains, munching on a packet of ready salted crisps. Neither of us has eaten and as I haven't had time to do a shop this week, crisps, nuts and an out-of-date packet of Twiglets were all I could find in the cupboard.

"Can you honestly believe that?" He shakes his head, "If it wasn't for the kids, I'd cut all ties. But I don't want them to suffer. I don't want them caught up in the crossfire. Do you know what I mean?"

He stuffs several crisps in his mouth at once. I glance at the TV screen. *Corrie's* just started, I wonder if he'd mind us watching it. "Leaving them this morning was absolute hell." I'll watch it on ITV-Plus later. "To think that I won't be seeing them every day, won't be tucking them in bed at night, playing with them in the park." His thin lips wobble. "I just sat in the airport lounge and couldn't stop crying, Audrey."

I grab the remote control and change channels, I don't want any spoilers. Ronan glances at the flickering screen as he opens the last packet of *Quavers*. Between us, we've devoured half a dozen packets of snacks. My coffee table looks like it belongs in *The Maid of Muswell* down the road.

"So, anyway," he says, popping a Quaver into his mouth and offering one to me, "how're things with you? I heard you got yourself a new beau." He laughs lightly, "Rich and successful, eh?" He nudges me gently with his elbow, munching. I feel a pang in the pit of my stomach. If only he knew. Funny what can happen in twenty-four hours. This morning I had a wonderful man in my life, I'd rekindled my friendship with my ex, and was even bonding with my partner's rogue of a daughter; everything was softly falling into place. Now I feel empty, lonely and miserable.

NO WAY BACK

"Actually, it's not working out, Ronan." I scramble to the edge of my seat and reach for my wine glass.

"Oh." His face drops, Quaver in mid-air. "I'm sorry; I didn't mean to be flippant. Nick didn't say."

"Nick doesn't know. In fact, I haven't even told Daniel yet." I give a little incredulous laugh. "I mean, technically we're still together but the row we just had was a bit explosive." I take a large gulp of wine, "There's no going back from this. I'm going to call him later and end it."

There's a brief moment of silence. A car revs up outside, the familiar sound of next-door-but-one's alarm goes off in the distance, it's always on the blink. Then Ronan says, "Are you sure that's what you want? You look pretty damned upset to me." He narrows his eyes. "This isn't about Nick, is it?"

"Oh God, no." I shake my head. "Daniel's just got too much baggage, that's all. It's draining me, and I saw a side to him today that I didn't really like. I can't handle it anymore. I think he just caught me on the rebound, to be honest. I'm not ready for another serious relationship."

"Have you known him long?" He puts down his crisp packet and picks up his wine glass.

"No, not really, but I've spent a lot of time with him during our short relationship." I stare at the TV screen, there's a documentary on about sea creatures which I'm finding deeply hypnotic.

"Maybe you should just slow things down a bit." He strokes my back gently, kindly. "Give it a chance."

"No," I snap, recoiling. "I feel suffocated, Ronan, it's all happening too fast. I should never have got involved with someone so soon, I wasn't ready." He looks at me for a while in silence, hand still stroking my back, alarm still beeping in the distance.

"Oh, come here." He pulls me into his arms. "What are we like, hey?" I lay my head on his chest, he smells of tobacco and spicy cologne. "Why can't life be simple, eh? Why does it have to have so many twists and turns and hurdles?"

I stare at a dolphin on the TV, listening to Ronan's heart thumping against my face – lubdub lubdub lubdub. "Anyway," he says suddenly. My head bobs on his chest as he fills his lungs. "At least you and Nick are talking again." There's an octopus now on the screen surrounded by colourful fish. "He said you've both moved on now. He'll be upset to hear your news, I'm sure." He curls my hair around his fingers. Nick won't be upset at all. He's got Connie to keep his bed warm now. My stomach clenches. I pull away. I need to sober up.

"Coffee?" I offer.

Ronan nods, eyes fixed on me. "You okay?"

I look at him for a while, wordless. I don't tell him that the girl he gave a lift home to tonight is Daniel's daughter, that Nick went behind my back and slept with her when he promised me he'd stay away. That he couldn't do this one thing for me. "Yes," I say eventually. "I'm fine. I'll stick the kettle on." A sudden attack of vertigo hits me as I get to my feet and I sit back down, the room spins.

"I'm sorry," I say, holding his forearm tightly, "too much wine." Getting plastered this evening wasn't such a good idea after all, especially as I have to be in the office by 9 a.m. tomorrow for a meeting.

"It's okay," he whispers, putting his arm around me, "don't apologise." Then as I turn to look at him he kisses me lightly on the lips. I look into his big blue eyes, glazed with lust. We've both had too much to drink. We've both been horribly let down. I kiss him back, slowly at first but then hard and passionately. He slips his hand under my sheer cream blouse and undoes my bra, his

NO WAY BACK

right hand cups my breast. Then he unbuckles his belt and I sit astride him, pulling my blouse over my head hurriedly. My mouth finds his again and we kiss wildly, madly.

And this time, we don't pull apart. This time, we don't stop to consider others. This time, we don't think at all.

CHAPTER 30

THE RINGING IS INSISTENT. Brrr, brrr, BRRRRRRR. Someone is banging their fist so hard on my front door, I can feel the vibration pounding against my skull.

A small voice in the distance is calling out my name. Opening one eye, I focus on the alarm clock. 9.26. Oh shit! I throw the sheets back quickly. I should've been at work an hour ago. I try to swallow but the roof of my mouth feels as if it's about to crack into a thousand pieces. I can't believe I slept through my alarm clock. It's unheard of for me. I'll have to ring for a cab now, and hope to God that I can fob Raymond off with a good excuse for turning up two hours late.

The cool morning air wafts over my bare body as the pressure over my right eye slowly makes its sad journey across my head, sabotaging any notion I had of getting out of bed. What happened last night? How much did I have to drink, for goodness sake? Then suddenly it hits me. Oh, fucking hell, I had sex with Ronan. Shit. Shit. SHIT! I sit up too quickly and the room spins. I think I'm going to vomit.

"Audrey!" The banging and ringing is getting louder and louder. "Audrey." More banging and ringing. "It's me. Are you okay? Open the door. Audrey!" Swallowing back the bile, I slowly crawl out of bed, grab my dressing gown and shuffle to the front door. I can see Jess's silhouette through the patterned pane. "I've been ringing for the last ten minutes." She storms into the hallway, red-faced.

"It's almost nine-thirty, what're you still doing in bed? You look dreadful, by the way."

"Oh my God, Jess." I pull my dressing gown around me hurriedly as I walk along the hallway, tying the belt at my waist. "I was supposed to be at work ages ago." I hold my throbbing head, my heart pounds. "Will you ring the office for me, tell them I'm ill? We had a board meeting to discuss sales figures and two new clients. Shit. SHIT. Raymond is going to bloody well kill me."

"I already have!" Jess says, pulling her Beanie off her head. My heart does a tiny little leap of hope. She must've guessed that I wasn't well, called in sick for me. "I tried calling you at work first but they said you hadn't turned up. Then I called your home, your mobile." My shoulders sag, she was calling around looking for me. "I had to come round, in the end. I thought something might've happened." Damn. I'd forgotten to turn my mobile phone back on after I left Aliki's yesterday evening, and my landline is still unplugged.

Jess looks at me worriedly, "You okay? You look rough." She drops her holdall by the lounge door and places a hand on my shoulder, sniffing the air. "And you stink of booze."

I pull an exasperated face, admit that I had a bit too much to drink last night, but assure her that I'll be fine after a shower and a cup of tea. "Going somewhere?" I murmur, giving her holdall an absentminded glance.

"Well, where to start?" She unwinds her grey scarf from her neck. "The noise in the house is unbearable. Mum and Gerry are at each other's throats most of the time." She slips out of her biker jacket, "Mum's talking about adoption again. Did she tell you?" I shake my head and she rolls her eyes. "Well, I say talking but it's more like screaming. And she wants rid of poor old Roxy. I've fallen in love with that dog."

"Oh, no," I say, "that's not good."

"I know," she cries, barely drawing breath, "And if all that wasn't bad enough, Francesca, you know, Gerry's diva twin?"

"Oh, yes," I nod and my head hurts.

"Yeah, well, she's flying in from Paris this evening with one of her sprogs."

"Already? I thought she wasn't due for another week."

"Yeah, it was a last-minute thing. Change of plans or something. Anyway, I can't study with that lot in the house, obvs. So I thought I'd stay here. It'll only be for a few nights until she goes back. Is that okay, Aud?"

"What about Sky?"

"No can do," she sighs, hanging her jacket on the coat rail. "Besides, we'd never get any work done if I stayed there."

I lean against the wall, arms folded, as she straightens her grey hoodie top and ruffles her dark hair. "What kind of name is Sky, anyway? It can't be his real name."

"It is. Kind of." She thumbs over her mobile phone, "Family name is Dobransky, they're Slovakian. Which one's your ISP?"

"SKYE506E." I clear my throat. I feel as if I've swallowed a ball of wool.

"What about your password?"

"Vixen A1," I say. She glances up at me briefly, grinning. "Funny how you haven't introduced us to Sky," I comment.

She stops fiddling with her phone and looks at me, "Er…dear kettle, yours sincerely pot."

"Huh?"

"Daniel?" she retorts, giving me a look that says, "are you a complete doughnut?"

"That's different," I hit back quickly, "Daniel's busy. He's got a family, a business to run." She raises her eyebrows at me incredulously then returns to her phone with a "whatever" expression.

"So," I go on, nudging her arm, "is he a lot older than you, then?" She doesn't answer. "He's not your teacher is he?"

"Noooowaah," she snaps, eyes not leaving her phone, "we're both students."

"Okaaay." I gather the lapels of my dressing gown close to my chest and lean forward on my toe, wondering what's so fascinating about the text she's reading. "He's not married, is he?"

"No, Audrey!" She closes the screen down quickly. "I'm not stupid, you know. My God, you're beginning to sound like my mother! Jeez, Daniel's got you tied up in knots. I think I preferred you when you were with Nick."

"What?" I ask, chasing after her as she storms into the kitchen.

"You were less stressed out when you were with him - easy going. Fun!" She wrenches the fridge door open. I'm speechless. "So?" she demands, shaking a carton of orange juice at me. I look at her blankly. "Can I stay, then?" she asks, carton in mid-air.

"Yes, yes, of course," I wave a hand. "The bed's already made up in the spare room." I push my hair off my face and take a deep breath. "I'll just sort myself out with a couple of paracetamol and a shower then give your mum a call. Find out what's going on."

"She's not in," she says lightly, wiping her mouth with the back of her hand. "Tina had the morning off and they've gone to see some boring rom-com at the cinema." She rolls her eyes as she turns on the tap.

"At this hour?" I ask to the drum of water hitting the stainless steel sink.

"Tell me about it," she mutters. "Tina had an early bird two-for-one offer and wanted to treat Mum."

I follow her into the lounge, glass of water in one hand, two paracetamol in the other. "OMG, what's been going on in here?" She looks around the room wildly. The coffee table is strewn with empty wine bottles, half-filled glasses, and crumpled crisp packets. My shoes are lying haphazardly in the middle of the room and my blouse is hanging off the lampshade on the side table. "Someone had fun last night." Jess scoops something off the floor. I stare in horror as she dangles my black lacy bra on the tip of her index finger. "No wonder you look so rough."

I snatch the bra out of her hand and demand that she calls my office with a good excuse.

"Wow, that Daniel is red hot, man." She steps over my red *Prada* pumps, reaching for the phone, "For an oldie, that is," she grins, then holds the receiver away from her ear, pokerfaced. "The phone's dead."

Scrambling on my knees, I plug the main phone back into the socket. My head is throbbing like a low, dreary base beat in the depths of a dingy R&B nightclub.

"Oh, yeah, there's a dialling tone now," Jess confirms. "What's the number again?" She punches in the digits as I call them out. "I think mum and Gerry were arguing over adoption again. Oh, it's ringing," she says excitedly. "You do know that Gerry isn't keen, don't you? Oh hello, Stacey, it's Jess Miller again. Yeah, I'm fine, thanks…listen, just to let you know that Audrey isn't well and won't be in today. Oh, no, no, she's okay, she's just got…erm…her period."

"Jess!" I hiss, stamping my foot.

"What?" she whispers, covering the mouthpiece, "You still have them don't you? Yeah, Stacey, sorry, cat just got under my foot." Oh, God, I close my eyes and hold my aching head. "Oh, didn't you know? It's a rescue cat. Yeah, I know. She's only had it a few weeks. Yeah, okay, will do…bye."

"A cat?" I say in exasperation.

"It's the first thing that came to mind. Audrey, babe, just chill, will you. She bought it and she now thinks you're a heroine." I'm too ill to argue.

"What did she say?"

"Get well soon and don't worry about work."

I drag myself into my bedroom on a mobile phone search. It's not in my bag or in its usual place on the bedside table. Damn. My hands find my hips as I survey the room. Where the hell did I put it? Drumming my fingers against my lips, I suddenly remember that during our short session of acrobatic random sex yesterday evening my bag flew off the settee and landed on the floor, spilling a few of the contents. I totter back into the living room where Jess has made herself at home, feet on coffee table, laptop on her patterned legging-clad thighs. I bend down and she lifts her feet up.

"Lost something?"

"Yes, my phone." I stick my head under the sofa, and there, amongst my lipstick, two sanitary towels and a packet of chewing gum, my mobile phone beams. I scoop them all up in my arms and get to my feet, panting, hair wild. "What're you watching?" I sit down heavily next to her and switch on my phone. Within seconds it starts bleeping with messages and missed call notifications from Daniel, Nick, Louise, Stacey, Jess, Mum and …Ronan.

"Just something a friend from Uni sent me on YouTube. It's so funny you should…" But I'm not listening to her anymore; all I can hear is the soundtrack of laughter coming from the laptop and Ronan's voice.

"Hi Audrey. Sorry to call so early but, well…hope you're okay, and…er…just wanted to say that when I left yours yesterday I picked

Nick up from Gerry's and...erm...we had a bit of a heart to heart in the car and..." His voice is heavy, remorseful. "I didn't realise he was still in love with you." I frown, yeah right. "I thought you two were over. I just saw that girl getting dressed in his room and put two and two together. ...and oh, Jesus, Audrey, I just feel so bloody guilty now." Guilty? What's he on about? "I don't know how you're feeling, probably the same." The same? "Look, I'd better go. I'll try you again later. Bye for now."

I stuff the phone into my dressing gown pocket angrily. Guilty? I can't believe he said that. Is that what I am? A guilty mistake? Not that I want a relationship with Ronan or anything, but still. Has he forgotten what Nick and Catherine did to us? I look at Jess, chewing the inside of my bottom lip.

"Were Nick and Ronan round yours last night?"

"Yeah," she says, her eyes not leaving the screen, she's now playing a game of Words with Friends. "Saw Nick going in just as I was leaving. Don't know about Ronan though, doesn't he live in Scotland?"

"Ireland," I say dryly. "Actually, I could murder a cup of tea, Jess." She springs to her feet and hands me the laptop.

"Two sweeteners, right?" I nod, tell her they're in the cabinet next to the hob. "Here, you can surf while I make them." How kind of her to allow me to borrow my own laptop.

I sit back and stare at an ad that's just popped up on the screen. Guilty? I shake my head.

As soon as I sign into Facebook the orange icon appears like a beacon in the corner of the page. It's from Nick:

Hi Audrey, I know that you won't reply to my text messages or answer my calls but I need to explain what happened yesterday with Connie. I didn't sleep with her. I kept my promise. That day when we were waiting for you outside your flat, we got talking. She told me she grew up in Crouch End and I said that's where I live, she asked me where - I told her. She then got excited and said a friend of hers lives on Nelson Road, what number was I? The next thing I knew she was on my doorstep telling me she was just passing and wanted to say 'hello'. She practically forced herself in for a coffee. Anyway, when I went off to the kitchen to make the drinks she stripped and got into my bed. Then the doorbell rang and you know the rest. I knew you'd get the wrong idea if you saw her at mine; that's why I tried to hide her. I didn't bloody know what she was up to. I was just as surprised as you were. Nothing happened, I swear on my mother's grave. I didn't have sex with her. I didn't do ANYTHING with her. When you left I had a right go at her and told her to do one. Ronan took her home, he's visiting, long story. Anyway, I just want you to know I'd never do anything to hurt you again. Ever. Love. Nick X.

I slam the laptop shut, face boiling, as Jess appears with two steaming mugs of tea. I twist my lips thoughtfully. Surely, he can't be telling the truth…can he? Connie. There was a message from Connie on my voicemail. I quickly retrieve her message as Jess whips the laptop off me, all the while droning on about how their house has turned into a bloody hotel. Connie's voice is loud and clear on the voicemail.

"Hi Audrey, it's me. Obviously, you don't want to talk or your phone's in your bag, as per. Whatever. Anyway, I wanted to say that Nick got really narky and went all weird on me…" I can hear her taking a long drag on a cigarette. *"He made me promise to call you and explain. Well, I'm calling but you're not…"* the line goes fuzzy, oh crap, not now, *"and I wanted to but he didn't…haha. Is he gay or something? Look, I don't know what's going on between you two but my dad thinks the world of you so… just don't hurt him, okay. Oh, and thanks a bunch for spoiling his birthday surprise, by the way, it's off now. Laters."*

"Shit, fuck. Shit"!"

Jess gives me a curious sideways glance, then turns her lips downwards and nods. "Nice choice of expletives."

"Sorry, Jess." I take a gulp of tea. The heat scolds my mouth.

"Hey, take it easy, tiger," she says, the glare of the screen lighting up her fresh, smooth, rosy-cheeked face. "That's bloody boiling."

My hands tremble as I retrieve Daniel's voicemail.

Audrey, where the hell are you, for heaven's sake?" he sighs heavily, *"I've been calling and texting you for the last hour. You should be home by now."* More sighs, *"I'm sick with worry."* A heavy pause. *"Look, I'm sorry about what happened at my flat. I really mean it. We need to talk. I want to explain. I spoke to Aliki, she told me you went round. I promise you on Lily's life, there's no one else. But Aliki's right. I need to tell you everything about my past. Just call me. PLEASE. I don't want to lose you."*

Later, as I take a shower, washing away my infidelity, I think about what I've done. I shouldn't have had sex with Ronan last night. He's right, it was a mistake. We were drunk. I was upset. Daniel had been so harsh with me, lying to me, playing me. And then there was Nick sleeping with Connie, well at least that's what I thought at the time. Oh, hell, it's *all* such a mess.

I turn the shower off and lower my dripping body onto the bathmat, guilt seeping through the pores of my skin, so powerful, almost asphyxiating. I dry myself off, the steamed mirror in front of me masking my shame. I can't even look at myself. It felt all right when I thought that Nick had slept with Connie, when I thought Daniel had another woman on the go, a mistress, an ex.

Now I just feel like a vindictive cow. I've got to talk to someone. My first thought is Louise but I can't burden her with my problems now, she's got enough on her plate, what with Gerry and the adoption and Francesca visiting. And how will Tina react if I tell her that I shagged her ex-boyfriend last night? I decide very quickly that there's only one person that can help me. One person who won't judge me.

CHAPTER 31

"OH, VICKY," I sob into her red cardigan, "what've I done?" We're sitting on her worse-for-wear blue fabric three-seater sofa, which also doubles up as a trampoline for the kids.

"Shhhh," she soothes, stroking my hair, "it'll be all right. It was just a buddy-shag, that's all."

"A what?" I sniff, pulling away from her, "I don't do those."

"Well, a one-night stand, then." A pink tinge sweeps over her face as she leans over and refills my mug from the cafetiere. Vicky never has instant coffee, which is a bit of a nuisance when she comes round to mine because that's all I have.

"Oh, Vicky." I rub a hand over my face. "If only I could highlight the last twenty-four hours and press delete."

"If only," she smiles. "What're you going to do about Daniel?" She leans back and curls her legs beneath her on the sofa.

"I'm seeing him on Sunday," I sigh. I called him on my way here, agreed that we should meet-up and talk. "He says he wants to explain. I owe him that at least." She nods thoughtfully, says at least that gives me a couple of days to sort my head out.

"Are you going to tell him about, you know, what happened?"

"That I was unfaithful to him, you mean?" I say rhetorically. "There's no need. I've decided to call it a day with him, anyway. It's not working out. There's no point in hurting him anymore." Vicky's eyebrows rise and fall.

"Shame, he seems like a pretty decent guy." She takes a sip of

NO WAY BACK

coffee. "Am I allowed to ask why?"

"I'm not right for him. We're not right for each other. We just don't fit. He's just too intense, fast-moving. I mean I like him, but…" I trail off.

"And what about Nick?" She eyes me carefully over her coffee mug.

"What about him?"

She puts her mug down and takes my hands. "Look at me." I lift my head and meet her gaze. "You know you're like a sister to me, don't you?" I nod, it's true, Vicky's been like the sister I never had, "and that I only want what's best for you?"

"Yes, of course, I do." I look at her searchingly. Where are we going with this?

"Okay." She takes a long breath through her nose. "Are you sure that Daniel isn't just a smokescreen? That you're still in love with Nick, that -"

"No, no, NO!" I cut across her sharply and pull my hands away, leaping out of my seat. "I care about Daniel." Her eyes widen. "I do!"

"Then why are you dumping him at the first hurdle, hmmm?"

I start pacing up and down, wringing my hands. "Because… because of other stuff. He's got too much baggage. He's too full-on, suffocating. And God knows what bombshell he's going to drop on me tomorrow. And he's got a temper on him." I run a hand through my hair, "I don't need all that. I've had enough of being lied to by men."

"I mean, let's face it," she exhales loudly, ignoring everything I've just said. "Nick only strayed with…" She waits for me to fill in the gap.

"I dunno." I throw my hand up haphazardly and look out of the window at the thick, grey skies. "Some girl he met in a pub."

"Well, anyway, you were actually on a break when he went off with pub-prossy. As far as he was concerned you two were over. It's not entirely his fault she fell pregnant, is it? It does happen. Spontaneous sex, I mean, especially if you're half-cut, as you know." She leans forward and adjusts the baby monitor on the table in front of her, glancing up at the clock on the wall. It's a quarter to two. "I'll have to wake them soon or they'll be up all night, and I need to take my meds." I nod, wordless, arms folded.

"He could've used something," I protest as she pushes her feet into her slippers.

"Well, we're not all as sensible as you, are we?" She gets to her feet, we're face to face. "Won't be a minute."

"He messed me around, Vicks," I say into her back as she heads for the kitchen. "Then he left me, abandoned me."

"I know, love." She saunters towards me, pops a yellow pill into her mouth and necks a glug of water straight from the bottle.

"I can't just pretend it didn't happen." I rub my forehead, the painkillers are wearing off. "And now he's having a child with another woman."

"Some couples get through it." She shakes her slippers off and sits back down. "How many people do you know who have children with other partners?"

I let her words settle in my mind like fresh fallen snow, and then I say, "But even I was still in love with him, hypothetically speaking, that is! What if I can't love his child?" I look up at her desperately. "What if he doesn't love me with the same intensity once his baby is born? I'm scared, Vicks," I gulp. "My heart can't take any more punches."

"Well." She pushes my hair off my face gently, "Yes, Nick will divide his love between you and his child, but it's a different kind of love, honey. And as for loving his baby, remember, he or she is a

NO WAY BACK

part of Nick, and if you love him you'll…"

"No," I snap, feeling as if shutters have shot up around my heart. "I can't be doing with all that. If it was just an affair, a one-night stand." I wave a hand in the air as Ronan's face bounces into my mind. "Then maybe we could have worked things out, but this is too much." I close my eyes briefly. "I can't, Vicky, I just can't."

I'm almost home when my phone buzzes with a message from Louise – have I got time for a quick catch-up at *Strawberry Court Cafe* in Muswell Hill. I could do with another friendly ear. Much as I love and respect Vicky, I left there feeling more confused than ever.

Louise spots me as I walk in, stands up and waves madly. I weave through a few customers waiting at the till to the hiss of the coffee machine, the chime of the cash register. I can't wait to confess my infidelities to Louise, cleanse myself of this burden.

"Hey," Tina trills scrambling to her feet. Images of me and Ronan on the sofa flash before me as she gives me a warm hug. Damn, I didn't expect Tina to be here too.

"Hey, yourself." I unbutton my mac, giving them an inquisitive look. They're both brimming with delight. "What've you two been up to?"

"You'll never guess where this one took me this morning," Louise giggles, sitting back down next to Tina.

"Jess said you went to the cinema. What did you see?"

"What we saw were big, fat boobs!"

Tina gives Louise a playful slap on the hand. "Only one pair of boobs, Lou."

"You went to see a porn movie?"

They're now laughing so hard they can barely string a coherent sentence together. People at nearby tables are looking and smiling.

I wait out their bout of the giggles with a frozen smile. I hate that feeling of exclusion, you know, where friends are enjoying a joke which you can never be a part of, no matter how hard you try.

"No," Tina manages, between outbursts, "a woman feeding her baby."

"Oh, a nursing mum." What's so funny about that? I'm beginning to wish I'd gone straight home.

"She," Louise points at Tina, wiping away tears of mirth, "took me to a Newbie screening."

"A what?" I lean forward, trying hard to join in.

"Exactly," Louise says firmly, dabbing at her eyes with a *Strawberry Court* serviette.

"Oh, stop it, Louise, people are staring, you're going get us thrown out. It's for mothers with their new babies, that's all. But I didn't know, did I? We only found out when the usher told us that there may be a few new mothers in there with their babies and..."

"Audrey," Louise intervenes. I force a smile but all I can think about is what I did with Ronan. Each time I blink I can see his face, feel his touch, smell his scent. "We could barely hear the film because it was on low sound, the lights were on, prams everywhere." I'm glad she's seeing the funny side of it. That she's getting over her loss.

"So, were you okay, Lou, with all those new mums, I mean?" I look up and acknowledge a waitress as she places our drinks on the table.

"Actually, it's just what I needed," Louise says, smiling up at the waitress, "life goes on and all that." She spoons the froth off her coffee. "Besides, I've got some news!"

"Oh?" I search for a sachet of sweetener in the bowl. Tina checks for messages on her phone.

"We've decided to adopt again." So Jess was right. "And guess

NO WAY BACK

what?" she says excitedly. "There's a baby waiting."

"Blimey, that was quick." I'm dumbfounded. "I thought these procedures took ages."

"Well, we applied ages ago, didn't we?" She leans back in her seat, cup and saucer in hand. I want to tell her that it's too soon for her, she's still grieving for her loss, but I'm not sure if I can burst her bubble right now, she seems overjoyed.

"Great, isn't it?" Tina pipes up, slipping back into the loop of our conversation. "And I've got some news too. Guess who I saw last night?"

"Who?" I ask brightly, taking a sip from my cup.

"Ronan!" Oh, bloody hell! I want to die.

"Louise and I decided to go for a pizza yesterday evening. You know, the one on Park Road, anyway, when I dropped Lou back home I popped in for a bit and there he was, leaning against the doorpost looking handsomely dishevelled." Oh hell, if only she knew why. "He said he'd just popped over to pick Nick up." Her voice drops a few decibels, "He did say Nick had a new girlfriend." I press my fingers against my lips. I want to leave. "You are okay with that, babe, aren't you? I mean, now that you're with Daniel."

I tell her that I am. "I don't care who Nick goes out with." Just as long as it's not Connie, but I don't say that, obviously.

"Anyway," she goes on, "you should've seen him, Aud, you won't believe how much he's changed." Oh, I will, Tina, I will. "He's shaved his hair, grown a goatee. He's even had his teeth done. Phwoar, he was just dripping with sex appeal." Oh God, please make her stop.

"Really?" I feel a slight tremor in my voice. "Did he ask you out again?" I smile at a toddler who's wobbled up to our table. He stares back at me with a deadpan expression, twisting his left ear with one hand and clutching the leg of a worn-out teddy bear with the other. He knows. He can feel my tension. Children and animals have a sixth sense, don't they? I close my eyes and take a gulp of air. I'm being paranoid. I've got to pull myself together.

"Jensen, leave the ladies alone," says his mother, scooping him up in her arms and giving us an apologetic smile.

Tina smiles at the mother and then turns her attention back to me. "Nah, I only saw him for a few minutes, but I said I'd give him a call and he seemed REALLY pleased, didn't he Lou? We exchanged numbers."

"You do know he's still married," Louise replies cynically.

"Divorcing, babe."

"Yeah, well he's not divorced yet. You'd be the 'other woman' if you started dating him now." I give a nervous little chuckle. It's getting quite hot in here. Jensen has now thrown himself onto the floor and is screaming the place down.

"Oh, relax, Lou, will you." Tina winks at me as Jensen wails in the background.

"Oh, come on, enough about bloody Ronan," Louise interjects and I feel my muscles relax. "Is Jess okay with you for a few days, Audrey? Francesca will only be staying a week." I nod, tell her it's fine. "You okay? You seem a bit agitated. If it's a problem…"

"No, no, it's not Jess, that's fine." I begin, and then go on to tell them how Connie coaxed me into waiting for a delivery at Daniel's flat, how he went berserk when he found me there, and about my visit to Aliki's.

"Oh my God." Tina's hand shoots to her mouth, she's on the edge of her seat.

"That's awful, honey." Louise lays a hand on my arm, "No wonder you're so upset. And here's us babbling on about our good news. What're you going to do? I mean you don't really know the facts, do you? There might be a perfectly good explanation for all this."

NO WAY BACK

"Yes, but if he's lying to her already," Tina says, "I'd cut my losses if I were you, Hun." Tina's always been team Nick.

"Just give him a chance to explain before you make any rash decisions," Louise says, giving Tina an annoyed glance.

"So, what's the latest with Nick, Louise?" Tina asks "Has his slut had the baby yet? He looked well peeved last night."

"Tina!" Louise snaps, her face tight. "Audrey doesn't need reminding about what that bastard did to her." My stomach twists as Louise continues to slate Tina, her incipient fury bubbling away at the surface.

"Yeah, I know, I know." Tina holds up her hands. "Sorry, Audrey. That was a bit insensitive of me. I just got a bit carried away."

"Carried away?" Louise says incredulously, "You make it sound like it's…"

They're both talking at once, over each other, as if I were invisible, their voices louder and louder in my ears.

"Oh, will you please just shut the fuck up!" Shit, did I just say that out loud? A heavy silence hangs in the air, a stillness, as if someone has hit the pause button. They're both staring at me, mouths agape, cups in mid-air.

I inhale deeply, taking in the smell of fresh coffee. "Oh, God, I'm sorry," I mutter, pressing my palm against my forehead, "it's been a tough twenty-four hours. Of course, I'm not okay with Nick and the baby. But he's apologised and I've accepted. I don't want to keep talking about it."

Tina grins at her ringing mobile phone, Ronan, no doubt, by the look on her face. Louise looks at me gravely over her coffee cup, picking up on a vibe, and I deflate into my seat, shrinking into my shoulders – she knows me so well.

CHAPTER 32

"YOU LOOK TERRIBLE."

"That bad, huh? I've had a rough couple of days, haven't been sleeping well."

"Well, I can't stay long," I stress as we walk along the golden leafed path. I love Highgate Woods at this time of year, there's just something magical about it.

"I know," Nick says, sounding grateful, "Thank you for coming. And at such short notice too."

His text buzzed through this morning while I was still in bed having a much-needed Saturday morning lie in.

Can we meet in usual place at 12.30? It's urgent. :/ xx

I didn't have the heart to turn him down. It wasn't his fault that Connie turned up unannounced, was it? What was he supposed to do if she barged into his flat, throw her out onto the streets? That wouldn't have gone down well with me either.

We walk in companionable silence, leaves swishing around our feet. A sixty-something jogger trudges past in black shorts and worn out running shoes, his blue vest soaked in sweat, his grey, wiry hair damp against his leathered skin. Jesus, where does he get the energy from? I practically crawled out of bed this morning.

I fill my lungs with the earthy, foresty air. It's a great day for outdoor activities – sunny, warm, fresh.

"I'm seeing the neurologist on Tuesday," Nick says, breaking the silence, "for my headaches and…"

"Headaches?" I cut in. "You didn't say."

"Well, we don't really talk much these days, do we?" I stare at my feet rustling in the leaves. I knew I should've worn my wellies instead of these pointed knee-high *L.K. Bennet* boots – a gift from Daniel. He still buys me shoes, by the way, says it's an emblem of our union. I wonder how he's feeling now, distraught, no doubt. But at least tomorrow he'll have the opportunity to explain everything, put it all to bed. Then we can both move on, get on with our lives. "Anyway," Nick's voice wipes Daniel from my thoughts, "they started after the accident, they're quite bad sometimes." He rubs his temple.

I'm about to ask if he's having one now when a man's voice calls out "Spike! Spike, where are you?" A little grey, curly haired dog appears from the depths of the woods, lifts its leg up against a huge root exposed tree and wees all over the moss before bounding towards its owner. "Oh, there you are, Spike," the man bellows in the distance, "good boy."

"I told them all about my out of body experiences," Nick continues, as Spike totters off with his owner, "and they want to run tests."

"But you don't have them anymore, do you?"

"Wellll…" I stop walking and look at him. "I still astral project sometimes. But I just float close to the ceiling." He hovers his hand in mid-air, "Sometimes I go outside but I can't travel at will, like I did when I was in a coma. Like when I came to you in Cyprus." I don't answer. The last thing I want to do is encourage him.

We start walking again. "So what does that mean?" I clear my throat, trying to sound supportive.

"They reckon I'm hallucinating." Now that sounds more like it. "That the blow to the head has rattled things around. They probably think I'm bonkers," he laughs, throwing a glance at me.

"Seriously, though, my consultant thinks I'm having something called sleep paralysis. Do you know what that is?" I shake my head. "Okay." He licks his lips. "At a point during REM sleep, our brain stops sending signals to our voluntary muscles and they become paralysed, just so that we don't act out our dreams. For example, if your limbs weren't paralysed and you were dreaming that you were strangling someone you could actually wrap your hands around Daniel's neck," he chuckles, clearly enjoying the joke at Daniel's expense. "Well, with sleep paralysis you wake up during this state, and because your muscles are still paralysed you can't move or speak. They say that some people have hallucinations during these episodes, too."

"It sounds horrifying." We bear to the right, the path ahead is carpeted in crisp golden and amber leaves, the branches above us woven together like a heavenly arc, hissing in the wind to the warble of birds. "Will you be okay?"

"Yeah, course I will." He pulls his signature puzzled expression, but it doesn't irritate me this time, "It's nothing serious," he assures me, grinning kindly. He knows I still care.

We continue our trail in silence. I can't help wondering why he thought that telling me about his neurology appointment and dreams was so urgent, perhaps, he was just a bit frightened, wanted a friendly ear. The leaves are falling like snowflakes. It's all so peaceful, so beautiful, so calm, and then suddenly I feel something crawling on the top of my head.

"Arghhh, arghhh," I flap my hands about hysterically, an enormous spider making its way across my skull. "Get it off, get it off, arghhh."

Nick is convulsing with laughter. "Come here." He gently picks a twig out of my hair. "You're such a girl." He taps the tip of my nose endearingly and for a few moments, our eyes lock.

I smooth down the static mop on my head. "I didn't know what that was," I say defensively, looking away.

"A bat," Nick teases, while I protest that we *are* in the middle of the woods and that anything could be lurking around in here.

I tug at the collar of my top, "I'm hot," I complain.

"I've been telling you that for years."

"Oh, you know what I mean." I unbutton my mac, letting in the cool breeze.

"I'll get my shorts and flip flips out then, shall I? You know, cos I've got two left feet. That's what you always told me whenever we hit the dancefloor."

"Ha ha." I give him a playful slap on the arm and call him a numpty. I really miss our banter, his humour. Daniel is great company but his demeanour is more serious.

"I'm not hallucinating, you know," Nick says after a while, "I don't care how many tests they run. It really is happening. My spirit leaves my body. I can feel it, Foxy."

I laugh lightly. "Will someone please take away this imposter and bring back the real Nick Byrne?"

"I know," he sighs, as a dog barks in the distance, "bit rich coming from a cynic like me, isn't it?"

"Just a bit," I grin, scrunching my nose. "I suppose you're going to write a book next. I can just see it." I wave my hand across the air, "*There is Life After Death (even for cynics)* by Nick Byrne."

"You're not taking this seriously, are you?" he complains.

"Well, what do you expect?" We walk past a crowd of people at the kiosk. A little black dog looks up at Nick; a choccy Labrador trails around me.

Patting the dog's head, Nick smiles up at the owner, and then suddenly his eyes light up. "Oh wow, look at this table." He's spotted a photo opportunity, I recognise that eager look in his eyes, "What a beauty." He lets out a low whistle, stroking the wood. "It's made out of railway sleepers, you know."

I stop and look at the table. It's dark and stout with long bench seats on either side. There's an electric blue grubby thermos plonked in the middle that someone must've left behind, and, for all its beauty, it's smeared in mud and dried coffee.

"Very expensive wood, that is." He whips out his mobile phone and starts snapping. I knew it. "Just a few shots for Instagram."

I leave him in his glory and browse around. The smell of food wafting from the nearby restaurant reminds me that it's lunchtime. It's almost ten past one and, having missed breakfast, I'm starting to feel lightheaded.

"So, come on, then." I pull him away from the table and hurry him towards the field, arm threaded through his. "What is it that you feel when you have these out of body experiences?" I glance at a man approaching. He smiles at us as he warns his little girls not to step in the puddle. I suppose we look like a normal, happy couple to onlookers, enjoying the autumnal afternoon.

"It happens when I'm just nodding off or waking up," he begins as the little girls squeal happily in the distance. "I get this vibration running through my body and then I'm awake but I just feel paralysed. I can hear everything that's happening around me. The sound of traffic outside, the TV, Ronan wandering around opening and closing doors but I can't move or speak." I feel a sudden surge at the mention of Ronan's name. I still haven't spoken to him since that day. "Then I leap out of my body," he goes on, "glide towards the ceiling, spin around and watch myself sleeping."

"That sounds very scary!" I carefully curl my hair behind my ears. "What happens next?"

"After a while, I feel myself descending towards my body," he says excitedly, pleased that I'm showing an interest, "then there's

NO WAY BACK

the sound of my heartbeat as my soul slides through my skin and syncs with my body, and then the breath of life." He stares into the distance, lips slightly parted, spellbound. "And then I open my eyes."

"Jesus, Nick, where's all this coming from?" I grin at him, shaking my head. "Come on, spill. What is it, a chapter out of the latest James Herbert novel?"

"No!"

"Stephen King?"

"No, it's all true. And stop taking the piss, will you." He sounds annoyed. "I'm NOT winding you up. This means a lot to me. I'm a changed man." He gives me a sideward glance. "I'm having more and more telepathic incidences as well."

"What, you mean like when you dream of someone and then see them the next day, think about them and they call?"

"Yes, but mine are more profound." He drags his top lip between his teeth. "I told you all about my dream premonitions, didn't I?" I nod. "There's no way a scientist can explain that away, is there? I had one about you a few days ago." Right, he's really starting to creep me out now. "Do you want to know what it was about?"

"Go on then," I groan, humouring him.

"I saw you holding a gold coin in the palm of your hand. You looked, I dunno, it was kind of weird." He stops and inclines his head thoughtfully, gazing at the trees ahead, "I'm not sure if you were indecisive or upset, anyway." We start walking again. "Then I saw a flash of you losing the coin, a splash, a well of water. This is going to sound really weird, but you were crying on a toilet seat. Does that make any sense?"

"No, it doesn't! I don't usually cry on toilet seats," I laugh. "What happens to me next?"

"Nothing. I didn't see anything else. I'm not a bloody clairvoyant you know. But similar dreams I've had have come true so…"

"Well," I mutter, unconvinced, "sounds like another loss on the lottery for me tonight, then. The bathroom needs a clean too, that usually reduces me to tears, and MetOffice predict rain this evening." He knows that I play the lottery every week, he just dreamt of me buying a ticket and losing, as usual, the doughnut.

"No, no…you weren't even in this country. You seemed far away, somewhere warm and sunny."

Well, that's not going to happen for a start off. "There's no way I'm going on any more trips this year. I've taken all my leave."

"Ha, that's what you think, you just wait and see. I'm never wrong."

I bow my head, cover my mouth and try to suppress a giggle as he continues with his dream premonitions.

"Er, are you laughing at me?" He pulls my hand away from my mouth. "You are, aren't you?"

I try to cover my lips but he's too strong, he pulls my arms away, then starts tickling me. "Okay, okay, stop! I believe you!"

"Well, you can scoff all you like," he says, raking a hand through his hair, catching his breath. "I know what I saw. Here." He gestures at a bench, "Let's sit for a while." He slides a cigarette out of the packet and lights up. "Everything's changed now. My outlook, my values." He blows a cloud of smoke into the air and stares at it forlornly. "I wish I could turn the clock back." He reaches for my hand, his touch is electric. "I miss you."

"Nick," I warn, pulling my mac around me.

He clicks his tongue. "I know, I'm sorry."

I stare into the distance. A dad is kicking a football around with his two young children – a boy and a girl. They've used their bikes as goalposts. Dad used to take me and George to the park for a kick-about when we were kids. I'd score most of the goals, of course, George was useless at sports, and then he'd throw a tantrum. I can just see him now, throwing himself onto the grass and screaming at the top of his lungs. Sometimes, when I was in a good mood, I'd let him win, just to keep the peace.

"Well, I'm glad you've told me all this, thanks for keeping me in the loop." I lean forward and look at my watch. My stomach is rumbling. Dinner at Mum's isn't for hours yet. I really ought to eat something before I pass out. "And good luck with the neurologist. Text me, let me know how it goes."

"Actually, there is something else."

"Oh?" I say.

"She's had the baby." The thud of a football followed closely by a chorus of children cheering throws me. Did I just hear right? Did he just say that he's become a father? "It's a boy." I did. A shiver rips through me.

CHAPTER 33

"I SEE," I SAY STONILY as the wind blows my hair. So, that was the emergency, the urgency. Why he was so anxious to see me today. "And does *she* have a name, the mother of your child?"

He looks at me wordless for a few moments, face full of remorse, and then, "Yes, of course." He shakes his head, "It's…"

"Don't!" I raise my hand to stop the words from leaving his lips. I startle him but I don't care. If he tells me her name then she'll become a real person and no longer a nameless, soulless silhouette in my mind.

We're silent for a while. I watch the sixty-something jogger in the distance climbing the hill with fearless gusto and determination, then suddenly it hits me - that's how I should tackle this upheaval in my life. I won't let Nick or Daniel bring me down. I don't need a man in my life to be happy. I don't need to be anyone's wife or mother or partner to feel content. I lean my head back and stare up at the sky to the thump of a football and the soundtrack of foreign voices from a group nearby. "So," I say finally, as a boy ironically calls out "*Papa*", "Have you seen your son?"

He nods pensively. I imagine a bonny little boy, the spit of Nick, in a duck-egg blue woolly bobble hat, weensy mitts, and matching outfit. I can just see them, walking along Camden Lock - his son is in a harness and *her* on his arm, smiling contentedly. A happy family. "I'm arranging a paternity test," he says breaking my reverie. "I'm not giving her a penny until I see it in black and white." He flicks ash off his cigarette. I know we spoke briefly about whether he's the father or not, but it didn't occur to me that he had any real doubts in his mind. He seemed so convinced at the time.

"And if it's positive, what then?"

He shrugs. "Do the right thing, pick him up every other weekend, maintenance and all that."

"What about…*her?*"

"What about her?"

"Can't you try to make a go of it for the baby's sake, at least?"

He laughs. "You're joking, aren't you? She's bloody married for a start off." Oh, this just gets better and better.

"Well, if she's married then he might not be yours."

He takes a long drag on his cigarette. "Not much chance of that, I'm afraid. Her husband had the snip. They're separated now, going through a messy divorce. I'll probably be named and shamed."

"Oh, I see." The little girl playing football has just kicked the ball over her father's head and scored to the dismay of her younger brother.

"Anyway, I wanted to tell you myself, I know how quickly news travels," he says cynically.

"Oh, come on, Nick, Louise is my best friend, she tells me everything."

"If you say so," he scoffs.

"Stop it! Lou's a good friend. She's been there for me."

He raises his eyebrows. "Gerry's too good for her, she'd better watch it or else…"

"Or else what?" I ask, suddenly concerned. Does he know something? Is Louise's marriage in trouble?

"I'm just saying, that's all." Phew, just Nick having one of his Louise rants. It amazes me how much they loathe each other. "You okay?" He blows smoke from the side of his mouth. "You look a bit stressed."

"Yes." I run a hand over my face. I didn't expect the news of the birth to have such an impact on me. "Just tired. Look, I really should get going." I get to my feet and shoulder my bag.

"You will see me again, won't you?" he asks tentatively, stamping out his cigarette under his shoe. "The baby won't make any difference to our friendship, will it?"

I nod. "We'll see."

He stands up and takes my hands. "It kills me to say this but I hope that you and Daniel have a happy life together. I really mean it, Foxy." He squeezes my hands gently, his eyes fill. "I want you to be happy, I really do." He wipes the corner of his eye, blames it on hay fever, but we both know that's not true. "And I've heard he's a top bloke too," he sniffs.

"Yes, he is," I smile hesitantly. He doesn't need to know that we're estranged, it'll only give him false hope. "I'd better go. I've got a bathroom to clean, and Mum and Dad are expecting me for dinner. Chilli-con-carne night."

"I miss those family nights." He pulls me into a bear hug and I cling to him tightly, drowning in the familiarity of his scent, his touch, his breath. "I lost the love of my life when we broke up," he whispers into my hair, "but I also lost my best friend. I miss you so much."

I swallow back a big tear queuing at the back of my throat. I miss him too, more than he will ever know, but there's no way back for us, not now; everything has changed. He's got a son. I'm in a messy relationship with another man. I had sex with his cousin – his best friend.

"I love you, Audrey Fox." Our eyes lock, and then he leans forward, presses his forehead against mine. I close my eyes. "Always have, always will."

CHAPTER 34

THE NEXT MORNING, on my way to Daniel's flat to end it, second thoughts start creeping into my mind. I think about Nick and his son. I think about what Mum and Vicky said about Daniel last night as we cleared up after dinner – he's a good, decent, bloke, seems to care about me deeply; and whatever it is he wants to tell me about his past, his secret, might be something I can live with.

Okay, assuming that they're right, that's all good and well, but what about me and what I've done? Will he be able to live with my confession? Because if we're going to wipe the slate clean, if there's any future for us at all, then he needs to know about my one-night stand with Ronan.

"Come in, come in," Daniel says urgently, taking my raincoat. His flat is warm and bright and smells of freshly baked pastries. I didn't have time for breakfast, as per. My tummy rumbles. "I've bought some raspberry brioches from the bakery down the road, you know, those muffin shaped ones you like." His voice is dry, shaky. "Oh, and that reminds me, I've got some croissants warming in the oven too, better check on those." He limps over to the kitchen. "I thought you might be hungry. I know you're not big on breakfast. There's a pot of tea brewing too."

"What happened to your leg?" I ask, following him to the kitchen area.

"Ah." His tone is dismissive, "Achilles Tendinitis," he says, bending down to check on the croissants. "A sports injury." He straightens up, flushed. "From running." He seems uncharacteristically on edge, he hasn't even shaved, very unlike him. Whatever secret he's about to tell me must be quite a bombshell.

Over breakfast, we talk about Connie and Lily. He tells me that Connie has a talking part on *Coronation Street*. The gig was an unexpected surprise; she's travelling up to Manchester this afternoon and staying overnight. I'm impressed. He knows I'm a big fan of the soap. He apologises again for rearranging our date at the very last moment - he was meant to cook dinner for me this evening but called first thing to reschedule because he'll be child-minding Lily tonight. "Aliki's in Devon visiting her brother Vas with her mum and won't be back until tomorrow morning," he explains, "or she'd have had Lily." I tell him that I understand that his family comes first, and he smiles at me kindly. It isn't long before we get onto the subject of my impromptu visit to Aliki's.

"She's a very nice person." I sink my teeth into a raspberry brioche hungrily. The last thing I had to eat was a plate of Mum's chilli-con-carne last night. "Have they finished decorating yet?"

"Decorating?" He refills my cup from the teapot. "What makes you say that?"

"All that stuff everywhere," I say wiping a bit of raspberry compote from the corner of my mouth, "she said she…"

"Ah…I see, the mess," he interjects, tearing off a piece of croissant. "She's a hoarder, has been for years. But things got a lot worse after we split up." Christ, her house looked like a car boot sale. I take another bite of brioche. I saw a programme about hoarders not long ago on the telly. Many of them holding onto items they'll never use again, like old newspapers, clothes, kids' toys, tins of food. Some of the sufferers had rat infestations too. They even had to climb over boxes to get from one room to the

NO WAY BACK

next. Poor Aliki. I had no idea. I wonder if her depression stems from her breakup; because Daniel left her. How could he?

"Is that why you two split up?" I'm not going to beat around the bush anymore. If we're going to make a go of this I need hard facts. I came here today for answers. "Because of her problem?"

"No," he says indignantly, "of course not, what do you take me for?" That's true, Daniel wouldn't do that, he's not a callous man. What was I thinking?

"Well, what was it then? Anything to do with that old photograph I came across the other day?" I glance at his bedroom as my phone pings with a text in my bag.

"No," he sighs, "she knew about that from the start."

"So you were married before, then?" I root around in my bag for my phone. It's from Nick. I switch it off, I don't want any interruptions today.

"Yes," he confesses, as I hook the strap of my bag over the backrest of my chair. "Yes, I was." I knew it! "To a lovely woman called Sophie. The lady you saw in the photo." He inhales deeply through his nose then looks at me gravely. "Connie's mother."

"Whaaaat?" I don't even try to hide my incredulity. "You mean Aliki isn't…"

Swallowing hard, he runs a hand up and down his thigh nervously, then says, "That's right. Aliki isn't Connie's biological mother. No one knows, except Aliki's mother and her brother Vas. And now you, of course."

"Whoa." As I leap out of my seat, the weight of my bag sends my chair crashing to the ground, but I don't even give it a glance. "Are you telling me that Connie doesn't know that Aliki isn't her real mum?"

He shakes his head, face ashen as he lifts the chair off the floor. "That's why I freaked out over the *My Treasures* envelope." He hands me my bag as he gets to his feet. "I've got all my personal documents in there, birth certificates, marriage certificates, the lot. I thought you'd seen them but then Aliki assured me that you hadn't."

I start circling the table like a goldfish in a bowl, round and round and round, my mind racing. I wish he hadn't told me now. I don't want any part in this. I stop circling. "And so where's Sophie now?" Silence. "Daniel?"

He swallows hard and stares at the ceiling, fists clenched by his side. "In heaven." His voice is barely audible. I stare at him, mouth ajar, and my heart breaks a little. "The photo you saw was of me, Sophie and Connie." His voice cracks. I tell him to stop, that he doesn't have to tell me anymore. "No, I want you to know everything." He sits down, stretching his injured leg out, and then gently pats the seat of his 60s-style grey upholstered sofa, very sleek, very Swedish, very Daniel.

"It was a beautiful summer's day," he begins. "I was at work, Sophie was out in the garden weeding, she'd secured Connie in her high-chair on the patio with several toys to keep her occupied. A neighbour saw Sophie lying on the grass and called for an ambulance. We don't know how long she was there." He shakes his head. "The doctors said she'd had a massive stroke, that even if she survived she'd probably need care for the rest of her life. Anyway, she had another stroke during the night and didn't make it."

I clamp a hand over my mouth, the hairs on my arm on end. "But she was so young."

"I know," he sighs. "Apparently, it's quite rare. I found out later that her maternal aunt died of a stroke at the age of thirty-six, maybe that had something to do with it." I look at him, gobsmacked. "I promised myself that Connie would want for nothing. I swore I'd never remarry or have any more children. I didn't want to share

NO WAY BACK

the paternal love with another child, didn't want her to ever feel left out. It was going to be just me and her. But then when Connie was just two-and-a-half years old I met Aliki. She was a real tonic, just what I needed. A wonderful person, a beautiful woman, she helped me to heal. She made me realise that I was being selfish, depriving Connie of a mother. After a short romance, we got married. I wanted Connie to have a proper family, you know? Stability. A mum and a dad. Aliki and her family love the bones of her. I couldn't have wished for more."

I feel the brioche ascending towards my chest. "I'm so sorry, Daniel." The words slip through my fingers. We're both silent for a while. I'm glad he's being honest with me but now I feel burdened. How will I be able to look Connie in the eye again knowing this secret? Hearing her talk about her mum, her nan, her cousins, her Cypriot genes - which she's incredibly proud of, by the way - knowing that she hasn't got a Greek bone in her body. I rub my chin. "I can't carry this around with me, Daniel, it's too big."

"I know. Can you see now why I didn't want you to find out?"

I nod quickly. "You've got to tell Connie." I'm almost manic.

"I can't," he says urgently. I look at him aghast. I can't believe he's saying this. I thought today was supposed to be about honesty, put everything behind us. "It'll destroy her, you know how proud she is of her Greek heritage. Besides, it's been too long. She might hate me for it. I couldn't bear that."

"Daniel, she has a right to know who she is, for crying out loud."

"No, no, that's not going to happen. She's a happy, confident young woman. It'll break her," he says firmly, then he looks at me sharply. "Promise me you won't tell her."

"Daniel, you're being selfish." He covers his ears with his hands, blocking out my words. "You're going to have to tell her sooner or later."

"No, I'm sorry, Audrey. I can't risk it." He undoes two buttons of his red polo shirt, cheeks flushed, neck covered in blotches, beads of sweat trickling down his forehead. "And I understand if this means you don't want to be with me anymore."

I run a finger along the seam of the sofa, circling one of the buttons thoughtfully. Yesterday, I was secretly hoping for something as drastic as this, that he'd give me an easy way out, but now that the exit is staring me in the face, I'm not so sure I want to walk through it.

"Daniel, how could Connie get to almost thirty and not know? I mean, didn't she ever need her birth certificate?"

He shakes his head. "I always renewed her passport for her, you know what she's like." Yes, Daniel does most things for her. He's like her P.A. "And she's not married so never needed it for anything else." He stretches his leg and winces. "She did ask for it a couple of times," he says with a grimace. He must be in a lot of pain. I glance at my watch. I should leave. Let him get some rest. "Just out of curiosity, I think."

"And?"

"I fobbed her off. The first time I told her it'd been lost during a move and that I'd applied for a duplicate. Then recently when she asked me again I told her Aliki accidently burned it during one of her clear-outs. Aliki backed me up, of course, and that was the end of that."

"You can't let her and Lily live a lie, Daniel. It isn't fair." He drops his head and then, to my surprise, his body starts shaking. I wrap my arms around him and he cries and cries and cries.

"Shhh," I rub his arm, "Don't worry. We'll sort this out. Together."

He looks up at me then, face wet with tears. "Does this mean I'm forgiven?"

NO WAY BACK

"We all make mistakes." I brush away his tears with my fingers then place a hand on his knee. "Let's start again – a fresh slate."

"No more secrets." He cups his hand over mine, it's warm and damp.

"No more secrets." I brace myself. Confession time. "In fact, I've got something to tell you too."

"Okay," he sniffs, wiping his nose with the back of his hand. "Me first, though."

"There's more?" I ask, stunned.

"Just one more confession." He raises a finger, "I want you to know everything about my past if we're starting afresh. You need to know why my marriage ended." I'm not sure I can handle any more secrets. "The reason Aliki and I divorced was because she had an affair." I feel as if I've just been slapped across the face. Hard. "I know, shocking, isn't it? Who'd have thought it, eh?" He strokes my cheek with the back of his fingers. I gaze at him, wordless. "Well, not an affair as such, it was more of a one-night thing." I think I'm going to be sick. "It was my fault too." He leans back and grips his knees tightly. I can see he's still hurt by her betrayal. "We were apart a lot. I was too involved in our business, neglecting her. She was lonely. I get it, but…"

"Well, who was he? Did you know him? Are they together now?" I know I'm asking too many questions but I must know everything.

"His name was Fanos, married with three small children. And no, there was never a relationship. He was the top salesman of our Larnaca office. Aliki regretted it immediately and confessed the next day." He leans forward, rests his forearms on his knees and stares at his feet.

"And you couldn't forgive her?" I crane my neck to get a better look at him, gauge his expression.

"No, I could. I did." Phew, thank goodness. "We tried for a while but I couldn't get past it. I kept imagining them together."

"Oh," I gulp, "I see." There's a dark silence punctured by the sound of banging and then cheering through the walls.

"New neighbours." Daniel rolls his eyes, "Teenage sons. Anyway." He reaches for a box of ibuprofen on the coffee table, "That's my lot. Your turn now." I stare at him wide-eyed. I don't know what to say. He's just confessed to divorcing his wife over a one-night stand. He'll never forgive me. My breath quickens, my cheeks burn. "Hey, don't look so frightened. Whatever it is it can't be much worse than what I've just told you." He eases two tablets out of a blister pack and knocks them back with a glug of water, all the while regarding me.

"I saw Nick yesterday afternoon," I blurt out. His face darkens as he leans back in his seat, elbow on the wooden armrest, hand over his mouth. "We went for a walk in Highgate Woods. He just wanted to talk about his accident and stuff. He's having all these headaches, migraines, I think, and hallucinations and peculiar nightmares, and..." I'm blabbering but I can't seem to stop myself. "I think he needed a friend and a shoulder to cry on, that's all. I mean, you're still friends with Aliki, aren't you, so I -"

"Phew," he cuts in, "for a moment there I thought you were going to tell me you'd slept with him. I couldn't bear that."

"Don't be ridiculous." I giggle nervously, and he smiles, pulling me into his arms.

"I know, I know, I'm sorry." I lay my head on his chest and he strokes my hair. "My perfect Cinderella would never cheat on me." Perfect? Ha. If only he knew. I bite my thumbnail, listening to the thud of his heart. "You won't be seeing him again, though, will you?" I frown, why did he just say that? He still sees Aliki. He gently plays with my hair as I focus on the gold Buddha in the

NO WAY BACK

fireplace. "Connie said she went to see him about some photo gig." I go stiff in his arms. "Said she got the notion that he's still in love with you, wants you back." I don't suppose she told him that she stripped naked and climbed into his bed, though, did she?

"Promise me you'll tell Connie about Sophie, Daniel?" I say, veering off the subject of Nick.

He peels himself away from me, sits up, irritated. "We've been through all this, I thought…"

"I'm sorry, Daniel, but if we're going to make a go of this, you've got to promise me that you'll tell Connie the truth." Silence. "Daniel?" I touch his shoulder. "I think you know that it's the right thing to do."

He's silent for a few moments and then, "Okay, okay, if that's what it takes," he says, not looking at me, fist clenched against his mouth. "I'll tell her as soon as we get back from Paris."

"Paris?" I shriek as someone screams "Yesssss!" from next door.

"I booked the tickets weeks ago." He pivots towards me, takes my hands. "I never wanted a surprise birthday party. All I want to do for my fiftieth is sip champagne in a Parisian Cafe with you. I wanted to surprise you with the trip nearer the time but…"

"Daniel! You should've said." I snatch my hands away, he looks hurt. "When's it for? I've used up all my holidays this year and my schedule's really tight. I hope you took out some insurance."

"It's only a day trip on Eurostar, surely Raymond won't mind you having one extra day off. It's weeks away, he'll have plenty of notice." I look at him, speechless. Paris would be lovely, I'm sure Raymond would be okay if I took the day off unpaid, and it is a big birthday.

"I'll have a word with Raymond on Monday," I sigh, laying back in his arms. I've always wanted to see the Mona Lisa.

I'm still buzzing when I reach Muswell Hill. I decide very quickly that it's too early to go home and I can't wait to tell Louise and Gerry that I'm back with Daniel. They'll be made up for me, especially when I tell them about my Paris news. It's only midday, they're bound to be home, and Jess did say something about picking up a few things from there this morning.

"Hey, Aud." Jess ushers me in, phone in hand. "Thought you were spending the day with Daniel?"

"Change of plans. He's got an achy leg. Long story."

"Oh, right," she says disinterested as her phone rings. "Hi babe, yeah I'm just leaving now…should be about…" She covers the mouthpiece, "…go through, Audrey, they're all in the kitchen." She rolls her eyes. "Bloody Francesca. I'm going upstairs."

I walk towards the kitchen to the hullabaloo of laughter, banter, the clatter of plates and, I'm quite sure, the gurgling sound of a baby.

"Who is it, Jess?" Louise calls out cheerfully.

"Only me," I yell. I push the kitchen door open and the room falls silent. All I can hear is the sound of Roxy shuffling towards me, sniffing around my ankles excitedly. Gerry leaps out of his chair and looks anxiously from me to Louise.

The rest plays out as if in slow motion – Louise looks up at me from the table rocking a baby in her arms, face ashen. An arrogant looking woman sitting next to her is leafing through the Sunday papers. Then she looks up at me, one leg on top of the other, mug of coffee in hand.

I recognise her immediately. How could I ever forget that face? It'll be etched in my mind for eternity.

CHAPTER 35

"YOU," I WHISPER, my eyes fixed on the woman. "What's going on?" I drop my bag by my feet and take a step closer to Louise. "What's she doing here?" My heart is pounding hard, throbbing in my ears.

"Take it easy, Audrey," Gerry warns, hands raised. A heavy, palpable silence hangs in the air. Apart from the puppy sniffing around my ankles and the odd gurgle from the baby in Louise's arms, everyone is still, frozen. "This is my sister Francesca," Gerry explains, "Francesca, this is our friend, Audrey."

"I don't understand," I say with a wobbly voice. "This is the pregnant woman I saw at Nick's bedside."

Francesca doesn't bother to acknowledge me. Instead, she sighs tediously, licks a finger and turns another page. Louise is on her feet now, eyes filled with unease. She licks her dry lips as she takes a step towards me. Roxy, sensing the tension, starts barking, prompting the baby to moan and wriggle in Louise's arms.

"Audrey, you don't know how many times I tried to tell you," Louise says, handing the baby to a reluctant Francesca.

"Tell me?" I can't seem to take it all in, everything seems surreal. Then suddenly a bolt of clarity sears through me. I look at Gerry sharply, he folds his arms, covering his mouth, his fingers are trembling. Roxy weeps and groans around his ankles. Francesca is the mother of Nick's child. Louise and Gerry have known all along. My stomach heaves. I feel as if I've just stepped off a white-knuckle ride. I hold onto the back of the chair to ground myself.

"Yes," Louise's voice again, "I tried to tell you about Francesca and Nick, but…"

Her words slice through me like blades. "Is this some kind of sick fucking joke?" I stare at Gerry long and hard. He shakes his head, then reaches down and scoops Roxy up in his arms. My eyes dart around the room, their faces a blur. The kitchen feels as if it's spinning, faster and faster. The puppy is licking Gerry's face. The baby is gurgling. Louise's mouth is moving but all I can hear is the babble of her voice and Francesca flicking through the newspaper, louder and louder in my ears.

"Come into the lounge, Audrey." I flinch as Louise's cold fingers close tightly around my wrist. "I'll explain everything. Gerry, put the kettle on."

"Get off me!" I take a step back and in my haste trip over my bag as the stark reality of what has happened snaps into place like a missing piece of a jigsaw puzzle. My legs buckle, Louise reaches out for me quickly, asks if I'm okay. I shrug her off furiously as I regain my balance. These people that I trusted, that I thought were my friends, have been lying to me for months.

"Listen." Louise raises her hands as if I'm armed. "I tried to tell you, honestly." Her voice is trembling, frightened.

"Well, you obviously didn't try hard enough, did you?" I yell, my voice bubbling with fury. "What kind of people *are* you?" Francesca gives a little snort as she twirls a strand of dry, peroxide hair around her finger. I look at her, baby on her lap, Sunday supplements strewn over the table, and for a moment I imagine walking over, tearing that sheet of paper from her clasp, scrunching it up into a tight ball and shoving it down her throat.

NO WAY BACK

"Audrey!" Louise actually seems horrified by my outburst.

"What?" I cry. "Harbouring my ex-fiancé's…" I glance at Francesca in disgust, "…slut and love-child." Footsteps thunder down the stairs. Hot, bitter tears are rolling down my face. Why would Louise lie to me like this? Why? Why is she being loyal to Francesca, a woman she's never liked? How could she choose her over me? Her best friend.

"Oi," Francesca says, standing up, bobbing the child in her arms, "watch it!"

"Or what?" I say challengingly, taking a step towards her.

"I won't be spoken to like that," Francesca spits, bobbing the child faster. "Tell her, Gerry." My eyes flit from Francesca to Gerry. I can see the resemblance now. Their profile is similar only Gerry's features are slightly larger. Their lips have the same fullness. Their blue eyes the same blank stare. The baby is wailing now, face red, eyes screwed tightly shut. The puppy has freed herself from Gerry's arms and is barking the house down.

"Just shut it, Fran." He looks at Louise in exasperation, "Didn't I tell you this would happen. Didn't I? But, oh no, you'd handle it you said." He throws his hands up in the air, "Well? Go on then." His face is bright red, his eyes wild with rage, "Sort it!"

"What's going on?" Jess is at my side looking worried. "You okay, Audrey?"

"No, Jess, I'm not. It's your mum…I…" I falter. "Something terrible has happened." Jess scowls at Louise and pulls me into her arms, handing me a tissue which she salvaged from her rolled-up sleeve. "How could you, Louise?" I say between loud, noisy sobs, "How could you keep this from me when you knew what I was going through? You knew how much I loved him. How? We've been friends since school, for fuck's sake."

"I knoooow." She stretches her arms out to me. Does she

seriously think that I'm going to run to her? "That's why I didn't tell you. I was trying to protect you."

"You let him go, luvvie." Our heads swivel towards Francesca. "He was a free agent when I met him," she says in frosty tones, trying to calm the baby with a dummy. "It's not my fault if you don't know how to keep a bloke." Right, that's it. I shrug out of Jess's embrace and march up to her.

"You count yourself lucky that you're holding that baby in your arms." I'm inches from her face. I can smell the coffee on her breath and the faint whiff of stale perfume. She winces and jerks back. Jess pulls me away, tells me she's not worth it. Then suddenly I'm face to face with Nick's baby. He's looking at me, giggling, little legs kicking, almost dropping the blue dummy from his mouth. Without warning, I feel an instant pang of affection and my face softens. He has Nick's smile and warm grey eyes. Poor little mite, it's not his fault, is it? But his jovial demeanour doesn't last long; he's now red, hot and tense – clearly having a poo in Francesca's arms. Thank you, karma.

"Shut the fuck up, Francesca!" The shrill of Gerry's voice sets the baby off again. The dog starts howling, everyone's talking at once. The house is in turmoil. What began as a gentle, lazy Sunday has practically turned into a riot. Any moment now the neighbours will call the police, sirens will blare down this quiet residential road in Crouch End and we'll all be carted off, handcuffed, in the back of a van. I bend down languidly and pick up my bag.

"I need some air." I stagger towards the door.

"Audrey, are you okay? I'll come with you," Jess offers, hand on my shoulder.

"No, please…wait. I can explain," Louise cries, grabbing me by the sleeve of my trench coat, "please give me a chance. This isn't my fault." We scuffle noisily as Gerry tries to peel her off me, and in her haste, she scratches my hand, it stings. "You've got to remember that it's Nick and *her* that have caused all this," she yells over Gerry's shoulder, "not us!"

"Er, hello?" Francesca's voice is piercing. "Do you or do you not want to adopt this baby?" Silence thumps through the air.

I turn around slowly, face red, hair wild from the brawl, hand stinging. "You're going to adopt Nick's baby?" I gasp, rubbing my hand. She doesn't answer. "Oh my God." I cover my mouth and bolt to the sink.

"Are you okay, Audrey?" Gerry asks as I heave over the ceramic basin. "Come on," he says kindly, pushing my hair back off my face, "come and sit down."

"Does Nick know about this adoption?" I ask as Gerry shepherds me away from the stinking vomit in the sink.

He shakes his head. "We haven't told him yet. We just wanted to keep it between us for now…until we sorted things out."

"Jesus Christ," I say, wiping the back of my mouth with my sleeve. "You couldn't make this up."

"Nick's the father of your baby?" Jess says to Francesca, appalled. "OMG. Mum!" Clearly, Jess has been kept in the dark about all this too. They start to squabble but I'm not listening. All I can think about is how this could've happened right under my nose. And then the penny drops.

"That's why you didn't want me to see Nick." I point a finger at Louise. "Why you kept on telling me to stay away from him. You were afraid I'd find out, that he'd finally crack and tell me and mess things up for you."

"No." Louise shakes her head to and fro, to and fro, everyone's still talking, baby crying, dog barking. "That's not how it was."

All this time I thought she was protecting me from Nick but all the while she was just looking after her own interests. "You selfish bloody cow," I scream. A sharp hush stills the room. I've even silenced the baby and the puppy. All I can hear is the hum of a lawnmower in the distance, then the ticking of the clock above the door. I stare up at it. A fly buzzes around the doorframe before landing on the long hand. It's still only twelve-thirty. Half an hour ago I was happy. I'd made my peace with Nick. I'd salvaged my relationship with Daniel. I was looking forward to Paris, could barely wait to share my good news with my best friends and now...

Francesca sniffs the baby's bottom, pulls a face, and then announces that she's going up to change his nappy and settle him down for a nap. She shoves past me gaily, a smug grin on her face, that stale scent of perfume in the air.

"Come on, Audrey." I feel Gerry's hand on my back, "Let's go into the living room. I'll explain everything. Keep Roxy in here with you please, Jess." A tearful Jess nods as she takes Roxy from his hands. Louise makes to come with us.

"Not you, Louise," he says darkly.

"But...I..."

"Please, just for once listen to me, your husband." Louise opens her mouth to protest. "Louise!"

CHAPTER 36

IN THE LIVING ROOM, I pin myself on the edge of the armchair as Gerry talks me through what happened.

Nick met Francesca one night at their house after our fall-out. They were all drinking, except Francesca who's teetotal. Nick was knocking them back like there was no tomorrow. Gerry was worried, said he'd make up a bed for him on the sofa, keep an eye on him. But Nick wouldn't have it, of course. At around twelve-thirty, they decided to call it a night. Obviously, Nick was in no fit state to ride his bike. Francesca offered to drive him home in Gerry's car, she's insured, she often uses it when she's over. They didn't see her again until the next morning when she strolled in during breakfast.

"It wasn't all her fault, Audrey," he goes on. "She was in a bad way too. Her marriage was on the rocks. Jean-Pierre made some investments that went belly-up. They were on the brink of bankruptcy." He runs a hand over his tired face, eyes red. "It was just a one-night stand with Nick, they didn't see each other again. Several weeks later I got a tearful call from Francesca telling me she was pregnant and that Nick was the father. We didn't know what to do for the best." He rubs the back of his neck, a car swishes by outside; it's turning dark, gloomy.

"Go on," I say.

"Lou and I were stuck in the middle of it all. We didn't know whose side to take, my sister's or yours?" He smiles sadly, shaking his head. "Then Jean-Pierre found out she was pregnant and threw her out. She turned up on our doorstep with the kids, bar Marcel, in floods of tears. What were we supposed to do, Audrey? She's my sister." He looks up at me then, but I don't say anything. "You and Nick were back together, planning your wedding. In the end, Fran decided to have an abortion." So Nick was telling me the truth about that. "She'd spoken to Nick, they agreed. It was all settled. We decided there was no need to tell you. What you don't know can't hurt, right?" I shrug my shoulders and stare at my nails like a petulant teenager. "Then Louise had this brainwave - why don't we adopt the baby ourselves? I told her it was too close to home but she just wouldn't listen. That woman is unstoppable when she gets an idea into her head."

"But don't leave out the important bit, will you?" Francesca is at the door tying the belt of her purple raincoat fast and furious.

"Francesca," Louise warns, appearing behind her. She must've been in the doorway, listening.

But Francesca ignores her. "That you dissuaded me from having the abortion on the promise of fifty grand to have the baby for you on the quiet."

"Oh God, no." I close my eyes. I can't believe this. This only happens in episodes of *EastEnders*, surely.

"Francesca, stop. This isn't helping anyone," Gerry says wearily. Slipping past Francesca, Louise tiptoes into the room and quietly slides into the seat next to Gerry.

"No," I say in a tired voice, "let her finish. Go on."

"You had it all planned out, didn't you?" She glares at Louise before returning her attention to me. "I'd have the baby and they'd adopt it. But then, sod's bloody law, she only goes and gets pregnant herself, doesn't she? And whoosh." Francesca throws her hands up theatrically, "the deal's flipping off!"

NO WAY BACK

"You don't understand." Louise closes her eyes, hand out. "I couldn't…I didn't…"

"What the fuck was I supposed to do now, hey? I had no money, no husband, children to feed. Of course, I had to turn to Nick, it's his responsibility too, you know." I look from Gerry to Louise, their heads are bowed. They can't even look at me. "There was no way in hell I was going to agree to bringing up this kid on my own."

"So, wait a minute, if you didn't get pregnant," I say to Louise, "you'd have gone ahead with the adoption, and she," I point at Francesca. I can barely look at her, let alone say her name, "wouldn't have gone to Nick with her threats and demands. We'd have been married now."

"Yes, thank you, DCI Fox," Louise retorts. "But you'd have been lied to and manipulated. You still wouldn't have known about the baby."

"He was going to tell me," I claim, "he was just waiting for the right moment."

"And you'd have been fine with that, would you?"

"I might've been," I snap. I wouldn't have been, but that's not the point.

"Yeah, right," Louise hits back, folding her arms.

"Louise," Gerry says through gritted teeth, "we're supposed to be explaining everything to Audrey, apologising, for heaven's sake! Stop behaving like a flipping knob!"

"Well, I won't be cross-examined, this isn't *Midsomer Murders.* All I wanted to do was save a life. Give us a family." She raises her hands then drops them heavily in her lap, "How does that make me the bad guy, eh?" I shake my head. Louise has always had the knack of coming out smelling of roses. She should've been a bloody defence lawyer, not a chef. But she's not going to wriggle out of this one.

"Yes, but you're forgetting one vital thing," Francesca pipes up. "Nick may have told you about Thomas and you may have even agreed to get married, but…" She nods at Louise and Gerry sitting side by side on the sofa like two naughty children. "They'd have been bringing up his sprog."

"Oh, stop it, Francesca, you're making matters worse," Louise says impatiently, then looks at me with her puppy eyes. "He wasn't right for you, Audrey. I told you that from the start. He'd have strayed again and again."

"He was perfect for me!"

"Oh, really?" She leaps to her feet. "Is that why he fucked Gerry's sister the moment you fell out?"

"Excuse me! I am still here, you know," Francesca barks.

"So you thought you'd play God, did you?" I hit back, getting to my feet.

"For God's sake, stop it! You're doing my head in, the lot of you." Gerry's voice slices through the air, silencing us. Louise and I begrudgingly sit back down. I try to steady my breathing. My heart is pounding so hard that I'm surprised they can't hear it next door.

"Anyway," Francesca continues briskly, "as fate would have it, she lost her kid and so the deal's back on again! Whoopee." She cries in fake glory.

We're all speechless, the air dense with tension. In the distance, Roxy whines and scratches at the kitchen door. Louise looks at Gerry pleadingly, a tear sliding down her pale face.

"She is right about one thing, though," Francesca points at me as she crosses the room and picks up the baby monitor off the dining room table. "You are a bloody selfish cow," she whispers, bending down to Louise's eye level. "I've a good mind to keep Thomas. You're just lucky I need the sodding money." Louise

NO WAY BACK

winces as Francesca shoves the baby monitor into her hands. How can she speak about her own child as if he's a commodity?

"Right, that's it." Gerry stands up, fists clenched by his sides.

"Okay, okay, keep your hair on." Francesca straightens up.

"Leave it, Gerry." Louise gets to her feet and stands between them, arms outstretched like a referee. "Yes, okay, Francesca, you've made your point. Can you please just go now?" she says irritably. "We'll talk about this later."

Francesca huffs as she backs away. "I'm meeting up with some friends up West," she says blithely, applying a fresh layer of lipstick in front of the mirror above the fireplace. "He'll need a feed soon." She presses her lips together, then grabs her bag off the armchair. "Don't wait up."

When the front door slams Louise rushes over and kneels in front of me.

"Don't believe her." She wraps her hands around mine, they're cold. "You don't know what she's like. She's a liar, a cheat, a manipulator." I raise my eyebrows. "We'd have told you and Nick about the adoption once the dust had settled. Once we'd sorted out the loan with the bank. That was the plan, wasn't it Gerry?" She looks at Gerry for support but he just shakes his head. "Look, Audrey, please, you're my best friend. I did what I thought was best for everyone. I didn't tell you before because I didn't want to cause you any more pain. He'd hurt you enough." She looks at me pleadingly. But she's dug a hole that's too deep. A pit that she'll never be able to climb out of. "I mean, we didn't force him to have sex with her, did we?" Her eyes widen excitedly, she must be mistaking my silence for compliance.

I pull my hands away and she flinches. "Have you any idea what I've been going through? How many sleepless nights I had trying to work out why he suddenly left me? Hell, I thought that it was me, that I'd done something wrong, that he'd gone off me, that I was too old for him. I felt ugly, rejected, lonely. My confidence was in tatters. And to think you had the power to save me from all that anguish right from the beginning."

Louise jumps to her feet and starts pacing, biting her nails. "I didn't know you'd find out about the baby before I had the chance to tell you, did I? You weren't supposed to visit him in hospital, start seeing him again for crying out loud!"

"Oh, so all this is my fault, then, is it? Louise, will you listen to yourself? You want to adopt, no sorry, BUY Nick's baby. MY ex-fiancé's baby – that's insane!"

"YOU DON'T KNOW WHAT IT'S BLOODY LIKE!" Her loud, piercing voice almost bursts my eardrums. Gerry and I exchange glances. "You with your perfect relationship and smug, child-free contentment."

"Louise, that's enough," Gerry says firmly.

"I was desperate for a family with Gerry. Desperate!" I gawp at her in amazement. I had no idea she resented me and Nick for being happy. "I wanted to adopt Thomas right from the beginning, I'm not going to lie to you." How ironic. I want to laugh. "I only called off the deal with Francesca because Gerry didn't think I'd be able to cope with two babies, that's the God's honest truth," she says, as if Thomas is some kind of lucrative contract. "I'd have sorted it out for Francesca somehow, helped her, given her some money to help raise Thomas on her own. But she went off to Nick's all guns blazing before I could stop her." She pauses. "Of course, now we're in a position to adopt him again. Don't you see, Audrey? This IS a miracle, Thomas is Gerry's nephew, there's a blood connection, they share some DNA. It can't get any better than this for us. This is our last chance to be a proper family, and…"

"Stop it, Louise, I've heard enough." I stand up.

"But, Audrey, can't you see that…"

"I can't believe you betrayed me like this," I cut across her icily. "You're not the friend I thought you were. I'll see myself out." She rushes behind me, blabbering, crying.

"Come on, Louise," Gerry pulls her back gently, "I'll walk Audrey to her car."

Gerry asks me to cut Louise some slack as we walk against the cold, sharp wind, says that she hasn't been herself lately, that her obsession to have a family has taken over her life, is straining their relationship.

"Don't be angry with Nick. He was kept in the dark about most of this. Poor sod," he says as two giggling girls rush past us, mobile phones in hand. "And there's something else you should know too." Jesus, I'm not sure I can take any more surprises today. "I told him not to tell you about the baby."

I stop walking and look at him. This just gets worse and worse. We start walking again.

"I…" He closes his eyes briefly, "WE suggested that he postpone the wedding until we got everything sorted with Francesca, made her see sense. She was threatening to tell you everything herself if Nick didn't leave you and take full responsibility for their child, and she meant it, too. I love my sister but she can be a cruel bitch sometimes. I think she even called your number a few times, just to show Nick she meant business." So those anonymous calls were definitely her then. "We thought we could calm her down if you just put the wedding off for a while. At first Nick wouldn't listen, was adamant that you should know the truth. He somehow believed your love was strong enough to take it. He's still in love with you, you know that, don't you? You're in his blood."

I stare at the pavement, swallowing back the tears that are welling in my throat.

"Anyway, in the end I managed to persuade him that it was the kindest thing to do, that it'd be less painful for you than the truth. It was a big ask, I can see that now." He rakes his hands through his hair. "Christ Almighty, Audrey, what a bloody mess. I can't help feeling responsible for his accident, wondering if all this trauma sent him over the edge."

We've reached my car, the end of the road. "Well, say something, then." He laughs nervously, rubs his arms, then turns up the collar of his short-sleeved checked shirt, as if that will keep up the cold. "Please don't look at me like that." But I can't tell him what he wants to hear, not this time. I can't comfort him with words of wisdom, nor wrap him in a blanket of compassion. I don't think he understands the extent of damage that they've caused.

"Thanks for explaining Nick's involvement in all this, Gerry, we've only just rescued our friendship, it couldn't take another knockback."

"I shouldn't have let this happen. I shouldn't have let Louise manipulate me. I was weak. Stupid." He exhales loudly, his warm breath forming a puff of mist in the cold air. "I'm just so, so sorry." He blinks and a tear splashes from his eye and rolls down his face.

"Look, I'd better go." I unlock the car and climb in.

He leans over the open door as I clip in my seatbelt, "By the way, they're having a paternity test done soon," he says, his tears drying. I don't bother telling him that I already know. "But it's just a formality to keep Nick happy. Jean-Pierre had a vasectomy some time ago. I've told Nick it's a waste of time and money but he won't listen, you know what he's like." I nod silently. We all know he's stubborn. "But anyway," he adds quickly as I turn on the ignition, "that's all in the past now, isn't it, you've got Daniel now."

"Yes," I say, putting the car into first gear. "I've lost all my friends but at least I've still got Daniel."

CHAPTER 37

STANDING IN FRONT OF THE MIRROR, the sweltering spotlights shine down on me as if I were centre stage at the Wyndham's Theatre. Why do they make these damn dressing rooms so tiny? I pull off one dress and hastily climb into another. Nothing fits – NOTHING! I can't go to Paris tomorrow underdressed. I harrumph in exasperation, face burning. This is all Louise's fault. I always to turn to comfort eating when I'm stressed. I've put on half a stone since I fell out with her three weeks ago. Our friendship is over now – ruined. I will never be able to trust her again.

I zip up the back of the dress as far as my arms can reach, these are the times that I wish I'd listened to my mother and taken up yoga. Loud music pounds across the dressing rooms as I stare at my reflection in the mirror. Actually, although figure hugging, this black little number doesn't look too bad. I turn to the side. Shit. I look like I'm expecting. Yanking back the curtain, I grab the attention of a svelte, young assistant.

"Yes, can I help you, Madam?" My shoulders slump. Madam. Why did she have to use that word? WHY? She's just made me feel like I'm a-hundred-and-three years old.

"Have you got this in extra-large?" I ask discreetly.

"Erm…I think we have but I'll just check for you, Madam." That dreaded word again. "And can I just say that we've got this style in red, blue and…"

"No, just another black one please."

 NO WAY BACK

"But if we've no extra-large in black? Shall I bring you another colour?"

"No," I say wearily, "if there's no black I'll leave it." She smiles and scurries out of the dressing room to the loud thump of the music.

I lean my back against the doorframe, fanning myself with my hand as I gaze around the communal area. It's more like a nightclub in here than a clothes shop. I'm surprised they aren't serving cocktails. A willowy, young woman is twirling around in front of the floor-to-ceiling mirror. I wish I had her confidence. And figure. She's standing on her toes now to see how the dress'll look in high heels – a girl thing. That dress is way too big for her, by the way.

"I look like a sack of potatoes," she admits to an over-enthusiastic assistant. She is tiny. Whatever possessed her to try on such a large size? Mind you, they always look different on the hanger, smaller in my case. I often snatch a size 12 off the rail, convinced that it'll fit me. It never does. The young woman catches my eye and I smile but she looks away. Goodness, why are people so cynical?

I glance at my watch and start tapping my foot. How long is that dress going to take? Vicky will be having kittens. She doesn't do waiting around outside dressing rooms for longer than ten minutes.

"Black dress in an extra-large!" Jesus, did she have to shout that out loud?

"Yes, over here," I say dryly, sticking my arm out of the booth.

As I climb into the dress I hear the voice of the svelte assistant telling the sack-of-potatoes-woman that the smallest size they have is a six. SIX! And that they don't do extra-small. I've got to go on a serious diet once I get back from Paris. I don't think I've ever been this big.

Outside on Oxford Street, I link my arm through Vicky's as we brave the crowds. It's rush hour, people are heading home, pushing past us hurriedly, grabbing a free copy of the *Evening Standard*, talking loudly into their mobile phones. It's the first time Vicky and I have been alone since Francesca-Baby-Gate. It's been good, therapeutic, cathartic - she's a good listener.

We cross Regent Street and hurry along beneath the twinkling Christmas lights to the buzz of traffic and army of people heading for the underground.

"Are you looking forward to going to Paris tomorrow?" Vicky asks as we're practically carried down the stairs by a heap of commuters.

I tell her that I am, sort of, but peeved that I couldn't find a dress I liked today. Or at least one that would fit me, and will now have to resort to my safe jeggings and black blouse. "But I'm still feeling quite raw, Vicks, you know." A man jabs me on the shoulder, I turn to give him a look but he's gone. "About Louise and Francesca. Oh, and just everything."

"Well, at least now it's all in the open," she says as we step onto the escalator heading for the Central Line. "I did tell you that Daniel's secret would be one you could live with, didn't I?" She smiles smugly. Daniel made me swear that I'd tell everyone that his secret was Aliki's affair, just until he told Connie the truth. But I hate lying to Vicky. "And it must be a relief to know that Nick only called off your wedding because of the baby. Gerry must've really put the pressure on him, poor bloke. And poor Louise. Imagine how desperate she must've been. It can't have been easy lying to you." She steps off the escalator and I rush behind her, black *Manolos* clicking against the resin floor.

"Hey," I complain, trying to keep up, "Whose side are you on? I've been deceived and betrayed by my best friend and ex-fiancé."

NO WAY BACK

"Yours, of course." She stops to throw a coin at a busker playing the clarinet. "He's bloody amazing, isn't he?" I nod, he is very good. I've seen him here before, brightening up humdrum evenings with his beautiful sounds. "But you've got to admit, it all makes sense now, doesn't it?" She raises her voice as we step onto the platform. "Can't you see how hard it must've been for them?" A gust of warm air blows our hair in all directions, the distant sound of the clarinet whines in the background as the train thunders into the dark tunnel.

I look up at the LED indicator – 1. Hainault 3 minutes. I wait until the train disappears into the darkness before answering. "If they'd just told me the truth from the beginning I'd have…"

"You'd have what?" she cuts in as we walk along the platform, "Married Nick and lived happily ever after? Given Louise and Gerry your blessing and offered to be Godmother?"

"Oh, don't be ridiculous." Despite her natural counselling skills, she can be quite harsh sometimes. "Nick should've just told me. Why on earth did he listen to Gerry and Louise, anyway? They're not his keepers, he's a grown man, for goodness sake."

"He panicked. Obviously, the thought of disappointing you must've been unbearable." My bottom lip jerks outward as I mull over what she's just said.

"But how could Louise have been so selfish?" I protest.

"Desperate times, desperate measures," Vicky shrugs. "You'd be surprised at what lengths some people will go to have a family."

"Oh, come off it. She's not exactly childless, is she? She's already got Jess."

"That tells you how much she craved that family unit with Gerry, then. Oh, don't pull that face, you've seen how mushy she gets over the twins. I know she appears a bit aloof and independent, but behind the bravado lies quite a sensitive, nurturing woman."

She's right. I'm being unfair. Louise has always been maternal. She used to babysit for family and friends when we were at school. She even worked at a local nursery during the holidays. I remember her coming round to see me after work sometimes, full of beans, telling me little anecdotes about the kids and how she couldn't wait to have several of her own.

"Well, they could've just adopted like other normal couples instead of re-mortgaging their house to buy Nick's kid."

"He's Francesca's child too, Audrey. Gerry's nephew. There's a good chance that the child will bear some resemblance to him, that's probably why Louise did it."

"Hmm…" I grumble, "not much chance of that, Tommy's got his dad's Irish good looks."

"Anyway." Vicky elbows me on the arm, "We all have secrets, don't we?" She's referring to Ronan, obviously.

"Hmm…" I murmur sulkily, giving her a sideward glance. The warm gush of the approaching train makes me feel a bit giddy and I take a step back.

"You okay, Aud? You look a bit peaky." She places a hand on my arm, concerned. "Do you want to sit down? We can catch the next train if…"

"No, I'm fine. I've been overdoing it lately, that's all. I just want to get home. I've got a long day ahead of me tomorrow." The doors slide open and we hover like a couple of vultures as passengers take their time getting off, then lunge at a couple of vacant seats as if our lives depended on it.

"I've been feeling a bit queasy lately and bloody exhausted," I say as the train trudges out of the platform. "My boobs are all achy." I shuffle in my seat, "And I just feel irritable all the time. I'm probably coming down with a virus."

"Yeah, horrible feeling – I was like that when I was expecting,"

NO WAY BACK

Vicky says matter of factly. We smile at the thought, nodding, and then slowly look at each other – po-faced. "You're not…?"

My eyes widen. "I can't be…I…"

"When was the last time you had your period?" A man sitting opposite glances up from his paper and gives us a look as I quickly try to work out when I was last on.

"It's been…oh…er…oh God, Vicky, I dunno, my period's been all over the place lately. I've never really been regular."

"Come on, think…a week, a month?"

"Erm…wait, give me a chance…er…one, two," I mumble under Vicky's watchful eye. But I can't concentrate, my mind feels like a knot of cables. "About six or seven weeks or so…I think." I tap my lips, my hand is shaking.

"You've got to do a pregnancy test." She looks at her watch as the train pulls into Tottenham Court Road. "Shit, we've got to change here for the Northern Line. By the time we get home the chemist will be shut." She bites her bottom lip thoughtfully. "There's that all night one in Golders Green, though."

"No," I say, as we head for the Northern Line. "I haven't got time. I've got to be up at five. I'll do it when I get back."

"Okay, a day won't make any difference. Will you tell Daniel or wait until you do the test, just to be sure?" I throw her a fleeting look. "Oh, God, Aud." She stops walking, grabs my arm, stilling me too. "Please tell me that you used a condom with Ronan." I cringe and shake my head, panic escalating through my body by the second. "Oh God." She holds her head. "So it might be his?"

"Yes," I hiss. "There's a bloody good chance, especially as Daniel always uses protection." She nods, tells me that no birth control is a hundred per cent, so it still might be his. "Oh, fucking hell, Vicky. What am I going to do?" I can't breathe, the tunnel is closing in on me, I think I'm going to faint. Vicky ushers me to a nearby seat.

"Don't panic! Deep breaths. Come on, deep breath in, deep breath out, that's it."

"Are you all right, love?" asks a kind looking lady in a black woolly hat, long coat and leather gloves.

"Yes, we're fine." Vicky smiles up at her. "She's pregnant." I give Vicky a daggered look. The lady nods knowingly and smiles before continuing on her journey. "Sorry, that just came out. You won't see her again anyway. Are you feeling better?" She takes a tissue from her bag and wipes the sweat off my forehead. I nod. "Do you want to tell Ronan?"

"Are you kidding me? He's only just started seeing Tina again – she's stuck by me over this business with Nick and Louise, took my side over theirs. It'll destroy our friendship if I tell her this. Oh, my God, I can't believe this is happening," I cry, holding my head in my hands.

"Okay, okay, take it easy, Hun." Vicky puts her arm around me and stares around the platform searchingly as if we're a couple of fugitives on the run. "Go to Paris and do the test when you come home. Don't worry. I'll help you through this. Whatever the outcome – whatever you decide to do." I give her a sharp look.

"I can't keep it, Vicky. No way."

CHAPTER 38

"BONJOUR, MADAM," says the taxi driver as I climb into the back of his cab. We've just got off Eurostar and are heading for Notre Dame. It's an unusually warm, sunny day for the end of November. I wore my signature beige mac but I'm already starting to feel the heat, which means I'll have to lug it around over my arm all day. Great.

I stare out of the window as we speed along the busy streets of Paris all the while thinking about what will happen if I get a positive result on the pregnancy test tomorrow. Well, I've got to tell Daniel for a start, because we agreed, no more secrets, and, whether I'm pregnant or not, I've also got to tell him about my one-night stand with Ronan because the guilt is killing me.

Daniel leans across me and stares up at the city, "Isn't it wonderful?"

"Hmm," I murmur, smiling. He sighs contently, eyes sparkling with anticipation, then he leans back and whips out a map from his inside pocket, spreads it across his strong thighs and starts planning. His black-rimmed square glasses are perched on the bridge of his nose, he's gelled his hair and combed it neatly to the side today, reminding me a little of Clark Kent in *Superman*.

I ogle him, a little bewitched by his stunning good looks. Fifty years old today, who'd believe it? He doesn't look a day over forty. He's too busy talking to notice me staring. I cuddle up close to him, I don't want to spoil his day. It isn't his fault that I've been such an irresponsible twat.

He tells me that from Notre Dame we'll walk along the River Seine and then make our way to the *Louvre* so that I can see the *Mona Lisa*, then we'll find somewhere cosy to eat. There won't be time to do much else. He's got it all planned out. He's so efficient. So in control, it's good to see him smiling again. Am I really about to pull the rug from under his feet?

I lean back, enjoying the hustle and bustle of the Parisian streets. This is my third visit to Paris. I first came here when I was little with my parents when they had the travel business. Apart from a visit to the Eifel Tower on the last day, a disgruntled George and I got dragged from hotel to hotel while they carried out their research for their weekend break brochure. My second visit was with Nick when we first got together. He was on a photoshoot at the time. I followed him around like a crazed groupie from venue to venue, ogling at the gorgeous models as they strutted around the studio in their designer outfits. We took cabs everywhere; his sense of direction is worse than mine. There was no time for sightseeing but we did dine in some lovely restaurants and quenched our thirst in some snazzy bars and nightclubs.

Daniel grabs my hand and smiles brightly as the sun streams through the window, warming my face. I raise a hand, shielding the brilliant sunlight as the driver rides a kerb, almost knocking down a pedestrian. I quickly grab Daniel's arm for support as we bounce around on the back seat. Holding me in his arms protectively, he asks if I'm okay, then in a raised, annoyed tone tells the driver to slow down.

I pull away. "It's okay, Daniel, I'm fine," I say, but I'm a nervous wreck. I can't believe that I've treated Daniel in the same abominable manner that Nick treated me. Only worse, because I was only estranged from Daniel for a few hours and he wasn't even aware that we'd broken up! I squeeze his hand unintentionally and he reciprocates the gesture, grinning at me warmly.

We travel in companionable silence for a while, taking in the scenery. Maybe Vicky was right, I was a bit harsh with Nick. I can see now how one stupid mistake can mess up your life - how one mad, drunken night of passion can turn your world upside down. Daniel, clearly sensing my tension, stretches his arm across the back of my seat and pivots towards me.

"Are you still upset about your bag?" I'd forgotten about that until he just reminded me. Outside Kings Cross station this morning as I climbed out of a black cab, my fabric *Louis Vuitton* bag slid off my shoulder and landed in a huge muddy puddle near a drain. Once inside the station, we tried cleaning the muck off but it was no use. My bag was destroyed, but that's the least of my worries.

I shake my head and pat the bag on my knees. The stains have dried out leaving huge, dark watermarks. "No, it's okay," I say, "it's just a bag."

He studies me for a while and then, "Look," he sighs, face serious, "I know you're upset and I can understand how dreadful you must be feeling right now." My heart picks up a little speed. What does he mean? "But you needn't worry, you know. Look at me. That's my girl. It's going to be fine. I promise you." Our eyes lock and for a few hazy moments, I wonder if he knows. If he's somehow guessed, but how could he? The car swerves and I fall onto him again, the driver hoots his horn and swears loudly in French, so much for slowing down. We straighten up. "I've spoken to Aliki and we're going to tell Connie on Saturday night." Yes, of course, his confession to Connie. What was I thinking?

"Do you want me to come with you?"

"No, no." He reaches into his pocket and pulls out his wallet.

"We'll be fine." I nod as we pull into the taxi bay at Notre Dame, feeling a little like a third-party, a spare part. It'll always be 'them' and 'me', won't it? It'll never be 'us'.

We join the crowds of tourists snapping away at the huge Gothic cathedral with their cameras, mobile phones, and iPads. I gaze up the beautiful stained-glass windows, the intricate sculptures carved into the aged stone walls. Daniel told me earlier that many date back to the thirteenth century. Simply breath-taking.

Inside the cathedral, we wander around in awe. I wonder how much craftsmanship went into creating the interior of this epic building. I stare up at the high arched ceilings to the magical sound of a keyboard, wrapping me in an embrace of sanctuary. I've never been very religious but I find myself in front of Christ on the Cross. I close my eyes.

"Dear Lord, what am I going to do? I've betrayed my partner (although he did betray me too in a way because he didn't tell me about his first marriage and everything, just so that you know it's not ALL my fault). Anyway, I know you don't hear from me much and I'm probably not worthy of your grace. I'm sure you've got more important Godly things to do but please, if you've got a few spare moments, I just want some clarity, some direction. I'm not sure what to do about my dilemma. I've got no one to turn to. I can't confide in Ronan because then he'd tell Tina. And telling Nick doesn't bear thinking about. Louise is the only one who could really help me and she's off the bloody radar. Oh no, I said bloody. I'm sorry, Lord. Oh, I said it again. Oh, shit." I take a deep breath. *"Okay, sorry about that. The swearing, I mean. Right, where was I? Oh yes. Look, I'm not even sure if I'm pregnant, but if I am…"*

"Didn't have you down as being religious." Daniel's arms around my waist make me jump. He nestles his chin on my shoulder as people wander around, immersed in the architecture and

NO WAY BACK

tranquillity of the basilica, their voices inaudible whispers.

"I'm not." I clear my throat and face him. "Not really."

"Here." He presses a gold medal in my hand and I shiver. "This is for you," he says, dropping a kiss on my forehead, "it'll bring you luck." He winks mischievously. "You'll see."

I turn the gold Notre Dame medallion in the palm of my hand. It feels strong and cool, and somehow significant. I narrow my eyes as Nick's words jump into my mind. *"I saw you holding a gold coin in the palm of your hand. You weren't even in this country, you seemed far away."*

"Oh, my God," I whisper, staring at the coin in my open hand.

Daniel laughs. "Well, I knew you'd like it but it's not that grand. It only cost me two euros. Audrey? Are you okay? You've gone a bit pale. You're not feeling sick again, are you? We could go out for some air if…"

"No, no, I'm fine now. And thank you," I add quickly. "It's lovely." I close my hand around it and slip it into my side pocket.

"Come on." He grabs my hand. "We've still lots to see."

We stroll along the River Seine eating cheese crepes to the backdrop of a busker playing a Parisian tune on his accordion. When we finish, I lean over the wall and stare down at the green, shimmering river dancing lightly in the sun. Ahead, people enjoy the views from an open-topped deck of a river boat gliding under a bridge. I take the medal from my pocket and turn it around in my hand like a bar of soap as if somehow the answers to my troubles lie deep within the yellow metal. *You've really messed up this time, girl*, I tell myself, *I can't see you getting out of this one unscathed*. I give it one final turn and then slip it into the breast pocket of my blouse.

"You'll lose it there," Daniel warns, leaning his back against the wall.

"I won't." I pat it lightly. "I want to keep it close to my heart."

He smiles at me warmly, squinting against the sun. My mobile phone bleeps. I lower my bifocal sunglasses from my head. It's Vicky again.

How r you? Feeling any better?

With a shaky hand, I quickly text back:

A bit – sickness eased off. Feel awful. So guilty. xx

A few moments later another message trills through:

Don't worry! All will b well. xx

I slip my mobile phone into my back pocket and turn to Daniel. He's snuggled up next to me, arms resting on the wall, staring down at the river. "It's beautiful, isn't it?" I say, taking it all in.

"Almost as beautiful as you are." A cliché, I know, but it's nice to hear all the same. I stare down at the calm, velvety water, friendly and enticing on the surface but deep and murky beneath, a bit like me. My mobile phone goes off again. Daniel straightens up and tuts impatiently. I can see he's had enough.

"Sorry," I say, pulling it out of my pocket, "it might be important." It's Nick.

Bonjour mon ami! Hope ur having gr8 time. Nick X

I text back hurriedly.

Yes. At River Seine! Speak soon.

"Sorry about that, it was Callum from work," I lie.

Daniel turns my face towards his as my mobile bleeps again. His fingers are cold. I flinch.

"Leave it." He pulls my hand away from my pocket. "Can't you just switch it off? It's been going off all morning. I thought we were supposed to be celebrating my birthday."

"I can't, Daniel, you know that. Raymond only agreed to let me have today off if he could contact me at any time." I take a few rushed steps forward and in my haste I twist my ankle and start hurtling towards the floor. I grab onto a nearby post for support, then as I pull away I feel a tug on my shoulder then the sound of a rip. Daniel rushes over and snatches me in his arms.

"Darling, are you all right?" A little shaken, I straighten up and brush myself down as Daniel examines my shoulder. "It's just a tear," he says, sounding relieved, "and a small scratch. You'll live." He taps my nose. "Not your day today, is it?" If only he knew the depths of my misery.

Still holding tightly onto my mobile phone, I read the message – it's Nick again: **Enjoy. Call u tomz xx**

I take my glasses off and snap them shut in their case. I've got to stop texting. It isn't fair on Daniel.

"Marry me," Daniel whispers, as I slip my glasses nonchalantly into my open handbag. My breath catches in my throat. I can't believe it. Has he really just proposed to me by the River Seine on his fiftieth birthday? Music from a nearby restaurant drifts towards us as if in serenade. I can't speak. I open my mouth, then close it again and gawp at him in silence

"I love you, Audrey." He pulls me close to him. I can feel his heart beating fast against my chest, his warm breath against my face. "Please say yes and make this birthday the best ever."

"Wow," I manage finally, "Daniel. Phew. You are full of surprises today. I don't know what to say."

"Just say yes and we can go and buy the rings right now." He takes a few steps back and pulls my hand. "Come on."

"Daniel, no…wait…I…you…we…you," I mumble incoherently. His face drops the instant he realises his romantic gesture has backfired.

"Oh, my goodness," he says, "you don't love me, do you?" My mobile phone starts vibrating in my hand. I glance down at it. It's George. Thank you, God.

"Sorry, Daniel, it's work. I've got to get this." I answer the phone nervously, backing away for privacy. "Hi," I say in a high-pitched voice, my heart hammering against my ribcage.

"Hey, sis, how are you? Everything okay?" George sounds concerned.

"Yes, I'm fine. A bit tired from the journey. Is everything okay with you? Has anything happened?"

"I heard the news." I can hear the smile in his voice, "Vicky told me. Well, I overheard you two talking on the phone this morning and coaxed it out of her," he says smugly as if he's *Hercule Poirot*. It takes a while for me to cotton on. Shit.

"George," I whisper, looking over my shoulder. Thankfully, Daniel is leaning against the wall of the bridge, arms folded, staring into the distance. "I don't know what you're talking about."

"Oh, stop being coy. I just wanted to say congratulations, that's all. I bet Daniel's thrilled."

"George," I hiss. "I don't know what Vicky's told you but there is no news to be thrilled about."

"But I thought I was going to become an uncle – at last. Mum's over the moon." Oh, fucking hell. My life is over.

"What makes you think that I'd want to have a child with a man I barely know, hmm?"

"Okaaaay, maybe it's not the ideal scenario but Daniel's a top bloke, right? We all like him, and besides, I thought you two were all loved-up. Come on, sis, worse things have happened and you're not getting any younger, are you?" Closing my eyes briefly, I press my palm against my forehead. I can't believe what's happening to me today.

"George," I say through gritted teeth. "I can't talk now. I'll call you tomorrow. And don't you dare tell anyone else, do you hear me?" I feel Daniel's hands on my shoulders and I shudder slightly.

"Yes, yes, I promise. Bye."

"Was that George?"

"Yes, it was," I answer truthfully, wondering how long he's been standing behind me. How much he's heard. "He just wanted to wish you a happy birthday."

"But I thought you said it was work."

"Huh?"

"Just now…on the phone…you said it was work."

I laugh nervously. "You know I can't really see without my glasses on."

"So?"

"So, I misread the…"

He tuts. "So? Will you marry me?"

CHAPTER 39

"DANIEL, LISTEN." I swallow hard, faffing with the contents in my bag, "you're a wonderful man and I care about you deeply."

"Oh, here we go." He puts his hands on his head and turns full circle, "you're going to give me the 'it's not you it's me line', aren't you?"

"No, no, that's not what I was going to say." That's the exact line I was going to feed him. "This is all just such a shock, that's all. I mean, you hardly know me really… I…" He grabs my hands, I'm facing him.

"I know all there is to know." Er, I don't think so because if you did you'd turn around right now run for the hills. "God, Audrey, you're everything I want. Life's too short to waste time. We're not getting any younger, are we? I mean I know we're too old for kids but…" I give him a quick, sharp look. "You don't want kids, do you?" I shake my head, swallowing back my guilt. "We can stay engaged for a year or so if you like, if you want more time, that is. Just don't say no, not yet." Guilt sluices through me. I want him to stop. I can't do this. I've got to come clean. "At least say you'll think about it…Please."

"Daniel." I stare into his pleading eyes and I lose my nerve. "Okay, I'll think about it." Oh Christ, why am I such a wuss? He pulls me close and rocks me gently in his arms as a light wind sweeps over us, tugging at my conscience.

"Thank you," he whispers, "that's all I wanted to hear."

Despite the crowds, Daniel and I manage to get to the forefront of the *Mona Lisa*. I hold onto the wooden barrier and stare at it in utter awe, completely spellbound. I've waited a lifetime to see this. Tourists are pushing and shoving, taking selfies with the portrait. A Japanese man nudges me as he leans against the barrier grinning into the camera, and then, dissatisfied with the picture his wife has just taken, insists she takes it again before swapping places with her and going through the entire process again. And all through this mayhem Daniel and I stand hand-in-hand admiring the beauty of this incredible masterpiece in complete silence.

Later, in the restaurant, having whizzed by the *Opera House* and *Gallery Lafayette*, Daniel and I enjoy a light meal in a small brassiere.

"You haven't touched your champagne," Daniel complains, tucking into his steak provencal, "not like you. You okay?"

"I'm exhausted, Daniel." And I am, my feet are pulsating. I haven't walked this much in years.

"Come on, you've got to have at least one glass to celebrate my birthday. I can't drink all this on my own." He points at the ice bucket on our table with his fork. I smile and apologise for being so unsociable, especially on his birthday. I take a small, hesitant sip. Daniel frowns at me over his champagne flute. "Is it okay?" I nod and gulp half the champagne back in one go. The bubbles fizz in my mouth, making the back of my throat tingle, my eyes water.

Daniel takes one sip, then another, all the time regarding me suspiciously. "I've upset you, haven't I?" He narrows his eyes. "I knew it." He slams his hand down on the table, one of the waiters look around from the bar. "I've frightened you off with all this talk about marriage. Look." He leans across the table and takes my hand, "I'm sorry, okay, forget I ever mentioned it, we can…"

I press my fingers against his lips. "Stop it, Daniel, it's not you. I'm just stressed out, that's all. I've got a lot on my mind."

He looks at me curiously for a while. "You're not ill are you?" I shake my head. "You would tell me if there was something wrong, though, wouldn't you?"

"Yeah, course I would." I fork a piece of omelette and look up at him fleetingly before shovelling it into my mouth.

"I mean, if you *were* ill, for instance, or…" Oh, God. Oh, no. He knows. He's worked it out. He's such a clever man. My face tingles.

"Daniel, I'm fine. Don't worry. Come on, we've only got half-an-hour, drink up."

"Okay," he says lightly, refilling my glass with downcast eyes. I'm sure he knows, his tempo has dropped, always a sign that he's onto something.

Our ride back to the station is broken only by the French commentary on the radio and the blare of police sirens outside. We drive by the *Apple* store on *Rue Halevy*. I stare out of the window as the taxi driver beeps his horn and shouts in French. Ahead, the lights of *Gallery Lafayette* sparkle vibrantly, illuminating the city.

"Traffic jam," moans the driver. He yawns and then scratches the back of his head all the while complaining about the traffic.

It's rush hour and it's taking ages to get to the station. I look at Daniel but he's staring out of the window, deep in thought, chin resting against a clenched fist. Impatiently, the driver rolls down the window and the cool evening air washes over me. I know that I've spoilt Daniel's birthday but is it really my fault that he decided to propose to me today of all days? Must I feel guilty for his spontaneity?

Away from the traffic, we cruise along the crowded streets. I can't feel my feet. I'm exhausted and I need the loo.

At *Gare du Nord*, we check in and find two seats in the terminal. I ask Daniel if he's okay and he tells me that he's fine, that he's just tired. "Will you look after my mac while I use the loo? It's just there." I point at the toilet signs.

I dash into the cubicle and bolt the door. I've just made it in time. I hover over the toilet bowl and tug at the loo roll, mummifying my hand with it quickly. Phew, that was close. A murmur emanates from a nearby booth followed by a woman's voice making unpleasant straining noises as if she's about to give birth to a 10lb baby. Within seconds, a potent stench fills the entire bathroom making me retch. Goodness, could today get any worse? Then as I reach out to press the flush I drop my gaze into the toilet. I lean over and stare down into the bowl and then, as if in slow motion, the gold *Notre Dame* Medal slides from my blouse pocket, bounces onto the rim of the seat before plummeting into the red-stained water with a dull plop.

I briefly close my eyes as I flush the loo, then put the seat down, collapse my tired body onto it and hold my head in my hands.

I almost choke as a build-up of tears spill from my eyes and trickle down my face, some catching into the groove of my lips. Then suddenly Nick's words echo in my ears, *"This is going to sound really weird, but you were crying on a toilet seat"* I lick my salty lips and tear off some more tissue from the dispenser. I've got to get out of here. I've got to get back home.

Stumbling out of the cubicle, I gape at my reflection in the mirror. A bleary-eyed stranger stares back at me. What have I become? I was always so virtuous, so honest. My long fringe has curled against my damp forehead, my mascara smudged around my eyes. I press my lips together, the stench of stale urine makes me want to heave. I put my grubby, stained bag onto the counter and turn on the tap. Water gushes into the sink and then splashes out of the basin, making a small puddle against the pale green countertop.

There's a click, a door unlocks, and noisy-poo woman emerges. She smiles at me briefly in the mirror as I wash my hands feeling the cold, tired, duck-egg blue walls closing in around me. How on earth did I get myself into such a goddamned mess? Six months ago I was happily planning my wedding to a man I loved with every part of me. Now I'm hovering over a sink in a public toilet in Paris looking like a smackhead.

I dry my hands and pull up the drooping sleeve of my torn blouse but it's no use, my shoulder is poking out defiantly. I've got to pull myself together. I've been gone for almost fifteen minutes. Daniel will be wondering where I am.

I try to ignore the smell of piss by inhaling through my mouth. From the corner of my eye, I see a few more faceless women come and go. I wipe my mascara-smeared face with a damp piece of toilet tissue and then apply a splash of lip-gloss.

There. That's better. Satisfied, I toss my lip-gloss into my bag, then as I rummage around for a clean tissue I notice a bling-adorned hand sliding towards me, depositing three Euros onto the wet counter. I slowly look up at a heavily made-up middle-aged woman with a dark bouffant staring back at me. She's wearing a brown tweedy coat with a huge fur collar.

"Acheter quelque chose à manger," she says softly. I follow her eyes to my soiled bag and then my torn blouse.

"Excuse me?"

"Food, food." She gestures at her mouth. "You omless, non?" And she's gone.

NO WAY BACK

As I step out of the toilets, completely drained and depleted, Daniel is waiting for me, my coat clamped between his folded arms. He looks at me expectantly.

"Do you want to tell me what the hell is going on?" he says firmly, jaw clenched.

I can't lie anymore. "Daniel," I blub, almost collapsing onto my knees, "I'm SO sorry. It was a moment of madness."

CHAPTER 40

3 weeks later - 17th December - My birthday

"COME ON, OPEN MINE FIRST." Tina nudges me, excitedly. Oh, bloody hell, I hate opening gifts in front of the giver, especially when there's a crowd, like today. I'm convinced I won't show enough enthusiasm, that they'll think I don't like it, or, worse still, realise when I don't! So, what I end up doing is faking glee. I paint on a smile and whoop at practically anything and everything, which, surprisingly, doesn't always go down too well. Just the other day at work as Fearne and Stacey handed me a gift-wrapped box, I felt my knees give a little. With a fixed smile, I unwrapped it hurriedly, going red, then held the item in the palm of my hand before smothering them in grateful kisses, proclaiming my absolute adoration of it – it's was just what I wanted, you must've read my mind.

"She doesn't know what it is," Fearne complained, "I told you to buy her something from *The Body Shop*!"

"Of course, she does," Stacey laughed, giving me a hesitant glance, "don't be stupid."

"Yes, I do, I do," I lied, clearing my throat, "it's an…um… a jewellery stand." I glanced quickly at Fearne, her face dropped. "Isn't it?"

Stacey reached out, lips pursed, and swivelled the item in my hand. "A candle holder, actually. If you hold it up the right way!"

NO WAY BACK

As expected, they weren't too impressed with my performance but eventually saw the funny side and blamed it on the *Bollinger* that Raymond had bought me to toast my forty-two years on this planet.

Dad sneaks a peek over my shoulder as he lifts a few empty plates off the table, face pink and moist. He's taken off his heavy sweater and rolled up his shirt sleeves. I acknowledge him with a gormless smile, gift in hand, and he grimaces; he knows all about my opening-gifts-in-public phobia. Giving Mum a sly wink, he heads back to the sweaty kitchen where he and George have been working hard all evening, and she grins at him wickedly as she pulls up a chair next to Louise, the smile not fading from her lips. Honestly, you'd think they were newlyweds.

I carefully begin unwrapping the gift, all eyes on me. Oh dear God, the sooner I get this over with the better. I loosen the broad, satin pink ribbons, and they glide off the quality silver paper and pool around the box. It's so beautifully presented, Tina has a knack for gift wrapping. It always seems such a shame to destroy her work of art.

"I hope you like it." Tina's eyes twinkle as she holds her hands in prayer to her lips while doing a little jumpy dance. I hope I like it too. I'm feeling hotter by the second.

"What is it?" Mum leans back as Nathan whacks his twin brother over the head, abandons his Lego bricks and clambers onto her lap, causing Josh to wail at the top of his lungs in protest. "Come on, Audrey, hurry up, don't keep us all in suspense."

Mum cringes at the shrill of Vicky's voice berating Nathan for belting his brother, threatening the naughty step, which has now set him off, too. "There, there, my love," Mum coos gently, stroking Nathan's hair, "we'll put silly Mummy on the naughty step."

Vicky shoots me an exasperated look as she comforts Josh in her arms. I wish Mum'd stop undermining her like that in front of her own children. She's only just weaned herself off the antidepressants. We're supposed to be supporting her.

Armed with his grandmother's approval, Nathan's tears quickly dry up and Mum gently rocks her favourite grandson in her arms, ducking as Florian bounds towards her with a Nerf Blaster gun. "Shhhhh," she calls out to Josh who's now screaming and flinging Lego bricks across the room, "Auntie's trying to open her present. And put that thing down, Florian, you'll have someone's eye out."

"Kids, hey," Tina whispers, glancing quickly at Louise, who's now joined Vicky on the sofa, "who'd have them?" We grin at each other as a Lego brick smacks her on the side of her head.

"She's probably bought you a bloody vibrator," Louise grumbles, arms resting on her knees, flicking through the TV channels. "Why is there never anything frigging decent on the telly?" She tosses the remote control onto the coffee table angrily. "I'm bloody sick of these crap reality shows." Scrambling to her feet, she climbs over Josh and makes her way towards us. "So, come on, where's this vibrator?" Tina elbows her on the arm, tilting her head sharply towards Mum. "Sorry, Ruby, slip of the tongue." Then she covers her mouth and cringes, "Ooops, no pun intended." A chuckle of drunken laughter slips through her fingers. Oh, God, please make her stop before she makes a complete fool of herself. I try to laugh it off as a shared girlie joke but it doesn't seem to go down well at all.

"I think you should just shut up," Tina snaps, hands firmly on her Armani jeans-clad hips, "and don't have any more of that!" She points at the bottle of Merlot on the table.

"Get lost," Louise slurs, helping herself to a top-up. "I'm a single woman now. I'll do as I please." Lowering Nathan to the ground, Mum raises a disconcerted eyebrow as she gets to her feet. Louise gazes at him longingly, glass in hand, as he totters back to his mum and brother who're now sitting cross-legged on the floor building a house out of colourful bricks.

I glance at Tina worriedly, tearing off some of the thick wrapping paper. Louise has gone completely off the rails since Gerry walked out on her.

He blamed the breakdown of their marriage on her obsession to have a child. He couldn't understand why she was so intent on extending their family when all he wanted was a quiet, happy life with the family they already had - and Roxy, of course.

It all kicked off when Gerry packed Francesca and Tommy off to France a few days after our fallout, telling her that the deal was off. No amount of begging or pleading from Louise would make him change his mind. He booked and paid for Francesca's flight online and even drove her to Heathrow, just to make sure she got on the plane. On his way home he popped in to see me, looking as if he hadn't slept or changed his clothes for a week. All he kept saying was how sorry he was for lying to me, begged me to give Louise another chance, insisted that she didn't deliberately set out to deceive me. But I wasn't prepared to forgive and forget at the time; it was too soon, my wounds were raw. So he left with his tail between his legs.

However, the day after I got back from Paris I woke up with startling clarity and decided I was ready to stop judging and start listening. My unscrupulous night of passion with Ronan and subsequent pregnancy scare made me realise that most of us are guilty of behaving selfishly and irrationally at times, especially when under pressure, because when you strip everything away, we're all the same really – fallible human beings just trying to do our best. None of us is perfect, we all make mistakes, and forgiveness, not only of others but of oneself, as Vicky keeps reminding me, is a virtue.

To say that Louise was delighted to hear from me when I called her that very afternoon would be an understatement. She and I have been through a lot together over the years. I finally realised how desperate she was to have a family with Gerry, and people do the strangest things when they're desperate, don't they? I should know. We had a tearful reconciliation and she promised she'd never pull a stunt like that on me again. The next day Gerry walked out on her with Roxy under one arm and an overnight bag in the other. He told her he'd be staying at Nick's until he found a place of his own. But Nick said they only stayed the one night, which was just as well because Roxy weed and pooed all over his kitchen floor, chewed his precious remote control and howled all night. The next day Gerry moved in with a female work colleague, a divorcee with two teenage children. Nick said their affair started months ago.

"Well, there are children present, Louise," Mum says firmly, one hand on her trim hip the other holding a glass of red. "Mind your language please."

"What's a vibrator?" Florian shouts, causing Vicky to shoot up from the sofa.

"Florian! How many times have I told you?" Vicky storms over as the doorbell shrills in the background, followed by the sound of heavy footsteps clambering in the hallway.

"Oh wow." I gaze at Tina's gift in my hands. "Tina, I don't know what to say!" I trill as Jess breezes into the room, bottle in hand, filling the air with a heady scent of musk. "This is just amazing." I hold out a black satin and lace Camisole Set as a synchronised murmur of delight surges around me.

"Aw, do you really like it?" Tina squeals, linking her fingers with mine. Actually, I love it. It looks well made, expensive. "Ronan helped me pick it out for you before he went back to Dublin."

NO WAY BACK

Vicky gives me a fleeting look over her wine glass. "Reluctantly, obvs, you know what men are like."

"He's got good taste," Vicky says smoothly, glancing at me again. Much as I love my sister-in-law, right now I want to tie her to a chair and gag her.

"Happy Birthday, Aud." Jess's cheeks are freezing. "I got you this." She waves the bottle. "Shall I put it in the fridge?" Glad of the intrusion, I thank her and say it sounds like a wonderful idea. She quickly does the greeting rounds, then disappears into the kitchen.

But Tina's like a dog with a bone where Ronan is concerned. "I really miss him when he's away," she muses, staring dreamily into the distance. Delighted as I am that she and Ronan are giving it another go, I wish she'd just put a sock in it now. "I mean, I know he's no Tom Hardy but…"

"You can say that again," Louise mutters and we all gape at her aghast. "What?" she protests, grabbing a fistful of nuts and shoving a few into her mouth, "I'm only saying what everyone else is thinking." She takes a large glug of wine. "She just said herself that he's ugly…AND he's still married."

Mum and Vicky look at me, startled. I'm not quite sure what they expect me to do. We all know she's drunk. Louise would never say such nasty, spiteful things if she were sober. She may be bossy and opinionated but she's not inherently mean. I know she doesn't mean it. She'll feel like shit tomorrow morning and call Tina to apologise, I'm certain of it. And besides, Ronan *is* attractive, in his own way, and he and Catherine have already started divorce proceedings. It'll be finalised in a few months.

"Anyway," Tina continues, ignoring Louise, "I really feel like we've got a connection, do you know what I mean?" We all smile at her like proud aunties, our heads bobbing in synchronisation, including Mum who assures her that beauty is in the eye of the beholder and that Ronan is a fine-looking lad.

"Thank you, Ruby."

"We aim to please." Mum salutes her with her glass. "Just make sure he's divorced before any jiggy-jiggy takes place." Tina grins at me while Louise snorts with faked laughter. Mum really doesn't know Tina well at all, does she?

"Oooh, wait," Tina says suddenly, "I got you a gift receipt. It's here somewhere, erm…" She rummages through the pile of silver paper strewn on the table, "Here it is." I take the receipt from her hand. "In case you want to take it back."

"*Agent Provocateur,*" I exclaim, "this must've cost you a fortune."

"Oh, you're worth it, Hun, and don't worry, Ronan put it on his card." She hunches her shoulders at me and giggles with delight. Oh, bloody hell. I feel like the worse friend in the world. I hold her gaze. Is there really any point in telling her about our stupid, ridiculous, pathetic one-night stand? I open my mouth. And then close it again. No, it'll only burst her bubble, and what's the point in that? "Oh, come here." She squeezes me in her arms. Over her shoulder, I catch sight of Vicky widening her eyes at me knowingly. I glare at her. If she carries on giving me looks every time Tina mentions Ronan she'll make someone suspicious.

"Hmm," Mum grumbles, feeling the fabric of the camisole, "pity there's no man in your life to appreciate it."

"Appreciate what?" George springs into the room, hot and flustered, holding two platters of canapés and munching on a sausage roll. "Oooh, very nice, sis, but Mum's right." His eyes flick from me to Vicky. "You two are about the same size, aren't you?" If only.

I give George a thump on the arm, almost knocking the tray out of his hand. "Ouch, I was only saying." Josh starts crying the moment he sees his father. George rushes over, crouches down and starts building bricks with his sons.

"Oh, Mum," I whine, "Daniel and I are having a break, that's all." Daniel and I have split up but Mum doesn't need to know yet because the moment she finds out, she'll nag me to death. I buckled outside the public toilets at *Gare de Nord* station and confessed my betrayal in a flurry of tears. He took it as expected and we both agreed that I wasn't ready for a new relationship.

Our train journey home was in stony-faced silence. At King's Cross, we parted without as much as a hug. He could barely look at me. I walked off the platform, teary-eyed and deflated like a worn out, used balloon, wondering if I'd just made the biggest mistake of my life.

When I checked his Facebook status the next day he'd already changed it to 'Single'. I thought that was it, I'd never hear from him again. But then about a week ago a text pinged through – he'd told Connie about her real mother. Subsequent texts confirmed that Connie already knew that Aliki wasn't her birth mother, after all. The little minx got to the envelope shortly before I did and set me up!

"Connie didn't buy my excuse that her birth certificate was destroyed, and went on a secret rampage in my flat," Daniel said when I called him for a proper chat later that morning. There's only so much you can articulate in a text, isn't there? And I was curious to find out all the gory details. "I was seeing a client that morning," he continued, "so she knew that the coast was clear. She found the documents hidden in the drawer under a pile of t-shirts."

Naturally, she was devastated and shocked to discover that Aliki wasn't her real mum. Too anxious to confront him or Aliki, she masterminded a plan that would make *them* approach *her*. And that's where gullible ol'me came in. She booked the delivery, roped me in and, knowing how weak my bladder is, piled me with enough liquid to bring on hyponatremia before setting me loose in Daniel's apartment. Daniel said she'd gone to the flat just after Pranvera left; removed the toilet paper from the guest cloakroom, forcing me into his en-suite, and then jammed a sleeve in the drawer, placing the envelope next to it. Her plan was that I'd spot it (which I did) and, aware of the fact that I can't stand seeing things out of place (which I can't), go over and tuck it back in (which is exactly what I did). I'm transparent, I know, so shoot me.

"Pure genius," Daniel said proudly, "she could work for MI5." That girl can really do no wrong in his eyes, can she? "I'm really sorry I accused you of snooping, Audrey," he went on, "but you can appreciate how it seemed, can't you?" I said that I completely understood and to forget it. That is was all in the past and I was glad that they'd sorted it all out. And that was the end of that.

"A break?" Mum says, unconvinced, "I'm surprised he's talking to you given that you turned down his marriage proposal." She shakes her head. "A great catch like that."

"Well, I can't marry a man I barely know, Mum, can I?"

"You do realise that you're forty-two today, Audrey, and not twenty-two."

"Yes, thank you, Mother," I say flatly, "for reminding me."

"You look great, Audrey," Vicky smiles, brushing past me, "take no notice."

"Stunning, babe," Tina adds, "and thirty is the new forty, anyway."

"She's forty-two," Louise remarks.

"Oh, what's a couple of years?"

Mum shakes her head as they continue to squabble over my age. "Handsome, successful, reliable. Honest. What more do you want?" Honest? If she only knew how he'd deceived his own daughter all these years.

"Oh, Mum, just drop it, will you. We're supposed to be celebrating my birthday, in case you'd forgotten."

"You're unbelievable, Audrey," she mutters, walking away, "just unbelievable."

"She's not past it yet, Ruby," Louise says to Mum's back, "any bloke would be lucky to have her." I lay a hand on her arm affectionately. I'm so glad she's back in my life. "Any news from Nick?" she asks softly amongst all the chaos, her demeanour suddenly sober.

"Yes," I say hesitatingly, "he called this morning to wish me a happy birthday." And to tell me that he still loves me, but I don't want to tell her that.

I'm not going to lie, I still care about Nick. A lot. But things can never be the same between us. The dynamics have changed. He's a dad now. There's no room for me in his life anymore. And I can't play second fiddle to his child. I've been there and done that.

"I'm glad you're friends again," Louise says sincerely, emptying the last dregs of Merlot into her glass. "At least someone is forgiving." She means Gerry. I know she misses him terribly.

"Come on, everyone," Dad barges in with a birthday cake. It's covered in stripy red and white candles. The flames dance wildly as he slams it onto the table in front of me, a few candles threaten to go out. "Lights someone." Within moments we're enveloped in darkness, our only illumination a burst of orange haze from the burning flames. "Good boy, Florian. Now, gather round. George, fetch the bubbly from the fridge, mate. And if you don't mind, Jess, will you give him a hand with the flutes? They're on a tray next to the sink."

"Sure, Mr Fox."

"Vicky, bring the boys over too. Come on, Ruby, love." Oh, no. They're going to sing Happy Birthday to me. I don't think I've had a birthday like this in close to thirty-five years. I feel a lump in my throat. The candles are burning. George is on stand-by with the fizz.

"One, two, three," Dad prompts, and they all chorus together out of tune, "*Happy Birthday to you, Happy Birthday to you...*" I look at their smiling faces, gulping with gratitude. I'm going to miss my mum and dad when they emigrate to sun-drenched, smog-free Cyprus in the New Year. Whatever will I do without them?

"Make a wish, make a wish," Florian says excitedly when they sing the last verse.

"I doubt very much it'll come true, Florian, but here goes." I lean forward, close my eyes, make a wish and blow.

"What did you wish for, Auntie, the new iPhone?" Florian asks as everyone chants "hip, hip hooray".

"No!"

"What then? The Macbook Pro?"

"I can't tell you, Florian, or it won't come true."

"No point in making wishes now," Mum whinges as she lifts the cake off the table in front of me.

"Oh, Grandma, stop being so negative." From the mouths of babes. "Okay, Auntie, but whatever it is can I borrow it?"

My living room is in euphoric chaos – the kids blow on their party whistles, everyone's talking at once, my phone ping, ping, pings on the sideboard, the doorbell trills in the background. Giddy with delight, I grab my glasses from the mantelpiece as George pops the prosecco cork to a roar of cheers. Eight WhatsApp messages. Dozens of social media alerts. Five missed calls and a new text – from Nick. I retrieve the text message quickly.

Great news, Foxy. Paternity test results in – I'm not the daddy!!! Woohoo!

My heart does an unexpected backflip, cartwheel, and high jump in my chest.

"Audrey, Audrey!" Mum's excited voice shrills in my ears, "It seems like your birthday wish has come true, after all, look who's here to see you!" Oh, God, it can't be him.

Spinning on my heel, adrenalin tears through me, and then my heart stops. He's holding a white paper carrier bag, tied at the top with thick, white ribbon; his hair and shoulders wet from the rain. I look up at him, my eyes wide, my heart apprehensive.

"Happy Birthday, Cinderella," Daniel says softly, handing me the *Jimmy Choo* carrier bag.

I bite my bottom lip, now who was it that said, *"Be careful what you wish for"*?

NO WAY BACK

Acknowledgements

First off, I'd like to thank my readers for supporting me on my writing journey and for making it all worthwhile.

A big thank you to Joe, husband extraordinaire, for the reassurance, love and support, especially during my wobbly moments, and for being my personal barista. The coffee helped – a lot.

Huge thanks to my family and friends for their encouragement, for believing in me, and for putting up with me droning on about my book!

Thanks also to my fellow authors, you know who you are! Writing can be a lonely business and, at times, a bit of a roller coaster ride; having like-minded friends to share the ups and downs with, or to just have a good old natter and a giggle with is a haven.

A very special thank you to book bloggers for the generosity of their time, enthusiasm and support – it means a lot. You are all absolute stars and I can't thank you enough.

And finally, many thanks to Urbane for their dedication, hard work, and for making the magic happen.

KELLY FLORENTIA was born and bred in north London, where she continues to live with her husband Joe. *No Way Back* is her second novel. Her debut novel, *The Magic Touch*, was released in March 2016.

Kelly has always enjoyed writing and was a bit of a poet when she was younger. Before penning her first novel, she wrote contemporary short fiction for women's magazines. *To Tell a Tale or Two* is a collection of some of her short stories.

As well as writing, Kelly loves reading, running, yoga, necking coffee and scoffing cakes. She's currently working on the sequel to *No Way Back*.